EAR

MAGIC

Book One: The High King of Kambrya

By:

Kenneth Price

Aprhys Publishing

Copyright © 2018 by Kenneth Price

ISBN: 9781980326809
ASIN: B079VVJHLH

In memory of my father Arthur Price, and two of my brothers: Charles and David Price.

They left this world too early but will not be forgotten.

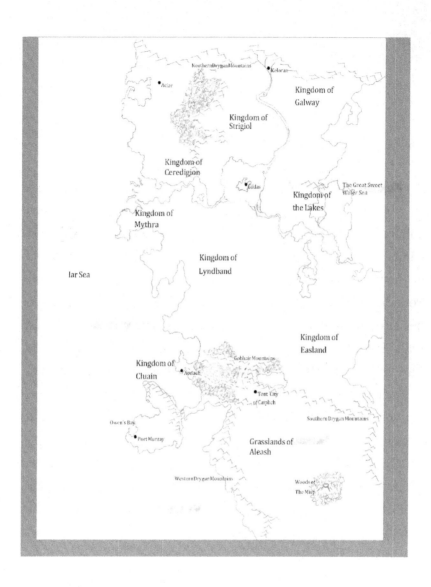

CHAPTER ONE

Elwin ap Gruffydd was at an age where he was not quite a man, nor could you honestly call him a boy. Stuck between childhood and adulthood, the young Gruffydd was lost in his thoughts. Hunched over a rather old cherry wood desk that had seen better days, the young man seemed oblivious to his surroundings. Before him was an extraordinarily old, worn, and a rather large book. Ever since he was very young Elwin had loved to read. True, a large degree of that love had come from the pride he saw in his father's eyes. Elwin's father had not been a learned man but had always encouraged his son's pursuit of knowledge. Partly to please his father, and part to quench his boundless thirst for knowledge, Elwin had always taken his learning very seriously. Slowly, he ran his hand across the large book. The black leather cover was worn thin in many places, and small pieces of the cover broke off under Elwin's fair skinned hands. Carefully, he opened it. The first page cracked in his hands. His eyes widened.

Despite the plain looking cover, the book had to have been made by a master craftsman. Wondering why such a book had been left in the dusty old tower library, Elwin stared at the page. Embellished upon the parchment were several golden red dragons. Encircling the page, the dragons' snake-like bodies twisted and curved together. After admiring the artist's illumination, Elwin turned his attention to the large graceful lettering. The golden colored print was in the old Kambryan dialect, which only a few scholars could still read. Elwin was proud of the fact that he had mastered the language at such a young age. His father had seen to it that he was given a first-rate education and was particularly insistent that he should know the language of his ancestors. Elwin had often wondered at his father's strange demand to know such an archaic script, but at the moment the boy appreciated his father's unorthodox demands of his tutors. It had been difficult even to find a scholar who could teach the old language. His father had to search all the kingdoms of Kambrya before he was able to find one. A few years after that, Elwin had mastered a language that he imagined he would never use. At the top of the page was the title in bold lettering, "**The Chronicles of Brother W...is**" Only the first and last letters of the scribe's name remained. The rest of the golden-red letters had faded and now lost to time. Elwin remembered that there had once been a local Saint Wallis in the Kambryan religion of the Three Gods. Saint Wallis had indeed once lived in Reidh County. Elwin was now in the same Reidh County that had once been home to Saint Wallis. He recalled that Saint Wallis had founded the Wallisinan Order of the Three Gods. The order's monastic center was not too far away. Running a hand through his long light-brown hair, Elwin wondered if he was looking at the writing of a saint.

Time had indeed taken its toll on the book. The golden lettering in some areas had faded or was gone entirely. Considering its age, the text was in amazingly good condition. Elwin brushed aside the hair from his eyes and began to translate the ancient text.

"THE HISTORY OF KING COINNEACH AP GRUFFYDD, HIGH KING OF KAMBRYA

by Brother Wallis

Brother Wallis! It really was written by Brother Wallis!

Elwin inhaled. Coinneach was the last king to rule over the Six Kingdoms of Kambrya. Shrouded in myths, King Coinneach was considered the greatest of Kambrya's kings. He was also Elwin's distant ancestor. The sword that hung at Elwin's side was believed to have once belonged to the great king.

In disbelief, Elwin read on.

> *"In the year 728, of Triesch, King Coinneach ap Gruffydd, High King of Kambrya passed away. With the passing of the High King, the world has emerged into a new age. The time of heroes, glory, and war are over. The age of peace has begun."*

The next several pages described the early history of King Coinneach. Some of the history Elwin was familiar with, and some he was not. Then Elwin came to the story of King Coinneach's death. The death of the great king was a part of the histories that had been lost. Elwin glimpsed an image of himself as a great scholar, the scholar who was going to bring back the lost history of Kambrya. His father's wish to have an educated son was going to make Elwin famous within scholarly circles, and Elwin was only seventeen.

Coinneach ap Gruffydd, High

King of Kambrya, had discovered a means of stopping the wars. With his discovery, King Coinneach (known as the Champion of the Blue Knight, Defender of Truth) set out to end the wars.

Carefully, Elwin turned the brittle page and read on. Brother Wallis had written of how the king and the Kambryan army had set out from Acair, and of the bloody summer that followed. Enthralled, Elwin read details of hard-fought battles, glory, and death.

By the end of that summer, the army had fought their way to Ban-Darn, the castle of the Overlord.

"Ban Darn."

Elwin took another deep breath. He had heard of both Ban-Darn and the Overlord. The myths and stories of the black walls of Ban-Darn and its evil master were often told and re-told. They were the tales of bards and gleemen. The stories were entertaining, but they were not usually believed. *Could they have been real?* Elwin wondered. Or maybe this Brother Wallis was mad. That seemed more likely. According to Brother Wallis, the Dark Overlord was the master of a cult called the Severed Head. Elwin had heard of the cult. A few years ago, he would have said that the cult was a myth as well, but now things were different.

Centuries after King Coinneach had died, the Cult of the Severed Head had returned and was challenging the doctrine of the Three Gods.

Elwin continued to read of a great battle that was fought at the walls of Ban-Darn. At the Battle of Ban-Darn, King Coinneach and the Overlord had killed each other. The wars had finally come to an end, and the Cult of the Severed Head disappeared into the mists of legends. Elwin touched the hilt of his sword at his side. Running his hand along the engraved silver weavings, he wondered if it had been the same sword that had killed the Dark Master of the Severed Head. But could Elwin believe what he was reading? Elwin shook his head. *It can't be true.*

Intensely studying the passage, Elwin did not see the count's son enter the library. He was a handsome young man with curly red hair and a cheerful round face and was dressed in the fine silk clothing of a lord. A silver brooch pinned to his light blue shirt sparkled in the light, and a plaid tartan draped over his left shoulder gave him a noble look.

The young lord cleared his throat. "I thought I would find you here. What are you reading now?" His voice carried the slight hint of the accent the county was known for, and his R's rolled gently off his tongue

Quickly closing the book, Elwin looked up with a start. "Oh, hi Pallas... Nothing. Just reading."

"Come on Elwin; I know you..." Pallas stopped short as Elwin's eyes narrowed into tiny slits.

"Okay, okay," Pallas, sighed. "I'm sorry. I mean 'Eoin.' What does it matter, anyway? Nobody can hear us up here. Other than you, nobody ever even comes up here. Besides, other than me, who would recognize you as Prince Elwin of Ceredigion?"

"Everyone, if you don't keep your mouth shut!" snapped Elwin. He knew Pallas was right, but one had to be careful.

"What brings you up here?" Elwin asked, his voice no longer sounding harsh. Like everyone else, Elwin found it hard to stay mad at Pallas. "You are not a common sight in libraries."

"I've been seen in them before," Pallas replied with a wry smile.

"Ha!" laughed Elwin, rubbing a cramp in his neck. "Only when Count Dovan makes you!"

"And not as often as father would like," laughed Pallas.

Pallas was the type of person that lived life to its fullest and was always ready with a joke and a smile. It was only with Pallas that Elwin was able to let out his sillier side. It was the effect the young noble had on people, and it was a quality that the stoic and scholarly Elwin envied.

"Well, what do you want?" asked Elwin. "You are not here to find a book, are you?"

"Heavens no!" Pallas feigned a horrified look. "Why should I do such a foul thing as to read a book? No, I am happy to leave the libraries of the world to you."

"Well, then why are you here?"

"I have news you might like to hear."

"News in Reidh County?" Elwin smiled as he pushed the book off to one side. "I did not realize things ever happened in Reidh, at least nothing that one could actually call news."

"Ha ha! Very funny."

"Well, out with it." Elwin grinned. "Did Widow MacKay's cow have its calf, or was there some other great earth-shaking event?"

"I don't know if I should tell you. You keep insulting me and my home!"

Elwin rolled his eyes, praying for patience. "Okay, I'm sorry, it's a lovely place. Now, what's up?"

Pallas ran a hand through his thick, curly red hair. "That's the poorest apology I have ever heard, but I'll let it go this time. A ship has come in. It's the first of the year."

Elwin jumped to his feet as if his chair had been kicked out from under him. With long strides, he raced to the window. A ship meant there would be news of the world beyond the Southern Drygan Mountains—there could even be word from Ceredigion, or better yet, his father. Last summer, Elwin had hoped to hear from his father, but no word had come. Elwin had different ideas this year. Word or no word, he was taking that ship. He was going home!

From the keep's tower window, Elwin looked out over Port Murray. Port Murray was not a large town, but it could not be considered small either. By the county's terms, it was a bustling city. To the rest of the world, it was a small fishing village. From the library window, Elwin could see down the main street. He saw the people going about their lives; running errands, buying goods at the market, or whatever else had to be done. At the moment, the street was rather quiet, but past experience told him it would be crowded tonight. The first ship of the year always caused excitement. It was a reason to celebrate. In Reidh county every ship was a major event, but the first of the year produced an almost carnival-like atmosphere.

The ship had lowered its anchor in the center of the harbor. Typically ships preferred to tie up along the wharf where it was easier to load and unload cargo. But this ship was made for the deep waters of the ocean, and the water along the pier was too shallow for it. Slowly, the ship rocked in the swells that rolled in from the Iar Sea. On board deck, the crew was busy furling sails and coiling lines. Elwin wondered what the ship's cargo would be. He knew there would be cargo because no ship entered Port Murray empty. Goods from beyond the mountains brought a good price in this isolated part of the world, especially when the mountain passes were still blocked with snow. Beyond the harbor and bay was the Iar Sea. The jagged waves made the horizon look like a row of sharp points. Sailors called such a horizon 'shark teeth', a sure sign of rough seas. No doubt the ship and its crew had a hard voyage.

"Any news?" asked Elwin, still looking out the window.

Clearing a spot on the desk so he could sit down, Pallas shoved a pile of books off to one side. Sitting on the desktop, the lord looked carefully at Elwin's back. He could sense Elwin was planning something, and Pallas was determined to be part of it.

"I don't know," admitted Pallas with a shrug of his shoulders. "I came here first. Thought you might like to head into town with me. Besides, the Dryrot won't be open for a couple of hours."

Elwin turned to face Pallas. "You want to go to the Dryrot? War could have broken out, and you think of beer? Your priorities seem to be a bit confused."

Pallas shrugged. "They seem proper to me. Besides, in Reidh you learn not to worry too much about the outside world. By the time news reaches here, it's already history."

Elwin laughed. In the past three years, he had learned that things in Port Murray rarely changed and never fast. Elwin had grown up in Acair, the busy capital city of Ceredigion. With its slow and stress-free life, Reidh was not a bad place to live, but Elwin was frustrated by the county's isolation. He had been on edge all winter, waiting for spring and news of Ceredigion. Late last summer there had been rumors of war. People were saying that Strigiol had invaded Cluain. Then with the arrival of winter, the rumors stopped. It was impossible to tell how Lyon de Brodie, King of Cluain, would react to war. Would he stand up to King Jerran? Most people thought he would not. Elwin had never met King Lyon, but according to those who had, the king was less than impressive. Evidently, Lyon was a man more dedicated to drink, rich food, and elaborate parties than to his kingdom or its people.

Elwin didn't think he was in any real danger. The only ones who knew he was in Reidh County were Pallas, the count and countess, and Lord Rodan, the count's trusted man-at-arms.

What worried Elwin was that if Strigiol had attacked Cluain, would Ceredigion be far behind? In a bold move, King Jerran had already invaded and conquered Lyndand and Easland. The king of Strigiol seemed bent on conquering all of Kambrya. As a descendant of the last high kings, Elwin knew he would be in danger. That was why he was hiding here in this remote corner of the six kingdoms.

Elwin turned and looked out the window once more. The ship anchored in the harbor reminded him of another ship. A similar ship had brought Pallas and Elwin to Port Murray. Elwin had never wanted to leave his home. The whole thing had been his father's idea, and when King Artair ap Gruffydd wanted something, he usually got it. This was especially true when it came to his family.

Three years ago, shortly after King Jerran had invaded Easland, King Artair announced that he had to make a trip to the city of Llanbaedarn, and he asked if Pallas and Elwin wished to come along. Pallas, who was a squire learning to become a knight, had been at the Ceredigion court for a few years. It was during those years that Elwin and Pallas had met and become friends.

The two friends quickly accepted the king's offer. Standing at the library window, Elwin recalled the memory, as if it had just been yesterday. The trip to Llanbaedarn had taken several weeks. Elwin's father and his entourage were traveling slowly, visiting the local fiefdoms along the road. In some cases, they would stay a few days as the king met with the local nobility, but at last, they had reached the city. The ride into the city had been long and dusty, so Elwin and Pallas had a quick dinner, followed by a hot bath and then hurried off to bed. King Artair also went to his room, but he did not go to bed. That night, the king patiently waited until he was sure everyone in the castle had fallen off to sleep. He then silently slipped out of his bedroom chambers and crossed the hall to where Elwin and Pallas slept. Artair bent over his only son and gently shook him. Elwin's eyes fluttered open. The king's brown eyes were reflected in the brown eyes of his son; one pair full of power, the other with sleep.

Artair leaned closer to Elwin and whispered, "Wake, my son. You have a boat to catch." Elwin rubbed the sleep from his eyes. "What is wrong?" he managed to ask between yawns.

"There's no time for answers now," replied Artair. The king helped Elwin from his bed and handed him some clothes. "Here, put these on. We have to hurry."

Elwin fought off the desire to lie back down. All he wanted to do was close his eyes and sleep, but instead, he slowly began to dress. As Elwin put on his clothes, Artair woke up Pallas, who was sharing the room with Elwin.

While Pallas was dressing, Elwin again tried to question his father but stopped short when his father's eyes narrowed into tiny slits. He knew those eyes were a warning to keep quiet. Elwin could never remember his father raising his voice. There was no need to. King Artair had an air of authority about him. That authority did not come from being king, but rather from the type of man he was.

Outside the room the castle was dark and silent. Quietly, they made their way to the Great Hall where the Duke held his court. Signaling Pallas and Elwin to follow, Artair entered the Great Hall. As if the walls were a large map, the king began to study their surface carefully.

"What are you doing?" asked Elwin.

"Shhh," warned Artair. He reached up to one of the several torches that were mounted on the stone wall. "If I remember, this is the right one."

The torch, with its flickering flame, looked like all the rest in the hall, but as Artair slipped it from its brass mounting, the wall began to move.

With a dull grinding sound, a secret door swung inwards revealing a long dark passageway. Elwin could hardly believe that a door could have been hidden in that wall, but there it was.

With Pallas at his side, Elwin followed his father into the dark tunnel.

Artair held the torch before him, creating a small circle of light. "Stay close," he warned.

The secret passageway had apparently not been used for many years, as the floor was covered with a thick layer of dust. Cobwebs continually had to be pulled away from their faces. The tunnel suddenly came to an end, and Artair stopped. He stared up at the stone wall. He then extinguished the torch. In the dark, the king located a hidden lever. There was a click, and with a push, Artair slowly opened another secret door.

The door opened into a narrow alleyway. The passageway had taken them beyond the castle walls and into the city. Above his head, Elwin could see the walls of the alleyway disappear into a thick fog.

Now that they were out of the tunnel, their pace quickened. They moved swiftly along the empty streets of the city. They passed by homes that were dark and silent. It felt to Elwin as if they were walking through a deserted city. Nothing stirred or moved. Not even a breeze disturbed the foggy world. Pulling his cloak tighter, Elwin tried to keep out the night. It was not long before they reached the harbor. Unlike Port Murray's harbor, Llanbaedarn's harbor was large and filled with ships. In the fog, the ship masts looked like some strange forest where all the leaves and branches were stripped from the tree trunks.

At the end of the wharf was a two-masted merchant ship. At first, the vessel looked like all the rest. It was quiet and dark as if it was sleeping through the cold dark night. But as they drew closer, Elwin noticed that people were moving on deck. In the gray fog, the figures on deck looked like phantoms aboard a ghost ship.

Crossing the gangplank, the ship gently rocked under their feet. Elwin could now see that the phantom figures were sailors, and they were preparing to cast off. As Elwin stepped onto the deck, one of the sailors looked up from his work. With a look of authority, it was evident he was the captain. His weather worn and leathery face spoke of many years at sea. Despite his hard face and body that rippled with muscles, he appeared nervous and uncomfortable. His eyes quickly shifted to the wharf. As if he was looking for more unwanted visitors, he scanned the shadows. Only after he was sure no one else was stalking around his vessel, did he let his gaze shift back to the king and the two boys. Still nervous, the captain's gaze shifted and once more, and again he looked down the deserted wharf. A moment later, he turned back to the king. He hesitated, and then nodded toward the ship's stern.

"Come on," whispered Artair. At the stern of the ship was a small cabin. King Artair opened the door and ushered the boys through. The plainly decorated cabin had only two narrow cots, one large sea chest, and one chair. With a thud, the king closed the door.

Elwin was unsure why they were leaving, but he knew that it was serious. He sat down on a narrow cot. Now wide awake, he could feel a cold lump forming in his throat.

Lighting a lantern that hung from the ceiling, Artair sat down next to Elwin. Pulling his son close, Artair embraced him.

"I know you're confused," the king whispered, "but I cannot stay and explain. It is also safer if there are some things you don't know. It will be dawn soon, and you must be gone by then."

Elwin held back tears. "You're not coming?"

"No. I cannot."

"Where am I going?"

Artair let go of his son and rose to his feet. He looked sadly down at Elwin. "Port Murray," he replied. "Pallas' father, Count Dovan, is expecting you. Dovan is an old and trusted friend."

"I don't want to go," sniffed Elwin.

Artair knelt down before his son. "I know, but this is how it must be. When it's safe, I will send for you. Until then, Count Dovan will keep you out of danger."

Slowly, Artair unbuckled the sword from his side and handed it to Elwin. The sword was the ancient blade of King Coinneach, as well as all the High Kings before him. Elwin was no longer able to hold back the tears. He wiped his face with the backs of his hands and looked down at the sword his father had placed in his lap.

Artair rested a gentle hand on Elwin's shoulder. "I pray you will never need to use this sword," he said, "but a day may come when you must. Until then, always keep it close and safe.

When the danger has passed, I will come for you. Then I will explain this all to you." Dropping to his knees, the king again held his son. Then reluctantly, he came to his feet. "Never reveal who you are. If any ask, you are Eoin," Artair nodded in the direction of the redheaded boy, "...Pallas' companion."

Artair opened the cabin door to leave, then as if an afterthought, he looked back at Pallas.

"Take care of my boy," he stated. "I'm counting on you."

"Yes, Sire," responded Pallas.

"I am pleased that my son has such a friend as you."

Then Artair turned towards his son one last time. A tear ran down his hardened cheek.

"Remember, I love you and I always will."

"But,…" Elwin's father cut his son short with a hard glare.

"There is no more time Elwin! For now, this is how it must be. Don't argue with me. This is hard enough as it is."

Resigned to his fate, Elwin sighed; he knew when he could push his father no further. "Say goodbye to Leina! And—I love you too." The king's eyes met Elwin's one last time. In that look, the king said more than words could ever say. Then the door closed, and Artair was gone.

Elwin turned from the library window. He was no longer the fourteen-year-old boy he had been when he had last seen his father. In three years, Elwin had grown into a young man. The prince looked a lot like his father. Elwin's gestures, voice, and humor were all those of King Artair. Only the lack of a thick beard, a muscular body, and age separated father and son. Elwin had the soft complexion and the manors of a scholar while his father had the hardness of a seasoned warrior. Elwin's father had wanted to create a world where a leader's mind was of greater importance than his sword.

Elwin slowly turned and looked at Pallas. He gave Pallas a warm, grateful smile. Elwin missed his father and sister Leina, but Pallas and the count and countess made it easier. Since he had been in Reidh, Elwin had grown to love them all. They had become his adopted family, and Reidh his home away from home. Despite its faults, Reidh was not a bad place to live. The land was at peace with itself, a place where one was free and safe — a place where wars never touched. Elwin would miss the green hills of Reidh County, but it was time to go.

"I am taking that ship," Elwin announced. "I'm going home!"

Pallas' eyes narrowed. It was a trait he had picked up from Elwin, though it did not carry the same impact. "Your father won't like it."

Elwin smiled at the thought of his father's reaction. "I can handle father." Then just as quickly, the smile slipped from his face. "Besides, I should have heard something last summer. There's trouble back home. I know my father can handle whatever it is, but I am his son, I should be there to help, if I can. I'm no longer a child."

Pallas nodded. He could understand Elwin's need. "Okay, we'll find out when the ship is going to sail. Then we can sneak aboard the night before."

Leaning back on the windowsill, Elwin replied, "Why sneak onboard? I can afford passage."

"Princes are really ignorant at times." Pallas smiled, "There are two reasons." Holding up one finger as he explained. "First, it's a merchant ship, and they won't take passengers unless you have money, and it will take a good amount of it to get passage on a merchant ship. They don't have much room to spare for passengers."

Elwin shrugged his shoulders. "So? Money's not a problem."

"True," Pallas replied with a certain smugness to his voice. It was not often that the young lord could outthink Elwin. "But if you offer them a large sum, they'll be suspicious, and may even kill us once we are out to sea. It's hard to tell what kind of sailors these men might be. Money offered in large sums indicates there is more where it came from. Second." He stuck up a second finger. "You can't tell them who you are. War may have broken out in Cluain, and there is no telling whose side these sailors are on."

"Okay, you made your point, but I can't hide in the ship forever. What happens when they find me?"

"Eventually we will be discovered, then we'll tell them a story they will accept. We'll tell them we are orphans, trying to reach a city where we can find work. Not an uncommon reason for stowaways who are looking for a better life. They won't be happy of course, and will most likely put us to work, but nothing more. And a few days of hard work will put a little muscle onto those skinny arms of yours. They will also have no reason to think that we are anything than what we say we are. Then when they sail into their next harbor, they'll put us ashore and be done with us. After that, we can find our way north."

"It sounds reasonable, but there is no 'we.' I go alone."

"Alone?!" Pallas exclaimed. "You won't make it out of the harbor without me! You high lords have no sense. You will need me to keep you out of trouble. Besides, I told your father I would look out after you."

"You'll be nothing but trouble."

"True," agreed Pallas with a smile. "But you will still need me."

Elwin crossed his arms over his chest. "No! You're not going. Your father would have my skin."

"But..."

"No buts!" interrupted Elwin with a note of finality. "Now let's have a few of those beers and see what we can find out."

Pallas didn't like the idea at all, but Elwin had his father's stubborn streak, and Pallas knew there was no point in arguing. Besides, he would have time to figure out a way to convince Elwin to take him along. If all else failed, Pallas would simply hide in some other part of the ship, and once out to sea, Elwin would have no choice. *If you think I am going to let you go off and have a grand adventure, you'll need to think again*, thought Pallas. *Besides, I promised your father I would look after you, and one does not break his word to your father!*

Elwin and Pallas returned to their rooms. Elwin gathered up a few things he thought he might need. Pilfering some clothing from the servant's quarters, the two boys quickly changed. Now dressed in woolen clothes and long hooded capes, the two no longer looked like two young nobles. Instead, they looked more like two shepherd boys.

Leaving through the keep's side gate, Elwin and Pallas never saw the man entering through the front gate.

ELWIN COUNT: 128

CHAPTER TWO

Dovan Murray, Count of Reidh County, paced across his study. Back and forth, he crossed and re-crossed the room. His once red hair seemed to be growing grayer with every passing moment. The black leather boots slapped against the wooden floor. His kilt of red, green, and blue swirled with every turn the tense count made.

Besides the count, there were three others in the study: the Dovan's wife, Kytherin Murray, Lord Rodan Macay, who was the Dovan's most trusted advisor, and a young squire who was trying to put the finishing touches on the count's kilt.

"Who in the name of the three gods does he think he is, ordering me about in my county?!" ranted Dovan.

No one answered. Rodan stared out a window, lost in his thoughts, and the countess knew better than to respond to her husband when he was in such a foul mood.

"And why is he here?" the Count ranted on.

Again, no one answered.

The small study was one of Dovan's favorite rooms. It had a pair of large glass doors that opened out onto a small balcony. From the balcony, one could see the mountains, or look out over the Iar Sea. Usually, Dovan found the view a welcome distraction from his work, but today was not a typical day.

In the center of the room was a large desk. The desk's dark oiled surface lay hidden beneath piles of randomly scattered papers, papers that the count had been busy working on only a moment ago. Mostly, the papers were of local matters, land disputes, or grazing rights that are the mundane work of the landed nobility. Those duties were now forgotten. Most of the time, Count Dovan Murray was happy to be taken away from his

23

paperwork, but not this day.

As he paced across the room, Dovan glanced up at a pair of bagpipes that hung from the wall. Making musical instruments was a hobby of the count. Dovan had made an identical set of bagpipes for his friend, Artair ap Gruffydd, King of Ceredigion. Many years ago, he had given the pipes to the king to celebrate the birth of the Artair's son. The bagpipes reminded Dovan of the promise he had made to King Artair. By keeping his word to Artair, Dovan knew he might have to make some difficult choices that would likely be of conflicting loyalties.

The young page chased after the count. As if performing some ritual dance, the boy ducked and weaved as the older man paced on, carefully trying not to be run over. Frantically, the slender boy was trying to fasten a sporran onto the count's kilt. Made from the coat of a long-haired sheep, the sporran was a traditional decorative pouch which was worn on the front of a kilt. Several times, the boy almost had the ornament attached to the kilt, but then at the last moment the count would change directions, and the page would have to start the dance all over again. Finally, the page ducked when he should have weaved and was nearly trampled. The count's blue eyes bore down on the boy. "Aren't you finished yet?!"

"Sorry, my...my lord," whispered the page, almost too softly to be heard.

Stepping in to save the boy, the Countess Kytherin spoke up, "You do not have to take it out on the boy! It is not the lad's fault. If you would stand still, he could do his job."

"Yes, dear," Dovan replied with a short bow. Turning back to the page, the count reached out and patted the boy's head. "Sorry lad, just try to hurry."

"Yes, Lord Murray," the boy answered.

Kytherin's complexion was nearly as dark as the count's. In the capital city, the countess was frowned upon, as ladies were not supposed to have such a dark tone to their skin, but Kytherin did not care what the court thought. She enjoyed working in her gardens, taking long rides, and feeling the warmth of the sun on her face. She was even known to accompany her husband on hunts, and she was not about to give anything up just because the ladies of court (whom Kytherin called the 'Chatter Girls'), considered it disgraceful. Kytherin's long strawberry blond hair was pulled back into a braid. Her smile always seemed to fill the room with warmth, but today it also hid her worries.

Kytherin let her eyes drift across the empty study. "What happened to the chairs that were in here?"

"I had them removed," answered the count. Finding it hard to stand still, Dovan nervously shifted from one foot to the other.

"Whatever for? It looks dreadfully bare!"

"Perhaps, but I want our visitor to stand while I sit. I have the feeling this is no social call. This is my castle, let him stand."

"Are you worried about Elw ... I mean Eoin?" Remembering the page, Kytherin corrected herself. She did not suspect the boy would say anything, but there was no reason to advertise that the prince of Ceredigion was staying in their home.

"Yes, I think the Strigiol lord knows he is here. Why else would the Lord of Risca come to Port Murray?" The worry lines upon the count's face deepened. The stress was taking its toll on Dovan. Kytherin had never noticed it before, but suddenly Dovan looked old to her.

"But that's not all I'm worried about," continued the count. "As you know, we are at war with Strigiol. At least we were last autumn. If we are still at war, then our visitor is taking a great risk by coming here."

Stepping forward, Kytherin stood close to her husband. She slipped a small hand into his large one. With apprehension, she met the count's eyes and asked, "Do you think we have lost?"

Dovan shook his head. "No, I don't believe we lost the war. The Cluain army might not be a match for the Black army, but we could not lose this fast. What I fear is that our good King Lyon de Brodie has come to terms. I believe he has surrendered to save his own skin. The bloody coward!"

With his free hand, Dovan slapped his thigh. "I just don't get it! Where is Artair? Ceredigion should have come to the king's aid! Together we could have held Jerran in check for years."

Rodan Macay put his thoughts aside. As if suddenly realizing he was not alone, the tall, dark-haired man shifted his gaze away from the balcony. Turning to the count, Rodan said with his slight foreign accent, "You should try to relax, and if you can't, then I suggest you at least try to look relaxed."

"Blast it Rodan, what is he planning?" Letting go of his wife's hand, the count began to pace once more, then stopping himself, Dovan apologized to the page and tried harder to stand still.

Now that Dovan had stopped pacing, Rodan started. "He's here, and you can't change that by worrying."

"You should take your own advice," Kytherin said with a forced smile. "You're as bad as my husband!"

"I did not say it was easy." Coming back to the window, Rodan stopped. Crossing his arms over his chest, he stared out over the Iar Sea. Rodan Macay was a strong, handsome man in his late thirties. He was the most sought-after bachelor in the county, yet there was a deep sadness about the dark-haired lord. With a sigh, he turned his back on the view.

"Nothing is easy anymore."

Concerned, Dovan watched Macay. Rodan had always been a quiet, moody man, but in spring it was always worse, and with each passing year, he drew further into himself. With his dark curly black hair and slightly olive colored skin, Rodan seemed out of place in the Reidh county. Dovan knew him as a good and honorable man, as his father before him was. He was a man that Dovan could trust with his life, but Dovan also knew the lord had secrets, secrets that were as dark as his skin. Dark and moody, Rodan was not a happy man. He was a man who put honor above all else, and his deep-seated sense of honor had left scars on the man's soul.

"I am finished, my lord," came the page's soft voice.

"What?" asked Dovan. He tore his eyes away from Rodan and looked down at the boy. "Did you say something?"

"I have finished, my lord," the page repeated. "Should I go?"

Forcing himself, Dovan tried to smile at the boy. *He's so young*, he thought. *Too young to have to deal with all of this.* "Thank you. Yes, you may leave."

The page bowed and left quietly, closing the door behind him.

"Shall I get the Strigiol Lord?" Rodan asked.

"No, let him wait a little longer." Dovan adjusted the pin on his tartan. "Have you any word on the baron's strength?"

"A hundred men, maybe more. It's hard to say. Most of his men are still onboard the ship and so far, they are staying out of sight."

Dovan frowned. "I would have secured the town first. However, a hundred men could not take this castle, nor could they even sufficiently besiege it. Within two days we could have three times as many soldiers. They are either overconfident or up to something."

"Perhaps you are right, and they underestimated the abilities of a rural county," said Rodan.

"A pleasant thought," replied Dovan, "but I don't think so. No, the Lord of Risca knows what he is doing." Thinking to himself, the count paused, then after gathering his thoughts Dovan had made his decision. "After you let the Strigiol lord in, I want you to head for the garrison in town. If we have to move, I want to be able to move fast. If I give the order, I want you to secure the docks first. And no one is to get off the ship until you have word from me. A few dozen men should be able to keep them from landing."

"Yes, my lord."

"And where are those sons of mine? They should be here."

"I'll find them," announced Kytherin. "I would rather be somewhere else, anywhere else." After giving Dovan a kiss, she crossed the room, her long white dress flowing behind her.

Dovan wished he could go with her. Then he called to her before she could leave, "Kytherin, while you're looking for our children, find Elwin too. Tell him to meet Rodan in the stable. Rodan, I want you to take him to the barracks. Once there, I want you to hide the boy somewhere safe, and place a guard on him. I have a bad feeling about this."

"Yes, love," the countess replied and slipped quietly out the door.

Slowly, Dovan walked over to his desk and sank into his chair. Taking a deep breath, he started shuffling through the stacks of papers. After looking at several different documents, he finally picked one out. The paper was large and slightly yellowed. It had something to do with watering rights, but that really did not matter.

"Okay, Rodan," he sighed, "let's get this over with."

While Rodan was gone, the count closed his deep-set eyes and tried to relax.

A few minutes later, Rodan returned. Holding the door open, he stepped off to one side.

Bowing, he said, "Lord, Count Dovan Murray of Reidh, I present his Lordship, Raytand Stanford, Baron of Risca."

Like a conquering hero, the baron entered the room. Eyeing the count, he slowly removed his black leather gloves, shoving them beneath his elaborately engraved silver belt. With a sour look on his face, Rodan pulled the door closed, leaving the two lords alone.

Looking over the top of the document, Dovan studied the baron. He was a big strong man in his mid to late thirties and carried himself like someone who demanded respect. His eyes were dark and cold, suggesting a cruel streak.

Swaggering arrogantly across the room, Raytand came up to the desk. Dovan had seen his type before. Stanford was the kind of man that tried to belittle others to make himself appear bigger, in truth, Stanford was a small man. Not in size, for he stood over six feet tall, but in spirit.

Ignoring the baron, Dovan pretended to be reading the document. The count, who was an excellent judge of character, knew he was not going to like this man.

The Baron of Risca was not accustomed to being kept waiting, and he quickly became impatient. Irritated, he finally asked, "Count Murray?"

"I'll be with you in a moment," replied Dovan, his eyes never leaving the document.

Lord Stanford's attire matched his personality. He wore a dark brown silk shirt with embroidered decorations that was woven in silver thread running along the sleeves. The embroidery was matched by several long silver chains that hung from his neck. Upon every finger was a large, tasteless ring. Blazoned upon his breast was the green boar of the Stanford coat of arms. He wore no sword, but an empty sheath as extravagant as his dress hung at his side. Rodan would never have allowed the baron in with a weapon. Count Dovan took his time with the document. *Let him wait. This is still my county...for the moment, at least.*

"Count Murray!" snapped the baron. "If you please! I have waited long enough!"

The count looked up at the impatient lord. Slowly, he put the document aside. "Yes, can I help you?"

"I hope I have not called at an inconvenient time," replied the baron, regaining some of his arrogant composure.

"Actually." Dovan waved a hand over his desk, "you can see, we are busy today, very busy. It would be more convenient if you could call another day. Tomorrow perhaps, or the next day." *Or never.*

The baron looked down his hawk-like nose. "I regret that's quite impossible. My business requires your immediate attention."

The count looked displeased, but not surprised. Dovan sat back into his chair, folding his arms across his chest. His deep blue eyes met Stanford's. "Then," said Dovan, sounding a little irritated, "I shall ask again. What can I do for you?"

"I am not here as your enemy. You need not be hostile."

"Hostile? Of course not, but one must wonder why such a distinguished lord as yourself would visit our small county."

"The war, as you may or may not know, is now over. Peace has been restored. Now order must be restored as well."

"To what war are you referring? We get little news out here." Dovan, of course, knew of the war. As soon as the mountain passes were clear of snow, he would be marching himself off to war. He and his knights would lend what aid they could offer to their king and country, but for now, he wanted to see Raytand's reaction.

Raytand Stanford frowned. The thought of being stuck out here in a county isolated from the rest of the world obviously did not appeal to the Strigiol lord. Dovan found that unsettling. It suggested that Raytand Stanford was planning to stay for a while, at least longer than either one would like.

"There was a brief war between our two countries," explained Stanford, "but as I said, it is now over. The war was a misunderstanding that thankfully has been corrected. Cluain and Strigiol are now friends and allies. I am simply here to help restore order."

Doubtful, thought Dovan as he nervously tapped the desk. *Sounds like our good King Lyon has buckled under to King Jerran...just like him, too.*

"As you can see, we have no disorder," pointed out Dovan. The count sounded much calmer than he truly was. "We were not even aware there was a war. Reidh is a quiet place. We have no need of your help." Noticing his tapping, Dovan nonchalantly put his left hand over his right.

"Perhaps," responded Stanford doubtfully. He turned and walked towards the glass doors. With his back to the count, the baron went on. "And perhaps not. We have reason to believe there is an enemy of the crown in your county...an enemy that poses a threat that could disrupt the peace that both our kingdoms have and continue to strive for. That is why I am here. I am to apprehend the individual and see that peace is maintained." The baron quickly spun around as if trying to catch the count's reaction. He found none. Despite what he was feeling, Dovan managed a lethargic expression.

That's it, thought Dovan. *He knows Elwin is here, but how!?* Then he said out loud, "Of course we shall help you locate this person. If on your way out, you would give what information you have to my sergeant-at-arms, we will then conduct a thorough investigation. Reidh will not rest until this threat has passed."

"I don't think you understand what I mean. I am here to take over." A sly smile crossed the baron's face. The smile reminded Dovan of a weasel in a chicken coop. Then, as if Stanford were grinding the count under his heels, he walked back to the desk. Looking down at Dovan, Raytand's smile broadened.

"Since when does a Strigiol lord give orders in the Cluain Kingdom?" Dovan demanded.

"High King Jerran's orders are all the authority I need!"

"High King Jerran?!" Dovan leaned back into his chair. "What is this nonsense?"

"I hope I will not be forced to confine you to your private chambers," Stanford said bluntly.

"Confine me!" shouted Dovan, coming to his feet. "This is my castle! My land! You have no authority here!"

Once more, the baron's thin lips curled into a smile. "Very well, my good lord," gloated Stanford as he pulled out a scroll. "I think this might answer all your questions."

Dovan snatched the scroll from Stanford's outstretched hand. Immediately, he recognized King Lyon's seal. He broke the wax and unrolled the scroll, his hands shook slightly. As Dovan read, his eyes widened.

To our dear lord, *Dovan Murray,*
Count of Reidh.

The kingdoms of Kambrya are

*once more blessed with a High King.
King Jerran of Strigiol has graciously
accepted the burden of High King. The
land cries out in joy and praises the
peace of the High King. We (the crown
of Cluain) have gratefully and warmly
embraced our sovereign, the High King
Jerran. This is welcome news. Rejoice,
my count, for peace has been restored!*

*The days of old are back. The
High King has returned! You and your
sons are to go to Gildas at your earliest
convenience and swear fealty to the
High King. We also request you give his
Lordship, the Baron of Risca, every
respect, and courtesy. Lord Stanford
speaks for High King Jerran, and you
are to obey his word as you would
mine.*

Long live the High King.

*Signed,
Lyon de Brodie, King of Cluain.*

Crumbling the scroll in his hand, Dovan dropped back into his seat.

After a long hesitation, Dovan composed himself. "What is it you wish, my ... my lord?" he asked, nearly choking on the words. He knew he could have Raytand imprisoned, and he could probably do the same to his men still aboard the ship, but that would only be a short fix. When news got out, King de Brodie would label him an outlaw and traitor, and more soldiers would be sent, more than the count's small county could hope to deal with. No, Dovan would have to find a more subtle way of dealing with the baron, and to do that he would have to play along.

"It is not all that bad, my count. This need not be a permanent situation. The sooner I find my man, the sooner I leave. So, you see, by helping me you'll be helping yourself. If somehow you could hand him over today, then I could be gone by morning. A pleasant prospect, no doubt."

No doubt, thought Dovan, *but unlikely. You will get no help from me. Do you really think I would betray Elwin just to have my county back? Fool!*

"What is it you want from me?" Dovan asked out loud.

"Good," replied the baron. "Shall we cooperate then?"

"It seems I have little choice."

"Ah yes, that is true," said the baron as he adjusted one of his rings. Then he looked straight at the count. "Let us start with the traitor prince of Ceredigion. Where is he?"

Dovan raised both his eyebrows in what he hoped was a look of surprise. "Prince Elwin, here? What makes you think a prince would be here in Reidh?"

"Cooperation, remember?" Stanford patronizingly. "I know he is here. How I know does not matter. What I want to know is where he is."

"I have no idea where the prince is," lied Dovan. Actually, it was not truly a lie. He did not know "exactly" where the prince was.

Suddenly and unexpectedly, Raytand Stanford went into a rage. The veins in his neck bulged and pulsed. Violently, he cleared the desk with a sweep of his arm. Papers went flying across the room. Placing his hands flat upon the desk, he leaned forward, his face only inches from Dovan's.

"Do not play games with me!" threatened the baron.

Trying to stay calm, Dovan swallowed his anger and replied, "I told you, I do not know."

"WHERE IS HE?!"

Dovan frowned. "Do you doubt my word?"

"Yes, I do! You are a liar and we both know it!" Stanford's eyes were hard and cruel. Then just as unexpectedly as his sudden rage, his eyes softened, and the baron stood back up.

Surprised by the baron's sudden mood change, Dovan stared silently, not knowing what to say.

"Yes, you are lying, but I expected no less," the Baron said, becoming so calm it was eerie. "That is where the challenge lies, does it not? And in the end, it will not matter. I will find and take what I want."

"You cannot find what is not here."

"Oh, he is here, all right." smiled Stanford. "We both know that. But for now, all I need is your obedience."

"You shall have it."

"Of course, I will. I demand nothing less," declared Stanford, "and you will begin by ordering your men to obey my soldiers. I would hate to have a conflict."

"You brought soldiers?" Again, Dovan already knew about the soldiers.

"Yes, and it was a wise choice on my part. I doubt if your men would be any more helpful than you have been."

Dovan shrugged as if it did not matter. "You, of course, may do as you like, but I have held nothing from you. I can only tell you what I know. Search the castle if you like."

Stanford gave him a doubtful look and laughed. "You cannot fool me, my count! I see right through you!"

"If there is nothing more," said Dovan, coming to his feet, "I should get word to my men that you are in charge and to obey your soldiers. As you said, we do not want a conflict. I will have the east wing prepared for your stay."

"Yes, that will do."

With a smirk, Raytand added, "Oh, there is one other thing. Have this study cleaned out by tonight; I will be needing it."

Dovan bit his lip. Using the pain to control his anger, he answered with a stiff nod of his head and hurried out of the room.

CHAPTER THREE

Taking advantage of the warm day, Elwin and Pallas decided to walk into town. It was only a few miles from the Keep to Port Murray, and they figured it would only take a couple of hours.

"I don't want to get muddy," said Elwin, looking at the road that lay before him. The warm sunny day had melted much of the snow, turning the dirt into mud.

Pallas pointed to the grassy edge of the road. "If we walk along the edge, we'll be alright."

But Pallas was wrong. They had only gone a short distance when a wagon headed for the keep approached. Heavily loaded with barrels, the wagon kicked up a thick muddy spray.

Realizing what was about to happen, Elwin shouted, "Watch out!"

Elwin's warning came too late. The passing wagon showered them with a wave of muddy water. Elwin and Pallas looked down at their soiled clothes and laughed. From head to toe, they were covered in mud. From a glance, they looked like a pair of vagabonds.

Laughing, the two youths had almost forgotten why they were headed into town. Elwin and Pallas were on their way to the Dryrot Inn. At the inn, they figured on finding one of the sailors that had arrived aboard the cargo ship. The Dryrot was a gathering place for fishermen and sailors alike. It would not be too hard for the boys to discover when the ship was going to sail. Once Elwin determined when the ship was to weigh anchor, he planned to become a stowaway and began his journey home.

Ignorant of what was happening back in the castle, and in high spirits, Elwin and Pallas had started off towards town, but their mood quickly changed. Their short walk to town was taking much longer than they had originally thought. The wet, muddy conditions were slowing down their progress, and the two-hour stroll was already into its third hour. As the sun sank over the horizon, the first day of spring was coming to an end, and the temperature began to fall. To top it off, clouds rolled in over the mountains, bringing rain. Weather in Reidh often changed quickly. Overhead, a thunderbolt cracked, releasing the rains that now poured down. Muddy, wet, and cold, they pulled their hoods tightly over their heads and struggled on.

"We should have ridden into town after all," Pallas murmured beneath his hood. "This rain will be changing to snow before long." As if to make his point, Pallas pointed up at the darkening sky.

"Wonderful!" shivered Elwin. He began to walk faster. Elwin knew that if Pallas said it was going to snow, it would, and the sooner he was in a warm, dry place the happier he would be.

The rain made a constant slapping sound as the large drops hit the already-drenched earth. Miserable and soaked to the skin, Pallas and Elwin walked in silence. Both were too cold and tired to hold a conversation.

Hearing something, Elwin lifted his head. He glanced over his shoulder. "There's a rider coming," he announced loud enough for Pallas to hear over the rain.

Pallas stopped. "Coming from the keep," he observed, looking back the way they had come. "And he is in a hurry, too."

Kicking up mud, the horse and rider were rapidly approaching. Already soaked to the skin, Elwin and Pallas did not try to move out of the way. It did not seem possible that they could get any wetter.

Without slowing down, the horse and rider raced past.

"Hey, that was Lord Rodan!" Pallas exclaimed. "I wonder where he is going in such a hurry."

"Someplace warm, no doubt," returned Elwin between chattering teeth.

Pallas tried to laugh, but he was too cold. "I'm surprised he did not recognize us."

Elwin smiled weakly from the dark shadows of his brown and muddy hood. "Dressed like this," he pointed to their muddy-looking clothing, "who would?"

Pallas nodded in silent agreement. But why was he in such a hurry? Pallas had a strange sensation that something was not right in town. "We better hurry, if we are going to beat the snow."

By the time they reached the outskirts of town, night had taken a firm hold over the countryside. The streets of Port Murray were deserted and quiet. The weather seemed to put a damper on the activity. The first ship of the year was securely anchored in the harbor. Typically, the first ship of the year caused excitement. The town should have been alive with festivities and merrymaking, but on this night the citizens of Port Murray seemed to be more concerned with staying warm.

"Something is wrong," whispered Pallas. His feelings became stronger with every passing moment.

Elwin looked at his friend in mild surprise. "Wrong?"

"I know it is a miserable night," Pallas continued, "but cold or not, Port Murray should be celebrating. We are used to this type of weather. It would take more than a rainy night to keep people home."

"I think you're crazy. It is cold and wet. If we had any brains at all, we would be home sitting before a roaring fire."

"I guess," consented Pallas, but still, he could not shake his uneasiness. *Maybe Elwin is right,* thought Pallas, trying to convince himself. *Perhaps it is just the weather,* yet something told him it was not.

The Dryrot Inn was near the harbor, so Elwin and Pallas had to cut through the center of town to reach the inn. At first, Elwin was convinced that Pallas was imagining things, but as time went on, he began to wonder as well. Each house they passed was dark and still. It was as if everyone was asleep. Wanting to be someplace warm and dry, Elwin could believe that the weather was keeping people home, but it was too early to be putting out the lights and going to bed. It was as if the whole town was frightened and hiding behind locked doors.

The wind whistled down the deserted streets. Elwin started peering down every alley they passed. Elwin had the feeling that they were being watched, as if eyes from every window and alley stared out at them. It was a silly notion, nothing more than an unfounded fear of the darkness. But still, Elwin shivered, and no longer from just the cold. Slowly, they were making their way along the streets when something just ahead of them moved. The strange night was making both boys a little edgy, so when they saw something among the shadows, they nearly jumped out of their skins. Something before them stepped out into the street. Elwin began to pray. Slowly, the form crept out of the shadows and into the light of a streetlamp. Only then did they see that it was only an old woman. Relieved and feeling a bit foolish, both Elwin and Pallas let out a long sigh. Elwin smiled at himself for letting the dark night get to him. He was no longer a child, he told himself. He should not jump at the sight of an old lady, or cringe from every dark shadow.

The old woman, bent with age, was carrying an armful of firewood; she slowly crossed the street.

"Hello, there!" Pallas called out.

The old woman looked up with a start. She had not seen them approaching. Her eyes opened wide. Elwin saw her haggard face in the dim light. She was terrified. Dropping her wood, she gathered up her skirt and ran. For an old woman, she ran much faster than Elwin would have thought possible.

"Hey! Stop!" yelled Pallas. But the woman did not heed his call, and she vanished into the night.

"Well," said Pallas. "What do you make of that?"

"I think you were right before," murmured Elwin. "Something is wrong. Let's get to the Dryrot. I want to get off these streets."

Pallas and Elwin hurried on as they cautiously kept their voices low and tried to stay off the main streets.

"The inn is just ahead," whispered Pallas.

Turning a corner, Elwin gasped and came to a sudden halt. Coming down the street was a squad of soldiers. A dozen armed men marched towards them in military formation. Over their chain mail, each man wore a long green tunic. Blazoned upon the tunics were the emblems of a boar. The boar was not the insignia of the Murray clan, nor any other noble family in Cluain. The boar was the device of the Stanford's, a powerful family in Strigiol.

Strigiol men in Reidh County could only mean one thing— Elwin had been discovered. Elwin felt a wave of panic and a shiver run down his spine. His first thought was to run.

"Stay calm," murmured Pallas, as if he knew what Elwin was thinking. "They won't recognize you."

Following Pallas' lead, Elwin stepped off to the side of the street to let the soldiers pass.

"Are you sure?"

"No," admitted Pallas.

In all his life, Elwin had never found it so hard to stand still. All thoughts of the cold and rainy night were gone. Now he was filled with a different kind of chill—fear.

Lord Rodan didn't recognize us, Elwin reminded himself, trying to stay calm. *But he was on a horse and riding fast. Would these soldiers be fooled by muddy clothing? What if they ask me something?* Elwin knew that his accent would give him away. He did not sound like a native of Reidh County, and he definitely did not sound like the common folk he was pretending to be. Fear again urged him to run, but now it was too late. The soldiers were upon them, and there was no place to go.

With their backs against a wall, Elwin and Pallas sank into the shadows. From beneath their hoods, they gazed out at the soldiers. Pulling his cloak tighter about him, Elwin prayed that they would not stop, but of course, they did. At the head of the patrol was a heavily built sergeant. As if he could read Elwin's mind, the sergeant raised his hand. The gesture brought the patrol to a halt. Slowly, the sergeant turned his large head and looked at the two boys. He had the look of a seasoned veteran. His skin looked as tough as leather, and across the right cheek was a long ugly scar. Unsnapping his sword hilt, the sergeant approached. He seemed to be twice the size of Elwin and Pallas. His hard-dark eyes glared down at them. Rain ran off his iron helmet and down his once-broken nose to dance across his war hardened face. Somewhere above, a thunderbolt cracked and lightning flashed, turning night into day then back to night.

"What are your names?" the sergeant demanded in a harsh gravelly voice. "And what is your business here?"

Pallas looked up at the sergeant. "I am Gavin, and this is me brother Eoin. We have come from our Pa's farm to celebrate the first ship of the year. Our farm is on the coast."

Pallas pointed to the south. "We saw the ship sail by earlier today."

Elwin was amazed at how quickly Pallas had come up with the lie. Also, to his surprise, Pallas had suddenly acquired a thick country accent.

The sergeant nodded his head as if he had heard the same story more than once this night. Pallas knew he would have. Once the countryside folks heard that a ship was in the harbor, they would be heading into town. In a few days' time, the city would be busting at the seams.

"You, rural folk are easily entertained," the sergeant growled.

"Aye, me lord," Pallas smiled. "We indeed live simply here in Reidh. A ship to us is a mighty impressive thing."

"I am a sergeant, not a lord!" snapped the man. Timidly, Pallas bowed his head. "I meant no offense."

"Soldiers do the work, while lords stay dry. That is the way of this world, boy."

"Aye—sergeant."

The sergeant turned his eyes on Elwin. "And what's your story, boy?"

"Sorry?"

The sergeant's eyes took on a hard look as he stared down at Elwin. "Is this brother of yours, Gavin, telling me the truth?"

"Aye." Elwin, despite the cold night, felt himself beginning to sweat. Keeping his answers short, he hoped the sergeant could not tell that his and Pallas' accents were different.

The sergeant curled his thumbs around his sword belt. "You seem nervous, boy. Am I making you nervous?"

"Aye—I mean no."

"He has always been that way," Pallas added quickly. "He is

a little slow, but a good worker all the same."

A scowl crossed the sergeant's face. "Well, you two had better get moving. Either find some rooms or head on back to that farm of yours. Port Murray is under a curfew. In two hours, no one will be allowed on the streets." With that, the sergeant spun on his heels. Apparently, he was in a hurry to have his patrol over with. He too wanted to find a warm place to dry out.

Unaware that he had been holding his breath, Elwin let out a long sigh. Relieved, he watched the soldiers march on. Taking what seemed like a very long time, the soldiers finally turned down a side street and disappeared. With the sergeant and his men gone, Elwin leaned back against the wall. "That was close."

"Those were Strigiol men, weren't they?" asked Pallas. "They seem to think that this is their country."

Elwin nodded. "They belong to Lord Stanford of Risca. I recognize the coat-of-arms."

"Are you thinking what I'm thinking?"

"That they are here because of me? Yes, I am. I can think of no other reason for Strigiol to send men into Reidh."

"And what are they doing patrolling Port Murray like it's theirs?" asked Pallas angrily.

"I don't know." Elwin shrugged. "But I bet that's why Lord Rodan was in such a hurry when he raced past us earlier on the road."

"Well, the ship is definitely out of the question," agreed Pallas.

Elwin had forgotten about the ship. It had to be from Strigiol, and the last thing he wanted was to stowaway on a Strigiol ship.

"Father would know what to do," added Pallas. "But I think it would be dangerous heading back home."

"I agree," added Elwin. "But what should we do?"

"We have to get you off the streets," continued Pallas. "So, I guess we should go ahead and visit the Dryrot Inn. It's right here, and if there is news to be had, it will be found there. After that, we better find a place to hide you."

Elwin nodded.

"Where did you learn to lie so fast?" added Elwin as they came up to the two large doors of the inn. "You were pretty quick back there. And what was that about me being slow?"

Pallas laughed. He was almost enjoying this. "You're a prince. Do I need to say more? All princes are slow. As for the lying, I think Aidan taught me that, remember?"

Elwin could not help but smile at the thought of their friend. Pallas was right, and this was the type of adventure that Aidan would have thought up. Elwin could remember the elf talking them into all sorts of things, like sneaking into the temple of the Three Gods to steal some of Priest Quadroon's ceremonial wine. And when they were caught, which was all too often, it was always Pallas who came up with a reason for being where they were not supposed to be. Elwin wished Aidan was here and that this was all just one of his adventures. But he was not. Elwin's smile turned into a frown. As children, the exploits had always been fun. He feared that this real-life adventure was just beginning, and it was certainly not fun.

Grateful to have finally made it, Elwin and Pallas pushed through a pair of doors and into the Dryrot Inn. As they entered, they were greeted by a wave of warm air. The large room glowed brightly, and a blazing fire crackled in the hearth. Few people had ventured out this night, and only a handful of men occupied the warm room. Most of the tables stood empty with their chairs still sitting on top of them. The proprietor would make little profit on this night. Those who had come out to the Dryrot huddled close to the blazing fire as if its warmth could ward off the dark and evil night that lay just beyond the doors. In soft, quiet voices, the few patrons of the inn talked among themselves.

Elwin looked around the room. The patron's soft voices went suddenly quiet. Every face turned towards Elwin and Pallas. In the kitchen door stood a young barmaid, her wide eyes were glued to the two boys, like a statue, she stood motionless. It was as if she had suddenly sprouted roots. Behind the long narrow bar, a slightly overweight barkeep slowly dried some mugs. Putting down his towel, the heavyset man wiped his hands on his dirty apron. Elwin's eyes drifted from face to face. Like the old woman the two had seen earlier, the faces of the inn's patrons were filled with fear. They looked at Elwin and Pallas as if they were witnessing some evil manifestation of the night—an evil that had just walked into their hiding place.

Closing the doors, Pallas shut out the night. With the sound of the storm removed, the room seemed to grow even quieter. Staring over their mugs, the men that were huddled by the fire watched and waited to see who these newcomers might be. The barmaid trembled slightly. She looked like she wanted to run, but her feet refused to move.

"A warm welcome," Elwin whispered to Pallas. Taking off their wet cloaks, Elwin and Pallas shook off the rain and hung them up. Only then did the faces in the room transform into smiles. Everyone in Reidh recognized their young lord and his companion whom they knew as Eoin. The barmaid stopped trembling, and the barkeep turned back to his dishes.

Once more, the sound of the bar came back to life.

"Oh-ho," called one of the men by the fire. "It's Lord Pallas and his young friend Eoin. Did not recognize you dressed so—so un-noble like."

"It's a cold, wet night," Pallas offered as an explanation.

Several voices added their agreement and called them over to join them. Elwin and Pallas crossed the room and took a table near the others, yet one far enough away where they could talk without being overheard. Elwin leaned back into his chair, letting the heat of the fire sink in. The night had left him shaken, but the fire and closeness of others gave him a sense of security. It was more than simply the weather or the Strigiol soldiers that bothered the prince. There was a presence about the night. It was the kind of night where one is constantly looking over one's shoulder, the type of night that unexplainably felt as if some dark presence hid in the shadows and down every dark alley. Elwin was not the only one disturbed by the strangeness of the night. The Dryrot was a gathering place for those who did not wish to be alone. It was a protective place, or at least it felt like it.

Pallas ordered two mugs of the famed Reidh ale, but the barmaid smiled, saying she would be right back with two hot ciders.

When she returned, Pallas complained, "We are old enough for ale."

The barmaid placed the mugs down before them and gave Pallas a wink, causing the young lord to blush. "Your father might think otherwise. And speaking of your father, does he know you are here?"

Trying not to turn any redder, Pallas replied with a shrug, "Does it matter? Like I said, we are old enough to do as we wish."

Her smile broadened. "So, your father doesn't mind you visiting taverns?"

"Does yours?" Pallas returned. "You're not that much older than me."

She laughed softly and kissed Pallas on the cheek. "I guess he does mind, at that. But he's hoping I'll meet a nice young man, or maybe even a lord to marry." Pallas blushed all the more.

Elwin smiled but said nothing. The waitress' name was Lili, and she had been teasing Pallas for years, knowing the young lord had a crush on her.

Closing his eyes, Elwin listened to the murmur of the voices around him. The hot mug between his cold hands and the warmth of the fire felt good. As his clothes started to dry, Elwin felt himself relaxing. He reminded himself that he was not out of danger yet, and he needed to be making plans. However, his body was too tired and comfortable to listen. He felt as if he could fall asleep right there. Then something came between himself and the heat of the fire. Irritated at whatever was blocking the heat, he forced his eyes open.

The cause of his irritation was a man of medium height, who had extremely wide shoulders.

His firm, well-formed muscles rippled over his body. Elwin recognized him as a fisherman.

Fishing was a hard, grueling profession and Reidh had many such men like this one. Looking weather-beaten and as hard as stone, the fisherman bent over Elwin's shoulder to look at Pallas.

"Lord Pallas, can I have a word with ya?"

In Reidh County, there was a casual relationship between the people and the nobility. In a community as small as Port Murray, there was no room for false pride. In Reidh, being a noble was just another job.

"Sure, Jon," Pallas replied with a friendly smile. "Have a seat. Maybe between the two of us, we can keep Eoin here awake."

Elwin shook his head. How could Pallas be so carefree? His father's land had just become occupied; he was being hunted, and yet Pallas could still smile and make a joke. It was almost disgusting, and it certainly was not fair. Even half-asleep, Elwin could not stop worrying.

Through nearly closed eyes, Elwin watched Jon drop into an empty chair. Jon was built like a rock and was just as heavy. Elwin waited for the chair to give way under the fisherman's weight, but it somehow held together. The man tipped back his head and poured a mug of ale down his throat. With the back of his hand, Jon wiped the foam from his mouth. "There's trouble in town," Jon announced as if it was something they did not already know.

In Port Murray, everyone knew everyone. Jon was a likable sort of guy, but he tended to drink too much and was not the most intelligent of men, but his heart was as pure as gold. He was a lifelong bachelor and owned his fishing boat. Most fishermen worked on boats that belonged to others. Only about one in ten fishermen owned their own vessel, or in some rarer cases, two or more boats. Jon was one of those who had worked hard and had saved enough money to buy his own boat. He was a proud man, and prouder still of his boat.

"So, we have seen," replied Pallas. "We ran into a patrol on the way here."

Jon glanced worriedly at Elwin. "And you had no problems?"

"No," answered Pallas. "Have you heard anything?"

Jon shrugged. "We." He indicated the other men in the room with a wave of his empty mug. "We are kind of hopin' you could tell us somethin'—you bein' the count's son and all."

"I guess we left before father knew anything," Pallas

answered. Then he asked, "Have you heard anything at all?"

"Only rumors."

"And?…" Pallas asked, encouraging Jon to continue.

"I spoke to Kaev, one of the town's guardsmen," explained Jon. "He says they were told not to resist the Strigiol soldiers. King Lyon's orders or somethin' like that."

"That would make sense," Pallas said. "Father would not stand aside unless ordered to do so."

Jon leaned over the table and lowered his voice to a whisper. "Some are sayin' your father has sold out."

Pallas' lips thinned, and his blue eyes narrowed. Silently, he looked down at the table. Being of fair complexion, Pallas turned red easily, and at the moment he looked like a ripe tomato ready to burst. Elwin could feel the tension.

Jon too could feel Pallas' anger and held up his large callused hands. "Not me," he said quickly. "I know your father be a good man. 'Tis only the talk of them knuckleheads down at the docks. We Reidhens know that Count Murray is a true friend. He's done much for us. No matter what, Reidh will stick by your father. And those who won't, will get their heads knocked together."

Still angry, Pallas silently stared at the table.

"There's more," Jon went on. His voice took on a more serious tone. "I think Eoin is in some bit of trouble."

With that, Pallas looked up with a start.

"Me?" asked Elwin

"Aye," replied Jon. "The soldiers have been lookin' and askin' about a boy." Jon looked across the table at Elwin. "A boy who looks a lot like you. They say he be an enemy of High King Jerran." Jon spat on the floor as if King Jerran's name left a foul taste in his mouth. "None says 'tis you they are lookin' for, but it is. Don't need a name to know 'tis you they want."

"I appreciate the warning," Elwin responded.

"Good thing you were in that muddy cloak," noted Pallas, forgetting his anger.

"Yes," Elwin agreed. "But it is strange. That sergeant never asked us about this person. Though I can't say why they would want me," he added for Jon's benefit. "They must have me confused with someone else. But all the same, I think I should stay clear of them."

"Perhaps the sergeant was in a hurry to get out of the rain," Pallas offered.

Elwin nodded. So far, he had been lucky, but he was far from safe. "Now what?"

"We can hide you," Jon cut in. "We been talkin', me and the boys, and we don't care what you did. If Count Murray and Pallas say you're okay, that's good enough for us. Besides, we figure if you did somethin' to make an enemy of King Jerran, then you are a friend, and a might tougher than you look." Jon grinned broadly. He was obviously not taken in by Elwin's story.

"We may not be cultured here, but we know you are no Riedhen. You don't look, talk or act like folks around here. First time I saw you, I knew you were hidin' from somethin'. Most everyone in the county knows, too. We can recognize our own pretty quickly. But we said nothin'. Most figure if Count Dovan is helpin' you, it must be for some good reason."

Elwin frowned. He thought he had played his part well. *But if Jon could see through me, then the whole blasted place can!* Shaking his head, Elwin realized that in the past three years he had fooled no one. However, it was comforting to know that the whole town was keeping his secret. Reidh was indeed a very special place.

"Did I fool anyone?" asked Elwin hopefully.

"Sorry," Jon apologized as if somehow it was his fault. "If it helps, we don't know who you are or where you're from. We just know that you're not a Reidhen."

Pallas laughed. "And you thought I would blow your cover! You are some great actor!"

"That's not funny," retorted Elwin. "Nothing about this is funny."

Uncharacteristically, Pallas suddenly became serious. "You can't go back to the keep. They'll be looking for you there. We have to find a place where you can hide, someplace where they won't think of looking."

"I agree," said Elwin, "but where?"

"That's what I was sayin'," Jon cut in. "I have a place you can stay at."

Elwin looked over at the big man. "It could be dangerous."

"It already 'tis. But I want to help."

"Thank you, Jon. What do you have in mind?"

"I have a small workshop over on the north side of the bay. It's nothin' much, but it's isolated, and you can hide there until we think of somethin' better."

"But how am I to get past the patrols?"

"By boat," Jon answered. "The docks aren't far. We should be able to reach them. Once out in the harbor, you'll be safe. In the rain and dark, I don't think anyone will spot us."

"I will not forget this," said Elwin. "You are a good man, Jon."

Jon shrugged off the compliment. "It's what we folks do for one another, and you're one of us now." Jon slapped Elwin on the back, nearly knocking him out of his chair.

"I'll head for the town garrison," added Pallas. "That's

probably where Lord Rodan was headed. He can take a message to father. He'll know what to do. Then I'll come back here, and Jon can take us both across the bay."

Elwin thought about objecting to Pallas coming along but decided against it. He was scared and did not want to be alone. "Okay."

Pallas finished off his cider and rose out of his seat. "I'll be back as fast as I can."

Elwin watched his friend cross the room. Pallas slipped back into his cloak. Smiling, he glanced back at Elwin. Pallas looked like a child excited about playing a game. Elwin prayed, hoping Pallas would be careful.

Pallas turned and stepped through the door and disappeared back into the stormy night.

Standing on the stoop of the inn, Pallas wrapped his cloak tightly around himself. The cold wind was still whistling through the streets, and it was starting to snow. Turning his head one way, then another, he cautiously scanned the deserted street. Satisfied that no one was watching, he stepped away from the Inn and hurried off to find Lord Rodan.

CHAPTER FOUR

Elwin leaned back into his chair. *Relax*, he told himself. *Pallas will be back soon.* He took a sip of his cider. From across the inn, Elwin watched the barkeep and barmaid. Despite there being very little for them to do, the man and woman stayed busy. They found tables to polish, floors to sweep, and dishes to wash— anything to keep their minds off the stormy night. Once in a while, someone would call for more ale, and they would race into action, competing to see who could get there first. At other times, the two would suddenly begin to argue. The arguments would erupt spontaneously, and for no apparent reason, the two would simply stop whatever they were doing and start bickering. It was as if they were responding to some unspoken cue.

It was while watching the barmaid and barkeep exchanging an array of colorful language that Elwin noticed a stranger.

Funny that I had not seen him earlier, Elwin mused. *And I don't recognize him. I thought I knew everyone in town.* The man sat alone in the far corner. Long shadows made it hard for Elwin to see his face. However, he could see that the man was dressed in a long brown robe that was gathered together at his waist by a thin, darker brown rope.

Probably a Priest from the temple abbey, Elwin told himself. *That's why I do not recognize him. The priests and monks of the abbey rarely come to town. But do they wear brown?*

"He's been watchin' you," Jon said, interrupting Elwin's train of thought.

"What was that?" Elwin had forgotten that Jon was still sitting next to him.

"The man you be lookin' at," replied Jon with a nod of his head. "He has been watchin' you."

Elwin stared suspiciously at the priest. "Who is he?"

"Don't know. But I can tell ya he ain't from Reidh. He came in just before the rains started. Since then he's just been sittin' there. He's not ordered a thin'."

"Could he be from the abbey? A priest maybe?"

"'Tis not likely. They wear gray, not brown. Besides, them monks don't drink and would never visit an inn."

Looking back at the stranger, Elwin flinched. The robed man was staring back at him. The stranger's intense scrutiny made Elwin nervous. The priest, if that's what he was, never moved or shifted. He just sat there studying Elwin from across the room.

The man had both an ancient, and at the same time, an ageless look about him. Small bands of silvery gray ran through his otherwise long, dark hair. The well-groomed beard that covered his chin was also streaked in gray. He had a long face with leathery brown skin. But the most striking aspect of the priest were his eyes. From below a pair of bushy eyebrows were two deep set eyes. His gray eyes were cold and misty, like a stormy sea. Elwin shifted uncomfortably. He felt exposed under the scrutiny of those strange eyes.

Elwin looked away. "Could he be from Strigiol?"

A concerned look crossed Jon's face as he caught onto what Elwin was suggesting. "Has to be. How else could he have gotten to Reidh except on the Strigiol ship."

After some time, the priest closed his eyes and leaned back into his chair. When the priest did not open his eyes again, Elwin decided the man must have fallen off to sleep. Elwin took a sip of his cider. *I have an overly active imagination. There's no need to create problems where they don't exist.*

Jon got up. "I need more ale," he announced. "If you need me, just give a holler."

Taking another sip of his drink, Elwin tried once more to relax. He sat back, covering a yawn with the back of his hand. He placed his mug to his mouth and took a long drink. Just then the priest suddenly opened his eyes and stood up. Nearly spitting out a mouthful of cider, Elwin sat up with a jolt. Waiting to catch Elwin alone, the gray-eyed man had only been pretending to be sleeping.

Advancing across the inn, the priest walked across the uneven wooden floor, his silvery gray hair glimmered brightly in the firelight. In his hand, he grasped a wooden staff that thumped against the floor as he walked. With a final thump, the tall man stopped before Elwin's table.

Elwin's first thought was to call out for Jon, but he decided against it. *Don't act like a scared child,* he told himself. *It's only an old priest. He has done nothing to offend or threaten you. What is wrong with you? And what can Jon do anyway? Pick the old man up and toss him out? Nice way to treat a priest that has done nothing more than walk across a room.*

"Good evening, Prince Elwin," the priest said in a quiet voice so that only Elwin could hear. "May I sit?"

Elwin's mouth dropped open. The priest knew him! In the name of the three gods! *He is from Strigiol.* Now Elwin wanted to call out for Jon, but his voice was gone.

Not waiting to be invited, the priest settled down into the seat directly across from Elwin. His eyes sparkled as he leaned his staff against an empty chair. He gave Elwin a nod and a half smile. "It is not wise for you to be in such a public place."

Swallowing, Elwin responded, "I think you must have mistaken me for someone else." Even to himself, Elwin thought his voice sounded weak and unconvincing. "My name is Eoin, and I am a servant of Count Dovan Murray's household." He tried to smile. "And I am no prince."

"You are in grave danger." Ignoring Elwin as if his denial was too ridiculous even to consider, the priest went on. "I have been looking for you. I've traveled a very long way, and it seems I have arrived just in time."

"Who are you?" asked Elwin. He was sure this man was no priest.

The stranger pulled a pipe from beneath his robe. "I am called many things, but I prefer Faynn. It is my given name." Staring over the flickering flame of the table's candle, the man watched for Elwin's reaction.

"Faynn Catach? The Wizard?!" exclaimed Elwin, sitting forward and nearly knocking over his drink.

Faynn nodded. "Yes, but I'm a druid, not a wizard, and I would also advise you to keep your voice down. I am rarely a welcome visitor."

A shiver ran through Elwin. Despite the fact that he held the warm mug of cider between his hands, Elwin felt cold. He had heard of the Druid. Everyone in Kambrya had heard of Faynn Catach, but few had ever seen him. Elwin, like many others, thought the man was just a story to scare children into behaving. Elwin swallowed. Faynn Catach; it was a name of mystery, of strange powers, and of fear.

With long, narrow fingers, the Druid stuffed some tobacco into the bowl of his pipe. "The stories you have heard about me," Faynn went on, "are half-truths at best. Trust me, Elwin, I am your friend. May I call you Elwin? I have always had a dislike for titles. You must believe me. You are in greater danger than you think. Evil is returning to the land. That evil is growing stronger and will soon be free. Already, its foul hand reaches out, spreading darkness over the land like a plague. And some things have already awakened—things that should never have left their dark hiding places; things of great evil, and they are looking for you." Putting his pipe in his mouth, Faynn reached towards the candle. Taking the candle, he held its flickering flame to the bowl of his pipe and inhaled deeply, pulling the flame down into the bowl. He repeated this several times until the tobacco glowed brightly. The burning tobacco gave off a strange, yet pleasant aroma. After lighting his pipe, Faynn continued. "However, it is not wise to talk of such things on a night like this. We can talk later. First, we must find a place where you will be safe."

"What do you want from me?" Elwin gave up trying to pretend he was Eoin. It seemed everyone could see through his disguise—Jon, the druid, and the whole population of Reidh County knew he was not Eoin. The only one Elwin had fooled was himself.

"To help you," Faynn responded with a nod of his head.

Elwin peered at the Druid skeptically. "I think it is you that I need protection from, you and your Strigiol friends."

"Strigiol friends?" Faynn almost laughed. "If that were true, would I have told you my name?" He let out a puff of smoke. Before drifting upwards, the smoke seemed to dance around the druid's head. "Would I have approached you here in a public place surrounded by your friends? If I am with the Strigiol army, why have I not gone for the soldiers? And why am I here talking to you?"

Why indeed? thought Elwin. *You had to have arrived on the Strigiol ship. How else could you have gotten into the county? It has to be some trick. I have to be careful. If you really are the druid, I'm in great danger.* Yet Faynn seemed harmless sitting there, smoking his pipe. He talked of dangers, but looked kind and gentle, like a grandfather.

"Why do you want to help me?" Elwin finally asked.

"There are some who want to see you fail." Another puff of smoke danced around the druid's head before ascending towards the ceiling. "I do not wish that to happen." Elwin watched the rising smoke.

"Fail? Fail at what? And why should you care?"

The druid sighed, "There is much to talk about, but this is neither the time nor place.

You must go somewhere safe. Let me help you, Elwin. Before it's too late."

"How do I know you are not lying? You might take me to some dark alley and kill me. Besides, I have already arranged something else. I don't need your help."

Faynn's smoky gray eyes turned hard. Elwin felt as if he could drown in those eyes. The druid took his pipe from his mouth and set it aside. The grandfather image quickly vanished. Here was the Faynn Catach of the stories. Elwin shivered. "Hear me, young prince! The world lies in the balance. By staying here, it is you and not I that threatens. You think King Jerran is behind the wars? You are wrong! The king is but a tool of the Severed Head. Torcull, a false profit, rules over both the dark cult and the king. He is an evil and ambitious man, and will stop at nothing to attain power. Only one thing stands in his way, you and that sword that hangs at your side." Elwin opened his mouth, but the druid silenced him with a raised hand and a hard look. "Your sword is the key that can either stop Torcull or empower him. With the sword, Torcull would release a darkness so powerful that the world would be engulfed in a never-ending night. You cannot imagine the horrors that lie within that dark power. Only you can stop it, Elwin. Only you! You must keep the sword from him, you need to hide yourself and the sword before the servants of darkness can find you. Torcull already knows you are here in Reidh. He has sent more than just soldiers. He has sent a nightling. I've felt his presence, and trust me, my young prince, you do not want to meet a nightling. Even now the nightling is looking for you. He's out there," Faynn nodded towards the door. "Searching the streets and every house. He is looking for you, and in time he will come to this inn, and he will find you."

"A nightling? I have never heard of a nightling," Elwin said skeptically. Nevertheless, a shiver ran down his spine, and a cold dread made his throat feel dry. "What is it?"

"They are spawned out of darkness and are servants of the Dark One. In the days of old, before the Great Wars, they were called the Soulless Ones. The Soulless Ones were destroyed in the Great Wars, but the nightlings lived on through their master. Now they have been reborn and set free once more. They come to prepare the way for their master. They have new names now. They call themselves Red Robes, or monks of the Severed Head, but they are still nightlings." Faynn looked at the door, then looked back at Elwin.

"There is no time to explain more. We must go!"

"No," said Elwin, shaking his head. I am not going to let him scare me. Nightlings*? There's no such thing!* "If you will now excuse me." Elwin stood up. "I need to see someone."

"Elwin!"

Ignoring Faynn, Elwin walked over to where Jon was standing next to the bar.

Faynn remained seated for a moment, then he came to his feet. He gave Elwin a long hard look. Then the druid turned and left the inn.

Once the druid had gone, Elwin and Jon returned to the table. "What did he want?" asked Jon. "I was watchin' you, but he didn't seem dangerous."

Elwin shrugged his shoulders. "I am not sure what he wants. But I do not trust him. He was trying to scare me with some stories of the Severed Head. I think I had better get out of here. Maybe I can take a room upstairs until Pallas returns."

"Good idea."

"When Pallas gets back, come up and..."

Elwin stopped short. The doors of the inn burst open. With drawn swords, several Strigiol soldiers rushed in. A sergeant stepped forward. Elwin recognized the hard-faced sergeant that had stopped him and Pallas earlier that evening. The soldiers quickly spread out, covering all the exits.

The barmaid and barkeep stopped arguing and turned deathly pale.

"No one move!" ordered the scared faced sergeant. No one did. No one breathed.

"I knew it," muttered Elwin. "The druid is with Strigiol. He went for help, and now I'm trapped." *I am a fool. I should have seen this coming!* Careful not to be seen, he unsnapped his sword hilt. Elwin knew he could not win. There were too many soldiers, and he was too poor of a swordsman. However, Elwin was not going to simply surrender. He quickly decided his best chance would be to make a break for the door. If Elwin were lucky and caught them off guard, maybe he'd make it, and Jon and some of the others might help him escape. *It's now or never*, he told himself.

Elwin readied. His muscles tensed. Then he froze. A wind whipped through the open doors. The inn grew suddenly very cold. A figure appeared in the doorway. Cast in the dark shadows of the stormy night, the figure looked like a wrath that had risen from the dead. Covering a tall, skeleton-like body was a blood red robe that snapped in the wind. Moving with an almost graceful stride, as if it never touched the floor, the figure stepped into the light of the room. Cloaked in its red robe, the figure hid its face beneath the shadows of a large hood. Only the reflection of his eyes could be seen in the light of the inn. Around his neck and attached to a golden chain hung a ruby the size of a man's fist. Another gust of wind blew through the doors. Carried on the wind, snow whirled and twisted around the figure. Like a burning flame, the robe flapped in the cold wind. As if by command, the doors slammed shut. The room fell silent.

Terrified, Elwin could not move.

The crackling fire sputtered and went out as if it had been drenched in cold water. Wide-eyed and helpless, Elwin stared at the figure.

"A Red Robe," someone nearby breathed.

Elwin shivered. *A nightling?!* He could almost feel a dark aura radiating from the monk. The strange gleaming eyes within the dark hood stared out at Elwin, and he knew it was him that it wanted. Even the hard-faced sergeant looked frightened as he took a step away from the Red Robe. The sergeant then pointed at Elwin. "That's him, my lord."

But the Red Robe already knew it. His search had ended. The monk nodded to himself. His master would be pleased. It had all been so easy.

Elwin could feel the cold eyes bearing down upon him. Cold and deathlike, the eyes of the monk reached out across the room.

"Come!" boomed the Red Robe's cold voice. A voice that sounded as if it had been spoken from within a tunnel. It echoed in Elwin's ears and felt as if some web was being wrapped around him.

Elwin trembled at the sound.

"Come to me," the nightling repeated.

Elwin had no intention of obeying the Red Robe. He scanned the room, looking desperately for an escape. A cold hand seemed to wrap around Elwin's heart. Finding it hard to breathe, Elwin looked back at the Red Robe. "Come!"

Feeling the cold hand pull upon him, Elwin suddenly found himself standing.

"Come!" The Red Robe repeated. Slowly and deliberately, he drew back his hood, revealing the face that had been hidden within the shadows. The face was deathly pale, a face that spent its time hidden from the sun and had lost its color. The eyes that were locked upon Elwin were as black as the night. His head was shaved clean, making his features intense and unforgettable. With his death-like face and fiercely dark eyes, he appeared to be some type of wrath risen from his grave.

"Come, my prince. Our master waits."

Upon the chest of the Red Robe, the ruby started glowing.

Magic! Elwin knew the monk was using some type of magic to control him. Trying to break the bonds that held him, Elwin resisted, but they were too strong. To his horror, he took a step towards the monk. He could *feel* the nightling's voice. It burned within him. The cold hand reached deeper and touched his soul. With the touch came a searing pain. The inn began to blur.

Jon was suddenly on his feet. Elwin tried to force his eyes to focus. Helplessly, Elwin watched Jon race towards the Red Robe. It was as though he was looking through a thick fog. Jon bellowed out some type of war cry that Elwin could not quite hear. Racing forward, Jon raised a chair high above his head. He had only gone a few feet before the monk lifted a bony white hand. The Red Robe pointed a single finger at Jon. The big fisherman dropped his chair and was lifted from his feet.

"Fool!" growled the monk.

With a look of horror, Jon was hovering two feet above the floor. Then the monk flicked his wrist, and Jon was flown backward. Crashing against the wall, Jon's limp body sank to the floor. The monk's gaze drifted across the room. No one moved. Slowly, the nightling turned back to Elwin. A thin smile came across his death-like face.

"Come!" he demanded once more.

Elwin felt the hand pull upon his heart, but this time, he held his ground. Sweat ran down Elwin's face. Within him, the voice of the Red Robe grew stronger. The burning increased. He thought his heart was going to burst. Driven by the agony, Elwin took another step. The pain seemed to lessen.

"Come!"

Again, Elwin resisted, and the torture returned. The dark eyes seemed to reach out across the room, piercing Elwin with waves of searing anguish. The inn began to fade away. The sounds of the inn grew dimmer and dimmer. A strange dark mist rose from the floor. Through the mist, Elwin could see people, but they seemed to be moving very slowly and far away. Then everything except the monk disappeared into the mist. The face and the dark, blood-red robe of the monk had also vanished. Naked, the nightling stood before Elwin, revealing its true self. The monk was a creature of darkness that was clothed in the skin of a human; however, there was nothing human about it. The nightling was a monster that had stepped out of the darkest of nightmares. Its flesh glowed like red-hot coals on a windy day. The nightling's skin changed from black to red, then back to black again. Its eyes were dark pits of emptiness that could swallow you up with no hope of ever returning. In the monk's eyes was the promise of death. The hand upon Elwin's heart began to tighten.

Cold fingers squeezed, forcing Elwin's pounding heart to begin to slow. Those fingers were killing his heart, squeezing out his life. The raging fire that burned inside him grew hotter and hotter. Agony swept through his body. Elwin opened his mouth to scream, but nothing came out.

"Come," demanded the nightling. "Time is being wasted. Our master is impatient to meet you."

Elwin shook with pain.

"Come!"

The inferno was unbearable. Elwin stepped forward. With each step, the torture lessened. Elwin no longer thought of the danger or what stood before him. He only thought of going forward. It hurt less than it did to resist, and he just wanted the tormenting misery to end.

As the burning pain grew less intense, the voice of the creature changed. The monk's voice now came as a soft whisper. "Come rest."

Yes, thought Elwin, *rest. Rest would be welcome. Yes, I need some sleep.* The burning lessened.

"Peace at last," called the Monk. "How sweet it would all be to sleep, to rest. Elwin, look into my eyes. I will lead you. Come with me. It's time to go; it is time to sleep. Your new master awaits you." The voice of the monk was transformed into a soft, singsong rhythm within Elwin's mind.

Elwin felt the last of the burning fire leave him. His head began to swim, and his mind slipped towards a black void. The soft voice pulled him into the calm of the dark world. He felt so tired. *If only I could close my eyes for a second,* he thought, *then I could sleep, if only for a....*

"No!" called another voice. The new voice seemed to come from a faraway place. "You must fight!"

Fight? Elwin wondered. *Why should I fight? What is there to fight?*

"Sleep," came the Red Robe's soothing voice. "Rest."

Elwin could now feel the other voice as well. It had a familiar feeling, but something undeniably different. The voice grew, and it did not want him to sleep. That bothered the prince. Elwin wanted to sleep so very much. At first, Elwin tried not to listen, but the voice would not go away. It kept telling him to fight, to resist the other voice. Elwin started to become confused. The fog thinned a little.

"Sleep!" called the monk with a note of urgency.

Suddenly, Elwin saw the glowing red coals of the monk's flesh. Its distorted face was close to his own.

"Fight it!" came the other voice. It sounded so familiar. Suddenly Elwin could see clearly. Fear rushed back into him. He was dying! The nightling was killing him! The Red Robe, with its cold searing hands, was pulling him into a dark pit. He was turning Elwin himself into a type of nightling creature…dead but not truly dead.

"NO!" he shouted, struggling to be free. The last of the fog lifted and the sounds of the inn rushed back to life. Elwin heard shouts and the sound of fighting. The druid, Faynn, was standing in the doorway. Elwin grabbed for his sword. If he was going to die, then he would do so fighting. The hilt felt strangely warm in his hand. The sword was halfway out of its sheath when Elwin heard someone shout.

"Stop him!"

Hands seemed to grab Elwin from all directions. The half-drawn sword fell back into its sheath. He fought with all his strength, but he could not break free. The hands grabbing him were too strong. A bright light erupted, and then the world went black.

CHAPTER FIVE

Elwin opened his eyes. Lying on his back and staring into a black void, he blinked.

Still, there was only darkness around him. Vaguely, he remembered something about the Dryrot Inn. There had been a struggle, and someone had tried to kill him, but his mind was in a fog, and he could not think clearly. He placed his hand upon his forehead. It was hot with fever. *Am I dead?* Elwin wondered. *Can you be sick when you're dead?* Trying to think, Elwin lied still. Shivering and aching, the fever clouded his mind, making it hard to focus. *If I am dead, where am I?* Since there was nothing to see, he closed his eyes and tried to recall what had happened. Slowly, Elwin remembered. Trembling, he recalled the image of the nightling. The creature with its burning flesh was etched upon his memory. Elwin knew that the face of the monk would haunt him for the rest of his life, that was if he were still alive. The last thing he could remember was the distorted face of the monk. It had held him with its burning hands. The nightling's dark, lifeless eyes had stared into his. Elwin almost screamed as he remembered the searing pain. *The Red Robe has dragged me into this darkness. If I'm not dead, I soon will be.*

"No," he said weakly, shaking his head. His voice sounded wispy and frail, but things were starting to become clearer. *I remember something else...people yelling and fighting, and then there was that bright light. And I don't feel dead...at least, I don't think I do. Not that I know what dead feels like.*

Turning onto his side, Elwin began to see a yellow glow. It was only a thin line, but it was a light. Any comfort in this dark world was a welcome gift. He stared at the sliver of faint light.

Slowly, his eyes became adjusted. He sighed. The light was

coming from beneath a door. Elwin realized that the darkness around him was not the abyss he feared, but only that of the night. Relieved at discovering he was alive, Elwin tried to sit up. As he did so, his head began to throb. Groaning, the young man fell back. Laying there with his pounding head, Elwin wished he had died. Taking-in long deep breaths, he noticed that the throbbing slowly decreased. Soon, the young man drifted back off to sleep.

Elwin dreamt he was walking in the green, lush woods just south of Acair. Acair was his home, where he had always felt safe. The warm sun was beating down on his back, and at his side was his father. Smiling, King Artair looked down at him. Elwin could hear birds singing in the trees. Squirrels scampered and played across the ground and over fallen branches. Elwin felt happy. Then, just as suddenly as it appeared, the peaceful world began to crumble away. A dark cloud rolled overhead, and a thunderbolt cracked. The wind died, and the woods grew deathly quiet.

"What's happening?" Elwin asked his father.

"It is coming," Artair replied. "Stay strong and true, my son."

"What is coming?"

"The dark days. I am so sorry, my son. I should have warned you. I hoped you would be spared, but now the burden is full upon you. Still, remember that you have all that you need to survive. Believe in yourself, and you will overcome the darkness."

"I don't understand."

"In time, you will."

"Let's go home. I'm scared."

Elwin's father did not respond. The king's eyes were looking at something behind Elwin.

Feeling an evil presence, Elwin spun around. There he saw a

figure cloaked in a blood red robe, a nightling. Elwin tried to warn his father, but when he turned the king was gone. Elwin was alone. Frantically, he looked for his father. "Father!" he yelled. "Help me!" But the king was nowhere to be seen. Terrified and alone, Elwin turned and ran from the monk.

Leaping over dead logs and crashing through branches, Elwin ran with a desperate energy, but he could not escape the nightling. Every time he looked back, there he was with his robes blowing and twisting behind him. As he ran, Elwin could hear the cruel laughter of the creature echoing through the trees. He could feel his hot breath upon the back of his neck. Before Elwin's eyes, the beautiful forest was transformed into a black and menacing world. Twisted trees withered and died, becoming lifeless hulks. Strange creatures with glowing eyes stared out of the shadows, watching him pass. Cries echoed hauntingly through the darkness. Elwin ran on.

"You cannot hide from me," a strange new voice called out of the blackness. "I have touched your soul, Elwin. Through my servant, I have tasted the sweetness of your soul. You can never hide from me again. I can feel what you feel. See what you see. Hear what you hear. We are linked together. You know it is true. There is no place you can run to that I cannot follow."

Somehow Elwin knew the voice was not the nightling's. The sound was cold, but it was not that of the Red Robe. "Elwin, do you know where your sister is? I do. If you do not come to me, I will go after her. She will not resist me. She will do my bidding. She will take your place at my side."

"NO!" Elwin shouted. He stopped running and turned around. Elwin drew his sword and held it tightly in his sweaty hands. Filled with a burning rage, the youth wanted to kill whoever was talking. "Leave Leina alone!" Elwin demanded.

Elwin did not understand what the cold voice meant by Leina taking his place, but there was an unmistakable threat to the speaker's tone. Elwin lifted his blade high over his head and then stopped.

The nightling was gone, but the voice went on echoing through the dead, lifeless trees. "Good. You see, I know you well. In the end, you will come to me. You will bring me what I want, what I need. If not of your own free will, then you will come to protect those you love. Love is such a weakness, such a useless emotion. It will bring you to me."

"Where are you!?"

"Can you feel it, Elwin? We have touched. We are connected. You cannot escape. Come to me. You have no choice. Our destinies are linked. Together we will be powerful, and the world will bow before us. It can all be yours. With power, you can protect the ones you love. Come to me, Elwin, and the world will be ours."

"Who are you!?" Elwin screamed. For several seconds, his voice echoed through the silent forest.

"I am your friend, Elwin. My name is Torcull, the Prophet, and servant of the Great One. Through my monk, we have touched, Elwin. I did not mean for him to hurt you. The nightlings are difficult to control at times. Believe me, Elwin, I only wanted to talk to you. I am deeply sorry if the monk has hurt or frightened you. However, my monk has now made it possible for us to talk. Come to me. There is no need to fear. Together we will set the Great One free. He has been wrongfully imprisoned for too long. He will be grateful, and together we will be beyond powerful. It is the only way you can save your sister."

"I know your name. Y… you're the one that brought back the Severed Head!" There was surprise and fear in Elwin's faltering voice. "You're the one who has caused the wars, all the pain, and suffering!"

"I have restored the Cult of the Severed Head, the servants to the Great One. I have brought them forth to help liberate the Master of Life. But I have not caused the wars, Elwin. It is the ignorance of the world that has brought on the pain the world now faces. The Great One will heal the world and make it whole again. Elwin search your heart. It will tell you that I speak the truth. It is others that seek to deceive you."

Once again, Elwin felt a cold hand wrap tightly around his heart. However, this time there was no pain. The hand was simply there, holding onto him, connecting him to Torcull. Torcull was telling the truth. They were linked, Elwin could feel it. He could sense that there was truth to Torcull's words. Elwin did not know how to explain it, but he could feel the truth in them. Yet at the same time, he knew that this self-proclaimed Prophet was hiding much more. There was a darkness that was being hidden from him. One moment Torcull would try and seduce him. The very next moment he would threaten Elwin.

"NO!" he screamed, but he could not shake off the hand upon his heart. "I won't listen to you!"

Elwin tried to run, but the hand of Torcull held him fast. "Come. I want to show you something."

The dark forest suddenly disappeared. Elwin blinked. He was now standing in a barren and dead plain. Low rolling hills spread out as far as he could see. Here and there a lifeless tree reached up out of the earth like a lost citadel for a land that once had been alive. Their branches, now darkened as if a fire had scorched them clean of their leaves, reached heavenwards. The black branches of the dead trees appeared as if they were frozen in time. The unmoving trees stood silently, mourning the death of the land around them. Other than the trees, there was no sign that life had ever existed in this vast and empty land. Above, dark clouds blotted out the sun, creating a uniformed grayness to this sad world. Elwin pulled his cloak tightly around him, as a cold wind whistled across the lifeless landscape. Listening, Elwin almost thought he could hear words within the cold wind. To the young and frightened prince, the voices in the wind sounded like the soulful song of mourners. There was a great loss and sadness in the strange song that reached out to him. In the distance, Elwin saw a towering castle made of black stone. Rising out of the earth, the castle looked as dead as the land around it. It cast a dark and menacing silhouette against the horizon, and it appeared to be even darker than the land around it. It was a great wound upon the earth, and it was the focal point of the landscape Elwin now found himself. To the prince, it felt as if it were some great stone parasite feeding upon the earth itself, draining it of its life and power.

There is something in there, Elwin thought with growing fear. He could feel it. There was something too dreadful to comprehend behind its black walls.

Silently, the black walls of the castle called out to him. In response to the silent summons, Elwin began to walk towards it. He wanted to run away, but his legs would not heed his cry. He had lost all control and felt like a puppet on a string being pulled forward.

Stopping before the black iron gates of the castle, Elwin looked up. The craftsman who had created the entrance had it designed to appear as if a black spider web had wrapped around the iron bars. The web was as dark as the castle walls and crisscrossed the entrance, sealing off the doorway. Elwin could look through the web into a courtyard, but he could see no way to open the thing. At the top of the web sat a large silver spider. The spider sculpture had been set with tiny, black diamond eyes. The statue looked down at Elwin as if it was waiting for its prey to approach. Shaking, Elwin started backing away, his legs finally obeying his commands.

"Elwin," came the voice of Torcull. Elwin looked away from the spider. At his side was Torcull, dressed all in black. A large red ruby hung about his neck. His hair was light blond and contrasted sharply with his dark clothing and the gray landscape. Torcull looked down at Elwin with soft blue eyes. His face was flawless, and it almost seemed to glow. Elwin had never seen a more beautiful man in his life. And yet there was something terrifying about the way the man smiled.

"It is here you must come," Torcull continued. "When it is time, you will come; the choice has been taken from you. Here we will stand together. Look upon Ban-Darn and remember. My Master, the Great One, waits for you. You will come, and together we will remove the guardian and bring the black castle back into the world, setting our master free. If I must, I will come after you, but in the end, you will come. Remember the pain, Elwin. Remember the pain. There is no place you can run to that I cannot follow. Why go through the pain, when such glory and power can be ours? I can be your friend or your enemy. That is a choice you can still make. Come to me Elwin. I will take you to Ban-Darn. I will show you what needs to be done."

Elwin swallowed. Whatever was in that castle, he wanted nothing to do with it.

"Do not resist. I can be your friend. Let me help you. Let my master help you. The Great One can set you free. You do not understand what the sword will do to you, Elwin. It is an evil thing. The sword will use you, and in time it will destroy you. I can help you. By setting our master free, you will free yourself of the sword. You will never be free until you come and let the Great One set you free."

Elwin started shaking again. He wanted to escape, but Torcull seemed to be holding him in place. Trembling, Elwin fell to his knees and buried his face in his hands. "This is a dream," he whispered.

"Do not despair," said Torcull. "Once you have brought Ban-Darn back into the world of men and freed our master, he will help you. He will destroy the sword. Look upon—"

Suddenly Torcull's voice was gone. Elwin felt as if he had been snatched away from both Torcull and the castle. Just as suddenly, Elwin had the strange sensation of floating high above the earth. Gently, as if cradled in a mother's loving arms, he was lowered downwards. He felt his feet touch the earth and opened his eyes. A new landscape appeared before him. He was now standing on a ridge high above a valley. The gray clouds were gone, and a warm sun shone down from a deep blue sky. Below him, the earth was green and lush. Flowers of every imaginable color covered the basin floor. Cutting through the field of flowers was a stream that wound its way to a large silver colored lake. Sparkling in the sunlight, the lake was in the center of the bowl-shaped valley; on the far side of the lake stood another castle. This castle was made of white marble. Sky blue flags flew above the pointed towers and golden colored gates. Several figures dressed in long flowing white robes stood before the castle walls. One figure that was bathed in a blinding white light stepped forward and looked up at Elwin. Unable to look directly at the figure, Elwin blinked and turned his head.

"Do not despair," the voice was that of a woman. Elwin was filled with wonder. Her voice rang out across the valley like a bird rejoicing on a summer day. "Heed not the voice of darkness, "It speaks falsely. Before you are two paths: one of darkness, another of light. The darkness fears you. Come to us, Elwin. We can help you. The Dark One has touched your soul, but you survived. You are the one we have waited for. You have been chosen for greatness. Prince Elwin ap Gruffydd, the Lord of Light beckons you. Come to us. We can remove the hand from your heart. Come and see the glory of the Light." Elwin stood with his mouth hanging open.

"We know where your sister is," continued the singing voice. "She is here. She is safe with us, but still she needs you, Elwin. Come to her. The Dark One is searching for her. We cannot keep her hidden forever. Come before it is too late."

"Leina?" Elwin looked wildly about as if his sister would be standing next to him. "She's in Ceredigion!"

"No, she is here. There is a great danger in that land. Come to us."

Leina was in danger! "Leina!" Elwin cried out. With a start, he was awake, but the fever kept Elwin in a dreamlike state. "Leina!" he cried out again. "Leina!" The feverish prince did not feel the gentle hands that eased him back down into his bed, nor did he hear the conversation beside his bed.

"Is he having another nightmare?" whispered a woman's voice. The soft tone was riddled in worry.

"Yes," whispered a second voice that belonged to a man. "But I do not think the nightmare is his."

"What do you mean?"

"I fear the Red Robe or some other servant of the Dark One is invading his dreams."

"How can someone enter another's dreams?"

"There are different ways," said the man's voice. "In Elwin's case, the Red Robe did something to the prince that makes it possible."

"Can you stop it?"

"I will do what I can."

"He's so hot," said the woman.

"He will recover," reassured the man, "but the Red Robe hurt him deeply. Rest is what he needs now."

Burning with fever, Elwin could not hear the voices around him. "Leina!" he called. "Leina!"

"You must sleep," came the man's voice. A hand rested on his hot, sweaty forehead. "Sleep."

"Leina!"

"Sleep."

Elwin struggled to stay awake. "Leina," he called weakly.
"Sleep," repeated the voice. "I will guard your dreams. Rest now and sleep."

Unable to resist the compelling voice, Elwin drifted back to sleep. Again, he dreamed. He was lying in a field of tall grass. Above him was a mountain peak that stood out against a blue sky. Next to him was a river of crystal-clear water. Leaning over the bank, Elwin looked down into the clear water. Just beneath the river's surface, he saw a silver crown. He reached out, plunging his hand into the icy cold water. He stretched, but the crown was just out of his grasp. Elwin moved closer, but still could not reach the it. He tried again, and once more the silvery object eluded him. Each time he reached out, it seemed to sink deeper into the river, and when he pulled back, the crown appeared to rise once more. towards the river's surface.

Frustrated, Elwin sat up. As he turned, he noticed that he was not alone. Standing several feet away was a man in a brown robe. Elwin thought the man looked vaguely familiar, but the man's back was turned towards him, and Elwin could not see his face. Suddenly appearing out of nowhere another man appeared. It was as if the man had stepped through an invisible door. The man was tall and handsome, and he was dressed all in black. "Torcull," Elwin murmured fearfully, and he tried sinking back into the tall grass. As if he had come through some magical hole, Torcull stepped into Elwin's dream. Surprised at seeing the brown robed man, Torcull hesitated.

The robed man stood before Torcull, blocking his path to the prince.

With a menacing scowl on his face, Torcull took another step forward. "You!" he exclaimed, pointing an accusing finger at the man in brown. "You will not interfere! Stand aside, old man. The boy is mine!"

The man in brown stood his ground, keeping himself between Torcull and Elwin. "Are you challenging me, Torcull?" Elwin recognized the voice. It was Faynn.

Faynn? wondered Elwin. *He led the nightling to me. Didn't he?*

Torcull scowled. He looked past Faynn. His cold eyes fell upon Elwin. "In the boy's dreams? I think not."

"Then be gone," demanded Faynn.

"Meddling old man! You cannot always be at his side. And you would not dare do what I have done. The boy cannot hide from me. I will return."

"And I will be waiting."

"Fool! You cannot fight fate. You know the prophecies as well as I. The boy *will* set Beli free." Torcull briskly turned and disappeared.

The dream faded away, and Elwin slipped into a deep dreamless sleep. When he awoke, he discovered that it was light outside. Elwin felt weak, but the fever had broken. Lying still, he looked up at the ceiling. At first, the young prince thought he was in his own bed, and that the night's events at the Dryrot Inn were just a nightmare. But he soon realized it had not been a dream, and he was not in his own bed. He was in a small, unfamiliar room. The room had one window. The wooden shutters of the window were tightly closed, but narrow beams of sunlight streamed through cracks. Huddled in layers of coarse woolen blankets, Elwin twisted his head. Taking in the small room with a glance, he saw that it was a simple room with few furnishings. Aside from the bed, he was lying on, there was a small table with a water basin and a chair. Mounted on the white plaster wall above the narrow bed was a wooden circle with a triangle, the iconographic symbol of the Three Gods. Each of the three points of the triangle represented one of the three deities of the Trinity: Anthary, the father and the sun god, Epona, the mother goddess of the moon, and their son, Triesch, the earth. The order of the Three Gods was known as the Anthary Trinity and was the main religion of Kambrya. It was the only officially recognized religion in all the kingdoms, except in Aleash and the Green. At least it had been the only religion in Kambrya until the rise of the Cult of the Severed Head.

The only other decoration in the room was a fresco painting on the north wall opposite the bed. The painting was a religious work of art meant for meditation and reflection. Such paintings were not found in castle bedchambers. Wherever Elwin was, it was not the Murray castle.

The room was cold, so Elwin kept the blankets pulled up close to his chin as he studied the painting. It was of a saint and an angel. The angel had three large wings, making it a seraph angel. Studying the fresco, Elwin recognized it as the markings of St.

Wallis. St. Wallis was the same man that had written the chronicle Elwin had read just yesterday. To Elwin, yesterday seemed like a very long time ago. In the painting, the saint was kneeling before a mountain. Above the mountain was a silver crown which floated upon a misty cloud. Elwin immediately recognized the crown from his dream. *I must have seen this before and then dreamed about this painting.* It seemed a reasonable conclusion. Off to one side of the crown flew the three-winged seraph. Streaming out of the seraph were three narrow beams of golden light. The beams of light reached down to St. Wallis, who humbly stared upwards towards the heavenly vision. The lines were meant to represent the saint receiving divine inspiration from each of the gods of the Trinity. *I must be in the Abbey,* Elwin concluded. *But the Abbey is a few day's ride from Port Murray. How could I have gotten here so quickly?*

Throwing off his blankets, Elwin carefully sat up. His head still hurt, but it was no longer throbbing. He saw that new clothes had been carefully laid out. Hanging over the back of the chair was Elwin's sword. He sighed. At least he did not appear to be a prisoner. Stepping out of the bed and onto the cold stone floor, the prince hurriedly dressed, pulling a clean blue silk shirt over his head. Dressed, he washed his face in the water basin and stretched out his sore arms. Feeling refreshed, and his dreams now reduced to hazy memories, Elwin buckled the ancient sword of his ancestors around his waist. He still felt tired and sore, but there were things to do. The first thing Elwin needed was to find out how he had gotten there. He crossed the room and unlatched the window shutters. Anxious to feel the sun upon his face, he pushed opened the window. The day was blindingly bright, and Elwin quickly shaded his eyes. The bright white light reminded him of his dreams and of the white castle. *They were only dreams,* he told himself. *Leina is safe in Ceredigion.* However, deep inside himself, he feared the dreams were more than that, and Leina was in trouble. But how was he going to find the white castle?

"No!" he said stubbornly. "They were only dreams. She's safe. Father would never let anyone harm her."

When his eyes had finally adjusted to the light, Elwin looked out over the landscape. The countryside was covered in a fresh coating of clean white snow. Winter had returned with a vengeance. Elwin moaned, wondering if spring would ever truly arrive. A cold wind blew in through the window. Shivering, Elwin quickly shut the shutters.

"You're up," came a voice from behind Elwin.

Startled, Elwin jerked himself around. Standing in the doorway was a short, stocky monk, wearing the grey vestments of the Wallisinan Order. Elwin hadn't heard him enter.

"Sorry, Your Highness," the monk apologized with a short bow. "I did not mean to startle you. I was only checking in on and did not realize that Your Highness was awake. How are you feeling today?"

"Fine, thank you," responded Elwin with a frown. Like everyone else, the monk knew who Elwin was. It no longer surprised the prince. Nevertheless, it did irritate him. "Where am I, and who are you?"

"Oh my! Where are my manners?" the monk asked himself out loud. "I'm sorry. Of course, you do not know me. Your Highness has been asleep so long. You are in Saint Wallis Monastery, and I'm Brother Partinas, the abbot."

"How long have I been asleep?"

"Weeks," replied Brother Partinas.

"Weeks!?"

"Almost a full four weeks, so just short of a month, actually.

You had a very high temperature. It was touch-and-go there for a while. But late last night your fever finally broke."

"A month..." It was hard to believe he could have slept that long. *No wonder I'm so weak!*

"From what I hear, you're lucky it was not longer. But there is time to talk later. You must be hungry. You have been fed nothing but liquids and some gruel these past weeks. It was all we could get you to swallow."

Elwin's stomach grumbled on-cue. "I guess I am hungry."

"Good. Hunger is always a good sign." The abbot's blue eyes sparkled with a warm kindness that matched his glowing smile. "If you will follow me, I will take you downstairs and have the cook fix you something. While you are waiting, you can visit with the others. Then maybe I can give you a tour of our monastery. It's ancient, you know. Some say Saint Wallis himself stayed here. Can you believe that, the holy man himself!"

"Others?" Elwin inquired.

Brother Partinas did not respond. He was already out the door and bouncing down the hallway. Elwin had to hurry to catch up to the overly jovial man. When he did catch up, Elwin was too out of breath to repeat the question.

Brother Partinas never actually gave him many opportunities to talk anyway. The abbot was pleased to have a guest, something that was apparently rare at the monastery, as he talked non-stop. The warm-hearted abbot went on about this and that. He talked about his order and the history of the monastery, of which he was very proud. Usually Elwin, who loved history, would have found such a conversation interesting, but his head began to hurt once more, and it took all his strength just to keep up. Finally, the monk led him into a small sitting room with several chairs that faced an unlit fireplace. Grateful to have reached their destination,

Elwin fell into a chair like a man who had just finished a race.

"I shall have food brought shortly," brother Partinas said. He vanished back through the doorway, leaving Elwin alone.

Elwin sank deeper into the chair. Once more, his head was throbbing painfully, and he no longer felt famished. A few minutes later the door opened. Elwin looked up, expecting to find Brother Partinas returning with his food, but it was not. Instead of the smiling abbot, he saw the druid Faynn, who entered the room carrying a tray with a single mug on it.

"Faynn!" Elwin exclaimed, recognizing the druid. Elwin tried to stand, but his head hurt too much. "What are you doing here?"

"Helping you. Whether you want to admit it or not, you need it. You nearly got yourself killed once already."

Elwin frowned. He did not like being talked to as if he were a child. "Did you bring me here?"

Faynn nodded. "Yes." He set down his tray. Kneeling before the fireplace, he started placing wood into the hearth. "But I had help," Faynn added over his shoulder. "You are no longer safe in town. Strigiol now controls Port Murray."

Elwin's frown deepened. *Faynn Catach saved me?* "Where's Count Murray? Is he all right?"

"He is fine. Your friend Pallas reported that the count is pretending to help the Strigiol lord. The count will do his best to keep any Strigiol patrol from getting too close to this monastery."

In a short time, Faynn had a small fire going. He stood back up. "There. That's better. These old monasteries can be so drafty and cold. Do you remember dreaming at all?" Flynn asked.

"Some," Elwin responded. "I saw you in a dream. You and Torcull."

Faynn nodded. "You remember, then?"

Elwin shrugged his shoulders. "They were only dreams."

"No, they were not." Faynn stood up and handed Elwin the mug he had brought in with him. "Here, drink this."

Elwin looked doubtfully at the thick, dark contents of the mug. He turned his nose at the foul smell and then looked back up at Faynn. "What do you mean? Are you saying it wasn't a dream?"

"It was a dream, but it was also real. In a way, both Torcull and I were really there. I was able to enter your unconscious mind because I was right next to you. Torcull has found another way into sleep." The druid sank into a chair next to Elwin.

"Maybe now you will start believing me. You are in danger." Faynn looked at the mug in Elwin's hands. "Now drink. It will make your head feel better. Then we will talk."

"Then it was you who saved my life at the Dryrot?"

"I guess," Faynn replied, shrugging his shoulders. "But as I said, others helped as well. You played a part, too, but to be honest, that part still confuses me. I thought you were done for. You are a fascinating young man."

"Then you did not bring that... that Red Robe to kill me?"

Faynn smiled. "No, Elwin. I did not bring the nightling. I hope you can believe that. If you remember, I did try to warn you. Now drink."

Regretfully, Elwin shook his head. "You did warn me. I'm sorry I did not listen."

"That is now the past. Just drink up and we will talk."

Elwin looked down at the mug. "I can't drink this. It looks and smells awful."

"It actually tastes worse than it looks. However, it will help your head."

"By making my stomach sick?" asked Elwin, but he held his

nose and forced down some of the liquid which indeed tasted worse than it smelled.

"That's disgusting!" Elwin exclaimed.

"All of it," ordered Faynn.

"All of it!? I'll die!"

"Stop arguing and drink it."

Elwin groaned, but he managed to down the foul-tasting liquid. The drink worked fast, and Elwin quickly started feeling better.

"What was that appalling stuff? Magic?" he asked suspiciously. The thought of magic being used on him gave him a cold shiver. Throughout Kambrya, the teachings of the Anthary Doctrine had been banned, and all forms of magic outlawed in all the Kambryan kingdoms. The kingdom taught that all magic was evil, and all users should be put to death.

"A cure. Herbs and spices," replied Faynn, "nothing more."

Trying not to look too relieved, Elwin put down the mug and glanced over at the druid.

Faynn's gray eyes which had scared Elwin at the Dryrot Inn now looked soft and kind. Faynn confused Elwin. On one hand, the mysterious man frightened him, yet on the other hand, he liked the druid. *So, you came back to the inn and saved me from the nightling, but I still don't know why. You must want something from me.* Then out loud, Elwin said, "Thank you, I feel much better. That stuff works fast."

Faynn answered with a smile and a nod.

"I also want to thank you for saving me at the inn last night. I guess it was really longer ago than that. But it feels as if it was last night."

Faynn shrugged. "Actually, I did very little. It was your friends who fought off the soldiers."

"I meant the Red Robe."

Faynn shook his head. "That's the part that I am still unsure of. You see, I arrived too late. The nightling already had you linked to him. If I had attacked the Red Robe, as you call the nightling, you would have died. To tell you the truth, I have no idea why you are alive. You really should be dead, but somehow you broke the nightling's link. How did you do that?"

"It was you and what you kept telling me...to fight. I didn't want to listen at first, but eventually you got through."

"Me?" asked Faynn, with a look of surprise.

"I heard you," stated Elwin. He remembered the voice that called out to him, the voice that had called him back. Without that voice to cling to like a lifeline, Elwin was sure he would have died that night. He had presumed the life-saving voice had been the druid's. Who else would have used magic or even know how?

"You heard me? I said nothing to you, and you could not have heard me if I had."

"But I did hear you. You called to me. You told me to fight back."

Faynn's face took on a look of deeper interest, as he raised his eyebrows in growing curiosity. "Someone spoke to you?"

"Yes. It wasn't you? It sounded familiar, and it helped me resist the Red Robe."

"Well, that is very interesting. Perhaps you had better tell me everything."

Elwin leaned forward. He still wondered if he should trust the man, but he needed to tell somebody what had happened. Elwin also wanted answers, and just maybe the druid had a few. So, Elwin began to tell the story of his nightmarish encounter with the Red Robe. Telling it brought back feelings Elwin wished he had forgotten, he began to shake, and his voice faltered.

"Relax," Faynn said reassuringly. "You are safe. Take some deep breaths, and then start again."

Elwin nodded and tried to breathe in deep steady breaths. "That's better," said Faynn with a sincere look of compassion. Faynn watched Elwin compose himself. The nightling had affected the young prince in ways that Elwin still did not comprehend. No one could be touched by such darkness and not be affected. It was that touch that had made Elwin so sick with fever. The evilness of the nightling nearly killed Elwin. The fever had broken, and Elwin now looked healthier, but the Red Robe had left a residue. Faynn could feel it, but he could do nothing about it. "I know it is hard to talk about," continued Faynn, "but it might be important."

"I'll try," consented Elwin. He then told Faynn of the pain, and how the monk had tried to lure him into a darkness that he now knew was death. Then Elwin spoke of the mysterious voice; the voice that had called him by name and had taken away the pain. Elwin remembered breaking free of the Red Robe's burning hands and then coming out of the fog.

"Then I heard shouts, and there was fighting everywhere. I saw you. Then someone grabbed me. There was a flash of light, and that's the last thing I remember."

Finishing his tale, Elwin sat back into the chair. Taking a deep breath, he wrapped his arms around himself, trying to push away the dark memories.

Faynn shook his head. "Strange. Very strange indeed. I have no idea who you heard, but whoever it was is the one who saved your life."

Faynn fell silent. He frowned slightly, trying to figure out who the voice could have possibly been. Giving up, he shook his head once more. "Very strange."

"But what was that light?" asked Elwin.

Faynn looked up. "That part was me. Once you were free of the nightling, I could act against it. After struggling with you, it was in a weakened condition and did not put up much of a fight."

"Magic?"

Faynn nodded. "Yes, Prince Elwin. I used magic. Does that bother you?"

"I guess not," Elwin lied, and then asked, "Did you kill it?" He would sleep better at night if he knew that the monk was dead.

"No," replied Faynn. "Nightlings are very powerful. They are not easy to kill. Even in its weakened condition, I could do no more than drive it away. I am not even sure they can be killed. In truth, they are not actually alive. But they can be hurt, and for now, it's gone. It is hiding, licking its wounds."

"Who grabbed me?" Elwin asked, trying to change the subject away from the nightling, but the thoughts would not go away. The nightling is still out there, and not too far away. Just the thought sent a cold shiver down Elwin's spine despite the heat from the fire.

"Just about everyone in the room," answered Faynn. "You were drawing your sword and looked like you were going to run out of the inn. There were still soldiers outside, and some fierce fighting was still going on. You had just escaped one trap, and you were about to run into another. Then you passed out. The Red Robe touched you deeply. For a while there, I thought you were going to leave us, but you are made of some tough stuff, Prince Elwin. You survived what no one should have."

Still finding the whole experience terrifying, Elwin did not want to think of the Red Robe anymore, but he knew the nightling was not finished with him yet. Elwin had but one thought: to get as far away from the monk as he could. "Where can I go?"

"That has yet to be decided," said Faynn. "The nightling is still out there. Fleeing is our only hope. And now, the nightling knows I am here. Next time it will not be taken by surprise. But for the time being, you are safe. You need to rest and..." Faynn hesitated. "There is still more. There are things you must know. However, you should not hear them from me. There are others more appropriate for that."

"Others?" questioned Elwin. "Brother Partinas mentioned others as well."

Faynn stood up. "I shall get them."

CHAPTER SIX

The door swung open. Elwin's heart skipped a beat. Digging his fingers into the arms of the chair, he stared at his lap. Forcing himself, he slowly turned his head. In the doorway stood Pallas and Pallas' mother, the Countess Kytherin Murray. Kytherin was like a mother to Elwin. Elwin had only vague memories of his own mother. His mother had been a sickly woman and had died when Elwin was still very young, and his father had never remarried. In the past three years, Kytherin had become the mother Elwin never had.

Looking over his shoulder, Elwin stared at the two. Both Pallas and the countess had long, drawn-out faces. Two more people entered the room. One was a big, muscular youth with dirty-blond hair, and he beginnings of a beard. His course, thick hair was cut short, exposing his angular face. At his side stood a short boyish-looking youth who was no more than five feet tall. His long, golden-yellow hair was pulled back behind his head where it was fastened with a thick leather thong. His strange forest-green eyes stared across the room. His pointed ears and green eyes left little doubt that he was a wood elf. Standing next to each other, the elf and the big youth made a comical pair.

Immediately recognizing them, Elwin smiled as he came to his feet. Both were Elwin's and Pallas' childhood friends; Aidan, an elf from the Green, and Colin, son of the Earl of Llanbaedarn of Ceredigion. Momentarily, Elwin forgot his fear. It had been years since he had seen them. He gave each a long hug. Colin stiffened awkwardly at the embrace. Still smiling, Elwin stepped back and looked at each of his friends, taking in their welcome and familiar faces. Admittedly they were both a few years older now and maybe a bit hardened, but still, they were Elwin's closest friends, and it felt right to have his childhood friends once again in the same room.

"What are you doing here?" Elwin finally asked.

"We've come to see you, of course," piped-up Aidan's soft musical voice. The elf smiled, but there was an underlying concern that betrayed Aidan's true feelings.

Ignoring the worry written across Aidan's face, Elwin smiled in response. It felt good to be with his friends once more. It was almost like being home, but something gnawed at his mind. Something was not right. "How did you find me?" Elwin asked.

"The druid brought us," said Colin, his voice sounding gruff. "You may not remember, but we saw you at the Dryrot Inn. We surprised the soldiers from the rear. With the aid of the town's folk, the city guard, and Faynn, we were able to drive them off."

Elwin did not remember, but he did recall the sounds of a battle. As a boy, Colin had been the best swordsman for his age, and better than many of the older boys as well. It would not have surprised Elwin if Colin had single-handedly driven the soldiers off. However, the Red Robe was something different. Elwin doubted that even Colin's skill could affect the monk. The nightling was beyond the power of steel.

"They've brought sad news," Kytherin said suddenly, and Elwin's mood became dark once more.

Stiffening, Elwin looked at Colin, then at Aidan. Nervously, Elwin's eyes shifted from one friend to the other. His throat went dry and the smile slipped from his face. Elwin realized that Aidan and Colin were messengers.

"Come," Kytherin said. "Let us sit." She took Elwin by the hand and gently led him back to the chair. Falling into the cushions, Elwin felt as if he were plunging back into the dark abyss of the Red Robe. His world suddenly seemed to be crumbling apart.

"I wish we could have come with better news," stated Colin, his voice quiet and solemn. "Things have not been good in Ceredigion. Your father..." his voice faltered. Unable to go on, he looked down at Aidan for help.

Aidan gave Colin a short nod. With a great heaviness, the elf turned and faced Elwin. Unable to look into his friend's eyes, the teary-eyed elf dropped his head. "I'm so sorry, Elwin, but...your father has...died. He was murdered."

Elwin blinked. It took a moment, but slowly the words sank in. His body began to shake. He wanted to tell them they were wrong, and yet he knew they were not. His heart lodged in his throat. The weight of the truth was dragging him downwards. Actually, Elwin had known the truth for some time, but he had denied it. Now it was suddenly real. He could remember when he first realized his father had died. It had been several months ago, just after the first snows had sealed-off Reidh from the rest of the world. In a cold sweat, Elwin had awakened in the middle of the night. It was at that moment that he knew his father had died, but at the time Elwin could not accept it. A bad dream, he had told himself, and dreams aren't real, or so he had thought. Elwin had fooled himself into believing it was just his imagination. Yet, it was the reason he needed to get home. Elwin knew something was wrong, but now it was too late. He felt the tears he had been holding in for months swelling up. No longer able to hold them back, he began to sob. His young body shook with pent up grief.

Kneeling before him, Kytherin held Elwin close. She whispered words of comfort. Crying, Elwin held her as tightly as he could. Shaking uncontrollably, he was grateful for her arms and the sound of her kind voice.

After a time, Elwin finally pulled back from Kytherin. He

wiped the tears from his face.

"How?" His voice sounded empty.

"You should rest first," whispered Kytherin. She too had tears running down her face.

Elwin met her eyes. "Not yet. I need to know." His young voice sounded hoarse and yet determined. Aidan was still crying, so Elwin turned to Colin. "Colin, will you tell me?"

Colin had held his tears in, but he could not hide the grief in the look he gave Elwin. To Colin, Elwin was both friend and lord. Elwin was the Prince of Ceredigion, the heir to the throne. Once crowned, he would be king. As his friend, Colin wanted to spare Elwin the pain, but as his prince, Colin knew that Elwin had both the right and need to know the truth. Colin gave him a stiff, uncomfortable nod. He didn't want to be the one to tell him, but he knew he would be the one. His voice trembling, Colin started the tale of betrayal and murder.

--

Several months earlier and far to the north, a young woman with silky black hair had also mourned the loss of her father. Her long, straight hair shimmered in the evening light. It flowed over her narrow shoulders and cascaded down her back. Like every night since she had returned home, she stood before her bedroom chamber window. The beautiful young woman was no more than sixteen. She was too young to feel such sadness. From the castle window, her large, dark eyes stared mournfully out over the city of Acair, where beyond the city walls rose the Northern Drygan mountains. Sighing, she looked at the towering snowcap peaks. For as long as she could remember, she had looked out at those mountains. Once, she had found them beautiful, but not anymore.

There was a time when she thought of the Northern Drygan Mountains as a friend. The majestic peaks were always there to comfort her. Those were happy days, but those days were now gone. The mountains had not changed, yet somehow the mountains, like everyone else, had betrayed her. The mountains seemed to mock her. When she needed them the most, they refused to offer her any comfort. Instead, they were a constant reminder that she was a prisoner in her own home and that the happy days were gone forever.

An eagle soaring above the castle walls cried out. Standing out against the darkening sky, the eagle circled, searching the ground below. Then with mighty strokes of its wings, the great bird turned and raced off towards the mountains. From the castle window, the dark-eyed girl watched the eagle until it finally vanished into the distance.

Dropping her head, she moaned, "Everything is free but me." Sadly, she turned her attention back to the mountains. For the past three weeks, she had watched the peaks wanting to see if the strange lights would come again. Each night, just after sunset, lights could be seen high in the high country. It was only a little distraction, but any distraction from her sadness was a welcome one. As the blue sky darkened, stars began to pop out and the lights appeared. Among the high country known as the Land of the Eagles, tiny fires flickered and danced. Over two dozen fires dotted the mountain side above the city. *But who could be up there?* Leina wondered. She knew it could not be the dwarfs who never make their home at such altitude. No, the dwarves like the roots of the Drygan Mountains. They believe the high mountains are haunted and belong to the spirits. The Northern Drygan mountains were steep, and supposedly they could not be climbed, yet there were the fires. Standing at her window, she prayed that the rumors would come true. It was said that the fires were an omen foretelling of the death of the new king of Ceredigion.

There was little she wanted more than to see the new king dead at her feet.

In the outer chamber of her suite, a door opened. She did not have to guess who it would be. There was only one person who entered her rooms without permission, her jailer and cousin, Parlan. She heard his heavy footsteps entering her bedroom chamber.

"Parlan, can't you knock?!" she snapped, still staring out the window.

"Would you have let me in?" he asked.

There was a smugness to his voice that made her shake with anger. "Of course not!" Leina was not trying to hide her distaste for him. She turned and faced her cousin with a wrathful gaze. He wore the maroon and silver colors of the Gruffydd family. Seeing him in the royal colors only angered her more. His long dark hair was pulled and tied back into a ponytail so that his hair would not hide his handsome features. One did have to admit he was a handsome young man. But his eyes were as cold as any she had ever seen. Crowning his head was a thin silver crown of interlaced small leaves and vines.

"That is why I did not ask," Parlan added with a shrug and a wry smile. That wry, cruel smile destroyed all his good looks. "And a king should not need to ask."

"A king?" She threw her head back and laughed bitterly. "You are many things, *cousin*," she emphasized the word cousin with spite, "but you are no king. A pretender, liar, and murderer, yes, but a king? No, that you are not. You are no king, nor shall you ever be."

"Princess Leina," Parlan smiled. He nudged the thin silver

crown that encircled his head.

"What is this, then?"

Again, Leina laughed. "King Jerran gives a toy crown to all his puppets. Do you think a trinket can make you a king?"

"High King Jerran," corrected Parlan. "And yes, it does. I am after all the closest living male of the royal family, and you are still but a minor. High King Jerran has acknowledged my rights, as I have acknowledged his rights as High King of Kambrya."

"It takes more than a crown to make a king. You are my cousin from my mother's side of the family and have no rights to the throne. You do not carry any of the Gruffydd blood and are nothing but a shame on my mother's good name. May she rest in peace; though with a nephew such as you, I cannot see how she can."

"It is true. I do not have any of your so-called 'kingly blood'!" Parlan consented angrily. "You Gruffydds have always looked down on me, parading around, acting as if I was nothing more than a servant. Did you think I did not see you laughing at me?! But you're not laughing anymore. Are you? I played you for fools, but now I'm done playing. Once you are my wife, no one will question my rights to the crown, and our son will have the Gruffydd blood."

"Never!" Leina cried, "Never shall I marry the likes of you! Never will I have your son! I would rather die!"

Parlan smiled. "Now, cousin, is that any way to treat your lord and future husband?"

"I will not marry you!"

"You have no choice in the matter," Parlan replied smugly. "At the week's end, we shall be wed. The arrangements have been made. It will be a small ceremony." His smile grew. After years of cowing down to the pompous royal family, he was finally going to have his revenge, and he was going to savor every moment. "I would not like it if you made a public scene. People might think you are not a happy bride."

"You would force me..." Leina asked with a look of horror, and disbelief, "to marry you before the three gods, knowing how I feel? Have you no shame?!"

Parlan replied with a deep chuckle, "None, princess. Shame only stands in a man's way. If I had any shame, I would not be king now. I have grand plans and for now, you are a part of those plans."

"Let me go!" pleaded Leina. "You have your kingdom. Why do you need me?"

"Because of who you are. If I am to keep my hard-earned kingdom, I will need to legitimize my rule. You are the daughter of our *beloved* King Artair, so we will become man and wife. You are too dangerous to be left single, and far too dangerous to be set free. There are those who would use you against me. Your name could inspire the people to take up arms. Some nobles of the realm would gladly jump at the chance to oppose me, and you could give them the reason they are looking for. We . . . I cannot allow that." He crossed his arms across his chest as if in deep thought. "On the other hand, if you cooperate, and once my throne is secure, you may be sent off to a nunnery where the illusion of some freedom can be yours." It was a lie. However, if it bought the princesses cooperation, he would let her believe it. The truth was that once he had married her and she had given him a son, she would no longer be needed and would be more of a liability than an asset. He was growing tired of the little tramp, so once he had his son Leina would have to have a tragic accident.

"Do you think anyone would believe that I would freely

marry a man who butchered innocent nuns, kidnapped me, and murdered my father? How could I do anything but despise you?"

"I have told you, I had nothing to do with it. The elves attacked the abbey. If you remember, I was the one who saved you from them."

"I was there, and I saw no elves, but I did see you and Strigiol soldiers. *You* attacked the abbey. I saw you cut down women in cold blood. I saw you burn the abbey to the ground, and I saw you plant elvish arrows to cast the blame on them. Then you used me to get at my father. You made him think you had rescued me, knowing he would come."

"When he did, you killed him! You used me to kill my father! I hate you!"

Parlan shook his head. She had seen more than Parlan had realized. *At least in her anger, she has told me what I must do.* It would not be a pleasant act. Even for him, killing a woman in cold blood was deeply disturbing, yet Parlan had come too far to let morals get in his way. "Oh, Leina, I am sorry you saw as much as you did," he said as if he almost meant it. "If you had seen less and accepted more, you would not be a prisoner here. I think we could have lived happily together."

Leina's large dark eyes could melt a heart, but now they were as cold as ice. She bit her tongue. Silently, she promised herself that one day she would kill this man. Yes, someday she would see him dead at her feet.

Parlan walked over to the window to stand close to her. She shivered, fearing what he might do. But he was no longer looking at her, and his mood suddenly changed.

Parlan leaned against the windowsill. Staring out into the night, he watched the strange fires in the mountains. The lights had been haunting him ever since he had marched into the city of

Acair. In the city's large cathedral, High King Jerran had crowned Parlan the King of Ceredigion. That same night the lights appeared. Leaving part of his army behind, King Jerran had returned to Strigiol, but the fires remained. Rumors throughout the city claimed that the fires were the spirits of the dead and that the spirit's leader was none other than the late King Artair himself, who had returned to take his revenge upon Parlan. Parlan put no value in omens. Omens were only the talk of superstitious fools, but even fools could lead the city into rebellion. Parlan ruled all of Ceredigion, but only through fear of the Strigiol, soldiers, and the priests of the Severed Head. There had already been several disturbances, sabotage and one outright uprising that had only been put down in a bloodbath. The people now trembled at the sight of the soldiers and the black robed servants of the Severed Head. Parlan did not care if the people loved him or not. Yet he also hated the idea of having to live under Strigiol authority. He hated bowing to King Jerran, and he hated knowing it was Jerran and not him who truly ruled Ceredigion. *For now, I need Jerran and the Severed Head. But only for now. Then the people will tremble at the sight of me.*

Thinking of that, he smiled to himself.

The first step is to put an end to the question of my legitimacy. As long as I am seen as a usurper and a tyrant, I will never put a stop to the rumors or free myself from Jerran. The princess was Parlan's answer. With Leina, he would bring an end to the noble's talk of uprisings. Once married to Leina, he would be the legitimate king of Ceredigion. All he had to do was get rid of Elwin, and that was already in the works. But those lights haunted his dreams.

He wanted those damn fires put out. Parlan had offered a substantial reward for the man who put the fires out, but none had succeeded. Many had tried, and most had fallen to their deaths, the others simply gave up. Every night the fires burned on, and every night Parlan dreamed of the fires.

In his dreams, the fires would rise out of the earth and transform themselves into pale, white faced, demon-like ghosts.

The ghosts would come down out of the mountains in the thousands. They would race forward, each one searching for him. The city's defenses were useless against the army of ghosts. Running for his life, Parlan fled the city. Mounted upon his swiftest horse, Parlan raced across the grassy hills of Ceredigion. He ran and ran until he was finally free of the ghosts, but suddenly he would come upon a silver griffin. Without warning, the silvery beast would leap at him, tearing him from his horse, ripping at him with great talons and razor-sharp teeth. Parlan would then scream himself awake.

Turning from the window, Parlan tried to forget the images of his dreams. He would not let a few nightmares stand in his way. Coldly, he gazed down at the princess. "Your opinion of me does not matter, my lady. I will not have a civil war. We will marry, and you will legitimize my rule. Once I am the unquestionable ruler and King of Ceredigion, the nobles will fall into line. They will have no choice."

"You've forgotten Elwin," Leina retorted. "He is still the prince, and one day *he* will be crowned king, as he is the rightful heir of Ceredigion. He will return, and you will still have your war. The people will rise up against you. When that day comes, I will happily watch them trample you under their feet, and all of Ceredigion will cheer as one."

Parlan smiled. He reached down to touch Leina's face.

The princess jerked her head away. "Do not touch me!"

Parlan's smile vanished. "I had hoped to spare you this, but

Elwin will not be returning." If Parlan could not have the princess' love, he would have her hate. "We know where Elwin is. He has run off like a coward to a small isolated county in Cluain. When the snows melt, King Jerran will send a ship. Prince Elwin has run out of time. He is as good as captured. The prince has fled his country, making himself a traitor to this land and to the High King. There can only be one sentence for traitors, death."

"No! You lie."

"I fear not, my lady."

Leina began to shake. "Do not do this, Parlan. If there is any kindness in you at all, then please, I beg you, leave Elwin alone. You have taken everything from me. Don't take my brother as well."

"I cannot stop it, my lady. It is the High King's command, not mine."

Like a horse whose spirit had been broken, Leina dropped her head. "Okay, I will marry you, but only if you don't kill my brother. Please, Parlan, do not take him from me!"

"Princess, while it would please me to have your consent, you are going to marry me. You can accept that or not, but it will not matter in the end. As for your brother, I have no choice. He cannot be saved. My cousin is a threat to my crown and must be removed, and as I said, it is the High King's decision, not mine. I cannot nor wish to ask the High King to spare him. The High King has made all this possible." Parlan spread his arms wide, indicating his rule over Ceredigion. "The King and his armies have given me the power to take this country, and you will give me the authority to keep it. I will not be stopped now."

"You monster!" screamed Leina. She clawed at his eyes, but he was too fast and too strong. Effortlessly, Parlan grabbed her wrists and tried to pull her close. Leina fought him. Kicking and scratching, she tried to pull free. Parlan scowled. Then he tossed her down onto her bed.

"Poor child," he spat. "You are throwing everything away." With wild, angry eyes, Parlan looked down at her. Leina trembled, fearing that Parlan would force himself upon her.

"If you continue to resist my lovely princess, you, like your father, may have an unfortunate accident." He hesitated then added, "Once we are married, of course."

With that thin, cruel smile of his, Parlan's eyes glided over Leina's trembling body. His dark eyes were filled with a mixture of lust and hatred. "Think about it, my lady." Then he turned and left the room. The door slammed shut behind him with a loud thud, and the iron bar slid back into place that kept Leina a prisoner in her own rooms.

She buried her face deep into her pillow and cried. "Oh, Elwin, be careful," she murmured between her tears. "If only I could warn you." She then cried herself to sleep, but she was not to sleep through the night.

Morning came early, or so Leina thought. A bright white light filled the room. Tired as she was, she opened her bloodshot eyes. She thought she could smell flowers. At the foot of the bed was a tall, slender woman dressed all in white. To Leina's surprise, the light was not coming from the morning sun, but from the woman. Outside, darkness still surrounded the castle. Slowly, the light around the woman faded, but the woman remained. She smiled, and the room seemed to grow warmer, as she gracefully crossed the room as if she walked on air. "Greetings, Leina ap Gruffydd, Princess of Ceredigion."

Leina sat up. "Who are you?"

Now wide-eyed and awake, Leina stared at the women. For some reason, Leina did not fear the mysterious women in white.

"And how did you get in here? Are you an angel?"

"I am called Sileas." She smiled. Her eyes shone with an inner kindness. "And I am not an angel, but a Guardian of the Light. I have come to take you from this place of darkness. I am taking you home."

CHAPTER SEVEN

Elwin sat on the edge of his narrow bunk. Outside the abbey's walls, the wind whistled and howled as a new storm came over the mountains, bringing with it more snow to the already snow-covered county. Winter was refusing to give way to spring. Elwin rubbed his bloodshot eyes. He knew that he needed to sleep, but he could not stop thinking about his father. In his lap, he held a closed book. The book was a black bound chronicle of Brother Wallis' life. He thought that reading about the saint's life might help his grieving, but it had not worked. He just couldn't concentrate on the words. He scanned the fresco upon the wall that portrayed the image of Saint Wallis. Silently, he prayed to the saint, for his father, his sister, and himself. He prayed for the pain to end and to be given a chance to avenge his father. It had been a horrendous day. Elwin could not imagine a worse one. He had awoken that morning to find that he was hiding in a monastery. Somewhere in the county, an evil servant of darkness called a nightling wanted to kill him. He learned that his cousin had murdered his father. Parlan had usurped the kingdom of Ceredigion and kidnapped Elwin's sister. He then compounded his crimes by trying to force Leina into marrying him. Elwin sighed. It had been a very long day, a very long day indeed, and one Elwin would never forget.

At least there was some good news. Leina had not married Parlan. The princess had escaped, but when Colin and Aidan had left with Faynn, there was still no word about the princess' hereabouts. No one knew where she had escaped to; she had just vanished from within a locked room. With little success, Parlan had tried to keep the princess' escape a secret. He even went so far as to go ahead with his marriage plans even though there was no bride. On the phony wedding day, there had been a great celebration with music and feasting which was followed by a private ceremony. A week after the fictitious wedding day, Parlan announced that Leina, his queen, had taken ill and could not leave her bed. Most knew the usurper was lying. At first, it was feared that Parlan had murdered Leina, but soon it leaked out that the princess had gone missing days before her supposed wedding day. Though Parlan was known to be a fake and a liar who had stolen the crown, there was little anyone could do about it. With both Leina and Elwin missing, there was no apparent legitimate successor to claim the throne, and Parlan had the help and support of Strigiol and the Severed Head.

"Where are you, Leina?" Elwin asked in the silence of his room. There was no answer other than the moaning wind.

Exhausted from the traumatic day and needing to get some sleep, Elwin laid back into the bunk. "Goodbye, father," he whispered. The reality that he would never see his father again hurt. The man who had always been there was gone. Despite feeling that he had no more tears left, Elwin began crying once more.

Wondering if the pain would ever go away, tears ran down his face. Elwin clutched the black book to his chest and found some comfort in that. Holding the book in his arms, he felt himself relax. The book felt strangely warm against his chest. He never knew the reason, but holding that book helped him forget, at least for that one night. Temporarily escaping the pain and loss, Elwin closed his tired eyes and slipped into a peaceful sleep.

--

"Sire," called out Ruan Deuchar, Baron of Keloran. The

105

Baron nervously gazed across the hall as he entered the throne room of King Jerran.

Ruan was a handsome man in his mid-thirties. Tall, dark, with a well-trimmed black beard and intense eyes to match, he was the image of the dashing lord. With long strides, he walked down the center of the throne room. King Jerran was nowhere to be seen. The room was extravagantly decorated; architectural details were lined in silver and gold. Large doors made of glass ran across the southern, northern, and eastern walls, creating the sense one was standing inside a jewelry box. The glass doors were very tall, and they opened out onto a long narrow balcony that wrapped around the tower throne room. It was said that on a clear day, one could stand in the room's center and look out across Gildas Island, gazing from one shoreline to the other. However, that was no longer possible. In the last few years, curtains had been hung over the windows making the hall dark where it had once been bathed in sunlight.

At the far west end of the room sat the famed black iron throne of Strigiol. The massive chair was fashioned in the shape of a great black eagle. Trimmed in gold, the eagle's wings wrapped around the seat. The bird's proud head with its silver beak hovered perfectly over the seat. Its jeweled eyes were fashioned so that the eagle would appear to be staring protectively over the king's head and down at his audience. However, at the moment the king was not seated on the throne. Standing there in the dark shadows of the throne room, Ruan felt as if the black bird was watching him from the empty throne. Its jeweled eyes reflected what little light there was in the room, and at times they almost appeared to blink. In the dark hall, the stunning eagle had been transformed into a creature of the night.

"Sire?" There was still no answer. "King Jerran?" the Baron

106

called out again, trying to not to look at the black bird. Ruan had been informed that the king would be here and that he would be alone. Ruan did not think the young page would lie to him, but then again there did seem to be a conspiracy to keep him from seeing the king. Torcull, the king's adviser and confidant did not like Jerran's friendship with Lord Ruan, and the adviser made every attempt to keep them apart.

Ruan shifted uncomfortably from one foot to the other. Running a hand through his dark beard, he began to worry. He knew coming here was a risk, but he had to try. *I'll just have to be careful. The king needs to know the truth. But if I speak too openly, my life could be forfeited.* It was rare these days that Torcull was not at the king's side. Hoping to find the king alone, Ruan hesitated to leave. This was an opportunity that he could not let slip by. Ruan did not fear the king. He and Jerran went too far back. Like their fathers before them, they were close friends, or at least had been once. No, Jerran himself was not a threat. It was Torcull that Ruan feared. If one wrong word got back to the prophet, Ruan would simply disappear. Others had tried to talk reason to the king, and they had vanished without a trace.

Frustrated, Ruan was about to give up and leave. It seemed once again he had been kept from speaking to Jerran. Just then, the king poked his crowned head from behind one of the long, thick satin curtains.

"Is that you, Ruan?"

"Yes, Sire," replied Ruan, recognizing the king's voice.

"Well, it has been some time since you last visited, my old friend." Jerran pulled back the curtains, letting in a stream of bright sunlight. Brilliantly, the light bounced off the gold and silver of the room. The touch of the sun's rays brought the magnificent hall back to life. For a moment, the past years of darkness seemed to vanish.

"Come over here so we can have a look at you," invited King Jerran.

Ruan wanted to tell Jerran that he had tried to call on him several times before, but Torcull, the king's right-hand man, always had an excuse. According to the Prophet of the Severed Head, the king was asleep, too busy, or feeling ill, and could not be bothered at the moment. Torcull would then smile and tell Ruan that he should call on the king at another time, but of course each time the story was the same. Joining the king on the balcony, Ruan reminded himself of the need for caution, so instead of telling the king the truth, the Baron of Keloran smiled and said, "Your lordship has been busy of late."

"That is true," the king mused with a slight nod of his head. "With the added burden of being High King, my time seems short these days." He slapped Ruan on the arm and gave him a genuinely warm smile, "But there should always be time for old friends. Do you not agree?"

"Yes, Sire."

"When did you start calling me Sire? We're old friends, and we are alone. Please, Ruan. You know you can call me by my name."

"Yes, Si...Jerran." The name felt strange and caught in his throat. It seemed like years since he had last called the king by his name.

Ruan studied Jerran, looking for any signs that Torcull might be drugging him, but Jerran looked the same as he always had. The years under Torcull's influence had not seemed to have changed him. His dark hair, with touches of gray at the temples, gave him a look of distinction. In the courtly manner, he was clean shaven and kept his hair short and well-trimmed. He smiled broadly, and his presence had a reassuring influence. Jerran had the look of a kindly father that could always be trusted. His looks went a long way in his uncanny ability of persuasion. The king was a master at communicating ideas to the masses.

King Jerran could convince the people into just about anything. Unfortunately, that made him an ideal tool for Torcull.

"Is it not a beautiful sight?" asked Jerran. With a wave of his hand, he was indicated the view from the balcony.

The bright, clear, spring day bathed them in its warmth. From the height of the balcony, Ruan could look out over the Island of Gildas. Its fields were green and healthy. Gildas was a stunning sight. *Strange,* thought Ruan, *that such a bright, spring day should appear in a land of such darkness.*

"Yes, Sire...Jerran, it is a truly beautiful day."

"We do not see each other enough," Jerran commented. "I'm pleased you stopped by, but you did not come to talk of spring. What is on your mind?"

Ruan was silent. Now that he finally had the king alone, he was unsure if he should speak his mind.

"Come now," encouraged Jerran. "What can be so bad that you cannot tell your oldest friend?"

Ruan gave a solemn nod. *But are you still the same man you once were? You look and act the same, but are you really?* Then he said with a deep frown, "I am concerned about you and the kingdom."

Jerran never stopped smiling, "Concerned? But why? Things have never gone better for Strigiol. We are the capital of all Kambrya except for one last kingdom to conquer, and that problem will soon be solved as well. Strigiol is now the greatest nation that the land has ever seen. The king is bringing in a golden age that shall last a thousand years!"

"But do we have the right to dominate the other kingdoms?"

"Dominate?" Jerran looked confused. "We did not conquer the kingdoms to dominate them. We have brought peace to the land, Ruan. Kambrya cannot survive as separate kingdoms. Someone had to step up and take charge, to unite us once more. Do you think I enjoy the wars?"

"No," admitted Ruan. He believed that Jerran honestly did not like the wars, but he also knew a land can never be unified by war. Peace was not something that can be forced upon people. For a while, it might work, but in time it would fail. The other kingdoms resented Strigiol's strong-armed tactics. Fear was no way to rule a land, and how long would it be before Torcull decided he no longer needed Jerran? How long before Jerran disappeared like all the others, and then what? More wars, or something far worse?

"We are bringing an end to the wars," Jerran continued. "Kambrya rejoices in our rule and in the newfound prosperity."

"Whose prosperity? Certainly not the other kingdoms. They are oppressed, and their toil and pain are what is making us so wealthy. The kingdoms have become our slave states." Ruan shook his head sadly. "You need to leave these palace walls, Jerran. You need to talk with your people and see with your own eyes what their lives are like. Come with me, Jerran. Together we can tour the kingdoms. If you are to be High King, then let it be for the good of all."

"I cannot leave my duties here," objected Jerran. "And I have been to Ceredigion and spoke with Parlan. The people are happy. You have my word on it."

"Parlan hardly counts," Ruan said, finding it hard to hide his contempt for the puppet king. "Parlan is a fool. He would say anything to keep his crown."

"Ruan!"

"I am sorry, Sire, if my words offend you, but Parlan is not the true heir to the throne. Prince Elwin is..."

"A traitor to the crown," Jerran finished the sentence, cutting Ruan off.

"I do not claim to be Elwin's defender," Ruan added quickly. "If you name him a traitor and an enemy of Strigiol, then he is an enemy of mine as well. But what if this traitor rallies the people to rebel against you? Should you not know where the people stand?"

"Torcull assures me that the people love me, and that Elwin is no threat to the peace. None will follow him."

Ruan sighed. *Torcull has you fooled, my friend. Only here in Gildas do you still hold the people's affection, and that too is waning. Who can trust a king that has allowed the Severed Head to spread?* "Then you trust...the prophet?"

"Torcull? Of course. Do you not?"

Ruan swallowed hard. He had to be careful now. Perhaps Ruan had gone too far already. "It is just that he uses the Black Army and the Severed Head to control the people, and there are the stories. They are horrible. They say."

Jerran cut Ruan off with a wave of his hand. "I know what they say, and it is nonsense. Torcull is a great and holy man, and his wisdom has made our land prosperous beyond belief. Gildas is the richest city in all the Kingdoms."

"That is true," a voice came from behind them. Ruan spun on his heels. Standing just inside the glass doors was Torcull. His flawless face lay just within the shadows of the throne room. His cold blue eyes threateningly gazed out at Ruan.

Ruan met the Prophet's intense stare and wondered how much the man had heard.

Nervously, Ruan started twisting the coarse hairs of his

beard, and then he snatched his hand back to his side. *I can't afford to look as scared as I feel.*

"Gildas is indeed a wonder to behold," Torcull went on. "An inspiration to all of Kambrya."

"Greetings." smiled Jerran.

Torcull nodded his head towards the king. "Greetings to you, my Sire." He then fixed his cold stare on Ruan and gave another nod."And to you, Lord Ruan."

Ruan nodded, trying not to look nervous, meeting the Prophet's eyes with his own steady gaze. He was determined not to let the Prophet see his fear. "Will you come out and enjoy the day with us?"

Frowning ever so slightly, Torcull turned back to Jerran and stayed in the shadows. "I see the good lord has paid a visit to Your Majesty. I am glad you two had a chance to visit. I hope I have not interrupted you. Perhaps I should come back at a later time."

"Not at all," replied Jerran. "You two are my most trusted friends. And you may also be of assistance. Our good Lord Ruan is troubled."

Ruan felt his throat go dry. *Don't let your fear show!*

"Oh?" replied Torcull, raising his thin eyebrows. He clasped his hands behind his back.

"What is bothering our good lord?"

"Nothing, really," said Ruan, hoping the king would let it drop, but of course he didn't.

"Lord Ruan believes the people are not happy with my rule, and fears the traitor Prince Elwin will lead an insurrection."

"Ah, I see," Torcull said. Looking from the shadows, his eyes never left Ruan's. "You may be assured that our sovereign is well loved, Lord Baron. And in time, Elwin will be captured and brought before King Jerran for treason. The rebel prince cannot elude the High King's justice forever."

"Of course," said Ruan, trying to undo the damage. "I'm sure that I am just worrying too much. I can see things are in good hands." Ruan bowed to the king. "If my Sire will excuse me, I have matters I must attend to."

"As you wish, Ruan," replied the king. "I hope your mind will rest easier."

"It shall, Sire."

"Good," Jerran responded, "and do not be a stranger. My door is always open to my friends."

"Your Majesty does me honor." Ruan bowed once more and backed off the balcony, slipping past Torcull. Ruan tried not to meet the prophet's eyes again. He could almost feel a threat behind his unblinking eyes. Turning, Ruan hurried across the throne room, suddenly anxious to escape the hall.

"Ruan is a good man," Jerran said as he watched the Baron retreat. "Is he not?"

"Does he not tend to be overly critical of Your majesty's policies?"

"Nonsense," replied Jerran. "Ruan is a cautious man. That's all. There is none more loyal to me than the Baron of Keloran. That is, except for you."

"As you say, Your Majesty. May we go inside, Your Majesty?" Torcull added, shading his eyes with a raised hand. "The sun is bright today."

"Oh, yes. I keep forgetting your sensitivity to light."

"A small enough sacrifice," mumbled Torcull under his breath as he followed the king into the throne room. The prophet stopped momentarily to close the curtains. Dark shadows once more reclaimed the chamber.

Sitting down, Jerran leaned back into his elaborate eagle throne. "It is a shame about your eyes. It's such a lovely day."

"I have lived with the ailment a long time, my lord. It no longer feels like a disadvantage, and my night vision makes up for it."

"I know how you must feel, Torcull." Jerran nodded knowingly. "As you live with the burden of your eyes, I too have burdens. As High King, my work never seems to be done, and I always worry about my people."

"That is what I am here for, to help relieve you of some of the weight of being High King."

"Ah, yes. You are kind to help. However, sometimes I feel guilty for letting you do so much. Still, the ultimate decisions lie in my two hands." With a look of concern, the king gazed down at his hands. He slowly turned them over as if he was seeing them for the first time. "Perhaps these two hands." He held them up so Torcull could see them. "Have not been carrying their fair share of the burden. I see my people so rarely nowadays. I should see them more. Maybe I will do as Ruan suggested and tour the provinces and see for myself how things are. Not that I do not trust you, Torcull, but it is my burden and not yours."

"It is no burden, Your majesty. It's an honor to serve you." Torcull hated these conversations with the king. It tried the prophet's patience. More than once, he had thought of drugging the king or killing him and to be done with it, but Jerran still had his uses. And he still needed the High King to fulfill his dream and rise to ultimate power. Jerran was the perfect puppet king. The truth was, Jerran cared little for the responsibility of being a ruler. The king liked the public speeches and elegant courtly parties. Happily, he left the rest to Torcull, but every so often the king decided to indulge himself in the illusion of being on top of things. This appeared to be one of those times. *Lord Ruan put this idea into your head,* thought Torcull. *Perhaps it is time for the good Baron to have an accident.*

"I wish father was still here," the king said so quietly that Torcull could barely hear. "He was good at running the kingdom...better than I am. No great speaker, but he was a wise man and a great king."

"I wish things had been different myself, Your majesty, but the good King Conrad has passed from this world. May his soul be at peace." Torcull hesitated for only a moment. "It is a shame he exiled me. I feel that if I had been near, I could have cured his illness."

"I never did understand why father exiled you." Jerran took the golden crown off the arm of his throne, turning it slowly in his hands. It was a wreath of pounded gold. It was not the ceremonial crown, but the everyday crown. Even so, Jerran did not like wearing it. It reminded him of his father.

The king's death had come so quickly, and because of the disease, he could not even see the body for danger of contracting the deadly disease. Ever since the death of his father, Jerran had felt lost. *I wonder if this crown weighed as heavy for you father as it does for me.*

He rolled the crown in his hands, then reaching above his head, he hung the jewel covered crown on one of the eagle's outstretched wings. "Father would have been wiser to use your council, as I do. Perhaps if he had, he would still be alive, and the kingdom in his capable hands rather than mine."

"Remember it was you who called me back when your father grew ill," added Torcull. "It was too late for me to save him, but I was able to ease his passing. You are both a good king and son."

"I am not the wise king he was."

"You are indeed a very wise king, my lord. While your father was a truly great man, he did not possess your vision. It is you who has brought Kambrya under one sovereign. For the first time since the ancient kings, the land will be whole again. Within the next few months, you will launch your attack on Mythra and complete what others thought impossible. Peace will once more govern the land. Your vision has brought back the golden days of old."

Jerran nodded his head. Obtaining peace throughout the eight kingdoms was the driving force behind all his actions. Only Mythra stood in the way. *Yes,* he thought, *people have been hurt along the way, but what else could I do? It's for the people that I have conquered. The good of all has always been my goal. But still, I do not think father would have approved. Am I wrong?*

"Sire, you have done what is best," Torcull went on, as if he could read the king's mind.

Jerran met Torcull's light blue eyes. *Yes, Torcull is right, of course. This is all for the best. The suffering of a few cannot stand in the way of a better world.*

"How are things in Ceredigion?" Jerran suddenly asked, changing the subject. "Is Parlan having troubles? I will need to withdraw most of my men out of Acair soon, but perhaps I should keep a garrison behind."

"He has things under control. If you wish, you may leave some of the Strigiol regulars behind, but I will recall the Black Army. They will be needed against Mythra."

The king shifted uncomfortably in his throne. He disliked the idea that Torcull had full control over the Black Army. With its troops made up from the Severed Head's faithful, the Black Army was by far the strongest force in all the Kingdoms. It seemed wrong to Jerran that he, the king, should have so little influence over it. However, the Black Army was a religious force and was rightfully under the Severed Head's leadership.

"If you are concerned that Parlan will lose his grip over the kingdom, you need not be, Sire." A smile crossed Torcull's flawless face. "There is nothing to worry about. The Black Army has put fear into Ceredigion. They will not fight again...not even if Prince Elwin himself were there to lead them. And that will not happen."

"Oh!" said Jerran. "That reminds me. I wanted to ask you. Has the prince been captured yet? You said it would be soon."

"No, my lord."

"No? But I thought..."

"It is not something you need concern yourself about. Make your speeches and woo the people. I will handle the Prince of Ceredigion."

"I appreciate your help," Jerran said, trying to look kingly, "but these are things a sovereign needs to know. So, I shall ask again. Why has the prince not been captured? Were you able to speak with your monk? You said you would be able to."

Torcull sighed. "Yes, I can speak to the Red Robe through what is called a dream walk, and I have done so." And since the red monk created a link to Elwin, Torcull could also reach the prince through dream walking, but he saw no reason to tell the king that. Dream walking also has its limitations; the dream walk could not tell him where the prince was hiding. There was also something that bothered the prophet about the way the last dream had ended. It was as if the prince had been snatched away from him. *Someone had interfered with the dream, but whom? Faynn? No, he could not have done that. The old man might be able to guard his dreams, but he could not snatch him away like that, not without me knowing it. The Guardians of Light perhaps? In a few days, I'll try again, and I will find some answers.*

"And the prince, is he in Reidh County as you thought?"

"He is there. The Red Robe nearly captured him, but Elwin had some...unexpected help. The prince got away and is hiding somewhere."

"Oh, I see." The king nodded, but he had a confused look on his face. "But won't Elwin try to reach Ceredigion? Perhaps he has already left the county."

"No, Elwin has not slipped past me—us I mean. He is there hiding somewhere, and in a short time, his hiding place will be discovered. This time, he will not escape."

"How can you be sure? Reidh is small, but there are many ways over the mountains. You cannot guard them all, and there's always the sea. He could have taken a boat and be halfway to Ceredigion by now."

Frustrated, Torcull closed his eyes then said slowly, "He is there. Through the powers of the Severed Head, and of the Great Master, a winter storm has sealed off Reidh County. All the mountain passes have been closed off. The sea is the only way out, and we have total control over the coast. No, the young prince is still there, and he will not escape me. There is no way out."

--

Pallas, Colin, and Aidan sat hunched over a small wooden table, finishing off their lunch of potato soup and bread. The Monks at the monastery had made them feel welcome. Even Aidan, who did not practice the religion of the Doctrine of the Three, found the monastery and its inhabitants friendly. Yet the three friends were uneasy.

"There's no way to escape," Pallas said with a glum look. "Lord Stanford controls all the harbors along the coast, and all the passes are full of snow."

"I know," said Colin sounding frustrated. "But Ceredigion needs Elwin. We must find a way."

Aidan looked silently down at his empty tea mug. Studying the leaves, he wished he could read their meanings, that is if things such as reading tea leaves were not just wives tales. He too had need to leave the wintery county. Despite the fire in the hearth making the room comfortable and warm, his bones ached. Elves were not made for snow. Despite his wishes, the snow continued to fall outside the monastery walls. It was a strange spring, even for Reidh. They had been in the monastery for weeks. During that time, the snow just kept falling, and the winds piled it up into towering drifts. It was as if winter had been called back, and it was showing no sign of letting up.

"Spring will most certainly come soon," Aidan said, trying to sound optimistic, despite not feeling it himself. The elves were creatures of the earth, and the earth's power resonated through them. Through a kind of sixth sense, they could feel the shifting of weather patterns and could give accurate predictions within a few days' time. Beyond that, they were less accurate. Aidan was uneasy, since his senses told him it should be a warm spring day, and yet the snow was falling harder than before. Something was wrong. He could feel it, and he knew that magic had to be behind the bizarre weather.

"Besides," the fair-looking elf went on, "Elwin needs this time to heal. Ceredigion will just have to wait."

Colin frowned. "Time is something we can't waste." Colin was always uncomfortable when his large size and strong muscles could not offer any help. He could not fight or pull his way through the snow. Waiting with nothing to do was putting him ill at ease.

"Until the snows melt, we have no other choice." Pallas pointed out the obvious.

Colin pushed himself up from the table. "I fear while we wait, the trap around us grows even tighter. We may just wait ourselves to death." Despite this, the friends had little choice but to wait as the winter dragged on.

CHAPTER EIGHT

Elwin stopped before a pair of steep stairs. They looked rickety and unsafe. He held his lamp a little higher so that he could see the stairs better as he cautiously began to climb. The stairs appeared weak and worn. However, they were sturdier than they looked.

It had been over a month now since Elwin had learned of his father's death and his missing sister. Now that he could think more clearly, he knew what he should do—find a way to Ceredigion and regain the throne. However, he knew he wouldn't do that, at least not until he found his sister Leina—but where? In the white castle that he had dreamed about?

Elwin had told no one of the dreams. Maybe that is all it was—dream. Although, Elwin no longer thought of dreams as just dreams.

Twice in the last few weeks, Torcull had tried to enter his dreams, but Faynn was always there to chase him away. *So maybe there is a white castle, and maybe Leina is there. But how can I find it if I can't get out of Reidh? To the south, north, and east, snow blocks the mountain passes, and the coast is now in the hands of Lord Stanford. Even if I find a way out, I still don't know where to begin looking for the white castle. It could be anywhere!*

It was Faynn who had come up with a plan. He said that he could discover where the missing princess was, but to do so, Elwin would have to trust him. At first, Elwin refused.

Faynn's plan called for magic. The youth would have to allow Faynn to expose him to druid magic, which he called Earth Magic. Elwin had been raised through the trinity doctrine. The Trinity taught that all magic was evil and damaging to one's soul. After all, it was magic that had sent Kambrya into the dark ages, famines, and endless wars. The dark ages had torn apart the society, and the kingdoms were still trying to recover from those dark days. So, for Elwin, the use of magic was an unpleasant thought. But as all other hope faded, he reluctantly gave in to Faynn.

Trying not to think about what he was about to do, Elwin struggled forward. He did not find the narrow stairs especially difficult. The hard part would happen once he reached the top of the bell tower. Silhouetted before him were Aidan, Colin, and Faynn. Pallas would have been there too, but he had braved the storms and had returned to Port Murray to talk with his father. *Maybe Count Dovan could find a way to get me out of the county.*

The stairs creaked under their weight. Faynn had decided that the bell tower would serve their needs best. At the top of the tower, there would be little chance of being discovered. At this late hour, the tower would be deserted, and Faynn assured Elwin that they would be finished long before anyone knew they were missing. The brothers of the monastery would never need to know of this night's activities. The monks had been very understanding with their guests, but they would never understand or accept what Faynn planned. Magic was a sacrilege, a forbidden art that had been outlawed for hundreds of years.

Leading the way up the stairs, Colin pushed open a trap door. Several bats took flight as
they were disturbed by Colin's sudden and unexpected arrival.

Joining the others, Elwin was the last to climb out onto the tower's top. From the bell tower, he looked out over the dark, snow-covered valley. Below the tower, the monastery lay huddled in a blanket of darkness. Elwin hung his lamp on a rafter and pulled his cloak tightly about himself. The night was cold, and a stiff breeze whistled through the beams above him. The brass bell, now green with age, swayed ever so slightly in the cold breeze. For the first time in weeks, it was not snowing, and the night sky was clear leaving stars stretched out above them.

Faynn did not waste any time. First, he carefully studied the stars above. After assuring himself that he was facing north, he pulled a green piece of chalk from his brown robe and lowered himself to his knees. He briefly spoke words of a strange language that he alone understood. The wind died, and a silence fell over the tower. Wide-eyed, Elwin, Aidan, and Colin watched while Faynn began to draw long straight lines upon the wooden planked floor. Creating a large octagon, the druid drew each line carefully. At each of the eight points of the octagon, he placed the signs of the compass: N, NE, E, SE, S, SW, W, and NW. With the green chalk, he drew four lines that connected each point of the compass to its opposite direction. The octagon now looked like a strange wheel with green spokes. Within the wheel, he wrote runes and other mysterious signs and symbols.

"What are you doing?" asked Colin. He sounded worried.

"There are four universal powers," Faynn replied as he continued to draw onto the wooden floor. Taking great care to make sure each point of the octagon was pointing in the right direction, he often stopped and stared at the stars above before continuing his work.

"The Four Powers, or what is called Earth Magic," he went on, "governs our world. Whether we recognize it or not, the Four Powers are constantly at work around us. Contrary to common beliefs, these powers are neither good nor evil, but can be used to serve both. It is through the Four Powers that all things are possible. Without Earth Magic, life on this world could not exist. As an elf, Aidan already knows this."

"What do you mean?" asked Elwin. "Why would Aidan

already know?"

"The elves call Earth Magic the Power of Life." Faynn raised a bushy eyebrow. "And they are creatures of magic. Did he not tell you?"

Colin's eyes grew narrow. "The elves use magic!? I don't believe it! You're lying! Tell him, Aidan. Elves and magic are just stories."

Aidan looked pale and did not answer.

Faynn shrugged nonchalantly as he revealed Aidan's darkest secret. "The elves are a part of the Four Powers. Not only do they use magic, they are magic."

Aidan? Magic?! thought Elwin. It was hard to believe. Sure, they had all heard the stories of Elven magic, and they certainly were secretive people, but Elwin had dismissed them as just stories. He had grown-up with Aidan and had never seen any magic. Of course, the elves would never admit it if they did use magic. The church hierarchy would never tolerate it. If the church authorities ever found any proof, they would call for a crusade against the elves, and the kingdoms would support it. Magic users were to be persecuted and driven from the land. It was the law.

The druids lived on an archipelago far out in the Iar Sea, beyond the sight of land, in a place that was considered outside of Kambryan borders. They did so to avoid the laws that governed the kingdoms of Kambrya. Faynn was the only druid that Elwin had ever heard of visiting the mainland. Thinking of thousands of soldiers marching into the woods known as the Green: Aidan's home, Elwin shivered. Aidan too appeared sick, as if he too was having the same thought.

"Each element of the earth has its own properties and purpose." continued Faynn. "The elves have a great and wondrous gift, which they call the Power of Life. They are able to balance each of the powers in harmony with the others. In that way, they can maintain their forest's wondrous health. The power of all earth's elements are capable of great and glorious things, yet they are also potentially dangerous. One must be patient and work with the powers and not try to force them to the users' will."

Aidan's face tightened. It was widely believed that the elves used magic, but the race had always denied it. Elwin's father, King Artair, accepted that they did not possess magic. Though the Green was not a part of Ceredigion, it was within the kingdom's borders. The church was always petitioning Artair to allow an investigation into the supposed use of magic by the elves. Yet without proof, the king refused to allow the inquisitional branch of the church anywhere near the Green, claiming it would be insulting to elves, who did not welcome strangers into their forest.

"You have nothing to fear, Aidan," Faynn said, seeing the concerned look on Aidan's face. "No one here will turn your people in or judge them for using something they were born with. It is in your blood. I too am a user of magic and after tonight, we will all share in the same crime."

"Is this true?" Colin asked Aidan. "I've heard the talk, but I never believed it."

Aidan gave him a tight nod. "It's true." His voice shook. "That's why we don't let anyone into the Green. If anyone saw the inner woods, they would know. Our home is a magical place. We cannot help it." His eyes shifted, and he looked scared. "Our magic is different from Faynn's. It comes from within, and it is a part of being an elf. We cannot stop being who we are."

Elwin gave Aidan a slight smile. "The Green is not part of Kambrya. The church has no authority over you." But Elwin could not help the cold chill that ran up his spine. *Aidan uses magic!* He knew deep down that Aidan was not evil, but the church doctrine had always thought that magic was the work of dark forces sent to destroy the world.

Aidan sighed. "What would it matter? If they could prove it, the church would not care, and Ceredigion would not be able to help us. Not even if they wanted to."

"So, *you* can use magic!?" asked Colin.

Again, Aidan nodded. "But we cannot do very much unless there are many of us together. That is why so few elves leave the Green. Away from our home and people, we are cut off from most abilities of the Power of Life." He hesitated then said, "I would have told you sooner, but any elf that wishes to leave the Green must swear to tell no one. I could not break my word to my people."

He is still Aidan, Elwin reminded himself, *and my friend.* "Don't worry, Aidan. We won't tell. Look what I am about to do." *Magic?! What am I doing? What would my father think?*

Faynn turned back to his work. "As I was saying, the elves have learned to work with the powers, and not against them. If they tried to force the power to their will, disregarding the harmony of nature, their forest could be transformed into a wonderland of unbelievable beauty. However, it would not last. In only a short period of time, the Green would wither and die, or even worse."

Checking that his octagon had all the right alignments, Faynn gazed up at the sky once more. "The four sources of Earth Magic are water, earth, sky, and fire. Each of these four powers has immense and incomprehensible energy. The druids have dedicated their lives to understanding the nature of the Four Powers, and still, we are like children compared to the Ancient Ones."

"Ancient Ones?" asked Elwin, happy to turn the

126

conversation away from Aidan.

"The Ancient Ones were once our teachers," Faynn explained. "They were an old and wise race of mortals and were, in fact, the first humans to walk on this world. This first human race had lived in the times before the gods left this world, or at least a people that called themselves gods. It was the so-called gods themselves who taught the Ancient Ones the ways of Earth Magic. Or so it has been said. Yet, as the centuries passed, the first race grew old and their time on the lands drew to an end. This race gave way to the world of men, elves, and dwarves time was just beginning. Seeing they would soon they would have to leave this world to the new races, they gathered together a few humans and began to teach them. The Ancient Ones taught these men their lore, history, and wisdom so that their world would not be totally lost. These men became the first druids."

"I've never heard any of this before," Colin said.

"The Church has banned the druid's history and beliefs, and who is to say how much is factual and how much is myth." Faynn stated, "The druids keep it alive nonetheless, though not all believe it is true."

Faynn then took a deep breath and went on with his story, "It was the Ancient Ones, with the help of the gods, who made your sword, Elwin. The Ancient Ones forged the blade with Earth Magic, and the gods bestowed it with their power." The druid pointed to the sword that hung at Elwin's side. "They called the blade Saran na Grian, which in the old language means, 'The Sword of Light and Darkness'."

Shocked, Elwin looked down at the sword as if he had just been stung by a wasp. *First Aidan and now this! The Sword of Light and Darkness? Was it possible?* He had heard of it before, but like most believe it was just a story. For Elwin, another myth had suddenly come to life. "Why did you not tell me this before?"

Faynn shrugged. "At the time, it did not seem important."

"Not important?!" Elwin stared at the hilt of his father's sword as if he were seeing it for the first time. He had known it was old, but he had no idea how old. *Saran na Grian!?* It was almost too bizarre to believe, but something told him it was indeed true. Elwin shivered. If it was true, then it was worse than using magic. Elwin knew the legends of Saran na Grian, and he was aware that in the stories, Saran na Grian had another name as well. "It's also called the End Bringer."

Faynn frowned. "So, it has been called by men."

"And that is not important!?" asked Elwin angrily. "It is said that the End Bringer will bring death and destruction. If you're right, this sword is dangerous!"

"All things of beauty are dangerous, Elwin," Faynn calmly stated. "It is the nature of life."

Elwin shook his head. He looked up from the sword. "Did my father know?"

Again, Faynn nodded. "All the kings of Ceredigion have known. Going back hundreds of years, the kings have guarded and protected the sword. If time had allowed, your father would have told you, but now that duty has fallen to me. The druids and your ancestors worked together to keep the ancient blade safe. We have kept the sword safe until the time came for it to be used."

"You knew my father?"

"I called him my friend, Elwin. He was a good man. It was his hope to someday bring the order of the druid's home to Kambrya again. Elwin, your father, was a good man and this world is a much sadder place without him."

My father was a friend of Druids! Elwin could not help but
128

wonder what other secrets his father hid, and he knew he would need to learn those secrets if he was to stay alive. "You told me that the sword was a key of some type. A key to what?" *Not important?! This is madness!*

"Saran na Grian was created to protect the harmony of the world against the dark desires of Beli."

"Beli, the god of night and darkness?" Colin asked skeptically. "This is too much. The Sword of Light and Darkness, and now Beli! You cannot think we are going to believe all this."

Faynn shrugged, "Believe what you will, young Colin. But even you saw the Red Robe. An evil has been set free and if we do not stop it, more will follow. It will not stop until it has consumed the world."

"I saw a monk in a robe, nothing else," stated Colin.

At the mention of the monk, Elwin pulled his cloak tighter. He had seen more than just a monk and was starting to believe in things—things that not long ago he would have called foolish. Things were different now, or maybe he was different. Elwin wished that he could still be like Colin, and be able to disbelieve, but the nightling had robbed him of that ability.

"What do the gods have to do with the sword?"

With a look of astonishment, Colin exclaimed, "Elwin! You're not taking this seriously, are you?!"

Elwin glanced over at Colin. "Yes... I have to."

Faynn gave Elwin a nod of his head and a look that acknowledged that he and Elwin shared a common knowledge, and with it a shared responsibility. "To answer your question, Elwin, Beli hates his twin brother, Tuatha, the God of Light. Long, long ago, before man walked upon this earth, the God of Night somehow went mad. He desired that darkness rule the world. To accomplish this, he decided that Tuatha would have to be destroyed. Tuatha, known as the God of Light or Dawn saw that this was folly. Tuatha knew that if he or his brother were killed, the world would come to an end. Both darkness and light are needed to maintain the harmony of the world, but Beli did not seem to care. At first, Tuatha was able to stay away from his evil brother and avoided a conflict that could bring about the end of the world as we know it. But Beli grew in his power, and he was relentless in his quest to destroy Tuatha. Seeing that eventually Beli would catch him, Tuatha enlisted the help of the other gods. The gods asked the Ancient Ones to make a sword, forging it with Earth Magic. Then the gods took the sword and created Saran na Grian."

"What does it do?" asked Elwin. He was finally learning something about the sword, but now he was beginning to fear what it all might mean.

"The gods gave it two powers," Faynn explained. "The magic comes from the combined effort of the gods, who gave the sword the ability to imprison Beli. It was the only way the gods could preserve the harmony of the world. But by the time the gods completed the sword, the Ancient Ones had already passed from this world. The age of man had begun, so Tuatha gave the sword to Vladimir ap Gruffydd, who became the first High King of Kambrya."

"Why did they not use it themselves?" Aidan asked.

"They could not take the chance," Faynn replied. "If Beli were to kill one of the gods before the gods could imprison him, the harmony of the world would have been destroyed. It was just too great a danger."

"But not too dangerous for this Vladimir?" Colin asked sarcastically. "Is a man's life less important than these so-called gods of yours?"

"In life, choices are not always easy or fair, Colin. What the gods did, they did because it was the best for all. And I do not truly believe they were gods, just a race in tune to the powers of Earth Magic. Perhaps in ways similar to the Elves."

Colin gave Faynn a discontented grunt.

"Don't be rude, Colin!" snapped Aidan. Aidan then turned to Faynn. "Did the Ancient Ones also make the crown of Kambrya as well?"

Faynn turned away from Colin and looked up at Aidan. "Perhaps. Since the crown has been lost for so long, it is hard to say where it came from, or what its functions were. But it is said that no one can't become a true High King without it. The reason why is not clear. It is written that the gods themselves crowned Vladimir by placing the lost crown of Kambrya upon his head. So maybe the Ancient Ones did make it, or maybe the gods did. Anyway, as I was saying, the gods gave the sword to Vladimir. With Saran na Grain, Vladimir was to lead the fight against Beli. However, Beli discovered the gods' plans before Vladimir could act. To protect himself against Vladimir and the sword, Beli went into hiding. As the centuries passed, the sword and crown were passed on to the next generation. Each new king stood ready, watching for the time when Beli would return. During those years, Beli grew in his power and his madness and his hatred deepened. Finally, Beli did return. Deciding that his time of triumph was at hand, the mad god emerged from his place of hiding and built his castle of Ban-Darn. At Ban-Darn, dark and evil acts were performed and Beli started calling himself the Great Master and the Overlord. Those were dark days. It was at that time that the Cult of the Severed Head first emerged. Soon after that, the Great Wars began."

Ban-Darn! Elwin shuddered. He recalled the dream of the

black castle, Torcull, and the spider guardian. Elwin had stood at the gates of the Black Castle.

"In time," Faynn went on, "the mad god came to believe that he could defeat the High King and destroy the Sword of Light and Darkness once and for all. Saran na Grian was the one thing that could threaten the Overlord, so Beli decided to face down the High King. But Beli failed, and he was imprisoned."

"So," said Elwin, "the Dark Overlord is the god Beli, and King Coinneach at the Battle of Ban-Darn did not kill the Overlord but imprisoned him."

Surprised, Faynn turned his head up from his work and looked at Elwin. "How did you know about the battle of Ban-Darn?"

"I read it in the Chronicle of Brother Wallis."

"You have seen a copy of the Chronicle?" asked Faynn. "I did not realize another one existed. I thought the Druids possessed the only surviving copy. Where did you find it?"

"In Port Murray," Elwin answered truthfully.

"Interesting. I will have to see it sometime. And yes, you are right. Your ancestor, King Coinneach, used the sword's power to imprison Beli, and now Torcull wants that same sword so that he can release the Dark Overlord."

"But that would be madness!" exclaimed Aidan. "Why would he do such a thing?"

"I agree. It is madness," replied Faynn. "Perhaps Torcull is as mad as his master. But more likely, Torcull fell under the Dark Overlord's influence. Even locked away in his castle, Beli is powerful. He is not without influence upon the world, and he has always been a great seducer of men. Torcull wants power and the Overlord has promised it to him."

"You talk as if you know this Torcull," stated Colin bluntly.

"I have met his type before." As he talked, Faynn returned to working on the octagon. "There is a fine line between the search for knowledge and the obsession of power. Once you have crossed that line, you have become a servant of Beli."

"What happened to King Coinneach?" Elwin asked. "The book did not say."

"At the Battle of Ban-Darn?" Faynn shrugged. "It is not known. There is another ancient codex that says he was destroyed in the battle. Mortals were never meant to handle such raw power that the sword possesses. It is not known, but perhaps King Coinneach was consumed by that power when he cast the Overlord into his prison."

"How does the sword work? " asked Elwin.

The Druid shrugged. "It is not known, but that is of little importance now. We just need to keep it from Torcull and keep him from finding a way to bring Beli back to our world. So long as the dark god is imprisoned, his threat is limited."

"We have the sword now." Aidan pointed. "Why do we not destroy it or cast it into the sea? Then neither Torcull nor anyone else will be able to free the Overlord."

Faynn shook his head sadly. "I wish it could be that easy, but if the sword could be destroyed, which I do not think it can be, Beli would then be released from his prison. It is the power of the sword that keeps him safely locked away. And if it were thrown into the sea as you suggest, that would only buy us a little time. Eventually, Torcull would find it. The sword is extremely powerful. Such a power gives off something that is like waves or ripples of magic. Those waves of magic can be felt and followed to its source."

"I don't believe any of this," stated Colin. "But if Torcull can find the sword, why has he not found us here at this abbey?"

"It takes time," said Faynn. "It took Torcull years to discover that the sword was here in Reidh. The longer the sword stays in one place, the easier it is to find. Given enough time, Torcull or one his servants will find it here. The only way to hide the sword is to keep it moving from one place to another."

"Then it was the sword and not someone else that gave me away?" asked Elwin. "It was the sword that let the...Red Robe know I was in Reidh?" Elwin was relieved to discover that he had not been betrayed. He had been worrying about that. But it was also upsetting to know that the sword drew his enemies towards him, and as long as he had the sword, Torcull would follow him. Faynn nodded, and Elwin went on. "And that is also how you found me?"

Again, Faynn nodded.

Elwin frowned. *Does that mean that I will always be hiding, always running from one place to another?* Elwin looked up at a dark cloud that was drifting overhead. The cloud was being carried along on the cold mountain winds. Elwin wondered if he would become like the cloud, ever drifting with no destination. Would he be forced into a life of running and hiding? Would he ever be able to stay in one place without risking that Torcull would find him and the sword? The world suddenly looked grim.

Elwin looked down at the druid. "I have had the sword for three years." His hand rested on the worn leather hilt of the blade. He trembled slightly as he thought of the power the sword might hold. The sword that always hung at his side suddenly felt heavy and unwelcome. "Why in all this time, have I never felt any of its power? It looks and feels like any other sword."

"You have not been trained in the ways that Torcull or I have been," Faynn gave as an answer. "We can feel things that others cannot. You are not trained in the Four Powers, nor are you the High King. Therefore, there is no reason you should feel or sense the power of the sword. I would have been surprised if you had."

"Then if Torcull is to use the sword," Elwin concluded, "he needs a high king?"

"Yes," replied Faynn, as he put the final touches on his octagon. "Torcull cannot use the sword himself. I doubt he would even touch it. The sword is the enemy of darkness. It might strike out against him."

"So, he's using King Jerran," stated Elwin.

"Yes," Faynn said again. "But he needs more. To be a true High King, one needs the crown of Kambrya, but it has been lost since the Battle of Ban-Darn. If Torcull can find the crown and take the sword from you, he will force King Jerran to use Saran na Grian to free Beli. If that happens, we have lost. All of the gods of old are gone, except for Beli. If Beli is freed once again, the other gods cannot come to help us, and Beli will have no one with the power to stand against him."

"Then that must never happen!" said Aidan in a panicked voice.

Faynn stepped back from the octagon and nodded his head as if he were satisfied with it. "Quite right," he said, staring down at the floor. "We must never allow that to happen, and if the fates are willing, we won't let it." He pointed. "That should do it," Faynn said, referring to the octagon.

"You never said what the octagon is for," pointed out Elwin.

"So, I didn't. Sometimes when I get to talking, I become distracted. It's not often that I have such an inquisitive and attentive audience. The octagon is drawn according to the eight directions of the compass. In a sense, it becomes a miniature version of the world. The octagon is the primary form used when one must immerse oneself or join with Earth Magic. As I said earlier, before I wandered off, Earth Magic is composed of the four universal powers. Each one of the elements has immense and potentially deadly powers. If left unchecked, those powers would quickly get out of hand. The octagon contains perimeters that help keep the magic under control."

Elwin frowned. He did not like the idea of immersing himself with forces he did not even understand, but Elwin knew he had no alternative.

Faynn pointed at the octagon again. "You, along with myself will sit in the center of the compass, and we will let the powers flow through and around us. In a sense, we will allow ourselves to join with the magic. If we tried this outside of the octagon, we would lose ourselves to Earth Magic and never return."

Elwin's face paled. "Are we going somewhere?"

"You need not worry," continued Faynn. "Once inside, we will be connected to this spot. What we will be doing is called dream walking. Our bodies will remain here, but our souls and minds will be swept away. The octagon will serve as a lifeline if you will...a rope that will lead us back here. We will enter the world of dreams where reality is altered, and the mind has fewer limitations. In that realm, you should be able to locate Leina. If she is asleep, you should even be able to talk to her, but she will only remember it as a dream.

Trust me, Elwin, it sounds more complicated than it really is, and I will be with you." Faynn smiled. "Shall we begin?"

CHAPTER NINE

"May I have a moment with my friends first?" asked Elwin. He was in no hurry to be immersed in druid magic.

Faynn nodded. "But do not take too long," he warned. "We have time, but none to waste." Leaving the three boys alone, the druid retreated to the far side of the bell tower.

Turning his back to them, Faynn stared into the night.

Shifting uncomfortably, Colin's eyes darted from Elwin to the octagon, and back again. Grabbing Elwin by his sleeve, the big youth pulled the prince farther away from both Faynn and the octagon. Aidan followed along. Colin leaned close to Elwin. "I don't like this," he announced in a quiet whisper. "The druid is keeping things from us. He answers our questions, but there is more that he wants from you that he's not telling us. I do not trust him. And to use magic!?"

"I understand," replied Elwin. "But what other choice do I have?"

"There must be a better way than magic." said Colin. He looked over his shoulder. Faynn did not seem to be listening. Colin turned back to Elwin. "Pallas will be back in a day or two. Surely Count Murray will know what to do."

"Why don't you trust Faynn?" Aidan asked Colin with a frown.

Colin did not answer, but Elwin knew what he was thinking.

"Because he uses magic?" Aidan added, answering the question himself. "Like me?" There was bitterness in Aidan's voice that Elwin had never heard before.

"Your magic is different. You said so yourself," Elwin said, coming to Colin's defense.

"And we know you. You're our friend."

"Not according to your church. Magic is a sin, right?" Aidan met Elwin's eyes with a hard stare. "Magic is not evil. You humans have labeled it so, but that doesn't make it true. Magic is a power and is no more evil than a king's or even a prince's authority over their kingdom. It is how one uses power that makes a difference. If you are going to say the druid is evil because of his magic, then you must say that I—"

"I never said he was!" stated Colin, quickly cutting off Aidan. "But what do we know of the druid? That has nothing to do with you or magic. I just don't trust him. That's all."

Aidan's frown deepened. "He helped us find Elwin. He got us through the mountain pass just days before the snows hit. If it weren't for Faynn, we wouldn't have been at the Dryrot Inn to help Elwin when he needed us." Aidan looked up at Elwin. "I trust him, Elwin. Without Faynn, you might be dead right now. Maybe he is keeping things from you, but he is not the enemy."

Now Colin frowned. "I don't like it. I don't trust him. And it's not that he is a magic user," he added quickly, seeing Aidan's accusing look. "I just don't trust him. I am a knight...or will be someday, and a knight needs to trust his gut feelings. My gut says we should not trust him!"

"I'm tired of waiting." Elwin sighed. "I don't trust him much either, but he did save my life. I agree with Aidan. He is not my enemy. I don't think he would hurt me. He could have done that already if he had wanted to."

"But—"

Cutting off what Colin was about to say, Faynn called over, "Prince Elwin, the night is growing late. Are you ready?"

"Elwin!" came Colin's urgent whisper. "It is too dangerous!"

Elwin returned boy's intense gaze. "Can you give me

another option?" he whispered back.

Colin returned Elwin's look but said nothing. Elwin turned to Aidan, who nodded approvingly. "I know it was a shock to find out about me. But magic is not evil. Trust him, Elwin. Faynn can help you find Leina. That's what you want, isn't it?"

That was enough for Elwin. He would risk anything for his sister. Elwin turned and faced Faynn. "Yes. I am ready."

Faynn stepped forward. "Good. Then let us begin."

"What about us?" asked Aidan. "What are Colin and I supposed to do while you and Elwin are on this 'dream walk'?"

"We won't actually be going anywhere," answered Faynn. "Our bodies will remain here in the octagon. It is our minds and souls that shall enter the world of dreams. All you need to do is make sure that neither Elwin nor I am disturbed. And stay clear of the octagon. If any of the lines are broken, we will never be able to find our way back, and we will be trapped within the world of dreams forever. So, no matter what happens, do not attempt to enter the octagon, and make sure no one else tries either. In many ways, I am trusting you two far more than Elwin is trusting me."

Folding his strong arms across his broad chest, Colin gave Faynn a gruff nod. "I will not lie to you. I don't like this, but you have my word. No one shall pass. And I am holding you responsible for Prince Elwin. If anything happens to him, I'll blame you for it."

Faynn's gray eyes sparkled. He appeared amused. "Fair enough, young man," he told Colin. His eyes drifted back to the prince, becoming serious once more. "Shall we?"

Making sure he did not smear or step on any of the lines, Elwin crossed into the octagon and lowered himself gently to the floor. Imitating Faynn, he sat with his legs crossed and tucked up underneath himself. Faynn sat with his back to the north and

Elwin to the south.

"Just breathe deep and try to relax," Faynn told Elwin. "That's right... Good... You'll do just fine."

Wrapping his hands tightly around his staff, Faynn raised the staff before him. Faynn's hands, which were wrapped tightly around the wooden shaft, were like hard leather. Baked brown from years of exposure, Faynn's hands matched the dark wood of the staff, making it hard to tell where his hands ended, and the wood began. Both Faynn and his staff seemed weathered and worn, and both showed signs of the passage of time as if they had spent a lifetime under a glaring sun. Holding his staff in a vertical position, Faynn lowered it until the heel touched the center of the green wheel. As the silver-tipped end of the staff came to rest upon the floor, Faynn mumbled an incantation. Speaking in the mystic language of the Ancient Ones, Faynn began turning the staff between his hands. As if the floor were made of mud, slowly the staff began to sink into the wooden planks. Elwin gasped. Where the staff and floor had joined, a dull, glowing green light arose. Slowly, the staff went deeper and deeper into the hardwood floor and when Faynn finally ended his incantation, only half of it remained above the floor. Aidan and Colin took a nervous step backward. Faynn started to speak again, and the green light began to glow brighter.

"So, this is magic..." breathed Colin.

Faynn closed his eyes. Still holding the staff in his hands, the druid began to sway from side to side. In a soft chanting voice, he began to sing in the ancient words of Earth Magic. The staff sparked where it touched the floor and slowly the light began to move up the shaft. In moments, the entire staff had a green aura around it that illuminated the bell tower. The light intensified once more. Then it began to move outward and away from the staff. The eerie glow crept out along the chalk lines of the octagon until all the lines sparked and glowed with power. Faynn chanted and swayed, and the color brightened. The light grew brighter and brighter until suddenly the light at the outer edge of the octagon burst upwards. From each point of the octagon, thin green beams of light arched upwards, reaching into the space above Elwin and Faynn. Then curving inwards, they joined with the top of the staff, creating what looked like a bird cage. Elwin gave a yelp but remained still inside the bird cage. Faynn swayed and chanted, and Elwin, with his eyes wide open, looked deathly pale. The glowing light continued to increase in its intensity. Slowly, the magical bars of the cage began to widen. The bars grew wider and wider until they merged with the other bars, producing a solid dome of green glowing translucent light that danced and sparked with energy.

From what they hoped was a safe distance, Colin and Aidan watched as the dome of energy sealed Faynn and Elwin inside. As the dome closed, Faynn's chanting was silenced. Aidan and Colin could still see the two within the dome. Faynn's body continued to sway from side to side, and his mouth continued to move, but no sound could penetrate beyond the green dome.

"Is this similar to what you can do?" asked Colin, his voice shaking.

"No," whispered Aidan. He, too, seemed shocked, and his voice was no more than a whisper. "It's nothing like it at all."

Helplessly watching his prince being engulfed in magic, Colin groaned.

"They'll be okay," reassured Aidan, but his voice betrayed his own growing concern.

Within the dome, Elwin tried unsuccessfully to stay calm. All he wanted to do was to crawl out from under the green glowing thing, but he had no idea what would happen if the lines of the octagon broke. Faynn had warned Colin and Aidan not to disturb the octagon, but he had said nothing about what would happen if the lines were disrupted or broken from within. Trying not to panic, the prince took several long, deep breaths. But remaining calm was not easy with the dome sparking and snapping just above his head. From inside the dome, Elwin could just make out Aidan and Colin. His two friends looked strange through the wall of light. Colin and Aidan appeared to be wavering as if they were a mirage.

Faynn opened his eyes. "The area is secure. It's time, Prince Elwin."

Elwin stared into Faynn's eyes, hoping that he did not appear as scared as he was.

Nervously, Elwin waited for Faynn to explain what he had to do next.

Letting go of the staff, Faynn stretched out to Elwin. "Take my hands."

Elwin hesitated then did as he was instructed. Faynn's hands felt as rough as they looked.

"Now," continued Faynn, "I will draw the power into us. All you have to do is relax and try not to struggle. Let the power take you where it will. It's not dangerous to resist, but it can be unpleasant."

Faynn closed his eyes, and Elwin followed suit. The air in the dome became uncomfortably warm. Elwin tightened his grip on Faynn's hands as he felt a tingling sensation run up his arms and into his body. Immediately, he forgot Faynn's warning and his muscles tensed up and he became lightheaded. He could feel his body both rising and sinking at the same time. For a brief moment, he thought he was going to pass out. It seemed as if he was being pulled in several directions at the same time. His head throbbed, and his body ached.

"Relax!" came Faynn's stern voice. "You are resisting."

With difficulty, Elwin took a deep breath and stopped fighting the strange sensation and let himself go with the forces that were pulling at him. The feeling of movement became steady, and the lightheadedness and pain slipped away. A moment later and without warning, the warm air of the dome was suddenly replaced by a welcome wave of cool, moist air, making it feel like a dewy morning.

"You can open your eyes now," said Faynn. Faynn's voice echoed strangely as if he was talking from inside a cave.

Elwin blinked. All around him was a thick, grey-blue fog. Despite that there was no wind, the fog shifted and moved. There was a strange feeling to the mist in this murky world. It was as if the grey-blue mist had a life of its own. At one moment the misty air seemed to form into objects, but then just before Elwin could recognize the forms, the fog would disintegrate and swirl away.

Glancing about, Elwin was surprised to find that he was now standing and was no longer holding onto Faynn's hands. At his feet was the octagon, but the dome was gone. The lines still glowed brightly, but all the symbols and ancient ruins were reversed. Elwin frowned as he looked at the staff, realizing that the silver heel of the staff that had sunk into the floor was now pointed upwards. It was if they were now below the octagon and had turned upside down.

Faynn answered Elwin's confused look. "We are not truly here," his voice echoed. "We are both still in the monastery, and our hands are still holding each other. Only our minds and souls have traveled to this place."

"Where are we?" asked Elwin, looking about. He listened to

the sound of his own voice echoing in the fog.

"This is the world of dreams, the underside of reality, which is nowhere and everywhere at once. I know that makes little sense, but there is no other way to explain it. From here you can travel after your sister, or anywhere else that you wish. But first, you must find the way within yourself."

"You're right. That doesn't make any sense. Just tell me what we have to do, and let's do it." Thinking of Leina, Elwin had lost his fear of the magic and the strange place he now found himself. His mind was racing. Could this strange world really show him where Leina was? Could the druid find her in all this fog? "Do you know the way?" he asked Faynn, speaking his thoughts out loud. "Can you find her in all this fog?"

"Only you know the way. It is you who must find her."

"Me? How am I supposed to find her in this fog? You're the druid! You brought me here! You must be able to do something."

"I have done much already," Faynn responded calmly. "But I cannot find your sister for you, Prince Elwin. You will have to do that yourself."

"How?" Elwin asked, shaking his head. "I don't know where to look, or even how to look."

"Is she close to your heart?"

"Leina? Yes, we are very close. But ..."

"Then she is already with you. You and your sister have a deep connection that binds you together. All you have to do is follow that part of her that is inside you, and you will find her."

"You're still not making any sense. Do druids have to talk in riddles? Can't you just tell me what I have to do and be done with it?"

Faynn shrugged his shoulders. "I am trying to tell you. As I said, it is you who must find the princess. I will stay here. It is you who must walk the dream. As you walk, think of your sister. Imagine her as you remember her best. That is how you start. You will find her as she once was. It will be as if you are looking into the past, and the images you see will not be able to see you or hear you. The past is as it is and cannot be changed. What you will see at first will only be shadows of what has been. Once you have found an image of Leina, you will sense that which is her Life Force."

"Life Force?"

"Everything that lives has its own unique life force. Follow Leina's Life Force, and it will lead you through your sister's past until you reach her present consciousness. As you pass from the past into the present, you will hear a soft sound, like wind blowing through dried leaves. You will then know that the image you are seeing is your sister as she is now, and if she is sleeping, you may enter her dreams."

"How will I recognize her Life Force?"

"You simply will. As soon as you feel it, you will know it to be Leina's as easily as you know her face."

Elwin looked into the fog. "How will I get back here?"

"Take a step from the octagon and you will see."

Elwin was sure that once he was in the fog, he would be completely lost. He stepped out of the compass. As he did so, a green ball of light formed over his head. Wherever Elwin turned, the ball of light stayed between himself and the octagon.

"It is called a home finder," explained Faynn. "The home finder is connected to both you and the octagon. When you are ready to return, all you have to do is follow the home finder back here. I will be waiting. That is the best I can do for you."

Elwin nodded and turned away from Faynn. He did not like the idea of walking out into this strange, foggy world. There was something about this place that scared Elwin, but if it would help him find Leina, then he would do it. Holding his breath, Elwin stepped into the fog. Thoughts of his sister filled his mind as he moved deeper into the world of dreams. In only a few short steps, Faynn and the octagon vanished into the fog, and only the green glowing ball of light showed him where Faynn was as well as his only way home. Without the home finder, Elwin realized he would have been hopelessly lost. Pushing the thought from his mind, he tried to focus on his sister once more.

Elwin walked in what he thought was a straight line, but the home finder let him know that it was anything but straight. The home finder moved from one side to the other as Elwin zigzagged his way through the fog. At one-time Elwin even found himself facing the home finder and headed back towards the octagon. In this strange, sunless netherworld, there was no way to tell where he was headed. The fog seemed to be the only thing that thrived here; no birds or animals of any type disturbed the eerie silence. There were no trees, no rocks, not even a breeze, and the ground was always perfectly flat beneath his feet. At one point, Elwin knelt and examined the earth. The ground was covered in a fine, flawless white sand that was cold to the touch. It was like a large sand beach, but without an ocean, the sun, or the moon. The only thing to be seen was the strange mist swirling about. The fog twisted about his ankles, and slid around his body, gently caressing his skin. The fog at times almost seemed to have a solid appearance, and Elwin could swear that the fog parted just before him as if to allow him to pass, but it never parted enough for him to see more than a few feet. The strangest part about the fog were the images that it seemed to create. From out of the mist, places and faces would appear...then just as fast, they disappeared. At times, Elwin thought he saw people he knew: his father, his friends, a woman Elwin thought was his mother, and a large man dressed in brown leathered armor whom the young prince thought he had seen before but did not recognize. The images never lasted long, and before Elwin could be sure the things he saw were real, they vanished back into the fog, leaving him to wonder if it was just his nerves or imagination. Wandering in this world, Elwin felt lost and alone. This place was indeed nowhere.

Elwin no longer could tell whether it had been hours or only minutes since he had left Faynn. Time had no meaning here. He walked deeper and deeper into the fog. More of the illusive images appeared and disappeared; again, he saw the man in brown leathered armor. The man appeared worried and seemed to be guarding something or someone. Then the image vanished.

Elwin walked on, but nowhere did he see Leina. Then suddenly the fog around him began to lift. New images began to form. This time, the images did not vanish but became solid and more real. Stunned by the sudden change, Elwin stumbled to a stop. He found himself standing in a large bed chamber. A large canopy bed lay to one side of the room. Through a window on the far wall, he looked out over the Northern Drygan Mountains.

Immediately, Elwin recognized the place. It was his sister's bedroom. He was back in the Acair Castle. His home. Sitting in the large bed was a small child. The child was a young girl around the age of seven or eight. Her legs were tucked up under her in a position in which only a child could sit. In her arms, she rocked a small doll. Singing softly to her doll, the child brushed aside a strand of her long, silky black hair.

"Leina!" Elwin breathed.

She looked so real, yet Elwin knew Leina was much older now. The image looked so real that Elwin almost forgot that it was but an illusion. Elwin could even hear her voice as she sang softly to her doll.

Hearing someone approaching, Elwin gazed up from his sister. Feeling strangely nervous, he watched and waited. The door to the room swung open. A tall man with a well-groomed beard and broad shoulders stepped forward. Elwin gasped. The girl dropped her doll and leaped into the man's outstretched arms with a joyful cry.

"Father!" Elwin called.

"Fool," Elwin muttered to himself, "they can't hear you. None of this is real." Yet there was his father standing before him, and he looked both real and alive.

Watching the vision before him, a tear ran down Elwin's face. He wanted the image to be real. He wanted to stay here with his family. Yet at the same time, he wanted to run away and make the vision go away. As much as he wanted to believe, Elwin knew his father was gone. With a confusing mixture of emotions, he watched. Helpless to turn away, Elwin stared at his family. He watched as his father tossed Leina into the air. Leina squealed out in laughter.

"Do it again, father!" she cried. "Do it again!"

Shutting out the painful memory of what he had lost, Elwin closed his eyes. But the laughter and voices of the past still haunted him. Like ghosts, the laughter echoed in his head. With the back of his hand, he wiped away the tears. Opening his eyes once more, Elwin tried not to think of his pain and loss. Leina was still alive, and she needed him.

"Focus on Leina," he told himself, reprimanding. "Just once, try to be strong!"

Around the princess, a blue-green glow appeared. Without knowing how Elwin recognized this as Leina's Life Force. Like Faynn had said, there was no doubt that it was Leina's Life Force.

Strangely, his father had none. *Perhaps,* Elwin thought, *that is because he is dead now.*

One last time, Elwin took in the image of his father. Then he let the illusion fade away. Elwin was not sure how he did it, or even if he had done it, but slowly the images of his father and sister vanished back into the fog, but Leina's Life Force remained. Glowing brightly, the blue-green light pointed Elwin where he needed to go. Images quickly passed by. He saw Leina grow from a child into a beautiful young woman. The years had been happy ones, and Elwin smiled as he watched them pass.

His smile vanished as those sunny days turned suddenly dark. He watched as his father left Leina in a small abbey. Time slipped by. One month, two, three months passed in the abbey. King Artair had hoped his daughter would be safe within the abbey walls. And for three months she had been safe, but as Elwin watched he saw how wrong his father had been. Helpless, Elwin watched Parlan approach the abbey. He was mounted upon a smoky gray stallion. Elwin's cousin smiled wickedly. At Parlan's back were fifty Strigiol soldiers.

Parlan raised his sword above his head. "Other than the princess, there are to be no survivors!" he shouted. Licking his dry lips, he kicked his horse into a charge. "Victory!" he shouted. The Strigiol soldiers echoed his cry and chased after him. In a military formation, they stormed into the defenseless abbey.

The first nuns fell to the soldier's naked blades. Horrified, Elwin drew his own sword. "NO!" he screamed. With his sword raised high, Elwin leaped at Parlan. He could feel the hot breath of Parlan's horse upon his face. With a raging howl, Elwin swung his sword. In a strike of silver, the Sword of Light and Darkness arched through the air. Harmlessly, Elwin's sword passed through the image of Parlan. He was nothing more than a ghost of a dark past.

As if nothing had happened, Parlan spun his horse about and chased after a fleeing woman.

With no effect, Elwin struck at the illusions. Desperately, he attacked anew, trying to defend the nuns, but he could not stop the carnage and cold-blooded murder. Finally, exhausted from fighting with ghosts, he dropped to his knees. Like a statue, Elwin sat motionlessly. Unable to turn away, he watched the horror unfold around him. Caught in the living nightmare, Elwin witnessed the butchery and bloodshed. He wanted to run...hide...look away, but he could only stare in dismay. Nuns dressed in long dark blue robes tried to flee, but there was no escape. He could hear their cries of terror and smell the blood as the sun began to sink towards the horizon. Soon the screams fell to moans and then there was only silence. A silence so deep Elwin thought he would drown in it. Death lay everywhere.

Finally gaining his feet, Elwin walked through the courtyard. Stunned by what he had seen, he wandered aimlessly like a lost child and as he walked, tears streamed down his face. The prince tried to make the image of the abbey fade away, but they stayed with him. Still caught in the nightmare, he looked on as soldiers set fire to the abbey. As the blaze grew, Elwin made his way out through the shattered gates. Outside of the abbey, the soldiers were planting elvish arrows into the ground. Elwin realized that Parlan would blame the elves for attacking the abbey.

Then he saw Parlan once more. Elwin felt a burning hatred he had never known before.

Still mounted upon his stallion, Parlan stood out against the setting sun and the billowing clouds of smoke. Parlan held himself like a conquering hero. Approaching the figure, Elwin glared up at his cousin. Standing there, Elwin watched Parlan grab a young woman and dragged her off her feet. He swung the woman up and onto his black leather saddle. The young woman's face was hidden beneath a thick layer of dirt and ash. Her black hair was tangled and knotted. Only her Life Force told Elwin the woman was Leina. Looking up, Elwin pulsed with hate. Leina struggled, but Parlan slapped her across the face and easily brought her under his control. Howling like a wounded animal, Elwin screamed a bone-chilling cry of agony that he alone could hear.

With a thin smile, Parlan held onto Elwin's crying sister. Flames reflected in Parlan's cold eyes as he watched a soldier approach. The soldier reined in his horse next to Parlan.

Parlan asked, "Is it finished yet?"

The soldier dropped his head. Elwin could not tell if the man was showing respect to Parlan or was ashamed of what he had done.

"Yes," he replied softly. "It is finished...my lord. And as you ordered, there are no witnesses. The elves of the Green will be blamed."

"Good. Then let us get away from here. The smoke stings my eyes." With one hand roughly holding the princess and the other his reins, Parlan looked down at Leina. "Soon, my princess, I shall be king." Then with a dry haunting laugh, he spun his horse towards the west and raced off towards the red horizon.

Mercifully, the image then changed. Once more, Elwin found himself in Leina's bedroom chamber in the Acair Castle. Leina stood staring out her window watching the flight of an eagle. All signs of the child who had played upon the canopy bed were gone. Her childhood had been stolen from her. In the span of a single night, Leina had become an adult. The days of innocence were lost in the ashes of the abbey. The beautiful round face that had seen years of happiness was drawn out and sad.

Standing at Leina's side, Elwin watched the day fade into night. As the day grew dark, Elwin saw fires appearing in the mountains and he wondered what it meant.

As in the first illusion he had seen, Elwin heard footsteps. However, this time, they belonged not to King Artair, but Parlan. With growing concern, Elwin watched as Parlan leer at Leina's back. Parlan now wore a silver crown and the colors of the Gruffydd royal family, proclaiming himself king. Standing where Elwin's father had once stood, Parlan watched Leina with a hungry look. Parlan and Leina began to argue. Elwin heard Parlan threaten to have Elwin killed, as well as his plan to force Leina to marry him. Then Elwin was compelled to watched Parlan try to force himself upon his sister. But when Leina resisted his advances, Parlan threw the princess down upon her bed. Then thankfully, Parlan left Leina alone.

Bursting into tears, Leina cried herself to sleep. Elwin thought the image would then change, but it didn't. In the blink of an eye, there was a bright light. Elwin quickly raised his hand, covering his eyes as the blindingly bright light abruptly flashed at the foot of the bed. As the light faded away, Elwin lowered his hand and saw a tall, beautiful woman in long, flowing white robes.

His mouth fell open in wonder and disbelief.

The figure smiled down at Leina as if she did not see the sad woman lying upon the bed, but instead saw the child that the princess had once been. Then unexpectedly, the figure turned from Leina and looked across the bed. The mysterious woman was now looking straight at Elwin. Elwin had not heard the wind signaling him that he had moved into the present, and so he knew this still had to be the past, and yet the figure in white seemed to see him. It was impossible. The woman in white was only an illusion of the past, and yet her soft green eyes met his.

"This is an unexpected meeting, Prince Elwin." The woman's voice had a rich musical quality to it.

Elwin staggered backward. *This was not happening...it could not be happening.*

"How?" he stammered. "How do you know me? And how can you see me?"

"We have met before, Prince Elwin. Do you not remember?"

Elwin remembered. It was in the dream he had the week before. Elwin recalled the black castle of Ban-Darn and remembered both the Red Robe, and the perfect face of the Prophet Torcull. But that was not where he had met this woman. Elwin had seen her in the beautiful valley with the white palace that sat beside a silvery lake. Before the gates of the white palace, a woman in white had spoken to him. Elwin knew without doubt that the woman before him now was the same person.

"I remember."

"Yes. We already know each other. The dream you had was a kind of dream walk. As you slept, I reached out to you, but this is far better. This will be easier now. But tell me, my young prince, how did you enter the world of dreams? Did you do it yourself? Have you that ability?" The woman sounded excited. "Has He Who is the Light come to you?"

"He Who is the Light? No. At least I don't think so. I don't know any such person."

She seemed saddened, or maybe disappointed. "Then how did you get here?"

"A druid brought me."

"A druid!" she exclaimed. Then she became thoughtful and

calm once more. "Forgive me, but a druid? That was not foreseen. Though, I guess I should not be surprised. They are a meddling sort, and perhaps he will be useful. He did bring you here. But if I were you, I would be careful. Do not trust this druid. The druids are not one with the light, and what they proclaim as the truth are only half truths. If he is helping you, then he has reasons for doing so. He wants you for something, or something from you. Druids always want something."

"And what do you want me for?"

She looked hurt. Elwin immediately felt guilty and ashamed. He did not mean to hurt this beautiful angelic-like woman. Before he could apologize, she went on, "It is not I who wants you. All I wish is to help you and to serve He Who is the Light. In the dream when we first met, you were shown the two paths: one of darkness and one of light. Torcull tried to show you only the path of darkness, but we interfered and I showed you the one of light. The choice is now yours."

"I still don't see what this has to do with me. And who are you? How can you see me? Do you know where my sister is?"

"So many questions! But to start, I am Sileas, a guardian of light, and yes, I do know where your sister is. She is safe with us. Come to the Woods of the Mist and you will find her. Come to us, Prince Elwin. We can help you fight the darkness that has touched you. In the woods, the light awaits you and there you will be healed. We have waited so long. The day of the awakening grows near."

"Where are the woods?" Elwin asked.

"You will find it. But you must hurry my young prince but be careful. The servants of the Dark Overlord have many faces."

Elwin shook his head. "But I don't know the way."

"The light will show you the way. But now you must go.

The world of dreams is not as it once was. The shadows of the night grow stronger and it is no longer safe here. Your enemies have followed you here. The one who calls himself Torcull knows you have entered this world and is searching for you. I can confuse him for a time, but you must hurry."

Sileas and the room began to fade back into the fog. "How?" Elwin called out, "How am I to find the Woods of the Mist?"

"If you are the one, you will find a way." Sileas' voice sounded weak and far away. "Trust only the light, Prince Elwin, and it will see you through."

"I need to know the way! I have to find Leina!" There was no answer. The guardian of light was gone. Surrounded by the fog once more, Elwin tried to relocate Leina's Life Force, but it too had vanished.

Wandering aimlessly, Elwin decided to start over, yet nothing happened. He knew he should leave, however he still did not know how to find Leina. He had never heard of the Woods of the Mist. Covered in the icy dew of the fog, Elwin began to tire and still he refused to give up. He pushed on until he was too cold and exhausted to take another step. Slowly, he sank down to the cold white sand. He knew he should follow the green light back to Faynn, but he didn't seem to have the energy.

Suddenly a new chill came over him and he could feel a dark shadow pass by. Some evil force walked the world of dreams with him. Elwin was sure whatever it was, was looking for him. Yet, he still could not find the strength to rise. The dream walk had drained him. Surrendering, Elwin laid back and waited for the shadow to find him. He almost hoped it would find him and put an end to the ghosts that still haunted his mind. He closed his eyes. In the silence of the world of dreams, he started to drift off to sleep. At first, he tried to fight it, but found he was slowly fading into sleep. He feared his sudden drowsiness was some kind of magic, or the effects of the fog filled world, but try as he might, he could not resist the forces at work around him and he dropped into a deep slumber.

Elwin awoke to discover that he was no longer on the ground. With his eyes still closed, he could feel a pair of strong arms holding him close. He was being carried. The biting chill of the icy fog told Elwin that he was still in the world of dreams. Images of the nightling flashed through his mind. Forcing his eyes open, Elwin looked up, expecting the worst, however instead he saw the face of a living man. Covering the man's chin was a thick salt and pepper colored beard. The man had two deep-set grey eyes that stared into the equally grey fog. Somehow, the man seemed to belong in this strange world. Cautiously, the grey eyes swept back and forth as if the person was looking for something or expecting something to leap out of the fog. Elwin would not have called it fear, but there was a tension to the craggy face of the man and a sense of urgency.

For a brief moment, Elwin did not recognize the man. He only knew it was not a Red Robe or Torcull. For the moment, that was enough.

As a name attached itself to the face, Elwin whispered, "Faynn?"

"Prince Elwin," the druid sighed in relief. Gently, he lowered the prince to the ground. "How do you feel?"

"Weak, but better than I did a little while ago. How did you find me?"

"When you did not return, I became concerned and decided to go after you. We are both still connected to the octagon, so I simply reversed a few things and used my home finder to find yours."

"What happened to me?"

"It's hard to tell, the world of dreams is different for everyone. Perhaps it is this place, or perhaps other forces are at work here."

"Is it far to the octagon?" Elwin asked, suddenly feeling the need to get out of this world.

"Not too far. Can you walk?"

Elwin struggled to his feet. "I think so." He could see the two green balls of light hovering over their heads.

"Good. We should make haste. We are not alone."

"Torcull." Elwin remembered the dark presence he had felt. "I think I felt him pass by. He followed me here, didn't he?"

"Yes. I too have felt him. I should have guessed he would follow you here." Faynn shook his head. "I fear I am growing old and forgetful. The nightling has touched your soul and left his mark. He has tasted your Life Force. Through the nightling, Torcull has also seen your Life Force and can now follow it. So far, we've been lucky. He has not been able to find us. Several times he has passed close, but each time he went right on by. I don't understand it. He should have found us by now."

"The guardian of light," Elwin guessed. "She said she would help me by confusing him."

"A guardian of light?" asked Faynn with a concerned look. "You saw a guardian?"

"Yes. She spoke to me and told me about...Leina!" Elwin suddenly remembered what the woman in white had said. "Leina is in the Woods of the Mist! Wherever that is."

Faynn's frown deepened. "There is time to talk later. Now we must hurry."

--

Torcull stood up. A glowing red octagon flashed at his feet, then disappeared. Where the octagon had been, a black staff reached out of the floor. Torcull reached down. The black staff was carved like a twisting snake and located in the head were two ruby eyes that slanted like two crescent blood-red moons. Torcull's gloved hand wrapped tightly around the snake's head. Pulling upwards, he easily slid the staff out of the floor, leaving no trace where the staff had been a few seconds ago.

The dark Prophet smiled. "So," he said to himself. "You think you are going to the Woods of the Mist, are you?" The man dressed in black walked across the floor and sank into a high-backed chair. "The guardians think they can snatch you from me. Faynn thinks he can protect you and hide you from me. They are wrong, Elwin. They are all wrong. They have no idea of the power of Beli. The prophecies that are written shall be fulfilled. You will go to Ban-Darn. It is to me you shall come, and you and I shall free my master. The Guardians are fools! They are playing right into the hands of my master." Torcull's white teeth shimmered in the dim candlelight. His blue eyes flashed. Off to one side, a tall figure dressed in a dark red robe stepped out of the shadows.

Torcull looked up at the hooded figure. "Faynn is a fool. Did he think I could not feel the boy enter the world of dreams? Did he think I would not follow? Is he as big a fool as the guardians?"

When the nightling did not answer, Torcull went on, "No, Faynn is no fool. Then what game is he playing? I wonder...but the boy will try to reach the Woods of the Mist, that much was evident. Faynn will no doubt try and block the boy's Life Force from me. But it is already too late, we... I know where he is headed. Even Faynn cannot entirely block his Life Force, there are other ways to track him down. If he does escape from Reidh County, I will be ready."

Torcull looked past the silent figure of the monk. "Come!" He called as if he were speaking to a dog.

From behind the nightling, a creature crept forward. It hesitated for a moment, and then slinked out of the shadows. Hunched over, the twisted figure looked shorter than it truly was. It had a humanoid shape, but there was an inhuman quality to the thing. A black iron mask with no eye holes covered its head. Around the creature's neck hung a silver collar that was connected to a long chain. Through a small hole in the mask, the creature breathed, making a raspy sound.

With its nose held high, it sniffed the air, searching for its master. Finding the scent, the thing moved forward. Like a primate, the creature used its long arms as well as its legs to walk across the floor. At the end of its arms, where hands should be, were two metal claws. The claw-like talons were polished to brilliant silver.

Naked except for the mask and a black loin cloth, the creature walked slowly across the room, it's masked head swinging back and forth as it took in the smells of the space around it. For the most part, the creature had pale sickly, white skin, but where its arms joined the metal claws, its flesh was a raw red color.

As it reached Torcull, the masked creature tucked its razor-sharp talons under itself, and cowered at the dark Prophet's feet. Looking down at the creature, Torcull reached out a hand and placed it upon the creature's masked head. The creature sat up with a jerk. Maintaining his hold on the creature, Torcull forced it back down. Almost whispering, Torcull began to chant. The ancient words of the song he sang were dark and haunting, and filled the room with the smell of rotting fruit. The air grew thick. A shadow seemed to enter the room and then pass into Torcull. The Prophet's eyes changed. The sky-blue color of his eyes turned into glowing red coals. In fear, the Red Robe took a step backwards. Beneath Torcull's hand, the cowering creature began to shiver and whimper.

--

Elwin blinked. He was back in the bell tower. Before him sat Faynn, who was tired, but still held tightly to Elwin's hands. "We are back," the druid whispered. "The danger has passed."

Or just beginning, thought Elwin.

CHAPTER TEN

"Return to Port Murray?" gasped Colin. The tall blond youth came to a quick stop. He stared over the heads of Aidan and Elwin, down a narrow staircase to where Pallas led the way. At Colin's cry, Pallas stopped and turned. He looked up at Colin, forcing the others to stop as well. Pallas had only just arrived from Port Murray and was still covered in dirt and grime from the road.

Colin shook his head as if he were watching a mad man. "Why would we return to Port Murray?! We barely escaped last time. And that thing...the Red Robe, or whatever you want to call it is still out there. Have you lost your mind?"

Pallas scowled, returning Colin's intense stare. Sounding defensive, he replied, "I have not lost my mind or anything else. And for your information, my father has not made up his mind yet. Besides, he is not planning to have Elwin go right into town. He plans on Elwin going just north of it, to the marshlands that line the bay, but we have to hurry. Father and Lord Rodan are here. They are waiting downstairs with the druid. And I don't think Rodan likes Faynn much." With that, Pallas turned back around and started down the stairs once more, taking two steps at a time. Quickly descending the staircase, Pallas forced Colin, Elwin, and Aidan to hurry to keep up.

"It's the best way," Pallas said over his shoulder. "And of course, it's dangerous, but it might be our only chance."

Elwin groaned. Pallas always appeared excited when there was any mention of danger.

"Do you have to sound so blasted happy about it?"

Pallas laughed. "It looks like there is going to be an adventure. And I plan to be part of it."

"Why can't we just stay here?" asked Aidan. "The brothers are more like elves than men. They don't chatter and talk nonstop like most men. It's almost peaceful."

"That was suggested as well," replied Pallas. "But I think father will want to get Elwin out of the county. It's too risky to stay here any longer. The Strigiol soldiers and this Lord of Risca are determined to find you, Elwin. They are not going to leave Reidh until they do. My father has kept them busy so far," Pallas added with a wry smile. "You should see the Lord of Risca. He doesn't know if he is coming or going. Father has him and his soldiers running in circles and chasing after false rumors and reports of people claiming to have seen you. But it is only a matter of time before they catch on and think of looking here."

"That is why I have to leave soon," Elwin asserted. "I can't wait for it to stop snowing or for the mountain passes to melt. If I can't get over the mountains, then I will have to go by sea."

"Father has arranged everything. If father decides to get you out of Reidh, there will be a boat already waiting to take you. You know Jon."

Elwin remembered the strong sailor who had risked his own life attacking the Red Robe. Evidently the man was still willing to help Elwin despite the nightling tossing him around like a rag doll. Then again, maybe that was why Jon was helping. It was a matter of pride.

Pallas went on, "Just in case he is needed, Jon and his boat are already waiting on the far side of the marshes just north of town. His boat may not be a Strigiol man of war, but she is Reidhen built. Our boats, though on the small side, are the best one could ask for."

"Can she handle rough seas?" asked Aidan, looking suddenly a little green around the edges. Just the thought of taking a small Reidhen boat out upon the rough and unpredictable Iar Sea made his feet sway and his stomach sink. "Haven't the recent storms made the ocean too rough? Maybe we should wait for the storms to break. A week or two won't hurt, will it?"

They came to the bottom of the stairs and turned down a corridor. Still leading the way, Pallas replied, "The seas are bad, but I don't think we have the time to waste. Strigiol soldiers are everywhere. Another warship sailed into port two days ago. It was strange too...the weather seemed to clear up just in time for the ship to arrive. The seas calmed down as fast as you could blink an eye. Then another storm rolled in right after they set anchor. You would almost think they are controlling the weather. But you don't have to worry, Aidan. Jon's boat is a good vessel, and she can handle the seas. It's getting out of the harbor that is the problem. One wrong move and BAM!" Pallas slapped his hands together, making Aidan jump. "You'll be on the rocks! But Jon will be at the helm. If there is a man alive that can get her past the rocks, it's Jon." That didn't seem to help Aidan much, but Elwin smiled as he remembered the courage of the big man. Jon had stood up to the nightling at the Dryrot Inn. Jon would do just about anything to help a friend.

"We're here," Pallas announced as they came to a pair of big wooden doors. Pushing the modestly decorated doors aside, he led the way into the room. The room was brightly lit and was dominated by a large rectangular table. Count Murray, Lord Macay, and Faynn, sat around the table. As the four friends entered the room, the three seated men lifted their eyes towards them. Count Murray frowned. Dovan Murray had requested Elwin's presence, but he had not asked his friend's presence as well. Pallas smiled awkwardly. He knew his father's looks, and he knew his father would now ask them to leave, but it was worth the chance. Pallas did not want to miss out. It looked as if Elwin was about to set off on an adventure, and Pallas was determined to be included.

"They insisted on coming, father," Pallas offered as an excuse.

Dovan Murray nodded his head towards the door. "Out you go."

Aidan frowned, and Colin scowled. Pretending the words were not meant for him, Pallas took a seat.

"That means you too, young man," Dovan said with the authority of a father. "Aww, can't I stay?" asked Pallas.

"No!"

"But..."

"Out!"

Pallas grumbled something about always being left out. Nevertheless, he stood up and followed Aidan and Colin back through the door, slamming it shut behind him.

Elwin looked at each of the men. Lord Rodan, Count Murray, and Faynn returned his stare. There was a tension in the air, and Elwin became uneasy under their somber eyes. Something was wrong. Lord Rodan looked angry. His arms were crossed stiffly over his chest, and he appeared like a volcano about to blow. Count Dovan Murray frowned. His brow was wrinkled, and he seemed deeply worried about something. Faynn, as normal, could not be read. His face was flat and without a trace of emotion. Whatever might stir behind his gray piercing eyes, the druid kept to himself. Elwin brushed a long lock of brown hair from his face and silently slid into the chair at the end of the table.

Dovan looked down the table at Elwin, "Thank you for coming, Your Highness."

Highness? thought Elwin. *Something is wrong.*

"As you can probably guess," Dovan went on. "We have been discussing what should be done to assure your safety. Faynn here," Dovan gave the druid a short nod. "Has been trying to convince me that Reidh is no longer a safe place for you."

Lord Rodan looked at Elwin. Over the past few years, he and Rodan had become close. The tall dark-haired and olive-skinned lord had become like an uncle or older brother to the prince. The lord smiled weakly and gave Elwin a wink as if to say it was not him, he was angry at.

"The question is," continued Dovan, "are you truly in any danger? And if so, where should you go? My inclination is to agree that you are no longer safe here. The sooner you are away from here the better."

Rodan' voice was as flat as Faynn's face. "I still think the wisest choice is to wait until the passes open. The seas are too rough, and the harbor is watched both night and day."

"The mountain passes are not going to open up," Faynn said as if that should be obvious to everyone. Rodan scowled across the table at him.

"What do you mean?" asked Dovan. "Surely spring is coming soon. Never have I seen such storms this late in the year. The weather must break soon."

"As long as Elwin remains here, so will the winter storms." Faynn folded his hands on the table before him. "As you have said, they are unseasonably late, even for Reidh. The reason is that these storms are not natural. Dark forces are at work, creating the storms. Our enemies hope to keep Elwin trapped in Reidh until he can be captured."

"That's ridiculous," snapped Rodan. It was evident to all that Rodan disliked Faynn.

Ignoring the angry lord, Faynn went on. "What I am about to

tell you must not leave this room. Elwin and his three friends already know, but it is best not to talk about such things other than what is necessary. The less rumors and fears spread, the better. Dark forces are once more at work in the kingdoms of Kambrya. The Dark Overlord has awakened. Beli is attempting to free himself from his prison of Ban-Darn. The god wishes to return to the world of the living. The wars are just a tool to reach this end." As Faynn named the evil one, Elwin thought he saw and felt a shadow cross the room. The Count seemed to also notice it, as his face darkened.

"You are talking about myths!" retorted Rodan. "Storms can be nothing more than storms. I don't have to create demons and monsters to explain snow. The Dark Overlord is only a story to scare children and entertain old men, nothing more."

"Are these storms that will not leave normal'?" asked Faynn. Not waiting for Rodan to answer, Faynn went on answering his own question. "No, they aren't. Are the troubles spreading throughout Kambrya myths? Again, the answer is no. A prophet by the name of Torcull is behind the storms and the evil that is sweeping across the land. You no doubt have heard that the Severed Head has returned to Kambrya. Torcull is the hand that moves the cult of darkness. He has become a servant of the Dark Overlord. An evil that once poisoned the lands has been reborn. Torcull now rules Strigiol. The true king is nothing but a puppet. It is Torcull who is behind the wars and bloodshed. His ultimate goal is to have Elwin's sword. If he succeeds, he will free his master, and then these hard times will seem like the 'good old days'."

"It's true," Elwin added. "Torcull wants my sword. It's the Sword of Light and Darkness."

"Sword of Light and Darkness!?" Rodan exclaimed angrily.

"More myths! Do not be fooled Elwin. Your sword is nothing more than the metal it was forged from."

Rodan turned to Faynn. "Stop trying to scare the boy and fill his head with myths and lies."

"There is good reason to be scared," Faynn stated bluntly, "as Prince Elwin already knows." Faynn's voice staying ever calm despite Rodan's ever growing anger.

Rodan leaned forward. His fists were clenched, his face red, but before the lord could say what he was thinking, Dovan hit the table, cutting Rodan off. "Rodan, that is enough!" Dovan snapped. Then the count turned to Faynn. "If this Torcull controls King Jerran as you say, then he not only rules all of Strigiol, but most of Kambrya as well. If this is true, then why would he want Elwin's sword? What more could he want? What good would a sword do for him?"

"Power," said Faynn. "Unlimited power. It's as Elwin said. The sword is Saran na Grain, the Sword of Light and Darkness." Dovan seemed to flinch at the name.

"There is a prophecy," Faynn went on, "that says that one day Beli will return. It is said that he who wields the sword will free the Dark Overlord. And whether *you* believe it or not, Torcull *does*. He wants Prince Elwin's sword." Faynn nodded towards Elwin. "And Torcull will do whatever he has to, to get it." Elwin swallowed.

Dovan's eyes darkened, as if a distant memory had passed before him. The count looked down at the floor and became suddenly quiet.

"There is no Overlord," insisted Rodan. "Are we going to run from a children's story?"

"If the story was about the Dark Overlord? Yes, I would run," said Faynn. "I would run as fast and as far as my feet would carry me."

Elwin shifted uncomfortably in his chair. "I've seen Torcull and the Red Robe." His voice sounded soft and weak as if he were unsure if he should speak among these men. After all, he was still just a youth, yet he was also a prince and the heir apparent to the Ceredigion thrown. "The Red Robe, the nightling attacked me. Torcull has appeared to me in my...dreams. I know it sounds foolish, and I can't explain it, but they were not ordinary dreams, he was really there. He scares me more than the Red Robe," Elwin admitted. "I have felt Torcull's hate and have seen firsthand what a nightling is like and what it can do." Elwin wrapped his arms tightly around himself. "I don't know if the sword can do what Faynn says it can. I'm not sure if it is a magic blade or only steel. I've never seen or felt anything unusual. It appears to be just a regular sword, but it was my father's, and I want to keep it. If for no other reason, I'll keep it because Torcull wants it."

"It is wise to fear," Faynn said. "It's a fool who has seen what you have and is not afraid. Be afraid, young prince. In the end, that may be all that stands between life and death."

"Magic!" said Rodan, as if the word was a curse. "I have heard that magic users can alter one's dreams. I don't believe in this Red Robe's powers. The monk is just one of your druid tricks." Rodan's voice rang like steel striking steel. "Talk of this Red Robe is all over town, but where is this Red Robe now? I have seen nothing of him. Nor has anyone else since the druid left."

With an accusing tone, Rodan looked directly at Faynn. "In fact, no one has seen him except a few, and they were in the Dryrot Inn with you. I think you created an illusion to scare the prince here into trusting you. However, if there truly was a Red Robe, he's gone now. All that is left are Strigiol soldiers. They are the true danger to Elwin."

"Exactly," cut in Dovan. The count had an expression of a man who had made up his mind. He looked up from the table. Ignoring what Rodan was trying to suggest, Dovan went on. "I do not need to believe in robed demons, evil Prophets, or the Dark Overlord to recognize that Elwin is in trouble. Yet, I must admit there is some truth to what Faynn says." Rodan's mouth dropped open. Dovan raised a hand silencing Rodan, as he went on. "King Artair, Elwin's father, and my friend told me of this sword. He told me long ago that it was called Saran na Grian. He went on to tell me that the sword was a curse on his family and a key to darkness and that he and his ancestors had been given the responsibility to guard it and keep it from falling into the wrong hands. It had been passed down a long line of Ceredigion kings. Each king takes on the responsibility to guard Saran na Grian and to never let it fall into the hands of the servants of Beli."

"I asked him how a sword can be a key, but he would not or could not answer. However, I know it was a great burden to him. But even worse was that he knew that one day he would have to pass that burden on to his son." His eyes softened as they fell on Elwin. Elwin's eyes were moist. "He planned to tell you, son." the count's voice faltered, "he always thought... there would be time, but..." his voice trailed off.

After a moment of silence, the count found his voice again. "At the time, I did not know what Artair meant by the sword being a key, nor am I really sure I do now, but that doesn't matter. There are Strigiol soldiers here in Reidh, and more are coming. That I am certain of, and they are searching for you, Elwin. And...perhaps the sword you carry."

CHAPTER ELEVEN

The monastery bell chimed. Elwin woke with a start. It was already well past midnight. With the last ring of the bell, Elwin realized he was going to be late. He threw off his covers and leaped from his bed. The room was cold, dark, and silent. Elwin tried to shake off his drowsiness.

"I have to hurry," he mumbled to himself.

Using the hot embers from the fireplace, Elwin lit a lamp. The flickering flame took away the darkness and chased away the shadows. However, the room was still cold from the night. As Elwin shivered, he prepared for the long day ahead. Feeling the stone floor beneath his naked feet, he placed the lamp down upon the small wooden table next to the bed and pulled on his pants and boots. From a ceramic basin, he began washing himself, cupping the water in his hands to splash his face. The water was shockingly frigid. Gasping for breath, he quickly washed and dried himself. Now wide awake, Elwin began to hurry, using a wooden comb, he pulled the tangles out of his long brown hair. Satisfied, he set the comb down and finished dressing. Feeling a little warmer and ready to face the day, Elwin gathered together his few belongings. Laying out his coarse brown woolen blanket, he placed his spare clothing, a book titled 'Perun's Travels through Kambrya', another book on Aleash, and a map of Cluain, which he had found in the monastery's library. He took off his insignia ring and placed it into a small pouch that hung at his side. When he had finished, he rolled the blanket into a tight bundle and tied it with a piece of twine. Setting the bundle down upon the bed's edge, he strapped on his sword.

The bell tolled again, reminding him how late he was. Hurrying faster, he gathered his bundle under his arm. Covering a yawn with the back of his hand, he reached into his pouch and dropped a few coins onto the table, hoping it would cover the expense of the books and the map. Next to the coins, he carefully placed a note addressed to Count Murray. Elwin stared down at the note. It was so little after all the count had done for him. Elwin had written it the night before, explaining why he had to leave. He only hoped the count would understand and forgive him. He hesitated for only a moment, then grabbing the lamp from the table, he turned and crossed the room. Taking a deep breath, Elwin pushed at the door. It creaked open. Nervously, Elwin swallowed. The door seemed so loud. He poked his head out and looked down the long narrow hallway. No one was there. The hall was as dark and quiet as his room. Without wasting any more time, he carefully closed the door behind him and hurried off down the hallway. He quickly passed through the monastery. Stopping before a large door, he listened. Nothing. Closing the shutters to his lamp, he opened the door and stepped outside.

The still air felt cold against his face. Before him was a small courtyard. It was plain and had only a few barren fruit trees in it. In the spring the monks would plant a vegetable garden here, but for now, it was covered in a layer of snow. At the far end of the yard stood the monastery's stable. The barn was dark and quiet. Elwin wondered if the others had made it out yet. Maybe he wasn't late after all.

Still standing in the doorway, Elwin hid in the shadows until he was sure that he was alone. At this late of an hour, there was little chance that anyone would be in the courtyard, but Elwin saw no point in taking any risks. One of the monastery's brothers unable to sleep just might be looking out his window, and the courtyard offered few places to hide. The trees were bare and would provide little cover, yet it was a dark, cloudy night, and a few snowflakes were beginning to fall. Finally satisfied that no one was watching, Elwin pulled his hood up over his head and started across the courtyard. Twice Elwin stopped and looked over his shoulder. In the dark, the courtyard looked like a deserted garden of a dead and haunted castle. Elwin shivered and hurried on. The silence of the courtyard made him feel uneasy. It was as if he were being watched by something invisible.

From above, the lifeless trees looked down on Elwin as he passed below. A branch creaked, and Elwin started to run. Making it across the courtyard, he turned. Standing with his back to the stable doors, he panted heavily. The cold air made his lungs sting. He glanced over the courtyard. It appeared a menacing place, and Elwin could almost feel eyes staring out of the shadows.

Fool! he thought to himself, *there's nothing out there.* But still, he could not shake the feeling.

Trying to convince himself, Elwin whispered, "There's no one out there," as he slipped inside the stable doors. He closed the door and threw down the latch. He sighed, and then smiled to himself. Now that he was inside, he felt foolish and was glad that there had been no one to see him running from shadows and trees. It was warmer inside the stable, and the smell of straw and manure filled the area. Elwin turned away from the door. Somewhere deeper in the stable, he heard a horse nicker. He took a step further into the stable.

"Pallas? Aidan? Colin?" Elwin called out. For a moment there was no reply. Then a light flashed in his face, causing Elwin to jump.

Holding up a lantern, Pallas stepped out from behind a haystack. Seeing Elwin, he gave a relieved sigh. He rolled his eyes up.

"Don't do that!" stated Elwin. "You nearly scared me to death!"

"Okay, you can come out," Pallas called. "It's only Elwin."

Aidan and Colin dropped out of the hay loft. Brushing straw from their clothing, the two jumped down and joined Elwin and Pallas. "What took you so long?" demanded Pallas. "We've been waiting here for nearly an hour. We thought you had been caught, and that father was coming to drag us all back inside."

Elwin mumbled something about Lord Rodan keeping him up late and needing some extra sleep.

Nearby, four horses nickered and pranced nervously about the straw covered floor. They were saddled and ready to go. Elwin took the reins Pallas offered him and said with a yawn, "We'd better hurry. Did you get the supplies?"

"Sure did," replied Pallas with his wry smile. "Aidan and I did a little pilfering last night." He gave the elf a broad smile. "But we still got here on time. Unlike those of us who needed to sleep."

"Not funny," returned Elwin.

Aidan patted the side of his saddle bags. "We did not want to take a lot, but we should have enough food to get us to Jon's boat, plus a little extra."

Giving Pallas a look, Aidan then added, "And we didn't actually steal it. We left some money behind."

"More than enough, if you ask me," Pallas replied, disgruntled. "We don't have all that much money."

"We can worry about money later," said Elwin as he began to tie his bundle behind his mount's saddle. The horse was a lean, powerful looking animal. The chestnut horse seemed as anxious to be on its way as Elwin did. With pride in its big brown eyes, the stallion shook his cream-colored mane and watched him as if judging whether this youth was worthy of him or not. Stepping into the stirrups, Elwin swung his leg up over the chestnut's back and settled into the worn leather saddle. It was only then that the prince realized he was seated upon Count Murray's prized horse. A quick glance around the stable revealed that there were no other horses around. Elwin frowned. All the stalls stood open and empty. Yet the day before there had been nine or ten horses.

Pallas saw Elwin's silent question, and climbed onto his horse, giving the prince a devious smile. "Why are you looking at me?"

"What did you do?" Elwin asked sternly.

"Why do you always blame me?"

Elwin raised an eyebrow. "For several reasons. More than I care to count at the moment."

"Well, this time, you're wrong. It was Aidan's idea. Though I don't think father will mind." His smile broadened. "Do you?"

Casting a cold stare at Aidan, Elwin replied, "Yes I do. What did you do with the horses, Aidan?"

Seated awkwardly on his horse, Aidan appeared uncomfortable. As a rule, elves did not ride or own horses, and Aidan, though he had ridden several times, had never quite gotten used to it. Despite looking as if he would be happier with his feet firmly on the ground, Aidan mirrored Pallas' smile. "It was my idea, I'll admit it, but Colin was the one who took me seriously and actually did it."

Elwin sighed. It suddenly felt like old times. Colin grumbled and shifted in his saddle. He tried to maintain a stern face, and he was only barely succeeding. "Sure, blame me!" he snapped halfheartedly. "Some things never change! You two come up with some harebrained scheme, and it's always Colin who takes the blame." He no longer could hold back his own smile. "Fine, I'll tell you what happened. I kind of let all the horses go."

Elwin shook his head. "Kind of? How do you 'kind of' let horses go?"

"Well, I let them out and headed them towards the mountains," Colin answered. Then he added to his defense, "They'll be okay and it will slow down anyone trying to follow us. In the morning, the Count will discover that we're gone. He will probably know where we're going and why, but it will be another three or four hours before he can find where all the other horses have gone to. By the time he gets them back here and saddled up, we'll have a half day's head start. He will never catch us then!"

"But why am I on the count's prized horse?" asked Elwin.

"Because you were the last one here," Pallas said with unconcealed mirth. "Besides, did you really think any of us was going to ride him? Father would have our skin!"

Elwin shook his head in disbelief, and then laughed despite himself. "You had better hope it slows your father down. I've grown accustomed to my skin."

--

Outside of the warmth of the stable and back in the monastery's courtyard, the sky was dark, and the snow began to fall harder. A cold wind had come down out of the mountains, causing the snow to slap Elwin's face. The laughter and jokes quickly came to an end as they slowly rode through the monastery's courtyard and out the main gate. It would have been impossible to hide the horses from any watching eyes, but thankfully there didn't seem to be any. Elwin glanced once over his shoulder back at the monastery. He regretted having to leave so secretly. He hoped one day the count would understand.

Turning his back on the monastery, Elwin stared into the darkness, and with a kick he sent the powerful chestnut stallion forward. Trotting confidently, the horse took Elwin into the night.

The pre-dawn light found the four still riding hard. They had traveled throughout the night and planned to continue throughout the day. Count Murray would soon be coming after them, so they had to push on. As the false dawn turned the night into a shadowy gray, they stopped for a breakfast of cheese and bread. Tired and sore, there was little talk among them. Each silently ate their portions, trying to block out the cold. Sitting alone, Elwin thought of his sword and what Faynn might have meant by it being a 'key' and of his father and why he hadn't told him about the sword when he was alive. King Artair had told Dovan Murray about it. He had told the count he thought the sword was a curse, but he had not told Elwin. Why? Elwin had no answers.

After giving the horses rest and food that they badly needed, they set off once more. As the day wore on, the snow finally came to a stop. However, it started to grow colder. Wrapped in their blankets, they rode in single file across the snow-covered hills. The road to Port Murray was some miles off to the south, but they decided not to take it. Though it was faster, the road would be far too dangerous.

So far, they had seen no other living soul. Typically, by this time of the year, Reidh would have turned green. Shepherds usually could be seen out with their flocks of sheep, grazing them along the gentle rolling slopes. However, with all the recent snows, the farmers were keeping their flocks in the barns and kept themselves before warm fires while they nervously waited for the return of the long overdue spring.

It was noon when they came upon a small farmhouse. White smoke drifted up from its chimney. The thought of those warm inside the house made the four feel even colder. Elwin thought he could smell fresh bread cooking. "Will it ever get warmer?" he wondered out loud.

Colin answered with a groan.

Sinking deeper into their blankets, the four reluctantly circled the farm, giving it a wide berth. A dog barked as they passed. Soon the farmhouse and its white smoke faded from view. By the time the gray day began to turn dark, they were exhausted. They had slept little the night before and had ridden hard all day.

When it started to snow again, they decided to call it a night. Choosing a small grove of pine trees to make their camp, they dismounted. There were a few inns along the road, but they had opted to stay clear of them. Count Murray was not their only worry. Strigiol soldiers and the Red Robe were still out there somewhere, looking for them...hunting for them. The thought of encountering either of them kept them far from the road and the comfort of the inns.

They didn't stop a moment too soon. By the time they had unsaddled and taken care of their horses, the weather made a turn for the worse. The four boys made camp under the broad limbs of an unusually wide pine tree. The tree provided them with some shelter, but even within the protection of the low hanging branches, the cold wind whipped about, and the snow was coming down hard. Beyond their shelter and the small circle of trees howled a winter storm.

In the blizzard conditions, the cold began to creep into their bones. Their breath came out in puffs of white smoke. Trying to keep warm, Pallas blew on his hands and then shoved them back under his arms.

"It's too risky to light a fire," Colin voiced his opinion. Aidan dropped the firewood he had gathered and glared at Colin.

"It's cold and getting colder. Elves aren't built for this kind of weather. I need a fire!"

Colin snapped back, accusing Aidan of being weak. The freezing and constant blowing snow was getting on everyone's nerves.

Elwin, who held his blanket over his head, spoke up. "We won't survive the night without one, Colin. We will have to risk it. Besides, who's going to see any smoke with all this blowing snow?"

Colin mumbled under his breath but stopped arguing.

Elwin shifted uncomfortably. "Aidan, can you start a fire? Everything's so wet. Maybe you should use your um...elf magic?"

Aidan shot him a look. "I told you, my magic is not like Faynn's. Elves are different. We can't do anything without other elves around to help, and we can't make fire, anyway. At least not with magic."

"What good is magic if you can't use it?" asked Pallas. He had only learned about Aidan's ability earlier that day, but he seemed less concerned about it than either Colin or Elwin.

"Elves are not druids," Aidan snapped. "Now let me get this fire going. An elf doesn't need magic to start a fire, which you should be grateful for. Humans have no wood lore. You would die out here if it wasn't for me."

Aidan then turned to his work. In moments he had kindled a good-sized fire. Within the boughs of the pine tree, it was surprisingly warm. Colin could feel the fire's heat thawing his tired muscles. It also seemed to thaw out his mind.

"Sorry Aidan," he managed to say. "You were right. I don't think too clearly when I'm cold."

"Forget it," replied Aidan. "As far as I can tell, humans never think clearly." Colin laughed, and all was forgotten.

"Come on and help me gather some more logs," Aidan invited Colin. "I'll show you how to find the best wood for a fire."

After setting watches to keep one eye on the fire and the other on the night, one by one they fell off to sleep. Elwin rose early the next morning to find that the snow had stopped falling. The blizzard seemed to have ended, though it was still bitterly cold. The cold cut through his clothing like a well-sharpened dagger.

Stiff, sore, and cold, the friends ate the meal Aidan had prepared. Once they had eaten and the horses made ready, Pallas put out the fire, and they set out once more.

The day started out as the previous one: cold and gray. Deep drifts had formed during the night, and the traveling was slow. It was beginning to look as if they would have to spend another cold night huddled before an all too tiny fire, which none of them were looking forward to. But around noon the clouds broke, and the sun came out. As they went farther east, there was less snow on the ground, and they began to make up some time. Aidan stood up in his stirrups and pointed to the east. "The marshes...I can see them." Elves have a keen sense of sight.

"We should reach Jon and his boat before dark," Pallas stated reassuringly.

Feeling better than they had in two days, they picked up their pace. As they rode over the next few hills, the rest soon could also see the marshes. Beyond that lay Owen's Bay. In the sunlight, the bay looked like a greenish blue jewel against the white landscape. Aidan once more stood in his stirrups and looked back to the east.

Elwin reined in his horse. "What is it?"

"Riders, they are coming this way."

"It can't be father," said Pallas, trying to see what only

Aidan could. "We've pushed as hard and as fast as father could have done, and we had half a night and a half a day head start. How did he do it?"

"He must have ridden all night," said Colin.

Aidan shook his head. "Through that storm? I don't think so."

Elwin's eyes narrowed. "Maybe it's not the Count."

"Who else..." Pallas stopped short, and his eyes widened.

"Soldiers," breathed Colin, saying what everyone else was thinking. Colin's single word was all the warning they needed. They turned and kicked their tired horses and raced off towards the west, and away from the coming threat.

Over the wind, Aidan yelled, "More riders coming at us from the south!"

Pallas looked. He could see the riders and they were closing in fast. "They're trying to cut us off!" he shouted. "We'll be caught between them and those behind us. Jon is waiting on the northern side of the marshes. Our only chance is to reach the eastern edge of the marshes before they can cut us off."

Before long, everyone could clearly see the two dozen riders coming out of the south. Standing out against the white snow, they appeared only as dark spots that rapidly grew in size. The riders were closing in fast. Sweating and panting, the four horses struggled on, but the riders to the south kept steadily gaining. With each passing moment, the gap between themselves and their pursuers shrank. Time was now their enemy.

To the east, riders could now be seen as well, and to the south, they could pick out the armor of the soldiers that pursued them. A flag flapped angrily in the cold wind. The flag was brown with a green boar at its center...Baron Stanford's crest. The flag shattered all hopes that the soldiers were not Strigiol's.

As the four fleeing youths dipped between hills, the soldiers vanished from view, but they always reappeared as they mounted the next hill. With each new rise, the soldiers were that much closer. Using his left hand, Elwin reached back to the hilt of his sword. The soldiers were close now, and Elwin knew time was running out. The trap would close upon them by the next hill or two. Their luck had run out.

Elwin's panting stallion burst over the next ridge, and there before him was the edge of the marshes. Elwin ground his heels into the chestnut's heaving sides. There was only a small chance they would make it, but it was a chance. As if it knew danger was at hand, the powerful chestnut drew upon a hidden strength and charged ahead.

Elwin leaned forward. The wind pounded unmercifully in his ears. Then in a sudden burst of speed, the marshes were at his side and the soldiers at his back. Elwin glanced over his shoulder. The others had also made it and were close behind him, but their horses were not as strong nor as fast as Count Murray's powerful stallion. They had already been pushed beyond their endurance, and yet somehow the horses heroically raced on.

Fifty yards farther back, the Strigiol soldiers gave chase. Unlike the four they pursued, their horses had not been pushed for two long days, and they were slowly gaining ground. Elwin turned back toward the west and prayed for speed. As if the chestnut could hear his silent plea, the proud horse surged ahead. Wrapping his arms tightly around the horse's thick, sweaty neck, Elwin held on hoping the other horses would not falter and could somehow keep up.

Beneath him, he could see the ground racing past. Never had he seen a horse run so fast. To his left, the marshes were a blur of rushes and cattails that were blocking his view of the bay. Risking a quick look, he glanced back over his shoulder. The chestnut was actually pulling away from both his friends and the pursuing soldiers. Elwin wanted to help the others, but there was nothing he could do. It was all he could do just to hold on.

The rolling hills of the landscape began to level and flatten out. Before long, Owen's Bay came back into view. Elwin knew that was the finish line. If Jon was there, they had a chance... if not...

Another moment passed. Elwin scanned the shoreline, yet all he could see were cattails and rushes swaying in the bitterly cold wind. Then something caught his eye. Not quite inside the frozen marshes, he saw what looked like a tree trunk with all its branches stripped away. It was tall and thin and stood out against the choppy green water of the bay. It was a mast...Jon was there!

CHAPTER TWELVE

"JON!" Elwin screamed, "JON! JON! SOLDIERS!" His horse raced on down towards the shoreline. "Jon! Jon prepare to cast off!"

At Elwin's cry, Jon came out of the cabin. At first, he only saw Elwin. He recognized him but could not understand what the hurry was about. He couldn't see any soldiers. Still, he ordered his men to get ready to cast off. Then he saw the others crest the hill, and the soldiers close behind. He already had his small crew off the side of the boat. Straining in the waist high, icy cold waters of Owen's Bay, the crew frantically worked, trying desperately to move the boat off the shallows. The tide was out and the vessel had settled onto the mud flats.

Elwin galloped up to the beach and pulled back on the horse's reins. The chestnut slowed down and stopped at the water's edge. With his bundle tucked tightly up under his arm, he leaped from the horse's back, and briskly thanked the horse for saving his life. In response, the horse shook its mane and pawed the ground. Then Elwin gave the chestnut stallion a slap that sent the proud beast off to the north, along the beach. He knew the horse would be safe now and would find its way back to his master. As the horse hurried off along the shoreline, Elwin turned to the boat. Splashing through the shallow icy water, he reached the side of the small vessel. He threw his bundle over the gunnel. Then joining the crew, he put his back against the boat and pushed. The boat moved a few feet, then became stuck in the mud again.

"Harder!" ordered Jon.

Elwin heard the crew groan with effort. He locked his knees and shoved with all his strength. Elwin could not believe after getting so close, it would all end here...stuck in the mud. His muscles tightened. Elwin groaned, ignoring the pain in his legs he pushed harder and then with a final great heave, the boat slid free.

Unprepared for the sudden motion, Elwin lost his balance and fell face forward into the icy water. Sputtering and coughing, he emerged a second later and with some help from a crew member managed to pull himself up over the aft rail of Jon's boat.

Jon was there to meet him, but his blue eyes were staring off to the west where Colin, Aidan, and Pallas still raced for their lives. Elwin was surprised at how far ahead the chestnut had taken him. Perhaps that lead would save them all. The speed of the chestnut had given Jon enough time to get his boat off the shallows.

Being the lightest burden to his horse, Aidan was the next to arrive, closely followed by Pallas. Being the heaviest, Colin was last, and he reached the shore just in front of the pursuing soldiers. His panting horse sucked in air. Covered in sweat, the horse staggered and seemed to have taken its last step. Leaving his bundle and saddlebags behind,

Colin leaped off his horse's back and crashed through the waves. With an arm thrust forward, he grabbed hold of the boat's taffrail. The arrows began to fly as several hands grabbed hold of the large youth and heaved upwards.

Colin managed to swing one leg up over the rail before Jon started barking out orders. The small fishing and cargo vessel became a beehive of activity. Quickly responding to Jon's orders, sailors started hauling in lines, tugging on the wet, icy sheets. A rusty-colored gaffed-rigged sail slid smoothly up the boat's single mast. The wind took hold, and the sail billowed out. The boat suddenly heeled sharply over to one side. Still straddling the handrail, Colin rolled over and crashed onto the deck, landing on something soft, which turned out to be Aidan. With Jon at the helm, the boat spun easily away from shore.

Shouts of anger and frustration erupted behind them. With a 'twang' more arrows flew. Shafts of wood arched into the air. The boat was still not far from shore, but the high winds made it difficult for the archers to aim accurately. Elwin ducked as several arrows whizzed overhead and another arrow quivered in the deck beside him.

Now pointing out towards the bay, the boat quickly put distance between them and the soldiers. Rising and falling, the bow cut through the small choppy waves of the bay. In mere moments, the arrows stopped flying, and only the soldier's shouts assaulted them. Then they too began to fade away.

Hardly even noticing that their clothes were soaked through to the skin, the four friends sat together on the deck. Aidan mumbled something about knowing what it felt like to have a horse fall on him. Pallas smiled, and Colin grumbled. Relieved at their narrow escape, Elwin leaned back against the rail and watched the receding shoreline. Even Colin's horse had managed to stumble off to the north and out of harm's way.

Feeling that the immediate danger was now behind them, Elwin began to inspect the boat.

It was a common type of vessel found in Reidh. Like the people themselves, their boats were not the grandest or the most awe-inspiring. However, they were, if nothing else, extremely practical. The vessel had a dual purpose. It could function either as a fishing boat or a small cargo boat. Its handrails were low, standing only two feet above the deck, making it easier to haul in heavy fishing nets. All sleeping quarters were below, leaving the deck open for the crew, fish, or crates. From past experience, Elwin knew there would be two cargo holds. To keep the vessel balanced, one hold would be located towards the bow and the other in the aft. In between the two cargo holds would be a small cabin. The boat had only one cabin where both captain and a small crew of five would sleep and eat their meals. These were small vessels, and every inch of space was used practically, and there was no room for a captain to have his own separate cabin. In Reidh, there really wasn't much difference between the captain and his crew anyway.

A crew member on one boat could easily be a captain from another. The vessel, which Jon named the *Sea Bird*, was twenty-seven feet in length and seven feet in width. Forward of mid-ship was the boat's single mast, where its rust-colored sail was taut, straining against the strong winds. The *Sea Bird* was a gaffed-rigged vessel, having a spar that extended the upper edge of the sail out away from the top of the mast. On most spring days, the harbor would be dotted with gaffed sails, but the recent storms kept the sailors at their moorings. With the endless winter like conditions, it was hard for Elwin to remember it was now late spring.

The sun was beginning to set. Jon was holding the tiller with both hands, steering the *Sea Bird* towards the center of Owens Bay. They could not see either the harbor or Port Murray yet because both the harbor and town were hidden behind a long sandy spit of land. Along the shoreline were sandy beaches with great dunes which were now covered in snow and ice, lined with a few sporadic trees.

"Reef in that sail!" Jon ordered. "I don't want her to blow out! And sheet her in! She's luffin' a bit. We're headed for open water boys, so tie down anythin' that's loose. We're in for a real blow!"

By twisting the long wooden boom, the crew wrapped the

bottom of the sail around the boom. Now that the sail was shorter, the boat heeled a little less.

Aidan, who had his race's fear of the sea and had never learned to swim, was now terrified. He clamped onto the railing. His white knuckles were as pale as his face. "This is worse than riding!" he exclaimed. "Can't we hide somewhere? We could wait until morning...maybe this storm will lift... I really don't think we should be trying to go out to sea today... Do you?"

"Now's our chance," Jon answered. "Those soldiers that were chasin' you four will be ridin' for town and be warnin' their friends that you've put to sea. If that happens, those two Strigiol Man of War ships will haul anchor and block us in. It's now or never."

"But the Strigiol ships will see us anyway!" Colin protested. "Once we round that point." He pointed indicating a snow-covered strip of land off their port side. "We will be in clear view, and it's not dark yet."

"By the time they see us, it will be too late," pronounced Jon. "The Strigiol ships are faster than us, but she won't be able to get her crew aboard, raise her anchor, and set sail and still be able to catch us before we reach the bay's mouth. By that time, it'll be dark. The Strigiol captain is no fool, he won't try to navigate the mouth in the dark and in this kind of weather. She'd never make it. She'd be smashed upon the rocks."

"And we can?" asked Aidan doubtfully.

"We had better," Jon answered with a laugh. "Cause that's what we're doin'."

Jon turned his attention back to his boat. "I said trim that blasted sail!" A crew member leaped into action. Grabbing hold of the sheet that leads to the end of the long boom, he braced his feet against the rail. Putting his weight into it, he brought the big sail in tighter. The flapping stopped, and the boat leaned a little more to one side, picking up speed.

Aidan held on tighter and his pale, blanched skin took on a greenish tone.

As they rounded the point of land, they quickly saw that Jon had been right. They could easily see the Strigiol ships and the town behind them. The captains of the two Strigiol ships must have been able to see them as well. However, the ship made no attempt to weigh anchor. It seemed that the captain and his crew were content to watch and see if Jon's boat would clear the rocks or be dashed against them.

Just as the day was coming to an end and the evening light faded into darkness, Elwin peered off to the east. He thought he could just make out a dark line cutting across the horizon, which he realized were rocks. Above the dark line, Elwin saw massive waves—the largest he had ever seen. To see waves at that distance meant that they had to be huge.

How are we ever going to get through that? wondered Elwin. The light faded, and both the rocks and waves disappeared into the night.

Another night without stars or moon settled over Owen's Bay. The only sound was that of the boat pounding into the waves and the whispers of the hard-working crew. Elwin felt himself slip into the rhythm of the waves. The constant and rhythmic rise and fall of the waves was almost hypnotic.

"Blast it all!" shouted Jon, breaking Elwin's trance-like state.

With his feet spread wide so he could sway with the waves that tossed the small boat, Elwin stood next to Jon. From where Elwin was standing, one could tell that the water in the large bay was getting rougher, but he sensed that wasn't what was bothering Jon.

"What's wrong?" Elwin asked.

Jon pointed off to the east.

Elwin narrowed his eyes, but no matter how much he strained, he couldn't see what Jon was talking about. "What is it? I don't see anything."

"That's just it!" Jon shouted over the sound of the wind that was beginning to blow harder. "The lighthouse is out. There's no blasted light!"

Of course! Elwin suddenly realized, *They've turned out the light. Without the lighthouse to guide us past the rocks, they think we'll turn back. That must be why the warships never bothered to chase us. They're back there waiting for us to return.* Elwin looked at Jon. He knew Jon better than the Strigiol soldiers did, and he knew that they wouldn't turn back.

Lighthouse or not, Jon is going through. At best, they think we will be dashed against the rocks. Elwin couldn't help but wonder if they might be right. But, like everything else lately, there was no choice.

Elwin heard the rocks long before he saw them. The waves crashed against the spit of land and boomed in his ears. The constant pounding drowned out both the pounding of the *Sea Bird's* bow and the howl of the fierce cold wind. The sound became a constant reminder of what would happen if Jon could not keep them off the rocks. Huge waves now rolled in through the invisible mouth of the bay and tossed the ship about as if she were a cork. Despite the waves that washed over the deck, drenching the crew and passengers alike, Jon was sweating as he leaned into the tiller, trying to keep his boat on course. Since the lighthouse was out and nothing could be seen in the dark, Jon had to steer from instinct alone.

"There!" came a shout from a crew member who had been

stationed on the bow. He pointed off the port side with his left hand while his right arm was wrapped securely around the forestay to keep himself from being washed away as the bow dipped into the waves. He was following the old adage and rule of the sea: 'keep one hand for the boat and the other for yourself.'

"The rocks!" the bowman yelled. "Two degrees off the port bow!"

Elwin squinted into the dark. He raised a hand, trying to protect his face from the water that was constantly spraying and washing across the deck. There, he saw the faint outline of the rocks. With each wave, the small vessel was being pushed closer and closer to the deadly wall. In only moments, the gray boulders that could turn a ship into a pile of toothpicks could clearly be seen. They were too close. The large, gray menacing shapes rose twelve feet above the turbulent green water. The rocks were no more than two boat lengths away. Time seemed to slow. Jon struggled to keep them off the rocks, yet he hardly gave them a glance. Instead, he watched the sail and the next wave that threatened to shove them closer to the boulders. Wave after wave broke over the wall. Spray came down like a rainstorm driven by a fierce wind.

Every free eye watched the rocks, hoping that Jon could somehow keep them from crashing into them.

Shouting, the sailor stationed at the bow kept Jon informed of the distance between them and the rocks. He started at sixty feet, then it went to fifty, and then to forty. Every time he yelled, they were closer. Elwin began to cringe each time the bowman bellowed out. He almost wished the man would stop; it was never good news, but Elwin knew Jon needed the information.

"Twenty feet!" the bowman yelled.

Then suddenly Elwin could see the end of the rocky spit.

The dark form of the lighthouse stood before them. It looked as if they were going to just make it, but rounding the point was the hardest and most dangerous part. It was there that they would face the full fury of the storm.

They started to round the point. Just then, the biggest wave yet suddenly hit the boat. Without warning, the green water heaved upwards. The wave grabbed ahold of the boat and lifted her up higher and higher. Next it spun the vessel about, shoving her towards the silent dark lighthouse and the rocks. Pitching heavily over to one side, *Sea Bird's* starboard rail was buried deep into the wave. Icy water poured over the handrails and across the deck.

Elwin was hit by the force of the wave. Losing his balance, he was washed backward. Horrified, he realized that he was going to be swept over the side and into the angry sea. Frantically, he reached out for anything to grab, but he could feel nothing. Helplessly, he slid down the deck. Acting swiftly, Colin tied a line around his leg and leaped after Elwin.

Elwin saw a blur, then his descent stopped with a jerk. With his leg fastened to the line, Colin was able to wrap his arms around Elwin's ankles. Colin held tight.

From his new position, Elwin could look over the rail and down at the deadly rocks. The wave had taken them above the rocky spit. Elwin's stomach twisted.

Despite Colin's heroics, he was going to die... They all were. Once the wave let them down, they would be thrown against the rocks. They would be smashed.

He wondered how he was going to die; there seemed to be only two choices. He was either going to be crushed against the rocks along with the boat, or Colin would lose his grip, and he would be thrown into the icy waters. Either way, the end would be the same. In that icy water, one had little time and no chance. The frigid water would kill a man in moments, but in these huge waves, he doubted he would have even that much time. It would only take seconds for the waves to take him down to a cold watery grave.

Elwin braced himself for the crash he knew would come, but nothing happened. Jon, who hadn't been washed off his feet, was still at the helm. With an almost superhuman effort, he thronged his weight and pushed the tiller one way then heaved it back the other way again. Like a top, the boat spun and snapped upwards, righting itself. The *Sea Bird's* bow was now turned out away from the rocks. The wave crested just off the stern of the boat, and like a log in the surf, the small vessel was pushed away from the rocks. Like a sled in the snow, they raced down the green sloping wave. The white foaming crest danced behind them. Quickly they picked up speed. The wave that had nearly taken them to their watery graves now pushed them away from the danger, and out into the open sea.

Across the boat, there was a loud sigh of relief. The *Sea Bird* rose upon the next wave, and the crew saw they were clear of the rocks. The breakwall and lighthouse were now off their stern and the they dove into the next mountain of water. The spray was everywhere, but Jon held the boat on course, and the small vessel rose up upon the next wave. Letting go of Elwin's ankles, Colin rose to his knees. Elwin looked up at him.

"Thank you! You...saved my life."

"It is a vassal's duty to protect his lord."

Elwin sighed. It was just like Colin to reduce his heroics to that of duty. However, there was pride in Colin's eyes, pride of saving both his prince and his friend's life. Elwin smiled and slapped the big man on the shoulder.

"Thank you, all the same."

"Look!" Cried out Pallas.

Elwin twisted his neck to look back towards the breakwall. On the top of one large boulder stood a dark robed figure. Blood red robes whipped and snapped in the gale-force winds, but not a drop of water touched the Red Robe.

Elwin gulped as he felt the eyes of the Red Robe upon him. Elwin remembered the wave that had nearly killed them, and he knew without a shred of doubt that it had been more than the wind that had created the wave—much more. It was impossible for someone to have been standing out there. The waves should have swept him away, but each wave, as if it loathed to touch the Red Robe, parted leaving him as dry as if he were miles from any water.

The boat dove down into another watery valley, and when she crested the next wave, the Red Robe was gone as if he had never been there. Without a word, the crew turned from the impossible vision, hoping it had not really been there.

Though the waves were just as big out at sea, they now seemed smaller. The danger of rocks and the robed figure were lost to the darkness behind them. Jon now followed a new course that took them out to sea.

After a few hours of battling the storm, the winds suddenly decreased and the waves died down into gentle rolling swells. The sky cleared and stars that they had not seen in a long time dotted the night sky. Brilliantly, the bright stars stretched from horizon to horizon. It was as if the storm only surrounded Reidh County and didn't extend out to sea more than a dozen miles.

Elwin stared at the sky. A warm breeze blew in his face— the warmest breeze he had felt since he left the Murray Keep. That already seemed like a long time ago. Elwin loosened his cloak and let the warm night breeze begin to dry his clothing. He took in a long deep breath, letting the warm breeze, the stars, and the gentle rolling of the sea ease his tension. He almost felt happy.

Helped by Pallas and Colin, Aidan was eased down through a hatch and into the cabin below. Colin lifted Aidan onto a narrow bunk, and Pallas gave him a drink, telling him that it would make him feel better. Aidan moaned and claimed that he wanted to die. Soon the drugged liquid took effect, and the golden-locked elf fell off to sleep. Leaving Aidan to get his rest, Colin and Pallas returned to the deck and joined Elwin, whom they found staring out at the night sky.

"Wow!" breathed Colin, "I never thought there could be so many stars!"

"It's like this at sea," replied Pallas. "Once you are away from the lights, trees, and hills of the land, the skies come alive."

"Look," Pallas pointed to the north. A part of the sky glowed with streaks of red, green, and white. The colors waved and shifted like ghosts that drifted on the warm night air.

"The gods are givin' us a light show."

Turning his head, Elwin recognized Jon's deep, gravelly voice.

The big captain, having given the tiller over to one of his crew members, took a seat on the edge of the rail. He too looked at the strange and mysterious shifting lights. "Those are the Lights of Claidemmh, the goddess of music," Jon went on. "Some say they are a sign of good luck, and others say it foretells of dangers to come. Maybe a little of both. Aye?"

"I've heard," commented Pallas, "that in Aleash they say the lights are the ghosts of the dead and will reach down and steal the souls of the living."

"I think the nomads of Aleash are overly concerned with the

dead," said Elwin, thinking of what he had learned from the monastery's library.

Aleash was a harsh land of grasslands that sweltered in the summer and froze in the winter. The high grassy and arid lands of Aleash were beyond the kingdoms of Kambrya and were inhabited by fierce nomadic and rather superstitious people. It was where Elwin was going. In Aleash, he believed he would find the Woods of the Mist and the home of the guardians of light.

According to Elwin's research, in the heart of Aleash's expansive grasslands there was a forest surrounding a single mysterious mountain. For religious reasons, it was a mountain and forest that no one in Aleash ever visited. It was considered a sacred place in the Aleash belief system. According to Elwin's readings, the mountain is a dormant volcano. It was on that mountain that the young prince believed he would find Leina. Count Dovan had wanted to ship Elwin off someplace safe, but Elwin was determined to go after his sister.

Jon shrugged his shoulders. "Everybody has their own stories." He looked up at the shifting colors of the aurora. "But I prefer to see them as a sign of luck. At sea, one needs all the luck one can get."

Colin leaned against one of the stays that held the mast in place. "All I can say is that it's beautiful, and it's great to be away from that storm."

Elwin couldn't help but smile. It seemed so out of place for the big square faced Colin to speak of beauty. It was kind of like a troll talking about his rose garden.

"Never seen anythin' like it... that storm, I mean," Jon stated. "Almost unnatural, it was."

"Almost," Elwin echoed, thinking of the Red Robe, but he didn't want to talk about him.

He didn't want to even think about him, and he hoped no one else would either.

"I did not think your small boat could take those waves," said Colin. "They were so big."

"It was her size that saved us," claimed Jon. "We were small enough to fit between those waves. A larger vessel would have been twisted apart trying to withstand the force of two or more waves at the same time, but we did not have to withstand that force. All we had to do was to go with it. It be the smallness of *Sea Bird* that saved us, my young man. That and a little luck."

And your skill as a sailor, thought Elwin, but he kept that to himself. It wasn't something that needed to be said. It was already being spoken in everyone's eyes.

Recognizing the unspoken praise, Jon seemed to stand a little tall that night. Elwin smiled, *I wonder what he would feel if he knew it was the prince of Ceredigion he had saved? Then again, I doubt it would matter. To Jon, any life was a life worth saving.*

Colin nodded, giving the boat an admiring look.

"Well," said Jon. "I'm not goin' to ask you what you be runnin' from. That I guess is your own affair, but I be needin' to know where I be takin' you. If I was to guess, I would say to the south. King Jerran and his men can't reach you there. At least not yet."

"Did Count Murray not tell you?" Elwin asked.

"Nope, he only said you be in some trouble and might be needing me to get you free of the county. I was to wait for you in the marshes. If you showed up, I was to head for sea and ask questions later. The Count said that's all I needed to know, and I would be safer the less I knew. That was good enough for me. I already knew you were in trouble; that robed thing and all." He shook his head as if trying to forget what the Red Robe had done to him. The thing had tossed Jon around like a rag doll.

"Well," said Elwin, trying not to sound relieved. If Jon did not know where they were supposed to go, it would make it easier to get him to take them where Elwin wanted. "We are not going south. There's something I need to do. I can't tell you what it is, Jon. I can only ask you to trust me. I know without a doubt that you can be trusted, but the Count is right. What you don't know won't hurt you, and I fear if you did, it just might. All the same, you will need to be careful. Never let *anyone* know that you helped me...and you might want to stay away from Port Murray for a while."

Jon frowned.

Elwin let his eyes drift over the rolling waves of the sea. "I need you to take me to Aonach."

Jon, still frowning, said, "Eoin, if that is truly your name, though I'll be willin' to bet it isn't. But then I also be willin' to bet I'd rather not know your true one, now would I?" He gave Elwin a hard look. When Elwin didn't respond, Jon went on. "No, I don't think I want to know. As you were sayin', what I don't know can't hurt me none. Yet I still say that sailin' south, maybe to the Empire or the free cities would be the wiser choice, but if you say Aonach, then the city of Aonach I shall take you." He looked up at the sky. Then he looked back at Elwin. "May the luck of them northern lights shine on all of you... I have a feelin' you'll be needin' it."

With that, the stocky sailor came to his feet. "I better go check and see what damage that storm caused." Then Jon turned and began his inspection of the boat.

Colin watched him go. "He never asked why we were alone. Doesn't he think it odd we arrived with no escort? I mean we are only a bunch of teenagers."

Pallas smiled. "You come from the world of nobility," he pointed out. "Jon is from a different world, he has been fishing and working for a living since he was younger than us. To him, we are old enough to take care of ourselves."

"I don't think your father will see it that way," added Colin. "He must be pretty mad about now."

"Furious is more likely," agreed Pallas.

Elwin nodded in agreement. Dovan would be beside himself with anger and worry. For that, he was sorry. Dovan was a good man whom Elwin loved like a second father, but he was not going to be put up somewhere while his sister needed him. Elwin looked out to sea; *I'm coming Leina.*

CHAPTER THIRTEEN

Ruan Deuchar, Lord Baron of Keloran sank into a high-backed chair. He leaned his head back and closed his eyes. *I'm tired*, he thought. *So very tired.* The red velvet of the chair felt soft beneath his leathery skin. It was of royal design, and no less than two hundred years old. The wooden arms and legs were polished to a glossy reddish-brown. It was a royal chair fitting for the palace. However, the elegant chair only reminded the lord that he was not where he wished to be.

He did not belong in Gildas, the gold city of Strigiol. In the northern city of Keloran, there were no such luxuries as red velvet cushioned chairs—not even in the baron's castle. Like the Baron himself, Keloran was shaped by the harsh north country of Strigiol. The cities and castles of the north were built for protection and survival, not places of comfort or prestige. Similar to the castles, the northern lords were very different from their counterparts in the south. They were the defenders of the kingdom, and these warrior lords of the north always felt ill-at-ease in southern Strigiol. Ruan was no different.

In the south, nobles of both low and high status struggled and manipulated for power and position. It was a game to them, or so it appeared to Ruan. The north was a harder, yet simpler life. In the north, you knew who your enemies were and who were your friends, making things clearer. Gildas, the capital of Strigiol, with its shimmering towers and luxury, filled rooms was anything but simple. Gildas was a city of intrigue, luxuries, and games of power—games which could, and often did have deadly outcomes. Gildas was no place for Ruan. However, he had always been faithful to his oath of allegiance to the king, the same king who had been his childhood friend. That oath over the last few years had become increasingly strained, but still, Ruan had never broken it or even considered breaking it...until now.

Ruan opened his eyes. Try as he might, he could not sleep. In his hand, he gripped a folded sheet of very expensive parchment. Imprinted on its surface was the emblem of the black eagle, the royal crest of the Cameron family and king of Strigiol. Oaths were not easy to break, nor should they be broken—at least that is what Ruan thought and believed. Ruan did not want the title of oath-breaker. It did not help matters that the oath he was now considering breaking was to his king. An oath that only a few years ago, he had happily sworn to Jerran. The king was his closest friend, or so Ruan had thought. To break his pledge with Jerran would mean he had given up on the king. Ruan would be forfeiting a lifelong friendship. He knew once he decided to break his oath, there would be no turning back. *Ha! Who are you fooling? Is it not already too late?*

For what seemed like the hundredth time, he unfolded the tan parchment, written by a southern noble. Ruan himself had never been able to master the calligraphy of the lords of the south.

Participating in the southern courtly ways was less important in the north. In the north, southerners were considered manipulative, conniving, and overall a bunch of arrogant snobs. On the other hand, in the south, northerners were deemed ignorant barbarians and backward farmers, who had no idea what culture was all about.

Ruan held the parchment before him.

> *"Our good Lord Baron Ruan Deuchar of Keloran, we regret that your request to leave the capital and return to your lands in the north*

cannot be granted at this time. We are on the brink of war with Mythra. At such a time as this, we cannot spare you. Your advice and wisdom are far too valuable. Kambrya will soon return to the days of old... the days of peace will come again. Strigiol will be the creators of that peace, and our lands and people will be whole once more. Then will be time for homecomings.

Until that time, we need you, Lord Ruan Deuchar.

King Jerran Cameron of Strigiol,
High King of Kambrya,
Lord and Protector of the Peace and Justice."

Wearily, Ruan folded up the note. *Needed?* Holding the parchment between his thumb and forefinger, he began to tap the letter against the chair's wide arm. *How can I be needed? I can't even see the king. The guards are tighter than ever. This note probably wasn't even written by Jerran. No, it's not the king who keeps me here, but the Prophet. Well, Torcull, you may control the crown, but you do not control me. I will not stand by and disappear like all the others. If you want me dead, you'll have to come after me. I'll no longer do your bidding or play this game by your rules. With or without the king's promise, I'm returning to Keloran.*

The door to his room suddenly opened and Ruan was pulled

from his thoughts. He saw a woman with flowing brown hair step forward. She wore a long dark blue dress with white fringes on the collar and sleeves. Around her narrow waist was a belt of white cotton. She stepped into the room and softly closed the door behind her. There was a certain grace about her, not the forced grace of a Southerner, but rather the natural grace of one born with self-confidence and inner beauty. Here was a woman who knew who she was and had no desire to be anything else. Ruan admired that. He always thought that one of the most irritating things about southern Strigiol was that you never knew who anyone really was.

A small smile crossed her round face. "Good evening, Lord Baron. May I come in?"

Ruan weakly returned her smile. "Eilidh, when does a wife need her husband's permission to enter their home?"

Eilidh stepped fully into the room. She met Ruan's eyes. "Often of late, my husband. You have been distant lately, and this—" She hesitated as she looked about the room with distaste, "Is not our home."

Ruan let out a sigh and nodded. "You're right. Lately, I have not been the attentive husband I should be. Please forgive me. As you say, I've been preoccupied of late, and you are also right that this is not our home. I think it's past time we left here. I grow tired of this place, and we have been away from Keloran too long."

"The king's permission?" Her eyes tensed as they fell on the parchment in Ruan's hand.

"No, I'm afraid it isn't." He slipped the tan parchment under his wide gray belt. "The king, if it is the king's hand, has ordered me to stay here in Gildas."

"Then you…we will go without his permission?"

"Yes."

"You will be named a traitor."

"I know. But I...we...cannot stay. I do not wish to leave our daughter without a father, nor their mother without her husband. If I stay, that will be the end result. It might be the same result by leaving, but at least I will go down fighting. It is too much to sit here and wait for Torcull to come for me."

"Nor do I wish to be without you. But to leave will be seen as a threat to Torcull's authority."

"True, yet if I stay, I'm sure my life will be a short one. Torcull already sees my friendship with the king as a threat. I can stay here no longer."

As if the mere thought of his death was more than she could bear, Eilidh hurried across the carpeted floor. Her long white arms pulled the seated Ruan close. "Yes, my love, let us leave this place. Let us go home. I do so wish to see our daughter again."

"It won't be easy." He didn't try to pull away from her. He felt comforted within her arms. "We will be pursued and hunted. Even Keloran may not be safe."

"Why?" she asked, pushing back her long black hair.

"Once it is discovered that we have left the city and fled north, an army will be sent after us. Maybe even the Black Army. Keloran will be a threat to the invasion of Mythra. They won't allow a potential enemy to be sitting at their back."

She nodded sadly. "I had hoped once we left the capital, the king would see that we are not a threat. You would never raise an army against him—never! Even now, Jerran must know that you are faithful to him."

"It's not the king, but Torcull I fear, and the time of keeping to ourselves or ignoring that which is happening has come to an end, my lady. Torcull has marked me. I regret that my actions have brought you into this. I have entered into a game I cannot win, but must try."

She held him closer. "I've been in it since the day we wed, my love. I would have it no other way. You are a good man, Ruan. A good man. You stand up for what is right. It's wrong for the king to persecute you."

Ruan sighed. "Perhaps I am not as good as your eyes see me to be. Was I not in Easland and Lyndland? I saw things there. I saw horrible things. Things that no knight should let happen, but I did nothing to stop it, nothing at all!" There was bitterness to his words. "Oath or no oath, I saw those acts and knew it was wrong. Still, I did nothing." He let his head fall upon her shoulder.

"Hush! I will not hear such talk."

"What have I done?"

"Please, Ruan. Don't talk this way. Things will work out. You will make it so." She then jumped to her feet, "Oh, my!" Her face reddened as if she were a child. "I had forgotten. Forgive me my love, but I have brought someone who wishes to have an audience with you."

"Now? Could it not wait until later? Eilidh, I am not in the mood for visitors."

"No, it cannot wait."

"Who is it?"

Eilidh turned with her smooth inner grace, and before the baron could question her further, she glided back across the room with light, delicate steps. Opening the door, she moved off to one side. A tall and beautiful woman stepped through the open door. A deep pride could be seen in her watchful eyes. She moved with the air of authority.

At the same time, there was a hesitation, as if she was no longer as sure of herself as she had once been. Her dark hair was pulled back and held in place with strands of silver threads. From her ears hung diamonds of unimaginable wealth. In the lamplight of the room, her full golden silk dress shimmered. Next to this woman's dress, Eilidh's blue dress seemed understated and crude.

Ruan's mouth dropped open. He leaped from the chair. Before he had even come completely to his feet, he dropped to the floor. With one knee firmly planted on the floor, he kept his eyes on the carpet. He grabbed the hilt of his sword and placed his other hand on his chest. "Your Majesty, the Light of Strigiol," he breathed the formal address given to the Queen of Strigiol. Then he added a northern touch. "The march has begun, and I await the honor to serve."

"Is he always like this?" the queen asked, looking at Eilidh. Her voice was firm yet gentle.

"Yes, Your Majesty," Eilidh answered with a smile. "Most northern men are. Ruan is no worse than others and better than most."

"Men," the Queen of Strigiol sighed. "Must they always be so overly dramatic?"

"Yes," Eilidh responded wryly. "I believe they do."

"Please stand, my lord."

Ruan came to his feet. He gave a short bow. "Your Majesty."

"I will come to the point," the queen said bluntly. "Your wife tells me you plan to quit the city. Is that right?"

Ruan gave Eilidh a long, questioning look. He was not surprised that Eilidh had known of his plan before he had told her. Eilidh always knew what he was thinking, usually long before he did. But still, to tell Catriono Cameron, the Queen of Strigiol and wife of King Jerran. *This is madness*! All of his plans were coming undone.

"Be at ease, Ruan. May I call you Ruan?"

"Of course, Your Majesty. You do me a great honor." He gave the queen a slight bow of his head. "But you must know that your husband, King Jerran, has requested that I stay here. His Majesty says I am needed."

"No, Ruan, I did not know that. I have not spoken to my husband in over a month. We..." A sad look crossed her face. "We have drifted apart. You've seen him recently, or so I am told, so you should know what I mean. The king is less than the person he once was. Oh, I know he was not a great king like his father, but he was a good man, Ruan. He truly was. You were once his friend. You know he was good once." Her body was held with rigid dignity, but her eyes faltered as if she feared Ruan would argue over that.

Ruan swallowed. Regretfully, he did know what she meant. "Yes, Your Majesty, the king was a good man. I believe he still is. However, he has been misguided."

"I hope you are right," she sighed, relieved that he had not said she was foolish for believing so. "Though I fear I no longer have your faith. I still love him, but I can no longer trust him. Like you, I am no longer safe in Gildas." The words came out of Queen Catriono's mouth as if she could hardly believe they were her own.

The queen, not safe in Gildas?! It was almost laughable.

"Others now have the trust of my husband, and I have become an unwanted burden. Those who I once called friends now shun me." Her face turned red. Ruan could not say if it was from anger or embarrassment. "I have become a liability to the noble's ambitions, and though I no longer hold the king's trust, I still have enemies. Powerful enemies, Ruan. Enemies who fear I will try to sway the king...and I would if he would listen, but..." She let her words drop off. "And then there is my son. He is but five years old. I fear for him. I will do anything to see him safe and away from this madness. That is why I have come to you, Baron. You may be the only lord of the land who will still listen to his queen. If you cannot help the Queen of Strigiol, which I would understand, then I ask you to help a mother save her child." She let her eyes drop to the floor. "Will you help me, Lord Baron? You are my last hope. The danger grows, and I have nowhere else to turn." The proud woman almost shook. It was humbling for the queen to ask for help, especially from a northern lord.

Ruan was at a loss. He was not the best person to ask for help. "A safe place, Your Majesty? I don't know if there is a safe place, especially for the wife and the son of the king." Ruan was blunt. "What you are asking will be dangerous, Your Majesty. You are requesting help from the helpless. I may not be the best of choices. I fear the Prophet wishes me dead."

"You may not be the best of choices," the queen admitted, "but you are the only one I have. I know we have never been close, Lord Ruan. But I need your help." She seemed close to tears. "I have nowhere else to turn."

"I'm not refusing, Your Majesty. I only mean to warn you. I will be a hunted man, more so with you and the prince with me. It will look as if we are conspiring together, trying to bring forth an uprising to overthrow the king, and I guess they would be right." Ruan knew to survive he would need to find a way to overthrow the king and put the king's son on the throne, making the queen regent. It was not a likely scenario, but it was all he had, which was more than a few minutes ago. "It would not be the first time a child was used to overthrow his father. It could mean a civil war, or we might have to flee the country. However, if you still wish to join with me, I will not say no. We are few, but together we may survive. So, to answer your question, yes, Your Majesty. You may join our mad dash for Keloran. It would be an honor to be in the company of Queen Catriono, and it's nice to know that not all my oaths need be broken. If my queen and prince need my help." He gave a short bow. "I am theirs to command."

The queen smiled. "There is still honor left in Strigiol. We will flee together and we shall see what the future will bring, and perhaps others might join us."

"Yes," said Ruan, "We shall see."

CHAPTER FOURTEEN

The hall before Ruan was long, dark, and empty. It had been a long night. Dawn was still a few hours off, but for Ruan, the day had started several hours earlier. He moved cautiously yet swiftly with an unlit lantern from his hand. If there was anyone up this early, a light would surely give him away. It was not forbidden for a lord to be in the servant's quarters, however, it was not common, especially just before dawn. If he were seen, there would be questions and suspicions. People would want to know what Lord Baron was up to. At this hour, there could only be two reasons for a lord to be in the servant's quarters; one, he was returning from his lover's bed; or two, he was plotting something. For Lord Ruan, it was the latter.

As a child, Ruan had spent two full years and several summers in the Gildas Palace. It was during those early years he had met King Jerran. The king was only a prince then. Ruan and Jerran had played together, exploring the palace's endless corridors. He knew from those childhood days that the servant's gate was poorly guarded. With the help of the queen, the gates would not be guarded at all this night.

Evidently, she still had some friends and had helped out several times in making the plans for their escape. The nobles may have abandoned the queen, but many servants and guardsmen were willing to support their queen, if only secretively. So far, the plan had worked, but now he would have to hurry. Dawn was approaching and the hallways would be alive with activity. Servants would be getting up to prepare the morning meals, getting his or her lord's clothing ready for the day, cleaning the palace or one of the many other daily chores.

With the back of his hand, Ruan covered a yawn. He had

been up a good part of the night. Things had taken longer than he had thought or hope, but it would be worth it. The preparations for his escape were done. With the help of Imrich, Ruan's riverboat captain, he had spent the night hunting down his crew. To Ruan, it felt like he had been to every seedy inn and tavern that Gildas had to offer.

Through the long night, Imrich and Ruan had searched from one end of town to the other and by the time they had located everyone, it was nearly morning. They had found that most of the crew was in a sorry state of affairs. The majority of the men were found attempting to sleep off the night's drinks. Many needed to be threatened, prodded, dragged, and when all else failed, carried back to the *Fish Hawk*, Ruan's riverboat. Imrich complained continually that it was Ruan's own fault. For years, the one-eyed captain had been telling Ruan that he was too soft on the *Fish hawk's* crew.

"You pay them too well, my lord, and too soon," Imrich would say. "Silver in a sailor's pouch is the same as putting a mug in his hands, and neither one will last for long. It would be far better to pay them when we reach home. Their wives would see to it that their wages are not wasted on gambling, drink, or other foolish weaknesses."

Ruan turned a corner. The night was almost over. All that remained to do was to reach his rooms. His wife, the queen, and the prince would be waiting there for him. If all went well, by noon he would be back on Fish Hawk and be free of the city. They would be gone before anyone suspected what they had planned.

Ruan was unalert, Thinking the worst was behind him. He came to a sudden stop. Down the hall, someone, or something had moved. Coming out of a side passageway was the dark shadow of a man. Like Ruan, the man walked without the aid of a light. Crouching down into the dark shadows of a door frame, Ruan watched. The man was dressed all in black and seemed to be one with the darkness. With long swift strides, he walked as if the halls were not cloaked in the darkness of the night.

Ruan tried to sink further into the shadows. *Torcull! What is he doing here?*

Never looking in Ruan's direction, Torcull turned and quickly headed down the hallway. Ruan hesitated with a mixture of fear and curiosity. He knew he should get back to his room and to those who were waiting for him, but if leader of the cult were to see him now, hiding among the shadows of the servant's corridors, no one would likely see Ruan again. However, something pulled at him. Ruan's hesitation lasted only a moment, and then he was off after Torcull. Cautiously, he moved among the shadows, keeping close to the wall. As if he were hunting the Black-Horned Bear of the Northern Drygan Mountains, Ruan removed his boots and crouched low. He tried to not get too close or to fall too far behind. Like the Black-Horned Bear, Ruan was sure Torcull had a keen sense of hearing and could see better in the dark than in the daylight. Briefly, he thought of attacking the Prophet. If he could kill the man, then perhaps the king would listen to reason, but something told Ruan that to attack the Prophet was asking for death.

Ruan had not been following Torcull for very long when the Prophet abruptly stopped, turned, then disappeared through a door.

"Now, what could be behind that door?" Ruan decided to wait and find out. Across the hall, Ruan found a room that was unlocked and unoccupied. He searched the room from one end to the other. It was a small storeroom and was stuffed full of barrels and crates, and the smell of dust was strong. Satisfied that he was alone in the storeroom, Ruan returned to the doorway. He opened the door a crack, lowering himself to the floor, and began to wait and watch. He leaned back against a wooden crate and settled in.

What is behind that door? Ruan kept thinking and rethinking. He had a strange feeling that something horrible was inside that room. He knew he should be on his way, yet he waited. Something was keeping him there. Curiosity? No, it was more. Ruan had to find out what the Prophet was hiding. It had to be important. There could be no other reason for Torcull to be down here. The thought of the Prophet visiting a lover seemed strangely out of place. The Prophet was a lover of power and not of the flesh. Even the idea of Torcull embracing another body sent chills down Ruan's spine. *Torcull having a lover?* It was almost repulsive. *What woman could find the Prophet attractive?*

It was not that Torcull was ugly. The Prophet was actually the most perfect-looking man Ruan had ever seen. The man was tall, blond, and had the deepest blue eyes one could imagine. When he wanted to be, the leader of the cult could be graceful and charming. However, despite his looks, charms, and grace, women tended to avoid the prophet. Everyone did. It was as if his enchanting looks and charms were a mask that covered a hideous face. Torcull was evil. You couldn't see it, but you knew it was there. Torcull looked like an angel but smelled like a demon.

Ruan sat and waited. He watched the shadows of the corridor beginning to retreat. Dawn was approaching. *What is he doing in there? He's been in there a long time. I wonder if there is another way out? I should be going, Eilidh will begin to worry.* But still, Ruan waited.

So far, no one had passed down the hallway, but Ruan knew it would not be much longer until the castle would begin to wake up, and people would be going about their business. Ruan was about to stand up and stretch his cramped muscles when he suddenly froze in place. The door he had been watching swung open. Torcull appeared. Like a moving shadow, the Dark Prophet glided into the hall. He took two steps down the corridor, then he abruptly stopped. He swung his blond head back over this shoulder. He gazed down the hallway. The light of the false dawn caught his blue eyes. Ruan swallowed. He was sure Torcull was staring right at him.

Torcull's eyes narrowed into two tiny blue slits. "Who's there?" His voice was like the soft icy whisper of the grave.

Cursing himself, Ruan swallowed again, only to discover that his mouth was painfully dry. *Why did I follow him? I'm such a fool!*

Torcull took a step towards Ruan's hiding place. "I know you are there. Come out!"

In one smooth, effortless motion, Ruan came up onto his knees, as he rocked onto the balls of his feet. Crouching behind the door, he quietly began to draw his sword.

Northerners were trained to stay calm when confronting an enemy, but Torcull was not a troll coming out of the mountains. He was far more dangerous. Ruan took a deep breath, yet his heart refused to slow, and a cold fear clouded his judgment. A troll he could handle; he knew what to expect from them, but Torcull was something else altogether. Torcull was spawned from the darkest blackness that had ever existed. For the first time in his life, Ruan knew what it was to fear. To die in battle was something all northerners expected, but this was somehow different. Trolls were cruel, but they were not evil...at least not in the same way as Torcull.

To Ruan's surprise, a child's voice answered Torcull. "I did not mean to spy," came the soft whisper.

Torcull's face looked as surprised as Ruan felt. All but forgetting to be quiet, Ruan shifted his position so he could look down the hall to where the child's voice had come from.

Nervously stepping out of dark shadows was a thin twig of a girl. The child could be no more than seven or eight. The young girl's dress was a long brown cotton garment that fit as if it were a size too large. *An apprentice, or the child of a castle servant,* Ruan thought. *And very poor by the looks of her.*

Ruan let his sword drop back into its sheath and shifted back so he could watch the prophet. Torcull was still a threat.

"I…I was on my way to the kitchens…the ovens need to be stoked up for the day… Your…Your Holiness." The voice of the terrified child shook and stuttered.

Ruan could see the scowl on Torcull's face. "Never call me that!" the prophet spat at the shaking child.

Nearly in tears, the child whimpered. "I…am…sorry, Your…my…lord?"

Torcull seemed to dislike that title only slightly less. "Are you alone?" he demanded.

"Yes…my…my…lord."

The scowl on Torcull's face deepened as if for some reason he doubted her. "Never tell a soul you saw me here."

"I won't…I…promise."

"You better keep that promise, child, or you will wish that you had never been."

Strangely, the girl almost smiled at that, but Torcull did not seem to notice. Abruptly the prophet spun on his heels and stalked off back down the hallway, mumbling something under his breath, then he disappeared as he was swallowed up by the shadows.

Though the Dark Prophet was gone, Ruan remained crouching just inside the stockroom. The girl was still out there. He could not hear her, yet he knew she was still out there standing— waiting. He did not seriously think she was a threat, but it would be best for the girl if she did not see him. She already had seen too much for her own good.

Quick as the wind, the stockroom door was pulled open. Taken unaware, Ruan gasped.

The dark-haired servant girl stood looking down at the crouching lord. She had large, sad eyes.

"You are Lord Deuchar, aren't you?" she asked as if she already knew the answer, and she no longer sounded scared. She stared down at Ruan as a mother would after finding her son hiding in the broom closet to avoid doing his chores.

Ruan jumped to his feet. "Do I know you?"

"Yes and no, but I do know you."

"You look familiar in some way." Her face, her eyes, they all reminded him of somebody, but he could not quite figure it out. "Are you a servant of the palace?"

The girl smiled a smile that was both happy and sad, and she looked wise beyond her years. Ruan felt both sad and happy too, though, he could not say why.

"I am one who never was," she gave as an answer. "I have watched you for a long time. But this is the first time we have spoken."

Ruan frowned. *That isn't an answer.* "What is that supposed to mean? 'One who never was'?"

She was silent for a moment, then ignoring his question she went on, "Lord Ruan of Keloran you have very little time left. You must leave this city, but do what you are here to do. My advice is to do it fast and make your escape quickly."

"What are you talking about?"

"It is important that you remember, Ruan, that you are linked to the High King. In time, he will call for you. When he does you must go to him."

"That does not make any sense. Please tell me who are you and why are you here."

"Remember, Ruan, when the king calls, go to him. I can say no more." Before Ruan could say another word, the girl quickly closed the door on him.

Stunned momentarily, Ruan reopened the door. The strange child was gone. She had simply vanished. Hesitating, the lord considered whether he should chase after the mysterious child or not. He decided not to. He was not at all sure he would be able to find her, and he did not wish to consider what that might mean.

She saved my life. A child? Was she a child? Ruan turned to the door across the hall. It was the door that Torcull had just come out of. "Do what you are here to do" the words of the girl echoed in his head. He put his ear to the door. *I'm linked to Jerran!? He is the one I am trying to escape from!* Ruan could hear nothing. *I have broken my oath to the king. If he calls me, I will not be going anywhere. Blast it girl. Who are you, and why do I feel that she's the adult, and I'm the child?* Ruan tried to push the thoughts of the girl from his mind. The child made little sense. However, she had been right about one thing—he had very little time.

He tried the door. It was locked, but the door was poorly constructed. Taking out a long knife that Ruan kept in his boot, the bearded lord quickly pried open the door. Torcull would know someone had broken in, but by then Ruan hoped to be far away.

Ruan found his flint. With a quick jerk of his hand, he lit the wick of his brass lantern he had been carrying. The flame flickered once before a small flame firmly caught to the wick.

Ruan let the light spread across the room.

"A servant's room?" Ruan said in a whisper. He had not expected to find a servant's room. His eyes drifted across the room looking for what Torcull would have come here for. Like most servant's quarters, the room was small with only a few furnishings. Other than a narrow cot, a round throw rug, a small fireplace, and an old empty dresser, the room was empty. There was not even a chair to sit on. The room appeared to not have been used in a long time. A thick layer of dust lay everywhere. The fireplace looked as if it had been years since it was last used.

Strange, thought Ruan. Why had the Prophet come here, and why had he spent so much time here? Ruan searched the room three times, and still he found nothing.

"What could the Prophet have hidden in here?" He dropped down onto the cot. A cloud of dust rose. *Think, Ruan, He must have had a reason for being here. But what could he have been doing here for so long? I must be missing something.*

His eyes drifted across the room once more. At first, he noticed nothing out of the ordinary. Everything was covered in dust. Then he saw it. A smile crossed his face as his eyes fell upon the carpet. Everything in the room was covered with a thin layer of dust except for the carpet. Setting the lamp down, he grabbed hold of the rug and pulled it back.

"A trapdoor," Ruan breathed.

Coming to his feet, he grabbed the iron ring set in the floor and gave a firm tug. The trapdoor would not budge. *If Torcull can do it, so can I.* He planted a foot on either side of the trapdoor and snatched up the ring in both hands. Bracing himself, he took a deep breath, then heaved. Veins along his arms and legs stood out. Ruan groaned. Painfully and slowly, the trapdoor came up. The smell of old, stale air rushed up to meet him. Carefully, Ruan lowered the door off to one side. He wiped the sweat from his brow.

Torcull must be stronger than he looks to lift that trapdoor.

Breathing heavily, he retrieved the lantern from the dresser top. Holding the light over the black hole in the floor, Ruan stared down at a ladder that vanished into the blackness below. He leaned close and listened. He could hear nothing. He swung himself into the hole and climbed down into the dark. Not sure that the ancient-looking ladder could hold his weight, the lord slowly descended, carefully testing each rung before putting all his weight on it. It was a long process, but at last, he reached the bottom of the ladder. Letting go of the last rung, Ruan found himself standing on an uneven stone floor. Before Ruan was a vaulted tunnel that slanted deeper into the cold earth. Trying to pierce the darkness, he held the lantern above his head. The light helped create a small circle of light around him, but beyond that the darkness held firm.

Taking a deep breath, Ruan descended. The tunnel took him below the palace and deeper into the earth. The air was cold and moist. The only sound was his steady breathing and the slapping of his leather boots against the cold, wet stone floor. Not even mice or rats appeared to live in the tunnel. Ruan felt entirely alone and yet there was a strange feeling about this dark tunnel. Ruan could not help but feel that an evil lurked in the darkness ahead of him, and his small light was violating this dark nether world.

Deeper and deeper, Ruan went. Slowly the tunnel grew wider. Slipping on the wet floor, Ruan reached out to the wall to keep himself from falling. The wall was cold and slimy under his hand. Steadying himself, he wiped off his hand and carefully moved on.

Abruptly the tunnel came to a stop and opened into a round-shaped room. Ruan stood at the entrance. Like the tunnel, the room had a rounded arched ceiling that was made of roughly cut stone, though these walls were dry, and the room itself had only two features to it. Against the far wall was a desk, and in the center of the room was a well.

Ruan drew his sword. The sense of evil was stronger in this place. Slowly, he stepped forward into the room. With his head pivoting from side to side, he tried to see the whole room at once. As Ruan approached the chamber's center, he glanced over the stone wall of the well and saw that it was nearly filled to the top with foul stagnant water. He turned his nose at the smell. A thick layer of slimy green algae covered the water's surface. As the lord stared at the disgusting surface, a pocket of air rising from below broke the slimy surface with a splat. Startled, Ruan sucked in the cold, damp air of the chamber and took a quick step backward.

Still watching the surface, Ruan saw the algae begin to move. The green slime shimmered and started to flatten out into what looked like a large green mirror. Ruan gasped. Reflecting in the mirror was not his reflection, but that of four strangers who stared out at him. Ruan nearly jumped out of his skin, but being a stubborn Northerner, he refused to look away. It took him but a moment to realize that the faces could not see him but were created with some kind of magical illusion. Ruan took a step closer.

In the strange mirror, four young men, who were really only boys, stood on a wharf just outside a large city. Ruan didn't recognize the city, but he knew that it was not in Strigiol. *Maybe somewhere along the Iar Sea coast,* he thought while he watched their mouths moved as if they were talking. However, there was no sound. *If I were a Southerner, perhaps I could read their lips.*

His attention was drawn to the youth with a long thin face

and thick brown hair that was pulled back into a ponytail. The boy frowned. His deep piercing eyes stared out at the harbor. With his hands on his hips and his dark green cloak flapping in a brisk wind, the youth's face was drawn inwards, and he appeared deep in thought. Ruan decided he was their leader. Though he was a boy, and a weak-looking lad at that, he had the look of authority about him.

Despite your *peasant clothes, I would say you're a young lord. A Ceredigion, by his looks.* Ruan could not say what it was, but he felt as if he were being drawn towards the boy. It was not exactly a feeling, but the boy seemed to be in some type of trouble and Ruan found himself wishing there was a way he could help the long-faced youth.

Shaking off the strange sensation, Ruan shifted his gaze to the other faces. Waiting at the young lord's side stood three more boys. One of the youths had tight curly red hair. The redheaded boy was impatient and shifted from one foot to the other. A smile covered his round cheerful face, and he had a devious look about him as if he was always plotting something.

A redhead... Must be from Cluain, thought Ruan.

Scowling down at the redhead was a large muscular youth. The beginnings of a dirty blond beard wrapped about his square prominent chin. The scowl then turned into a laugh, and he playfully gave the redheaded boy a shove that nearly sent the Cluain boy off the wharf's edge. The big youth reminded Ruan of himself. He could easily be from Northern Strigiol or Galway, however with his dark blond hair, it was likely he was from Easland. Over his right shoulder protruded a leather-covered hilt of a large sword. Ruan watched as the big Easlander turned his eyes to the young Ceredigion lord. Now the big youth's stare took on an intensity, and there was a spark of pride that flashed in his eyes, but the spark quickly changed to one of concern.

The young lord's guard, Ruan decided.

The last boy was the strangest of all. This boy was shorter than the others and was as thin as a twig. The short, thin boy had long straight golden-blond hair that was almost white. Those eyes were not like any man Ruan had ever seen—sharp, narrow eyes that had a strange light-green color. He was dressed in off white cotton clothing and a cloak as green as his mysterious eyes hung behind his narrow shoulders. Hanging over one of those shoulders was a bow made of finely polished wood. The bizarre looking boy stared at the city as if it were the last place in all of Kambrya that he wanted to be. Ruan had never seen one, but if he was not mistaken the smallish boy had to be an elf.

An elf outside of the Green? This is a strange group indeed.

The images in the mirror flickered and began to shift and twist. When the mirror finally stopped moving, the four youths were gone. Another face now stared up at Ruan from the well. The face belonged to a tall, bronzed skinned figure with hair as black as night and eyes to match. The eyes were so dark they seemed to be absorbing the light around them. Never had Ruan seen such dark and intense eyes. They stared back at Ruan like shiny dark pits that hid the soul within. The black-eyed man had long coarse hair as black as his eyes. His hair was pulled back into a braid that was held together by a band of white gold. With his hair pulled back, it was easy to see his pointed ears.

"A black elf!" Ruan said in a hushed whisper. *A mountain elf! That's impossible! Black elves do not exist.*

The black elves were mythical creatures, also known as Yorns. The mythical Yorns were said to live deep in the Northern Drygan Mountains, and that the Yorns were as evil and as the dark overlord himself. *Black elves shouldn't exist. The Northern*

Drygan Mountains is troll and hobgoblin country. Trolls and hobgoblins did not like living with the other races, thus they had driven all other races out of the mountains thousands of years ago. The mountain creatures were a constant threat to Keloran and all of the north country. Ruan shook his head. *The mountain elves nor any other race could live in Troll and hobgoblin country. Black elves are just stories. Who is to say that anything in the mirror is real? Another one of your tricks, Torcull? I won't believe your mirror any more than your words.*

The elf in the mirror sat with his back against a large reddish gray granite boulder. Ruan was familiar with such rocks. These reddish-gray granite stones were common in the Northern Drygan Mountains.

High in the mountains, the black-eyed Yorn stared up at a cloudless blue sky where an eagle soared upon the mountain winds. As he watched the great bird, the elf oiled a long blade that lay across his lap. The sword was a long, deadly-looking weapon, forged from the same strange white metal that held the elf's braid. There seemed to be a union between the white blade and the emotionless face of the elf.

Never changing his flat, expressionless face, the elf shifted his position and gazed down the rocky slopes. Rising out of the rocky base of the mountain was a city surrounded by a large wall. The city was unlike any Ruan had ever seen. The buildings and houses were painted in bright, brilliant colors. Everywhere flags of different colors flapped in the strong wind. It was like looking down upon a rainbow.

Beyond the city was a small clearing, and beyond that was a vast forest that seemed to stretch out forever. Coming to his feet, the elf slid his long white blade inside a black sash. He started walking down a wooded trail. Without warning, the features of

222

the elf began to shift. Slowly they became distorted and grotesque. The elf seemed to be transforming into something else. At last, the elf's transformation was complete. In shock, Ruan pulled back from the well as he found himself gazing down at his own face. The reflection of his own face looked haunted and lost. That too faded away, and only the well remained. The visions seemed to have come to an end.

Rubbing his eyes, Ruan stepped back from the mysterious well. *A Ceredigion lord, an elf, a Yorn that somehow transformed into me... and a wonderfully colored city? What does it all mean? Are they related in some way? Fool! Do not let Torcull's tricks and lies distract you.*

He turned his back on the well and paced across the floor. The desk had nothing on it but a key and a single sheet of paper that looked as if it had been torn out of a book. Ruan turned the sheet over in his hands as if looking for something more.

The writing on the page was a rusty red color. Ruan held his lamp closer so he could read the writing. It was some kind of poem.

"*Blood thickens, blood thins, blood dries. All who are born must die.*

Two will stand in the place beyond the light. One of day and one of night.

Two will stand but who will die?

Blood thickens, blood thins, blood dries. All who are born must die.

From blood of old, he who was will be again.

Two in one and yet not whole. In the place beyond the light, only he may go.

Blood thickens, blood thins, blood dries. All who are born must die.

One without a king will find a king. Forced to leave, he will return.

An army will he bring.

Blood thickens, blood thins, blood dries. All who are born must die.

The one who was will have two guides. The sage who does not know.

The Seer, who cannot see.

Blood thickens, blood thins, blood dries. All who are born must die.

At his side, there will be three. The three will change, or all will die.

The three must stand then stand aside.

Blood thickens, blood thins, blood dries. All who are born must die.

Those who never were will show the way. Those who were and are

no more will sing the tune. Those who were never born will be the key.

Blood thickens, blood thins, blood dries. All who are born must die."

"Gibberish," Ruan said to himself. Yet he still folded the parchment and placed it into his leather pouch.

Feeling he had wasted enough time, Ruan turned to leave when he heard a sound. It was the first sound he had heard since coming down through the trap door. Ruan stood still. Again, he heard it. It sounded like a wounded animal. Trying to locate where the sound was coming from, Ruan slowly turned. The soft moaning was coming from behind a door. A small window with strong iron bars was fitted in the center of the door.

It was *some kind of cell. This must be some kind of dungeon. Why did I not notice this door before? It's like the door does not want to be noticed. A door can't hide...can it?*

As Ruan crossed the room towards the door, he felt a strange pulling and pushing sensation. It was as if he were being drawn towards the door and yet at the same time being told to stay away. The pushing sensation grew stronger. It was as if the door or something beyond the door was trying to keep him away. The closer he got, the stronger he wanted to look away. *It is just your nerves.* But Ruan sensed it was much more.

More of Torcull's magic, he realized. *But if you're hiding something in there, I need to find out what it is.* Ruan found it was growing harder to keep his focus on the door. He forced himself forward despite the growing fear of what Torcull was hiding. In a way, he did not want to know, and yet he also knew he must find out what it was. It took all his effort not to look away. It was like walking into a raging storm, but this storm was invisible. It took Ruan all he had just to move slowly forward against this invisible force.

Finally, he reached the door. His arms felt heavy. His heart was racing and sweat poured down his strained face. Ruan tried the door, but it was locked. With difficulty, he lifted his lamp. Straining from the effort, the northern lord let the lamplight spill into the cell. He spied through the square window. The cell was

225

dark and smelled of decay and mold. Ruan could see nothing but a pile of rags, but then he saw the rags move. He turned the light onto the corner. Whatever was there began whimpering and moaning. Lying huddled in the corner was an old man dressed in rags. Skinny as death, he looked like a skeleton. The bony man held a hand to his face and squirmed about as if the light was burning him.

"No!" the old man's whimpers formed into words. "Ask me what it is you want. Ask me something…anything, but please stop. I will…answer, I swear, just…ask what it is you want. I just want…the pain to stop! Please don't hurt me!"

Ruan nearly dropped his lantern. He knew this man. Skinnier and older by far, but still the same man. The cowering, whimpering shell of a man was none other than Conrad Cameron, the late king of Strigiol.

"In the name of the three gods!" Ruan exclaimed. "You are alive!"

Quickly Ruan raced across the round room to retrieve the key from the desk, but as he turned back to the door, he stopped. The door was gone. *Damn it! I know it was here!* He stared at the wall, but he could not find a sign of where the door he had stood at only moments ago. *I did not imagine it. It must be here. Doors don't just vanish.* Ruan knew it was Torcull's magic at work. Magic was keeping the door hidden from him. *You're not stopping me, Torcull.* Picking a random spot on the wall, Ruan placed his fingers on the smooth stone surface. *I cannot see the door, but maybe I can feel it.* Ruan slowly started walking, while dragging his hand across the wall. All the way around the room, he gently dragged his fingertips across the wall. As Ruan felt the wooden surface of the door, he came to a stop. Once he could feel the door, the door itself snapped back into view. It was now right in front of him, with his outstretched hand resting on the thin wooden surface. Ruan had broken the spell through a simple touch. He smiled to himself. *By the three gods, it was hidden by an illusion.* Once more he gazed through the window.

"He is alive!" he breathed, still only half believing what his eyes were telling him.

Once more the magical force assailed him. It tried to turn him from the door, but this time, he was already at the door and did not have to strain to reach it. Slipping the key into the lock, he turned it and with a click the door swung open. The man who was once king cowered in the corner, trying to melt into the cold stone wall. "No! Oh please, say something, ask something. Don't hurt me. I can't take it anymore!"

Ruan entered the room, and as he did so the force that assailed him suddenly vanished. The spell was meant to keep unwanted visitors away, but once inside the spell seemed to have been broken.

Slowly, Ruan crouched beside the old man. He smelled like overly ripe fruit and he was covered in dirt and grim. "Your Majesty," Ruan whispered softly, "I will not hurt you. It's me, Ruan."

"No more hurt. Oh please!"

"Your Majesty?" *He's gone mad. How could he stay sane down here with Torcull torturing him, and for no apparent reason?* "I will not hurt you." *Torcull will pay for this!* "I am going to take you away from here."

"You're not him?' The king looked puzzled, then suddenly turned to one of fear. "No! You must go!" There was panic in his voice. "He will come. He always comes…and the pain. He will hurt me for talking to you. He'll hurt you too! You must leave now!"

"He will hurt you no more. Not anymore, Your Majesty. I give my word."

"Why do you call me Majesty?" The panic in his voice was gone, but the madness in his eyes remained.

"You are my king," Ruan told him.

"Ha!" he howled. "King you call me? You are crazy, young man. Ha-ha! Crazier than I, you are. Ha! Ha-ha-ha!…" the king burst into loud hysterical laughter.

After a time, Ruan quieted him down. Sadly, Ruan gazed down at the king. *He was once a great man, and now Torcull has turned you into this. He will pay.* "We must leave, your…" Ruan cut himself off. Conrad had forgotten who he was. Torcull's sadistic torturing had destroyed the king's memory.

The king looked up at Ruan. "Do I know you? You look…familiar."

"My name is Ruan."

"Ruan?" the old man repeated. "I do not recall that name…wait… Yes, I sometimes dream of a man named Ruan. We fought together once…I think. We won great battles together. Didn't we?"

"That was my father. You and he were good friends. I'm named after him."

"Friends? No, it was a dream. I dream a lot, you know. Maybe you are a dream, yes? Once I dreamt I was a king. Ha! Me a king! I am but an old man, you know." His head cocked to one side. "Do you know me?"

"Yes, you are the...your name is Conrad."

The man smiled at that. "Conrad," he said as if he had never heard it before in his life. "I like that. It is a better name than Ruan. Don't you think?"

"Yes, your…Conrad. But come, we must go. Here, let me

help you stand."

With Ruan's help, Conrad slowly came to his feet. "You won't let him hurt me? You...you promise? You said you promised."

"Yes, Conrad, I promise. Please, we must go now." Supporting the king, Ruan guided the man out into the round room.

"Would you have tea with me, young man? I do love tea. Do I know you?"

"I am Ruan, and yes, I will have tea with you Conrad, but first let us get you out of here.

Okay?"

"That is a good idea, I think. I do love tea. It is excellent with honey. Ruan, you say?"

"Yes, Ruan."

"That sounds familiar. Sometimes I dream about a man named Ruan. Are you him?"

CHAPTER FIFTEEN

Standing on the harbor wharf of Aonach, Elwin stared out over the harbor. His dark green cloak blew behind him as a stiff breeze was blowing in from the Iar Sea. He had safely made it out of Port Murray, but not out of danger. Aonach was the capital city of Cluain and the weak-willed king of Cluain had caved to the power of Jerran. Cluain was now in the hands of King Jerran and Strigiol, and that meant he was in a land that was under the control of Torcull. Slowly, Elwin became vaguely aware that Pallas was saying something. Pallas was once more ribbing Colin over something. Pallas seemed to enjoy bantering with the big youth, particularly at the most inappropriate moments. *Some stress management*, thought Elwin. It was a habit they had both picked up as children. Perhaps it reminded them of better times and kept their hope alive, a hope that those times could come again. However, this time, Pallas' wit nearly got him tossed into the harbor's cold water. Elwin gave their horseplay little attention; he had other things on his mind right now, such as how to get in and out of the city. He wanted to do it as quickly as possible, without drawing attention to themselves. If it were possible, Elwin would have avoided the city altogether, but the road to Aleash would take a good two weeks of hard riding, and they need both supplies and horses.

Having arrived safely at Aonach, Jon had said his goodbyes and hurried off to find a buyer for his cargo. The storms that had raged over Reidh had brought a temporary halt to the sea trade. With his cargo of whitefish and Reidhen wool, Jon would make a good profit.

Unlike Reidh, spring had already arrived in Aonach and summer was quickly approaching. Sinking towards the horizon, the sun was still a dazzling bright yellow ball of fire and the spring afternoon was still quite warm. All along the crowded wharf, the pungent odor of fish permeated the air. The fishy smell mixed with the strong scent of sweat, tar, and rotting seaweed created an unpleasant odor. Those who lived here had grown accustomed to the offending smells and hardly noticed them. For foreigners, Aonach's harbor was more pleasant to see than to smell, yet it was hard to have one without the other.

Rocking at their moorings, ships from all over Kambrya filled the harbor, each waiting for its turn along the wharf to load or unload its cargo. The wharf itself was alive with activities. Sailors sauntered to and from the city, vendors cried out, and buyers and traders squabbled over prices. Aonach was on the trade routes of both sea and land, and thus was a thriving, prospering city, yet there was something wrong in Aonach. One could almost feel it in the air: Aonach was an occupied city. Tension and fear were visible upon every face.

Feeling the dark mood around him, Elwin stopped and stared at a large square rigger ship that was tied up to the wharf. Golden skinned sailors were hard at work. Sweating under the hot sun, the sailors rolled barrels down the square rigger's gangplank. A frown crossed Elwin's face. The flag flying off the ship's transom had a black eagle blazoned upon a field of white. The flag was that of the Strigiol, and every ship in the harbor flew the flag. Even over the city gates the white and black flag snapped and twisted in the wind. All of Kambrya seemed to be flying the black eagle.

Following Elwin's gaze, Colin stepped in close. "It is not wise to stare." Unlike Elwin, Colin had not been isolated in Reidh the past few years. "It flies everywhere," he went on, keeping his voice low. "And the Severed Head have temples and guards in every city; they do not take kindly to malcontents. If they suspect you are up to something, they may very well take you to the temple for questioning. You don't want to be there. Not everyone who enters the temples comes back out again."

As if the Severed Head could hear Colin, one of the guardsmen suddenly appeared. With his head held high, the guard came striding down the wharf, falling back out of his way, the crowd fell silent. The guardsman had an arrogant saunter to his step and seemed to be enjoying the effect he had on people. In his finely polished breastplate and black coat, his eyes drifted across the crowd. Painted upon his right breast, he proudly wore the red flame of the Severed Head. In mid-stride, he stopped and stared at a vendor. Patently the guardsman of the Severed Head waited until the vendor saw him and briefly met his eyes. The vendor began to sweat and quickly looked the other way. A thin smile crossed the guard's face. Satisfied, the guard let his eyes drift over the crowd once more, looking for his next victim.

Elwin had never seen a temple guardsman before, but there could be no doubt this man was one. Quickly, Elwin looked away from the flag, but not before the guard had noticed him. The man stared at him with intense and accusing eyes. A dark frown upon the man's face let prince know he was in trouble. Attempting to put distance between himself and his friends, Elwin took several steps towards the tall ship that was tied up along the wharf.

Pallas tried to follow, but Colin, seeing what Elwin was trying to do, stopped Pallas with a quick jerk. He pulled Pallas close and whispered. "Stay here. The guard will think Elwin is alone. If that guardsman makes any trouble, we'll have the element of surprise. Try to look natural but be ready." Sitting on a barrel, Aidan pulled his bow from his back. Slowly, he started casually oiling its wood. An arrow lay close by.

The guardsman stepped in front of Elwin and placed his hands upon his hips. "What are you looking at?" he demanded.

Trying to appear surprised, Elwin let his mouth drop open, and his eyes widen. "Who? Me?"

"No, I'm talking to myself," the guard replied with heavy sarcasm. "Of course, I mean you, boy! I don't see no other lowlife scum around here... Speak up, or do I need to take you to the temple for questioning?"

"The temple?! No... I mean... I wasn't doin' nothin'. Just admirin' the ship is all." Elwin tried to sound like the country boys he had heard in Reidh, though he was not nearly as good as Pallas, yet here away from the county it just might work.

"Do you disapprove of the High King's flag, boy?"

Elwin fringed a horrified look, "Good heavens, No! I am truly loyal...to me bones, I am."

"That's what all you troublemakers say. Maybe you're one of those renegades."

"Renegade?"

The guard shook his head and chuckled. "No, I don't think you are a renegade. A skinny boy like you? Even the renegades can do better than that."

"I am the cabin boy aboard the Falcon." Elwin remembered seeing a schooner by that name when they had entered the harbor.

"A cabin boy, aye. Where are you from? You don't sound as if you are a native."

"I be from Lowford in Reidh county. Ever been there?"

"Hardly. Having to patrol this stinking wharf is bad enough. So, you are a country boy coming to the big city, aye?"

"Yes, me lord."

The guard smiled at the title. "Well, get on with you. You can't just stand around here gawking."

Elwin gave a deep bow. "Of course...me lord." Quickly he backed away and moved into the crowd.

"Good act," said Pallas, catching up to Elwin. "I couldn't have done better myself. Well, maybe a little better. That accent was awful! Good thing he's never been to Reidh." Elwin sighed.

It was only a short walk from the harbor to the city gates. Aonach's double arched gates were tall and strong, built to withstand a long, drawn out siege. Still hours before sunset, the city gates stood open. Long lines of people and wagons were trying to make their way in or out of the city. On either side of the gates, two guardsmen stood watch. For the most part, they just kept the people moving along, trying to maintain the gate from getting congested.

The two guard's breastplates shimmered in the afternoon sun. Unlike the guard on the wharf, these men had dark green uniforms under their armor that billowed out at the sleeves. On their chests was an emblem of a white swan rising out of a chalice, which meant that they were city guardsmen. After a short wait, Elwin and his friends approached the gate leading into the city. A dark-haired city guardsman frowned and pointed at Aidan out to his fellow guard. The other guard's eyes narrowed as he watched Aidan suspiciously. This far south, elves were almost considered myths. Aidan's pointed ears were hidden under his long blond hair, but there was no hiding his facial features. His narrow face and slightly slanted green eyes gave him away. It was obvious that Aidan was different. After a long, suspenseful pause, the second guard gave a shrug and the first waved them on. "Keep moving," he ordered.

Once past the suspicious eyes of the guards, Aidan pulled his hood up over his head. "I don't like cities."

"We better find an inn," stated Pallas. "Aidan is going to

stand out and attract attention."

Elwin nodded. He too wanted to be out of sight. Dressed in his dark green cloak and a peasant cotton shirt, he looked more like a shepherd than a prince. Dressed so un-lordly, it was unlikely that anyone would recognize him as the Prince of Ceredigion, but there was no point taking any risks. "Do you know of an inn, Pallas?"

Pallas gave a noncommittal shrug. "I've only been here once, and that was a long time ago. We stayed with the king in his castle." He pointed to the inner city where a single tower could be seen over the rooftops. "And of course, father's guards were always making sure I did not wander off and enjoy myself, or some other awful thing like that."

"I do not think the king's castle is an option this time," said Colin.

Elwin looked up. Above the tower crenellations, the black and white flag of Strigiol could easily be seen flying above the flag of Cluain.

"Agreed," said Elwin.

Once through the harbor gate and away from the ocean breezes, the air had become still, and the temperature rose. Aidan let his light green hood drop off the back of his head. He loosened his shirt throngs. People were staring at him anyway.

A hooded man in this hot weather made Aidan stand out as much as his outlandish features. "I do not care where we stay, as long it's out of the sun, and away from all these staring humans. You would think they have never seen an elf before."

Pallas smiled, "They haven't. To them, you are a myth."

"A myth?! Never! Well if I am a myth, then I am a hot one in need of a cold bath. Can't we hurry? I think I'm beginning to melt."

Despite that none of them had ever been alone in the city, finding an inn had not proven to be difficult. Aonach was filled with inns and taverns. Elwin chose a small inn named the Silver Thorn. The inn had only two floors and appeared to be well kept. Compared with some of the inns they had passed closer to the harbor, the Silver Thorn seemed calm and had an almost homey appearance to it.

The innkeeper was a muscular heavyset man. He stood behind the bar like a lord before his court. Around his waist was a spotless clean apron. As the four youths entered, the keep eyed them. His tight angular face gave way to a wry smile that verged on open laughter.

"Farmers with swords," the keep laughed. "And a short boy with a big bow. I have seen your type before. Going to join the army, aye? Well, I have been around and seen enough of your kind to know you don't have any money. And times are hard. So be off with you. I can't give out any more charity, and I don't need any more kitchen help. Take old Ned's advice and go home. This is no place for you, and there is no more room in this world for four more country boys dreaming of adventure. Go home, this adventure of yours will only lead to some early graves and grieving mothers."

"We need a room, not a lecture," Elwin stated flatly.

Ned smiled. "Don't misunderstand my words, young man. They mean you more good than harm. The world has grown dangerous, it has. Ned here, that's me of course, has seen a thing or two in his day. Take my advice and go home." Then a strange sadness came into his eyes. "Dreamers like you four are rare and wonderful. Go home before this cruel world crushes it out of you. Go before it is too late."

With an unblinking stare, Elwin met Ned's eyes. "How

much for a room?"

The keep frowned and shook his head. "For the four of you? Eight coppers. More than you four could possibly..." Elwin reached into his pouch and produced the required coins.

"We need a room for the night and a bath."

The keep's frown deepened, but he scooped up the coins all the same then tossed Elwin a key. "The room is up the stairs and at the back. It's number 4. I'll have some extra cots brought up later, and there's a bath at the far end of the hall."

--

Elwin threw his pack on the bed. He sat down and dug out a piece of cheese and bit into it. "That keep irritates me."

"What does it matter?" asked Aidan. "We got a room for the night. Isn't that what really matters?"

"I don't know. I guess," replied Elwin. "It is just that he reminds me of someone...and I don't like being treated like a child."

Aidan replied with a shrug.

"Now what?" asked Colin. He walked over to the window and closed the curtains.

Elwin took a deep breath. Aidan was right—the innkeep did not matter. Still, the man reminded him of someone. He looked up. "Sorry. What did you say?"

"Now that we are here, what do we do next?"

Elwin took off his dark green cloak and laid it over his pack. "I guess we should buy supplies and horses."

"Do we have money for horses?" asked Pallas.

Elwin nodded. "I think so. Besides, it's a long walk to Aleash."

"Then let's go and get what we need," said Colin. "The sooner we get moving, the sooner we will get out of this city."

"I agree," said Aidan. "The sooner we are out of this city, the better. Tomorrow morning won't be soon enough for me."

"Not so fast." Elwin came to his feet. "We can't all go." Being in charge felt very uncomfortable. His whole life, others had chosen what was best for him. Now he had to make the decisions. He could feel their eyes watching him. He began to pace.

"Colin and Pallas will have to go out and buy what we need. Aidan and I better stay here, and out of sight." He stopped pacing and tossed Colin a small round bag of money. "Use that sparingly. That's all we have. We don't have enough to waste. While you're out there, find out what you can about the road to Aleash. And Colin, please keep Pallas out of trouble."

--

Colin leaned heavily onto the table. He was in a sour mood. "Elwin said nothing about stopping at every tavern we pass. We are supposed to be getting supplies and horses."

"We also need information," Pallas stated. "And taverns are the best place to pick that up."

"I'm supposed to be keeping you out of trouble."

Pallas smiled and threw up his hands. "What trouble?"

"Trouble follows you like the plague! If there is any to be had, it will find you. And taverns are the best place to find that too."

"Stop worrying. You sound like my mother." Pallas signaled the barkeep.

"Who has a lot more sense than you," added in Colin. "If

you had your mother's good sense, I would not have to worry."

Pallas only smiled at his friend as the barkeep came over to the table. "What can I do for you two?" Unlike Ned from the Silver Thorn, the apron around this man's waist was stained and greasy.

This was a harbor side tavern, and would typically be filled with unsavory patrons, but today the place was empty except for themselves and a table near the door where five men sat quietly talking with their heads close together.

"Ale," ordered Pallas.

"Nothing for me," grumbled Colin.

A few moments later the keep returned with Pallas' drink. "Anything else?"

"Some information. We have just arrived in town." Pallas took a long drink from the foam-covered mug. "Good ale. Reidhen I would say."

The barkeep smiled, "It's from last year's supply. Some big storm down south has been making it hard to come by."

Pallas nodded. "As I was saying, we are new to Aonach and my master, who is a carpet merchant, has just arrived by sea with cargo. We need to buy some horses and a wagon to take his carpets inland. He has sent me out to find where the nearest stables might be, one that won't rob him blind. My master is a good man, but not a rich one."

"Good luck to 'ya. Horses are scarcer than Reidhen ale. The Strigiol army has confiscated just about every available mount. Rumor has it that the High King will attack Mythra before the end of the summer, and he is building up the cavalry."

Colin looked up. "We have been to sea for some time. One must travel far to the south to the free cities to purchase fine imperial carpets. What other news is there?"

"Biggest news is the warrant."

"Warrant?" both Pallas and Colin asked at the same time.

"A thousand gold sovereigns for the man who can deliver the Prince of Ceredigion."

Colin's eyes widened, and Pallas gave a long whistle. "Big money! What has he done?"

From behind them came a deep rumbling laugh. Both Pallas and Colin turned to see a dark man standing behind them. He was one of the men who had been sitting by the door.

Snatching up the coins Pallas left on the table, the barkeep frowned at the man. "I have things to do," he mumbled and hurried off towards the kitchen.

Ignoring the barkeep's reaction, the dark-skinned man eyed Colin and Pallas. He adjusted the eye patch that he wore over his left eye. Hanging from his left side was a long, deadly looking blade, and on his right, a short knife with an elaborately carved ivory handle.

The man appeared capable of handling both. With the grace of a will trained dancer, he came to his feet and crossed the room. He walked with such a light step, he almost seemed to glide across the room. "You must have been at sea for some time if you don't know about the renegade prince."

Colin did not like the sound or the looks of this one-eyed man. "We have indeed. So, what has this Prince of Ceredigion done?"

"Done? He refuses to recognize the High King for one thing. And for another, the outlaw prince is behind the recent increase in the Renegade's activities, or so the temple officials are saying. Just yesterday there was a raid on a caravan only a few miles west of the city. The Renegades are getting bolder by the day."

"They're probably just rumors," said Pallas. "Why would a

Ceredigion prince be in Cluain?"

The one-eyed man nodded. "You're probably right. Yet the temple itself posted the warrant just two days ago. It is not like them to react to rumors. Then again, this prince might be in Mythra, the Free Cities, the Empire, or even hiding in Ceredigion like a scared rabbit. They say he is just a boy and a sickly boy at that. But like you said, it is probably just a rumor, but the temple wants him, and wants him badly."

"A thousand gold sovereigns," uttered Pallas. "That's a good price, even for a prince."

Pulling out a chair, the man swung the chair backward and dropped down into it. Setting his clay mug onto the worn wooden table, he leaned forward. "It is at that, lad, it is at that. I'd guess you'd take a share in that, would 'ya not? Even a third of that type of coin would set you up for a long time. You could even become your own trading master. Yep, that kind of money could change your life."

Watching the man over the brim of his mug, Pallas took another sip of his drink. "Sure would. You could buy a small kingdom with that kind of money or at least a county."

The man laughed and slapped Pallas on his back. "None are for sale, lad. All kingdoms, as well as counties, belong to High King Jerran now, 'ya know."

The man took a long swig from his own mug. With the back of his hand, he wiped the foam from his thick mustache. "You can call me Patch, everyone else does." He tapped the black patch that was over his eye. "A suiting name, don't you think? I don't even remember my given name. Let me buy you two a drink."

"No thanks." Colin shook his head and stood up. "We can't stay."

"Come on. What's one drink?" He then nodded towards his

companions who were now standing near the doorway, their thick muscular arms crossed across their broad chests. Patch's four friends were staring at them with a strange and rather disturbing intensity. "You see my friends over there think you are Renegades. I said you were not. Just a couple of boys having a drink, I told them. But with you rushing off like this, it makes me wonder. You seem nervous. Is something wrong? Maybe I can help. I can be a mighty good friend."

Sensing the danger they were in, Colin dragged Pallas up out of his chair. "Nothing's wrong. We just have to be going. It was a pleasure to have met you, Patch."

"Sit down." Patch's voice took on a cold tone to it. It sounded more like an order than a request.

Colin gave a shrug. "Can't. Our father needs us back at the farm. We only stopped in to wet our throats."

Patch looked up, a wry smile crossed his hardened face. "I thought you two worked for a carpet merchant?"

Colin shrugged again. "We do," Colin replied trying to think quickly. "Once we get some horses, we're be headed home. We have been gone a long time, and it is time my brother and I were getting back." He doubted that was going to cover up his mistake. Colin gave Pallas a shove towards the door.

"Brothers?" Pallas whispered as Colin guided him across the room. "A big clumsy blond and a handsome redhead? It seems unlikely to me."

Colin gave him another shove. "Shut up and keep moving. I think we're in trouble."

Patch was suddenly on his feet. "Hold those two!" he shouted. With one quick, graceful move, his sword was suddenly in his hand. He held the long blade with the ease of a master swordsman.

The four men near the doorway also drew their swords. With cruel smiles, they stepped out in front of Pallas and Colin.

"Nothing personal, lads," Patch said with his ever-smiling face, "but there's a reward for Renegades, even for young ones. And a man has to make a living, ya know. Now be good lads and come along. You're worth more to me alive than dead."

"We are not Renegades!" Pallas insisted.

Patch's smile broadened, and he shrugged. "Doesn't really matter, as long as the black ones think you are. And it's clear you're hiding something. Besides, if you are telling the truth, you will be put to a few questions then sent on your way. And I will already be gone with my reward. In the end, nobody gets hurt."

Just then there was a sudden bang. One of the men by the door fell with a thud. Where the man had been, the barkeep now stood. In his hand, the barkeep was holding a large cast iron frying pan. "No one's being taken anywhere," he announced. "Not in my tavern they're not!"

Surprised, the man next to the keep hesitated, then raised his sword to strike him down, but he had waited a moment too long. Not waiting to draw his sword, Pallas leaped forward. Throwing his weight forward, Pallas hit one of the men in the side with his lowered shoulder. At the same time, he brought his fist up into his midsection.

With a loud groan, the man hit the wall. Before the sword-wielding man could recover from Pallas' attack, the keep hit the next man over the skull with his pan like a club. With a thud, the man slipped to the floor as Pallas stepped back. The man's eyes rolled back into his head, and his sword fell from his hand.

Still moving, Pallas spun. Drawing his sword, he ducked. The other two men were on them. Lifting his blade, Pallas was just in time to parry the first blow that was aimed at his head.

The barkeep began to furiously swing his frying pan, trying to keep the other armed man at bay. Patch cursed at his men's slow reaction. Then like a stalking cat, he turned and approached Colin. He had a sword in one hand and a knife in the other. From above his shoulder, the big youth slid his long sword out of its sheath. Balancing the blade before him, he waited for Patch to attack. He did not have to wait for long. Feinting with the knife, Patch thrust forward with his sword and Colin parried. Patch circled, and drew his knife upwards, trying to get under his guard, but again the youth successfully parried the attack. Colin was good with a sword. He had a natural born talent where weapons had always come easily to him.

But this was different.

This time, he was not practicing, and these swords were not made of wood. Never before had Colin fought a man intent on killing him. Sweat ran freely down his face, as he nervously backed away from the one-eyed man.

Colin parried one way then stepped the other way, letting Patch's blade harmlessly pass by him.

Patch smiled and stepped back. "You have training, lad. Not often do I get a real challenge, but can you do more than defend yourself?"

Colin remained silent. He was not a sword master, but even a novice knows enough not to talk unless one thinks it will distract his opponent. Patch did not seem the type to be distracted. Crouching, his sword lightly held in his hand, Colin watched as Patch dropped his guard. On purpose, he was leaving himself open.

"Come on, Lad. let's see what you can do. Now's your chance."

Colin lashed out.

With lightning fast reflexes, Patch turned aside the attack. He laughed. "You'll have to do better than that, lad!"

Grabbing the leg of a table, Colin threw it at Patch, then lunged forward. Quickly sidestepping the table, Patch gave a quick twist of his knife, deflecting Colin's attack, then slashed with his own sword. A thin line of blood trickled down Colin's left shoulder.

"Innovative, lad, but hardly the result you were looking for."

Colin drew back. Patch was the better swordsman, and he knew it.

Patch slashed down, then up, then feinted and thrust. He would attack with his sword, then with his knife, never letting himself fall into a pattern, and never relenting. He was always on the offensive. Colin tried to hold his ground, but each time Patch forced him backward with a torrent of lightning fast strokes. He parried, ducked, and dodged each attack, struggling to avoid the razor sharp blades that were coming ever closer. Attempting to use his sword's longer reach to his advantage, He managed to keep Patch away, but only barely. He could do nothing to stop him from coming again. Colin knew he was in trouble. Sooner or later he would grow tired, and he would falter and make a mistake. And this sword master would finish him. Gasping for air, Colin was already bleeding from three separate wounds. None of the injuries were serious, but time was running out.

"Give in lad," Patch said. "You can't win. Do you want to die?"

Colin did not answer. Behind him, he could hear Pallas struggling with his own opponent. Pallas was Colin's only hope. If Pallas could finish off his man, then they might still have a chance. However, Pallas was not having any more luck than Colin. He too was fighting for his life, and the barkeep had been forced back against a wall and was doing no better.

"Come, now... Give it up," Patch said repeating himself.

Again, Colin gave no answer.

Patch cursed. "Damn it, lad! I don't want to kill you!"

Abruptly, the sounds of the battle behind Colin stopped. Lowering his sword, Patch stepped back. Fearing the worst, Colin risked a quick glance over his shoulder. A dozen more men had entered the tavern. They wore green coats under shiny breast plates; the city guardsmen. They stormed into the tavern and quickly overran Patch's two accomplices. Colin sighed in relief. Both Pallas and the barkeep were breathing hard, but they were alive.

The captain of the city guard stepped forward. "Patch!" A thin closed mouth smile touched his face. "So, we meet again!"

Patch returned the smile with one of his own and gave a long theatrical bow. "You remember. That is kind of you, Captain. It has been a long time."

"Your luck has run out. Hand over your sword."

Patch continued to smile. "I don't think so, Captain." He turned to Colin. "For a boy, you fight well. If you don't let that pride of yours kill you, you just might turn into a first-class swordsman."

"Patch!" snapped the captain. He singled his men to move forward. "Drop your sword!"

Patch raised his sword to his forehead and saluted Colin. "Until we meet again, lad." He then turned and made a dash across the room and away from the door that was blocked by the guardsmen.

"Stop him!" shouted the captain.

The guards surged forward, but they were too slow. Patch gracefully leaped to a tabletop then, with a mid-air twist of his body, burst out a window and into the street beyond.

"Bloody...!" exclaimed the captain. "After him! Do not let him escape again!" Four of the guardsmen gave chase.

The captain looked at Colin for the first time. "Are you hurt?"

"Nothing serious."

"You are either very good or very lucky. Patch is a rogue, a thief, and a master swordsman."

"Who was he?" asked Colin.

"He likes to call himself a bounty hunter. In truth, he is nothing more than a hired assassin, but he is a bloody good one. I wonder what he wanted with you boys." The captain's eyes narrowed. "Who are you? What did Patch want with you?"

"He thought we were renegades," Pallas said, joining them. His sword was back in its sheath. He looked tired but unhurt, "Whoever these renegades are."

"Renegades? You two? I think not. You look like an Easlander," he said to Colin. "And you have to be a native of Cluain. From the country, no doubt. Patch most likely was just trying to get you outside and rob you. He could not present anyone to the authorities without getting arrested himself. Strange, though, a Cluain and a Easlander together. Perhaps Patch thought the same. Who are you?" the Captain asked once more. "And what are you doing in Aleash with an assassin trying to kill you?"

"You said it yourself," Pallas pointed out. "He was trying to rob us."

The captain scratched his head in thought. "Maybe, but it is not like Patch to roll a couple farm boys. Now that I think of it, he must have seen an opportunity for a profit."

Just as Pallas was formulating a story to tell the captain, a soldier burst in through the door. He was limping and bleeding from several wounds. Leaning heavily on a table, the man addressed the captain. "Sir." He was breathing hard. "We have him cornered in an alley. But we need more men to take him."

"Blood and ashes! I won't lose him again!" The captain exclaimed, then he looked at Pallas, then at Colin. "I want you two out of the city before dawn. If I see you again, I'll put you both in chains. Understand? If Patch is after you, there's bound to be more looking for you, and I will not allow the streets bloodied up because one of you slept with some noble's daughter, or whatever it is you two did to put a price on your heads." Without waiting for an answer, the captain turned and leading the rest of his men rushed out of the tavern.

Pallas turned to the barkeep and shook his hand. "Thank you. You saved our lives."

"I run a business here," the barkeep said matter-of-factly, "and I can't make a profit if there is always fighting going on. This is a rough part of town, and I have a reputation to maintain."

"Still, we are in your debt," said Colin. He gave the barkeep a few coins. "I hope this helps to fix up your place." The barkeep took the money. "It wasn't your fault, but I doubt I'll be getting anything from that Patch fellow."

"Lucky thing the guardsmen came by when they did," added Pallas.

The barkeep smiled. "Luck has nothing to do with it, lads. Like I said, this is a rough part of town. I pay the guardsmen in free ale to stop by every hour." He shoved the coins into his apron. "I think it's a bit too rough here for you two. If I were you, I would be doing as the captain said, and be leaving the city."

Agreeing, the two youths thanked the barkeep once more and hurried out of the tavern.

Forgetting about the horses and supplies, the two rushed back towards the Silver Thorn. As they approached the Silver Thorn Inn, Colin hesitated.

Pallas looked up at Colin's concerned face. "What is it?" he asked.

"I'm not sure, but something is wrong." Colin looked up at the sky. "It's almost dark. I do not claim to be an expert on inns, but shouldn't it be a little noisy in there? And I don't see any lights."

Pallas frowned. "You're right. People should be wandering in, but the place looks empty."

Keeping a sharp eye open, they began moving down the street and towards the strangely dark and quiet inn. From the chimney, smoke slowly rose into the darkening sky. Somebody had to be inside.

"Boys! Over here!" a voice called softly. It came from across the street and from inside the inn's stable doors. "Hurry!"

Pallas drew his sword. "Who's there?" he demanded, trying to pierce the dark shadows within the small barn. The stable door stood halfway open. Pallas could just make out a pile of straw, but nothing more.

"It's me, Ned, the innkeep. Hurry! Please! You are in great danger!" Drawing his own sword, Colin carefully followed Pallas into the stable.

"Put those away," Ned whispered from behind the pile of straw. "It is not me you need to fear." Ned pointed across the street to his inn. "It's them." Colin and Pallas exchanged confused looks.

"Blast it all!" Ned cursed. "Get out of sight!"

Pallas shrugged, and they put away their swords. After partially closing the doors, the two boys joined Ned behind the pile of loosely stacked straw.

Using the pile of straw as a blind, they could see the inn across the street with no danger of being spotted themselves. "What is going on?" Colin asked.

Ned shushed him pointing towards the inn's doors. "Look."

The door to the inn opened, and a soldier dressed in a black uniform stepped out. Clasped about his neck was a small silver broach that was fastened to a long black cloak that just touched the tops of his black leather boots. The cloak was pulled back over his shoulders revealing a broad, well-formed chest. Upon his right breast was a red flame. His tanned face stood out against the black of his wardrobe. Standing before the inn, he looked up and down the street as if he was expecting someone.

"An officer from the Black Army," whispered Ned.

A moment later a black-robed priest joined the officer at the front of the door. He appeared to be mad, and the two quickly began to argue. The second figure was a head shorter than the first and his black robe fell just short of touching the inn's stoop. His head was shaved clean, and his cheeks were as red as the ruby that hung from his neck.

"A priest of the temple," Ned informed them in another whisper. "One of the Unholy Ones."

The three hiding figures laid flatter against the straw. The priests of the Severed Head practiced dark arts and deserved to be feared. They were the masters of the temples, where unspeakable acts were performed and untold suffering inflicted. The priest's souls might not be as tainted as the Red Monks, but none of the three wanted to be discovered by one of the Unholy Ones. Holding their breaths, the three kept still and listened.

"This is a waste of time," the officer insisted, his harsh voice carrying from across the street. "They are hiding somewhere, or have already quit the city."

"We have something they want!" replied the priest. His voice was growing louder. The officer did not seem to fear the priest and that maddened the black robed man. "But they will run and hide if they see you standing out here!"

"I'm telling you, they are not coming. We've already wasted two hours. There might not have even been anyone else, and we got what we really wanted and needed."

"Torcull himself said the boy would have three friends with him, so he will get the boy and his three companions."

"Perhaps your beloved prophet was wrong! Maybe there was only the elf."

"Our prophet," the priest emphasized. "Do not think you are not bound to him as we all are."

"Then our prophet is wrong!" the officer snapped.

"Wrong?" the priest almost laughed. "If he says there will be three, there will be three. He is never wrong!" The priest scowled up at the officer. "And I would advise you to think carefully before disobeying him. He has given you much, but what he has given he can also take back. The Dark Prophet is not a kind master to those who displease him."

The Unholy One then said something too quietly for those in the stable to hear. The officer's face paled. Triumphantly, the priest smiled wickedly. He then turned and went back inside. Composing himself again, the officer looked up and then down the street a few more times. Then he too vanished back inside. Quietly, Colin closed the stable door.

Standing up, Pallas looked at Ned. "What's going on here?"

"I could ask you the same thing." Ned lit a lamp. "Why is an officer of the Black Army and a Black Priest from the Temple looking for a few boys? What have you done? Who are you?"

"That doesn't matter now," answered Colin. "What happened to our friends?"

Ned nodded. "You don't have to tell me if you don't want to. But you're in some deep trouble. That is clear enough."

"And our friends?" Colin insisted.

Ned shook his head again. "I am afraid it is not good. The Black Ones came two hours ago. They just burst in and started searching the place. There are two dozen soldiers in there." He pointed in the direction of the inn. "And from what I could gather, they are waiting for you to return. The temple priest seemed fairly sure you would come looking for your friends, and it seems he was right. So anyway, when they stopped paying attention to me, I snuck out the back and came here to warn you."

"Thank you," Colin replied with a nod of his head. "You may have saved our lives. That seems to be happening a lot lately. But what about our friends? Did they escape?"

"I'm deeply sorry. I liked that boy, I truly did. He reminded me of myself when I was a young fool, but it happened so fast. I could do nothing for them, truly I could not."

Pallas paled. "We believe you. We only want to know what happened to our friends. Are they...are they dead?"

"If they're not, I fear they will be soon. They have been arrested and taken to the Temple. They are beyond your help. Come with me. I will take you to a place where you can hide for the night. The city gates are too heavily guarded for you to slip out tonight, and will be closed soon anyway. By now the whole city is looking for you two. Tomorrow we will think of something. I have friends that might be able to help you, but now we must go."

"Not before we get Elwin and Aidan out of the Temple," Pallas asserted.

"It is too late for them, boy... Elwin! The prince? Prince Elwin of Ceredigion?!" Ned looked shocked. His eyes were as wide as if someone had just unexpectedly slapped him across the face.

Colin gave Pallas a hard look, but it was too late. "Yes. He is the Prince of Ceredigion."

"In the name of the three gods! I should have known."

Avoiding Colin's angry look, Pallas opened the door a crack. "There is no one out there. We should get moving. Where is this temple? We have our friends to save."

CHAPTER SIXTEEN

Pulling on long oars, a dozen sailors propelled the lean riverboat against the gently moving current of the Clwyd River. Overhead, a large grayish-white sail filled with a warm breeze helped the boat move a little faster against the flow of the wide river. Keeping to the slower moving currents, the helmsman hugged the west bank of the river. The shoreline silently slipped by with a mixture of trees, freshly planted fields, and small farms.

Ruan stood at the stern of his boat. He found a certain calmness when he was on the water. The rhythmic sound of the creaking oars and the splashing of the water was almost hypnotic. He gazed off to the south. It had been almost a week since he had left Gildas. Off *Fish Hawk's* stern, the wide river stretched into the distance as Ruan searched the quiet waters. The past week had been quiet and uneventful. Ruan knew that he should be thankful for the past few days, but he wasn't. Things were changing in Strigiol. Once the river would have been busy with traffic, but now it was nearly deserted. Earlier that morning they had sailed past the small town of Crioch. Even there it seemed unusually quiet. As the boat approached the town, people vanished inside their homes, slamming their windows shut and locking their doors.

"Tomorrow," Ruan told himself, "tomorrow we will be home." Staring off to the south, Ruan found what he was looking for. He had been hoping that he would not find it, but the northern lord knew that he would. It was always there. Rising above the distant horizon, he saw a cloud of dust. *We have gained some more ground,* he thought, *But not enough. It will never be enough.*

Ruan knew that an army was chasing them up the river. The river boat was faster than any army could hope to match. Ruin had also set up rotating shifts at the oars so that day and night *Fish Hawk* made its way towards the north country. He would reach Keloran tomorrow, but what good would it do him? Ruan's boat was faster than an army, yet once he reached Keloran, there was nowhere else to run. He and those who were with him would be caught between the army and the mountains. Ruan figured that he would have a week or two before the army arrived, then there would be a siege. Ruan shook his head. He could not hope to hold out against the Strigiol army. There would be no allies coming to his aid. He was alone in his stance against the king and his prophet. Trying not to think of what the future would bring, he turned around, putting his back to the south and the troubles that pursued him. Looking across the boat's deck a young boy caught Ruan's eye. The young prince of Strigiol was slowly walking across the deck. Ruan followed him with his eyes. The child was enjoying his riverboat ride and seemed unaware of his situation. Ruan envied the child's ability to live for the day, but the prince's future was as bleak as Ruan's, and maybe worse.

The boy came up to the starboard side of the boat joining an old, bent and haggard looking man. Smiling, the prince looked up at the old man. Not noticing the boy, the old man stared with a vacant gaze as the shoreline slipped past.

Trying to get the old man's attention, the prince pulled on the man's gray cloak. "Sir?" The man looked down with haunted eyes.

"Are you my grandfather?" asked the prince. "I heard mother saying that you are."

He blinked. "Grandfather? I don't think so. I am Conrad. That is what I have been told is my name. It is a good name, too. What is yours?"

"I am Horik." the boy smiled up at Conrad. To Horik,

255

Conrad was not the man driven crazy by Torcull, nor was he the king. To Horik, Conrad was the grandfather he had never known, or at least could not remember.

Conrad's eyes narrowed. "Jerran? Is that you? Where have you been? I have been looking all over for you!"

Horik looked confused. "No," he said, shaking his head. "I am Horik. Jerran is my father, the king."

Conrad frowned. "Jerran?" he repeated as if he had not heard the boy. "Why did you do it?"

"Jerran is not here," Horik insisted.

"Oh," sighed the old man. "You look like... Would you drink some tea with me?"

"I don't think mother would let me, but it was kind of you to ask."

"I like tea."

"Why do you look so sad?" asked Horik with the honesty of a child.

For a moment Conrad's eyes softened, and the haunted look upon his face faded.

"Horik?" he said after a moment's silence. "You are Horik?"

"Yes."

"So many lost years..." The man who was once king began to show through. A tear touched his wrinkled check. "Horik," he repeated to himself. "Yes, I am your grandfather. I remember now. Sometimes I do. It hurts to remember."

Horik smiled, but Conrad's mind was gone again. The king turned away. Once more he stared at the passing shoreline. Horik did not seem to mind. Smiling, he took his grandfather's hand and together they stood and watched the world slide by.

--

"What?!"

The boy before Torcull cowered. "The k...king wishes y...your immediate p...presence."

"Get out!" demanded Torcull. The boy turned, stumbling, as he ran for the door.

--

Pacing across the throne room, King Jerran mumbled angrily to himself as he waited for the prophet.

When Torcull arrived, he found the door open. Without announcing himself, he entered the throne room with long strides of an angry man. Closely followed by a pair of Black Priests of the Severed Head, Torcull held his hands clasped tightly behind his back. As he entered the room, he came to a quick stop that nearly caused the two black-robed priests to crash into his back. The temple priests quickly adjusted and flanked out to the sides of the Prophet as Torcull crossed his arms across his chest and stood scowling at the king who passed before the eagle throne.

Taking a deep breath, Torcull transformed himself into the image of tranquility and calm.

"Your Majesty," he called, his voice echoing in the spacious room.

Jerran looked up. "Oh. You are here." The king stopped his nervous pacing and turned to face the three black-robed men.

"You wished to see me?" Torcull's voice was soft, yet there was a controlled harshness to it. Then as an afterthought, he added, "Sire."

The king did not seem to notice the tension in the Prophet's voice. "Yes. I have had some disturbing news. A misunderstanding, I am sure. However, it has been reported to me that you have sent a part of my army north. Is that true?"

"Who told you that?"

Jerran sat down upon his throne. "I do not rely solely on you for my information. Tell me, Torcull, is it true?"

"Yes."

Jerran crossed his arms across his chest. "Then you did send them? Without asking me first?"

"I said I did," Torcull replied coolly. "It was necessary."

"Necessary!? It was necessary to act behind my back?"

"Not behind your back, sire, but in your best interest." Torcull took a step closer to the king. "It is my duty to see to your interests."

"And what interest do I have in the north? I already control the northern half of Kambrya."

"It is imperative that we capture Lord Ruan before he can cause any more trouble."

"What do you mean?" King Jerran looked down at the Prophet. "Ruan is here in the palace."

"No sire, he is not. The lord has quit the city and is fleeing to the north."

"Fleeing!" Jerran's voice grew louder. "From who? Me! That is ridiculous! He was not ordered to stay in the city. Ruan can come and go as he likes. What's going on here, Torcull? I am the king! Not you! I alone send out the army! If Ruan wishes to return to the north, then he may go with my blessings. I have lost too many friends already." Jerran finally noticed the priests, but just as quickly dismissed them from his mind. The king had grown used to seeing priests of the Severed Head accompanying the prophet. "What do you have to say for yourself, Torcull? What reason have you for going behind my back?"

"I needed to act quickly, sire. Ruan has done more than quit the capital. He has also kidnapped your wife and your son." Torcull left out that he also had the true king, Conrad with him. However, Jerran did not know the man had imprisoned and had been torturing his father. Jerran still believed his father had passed away of natural causes.

"What?" Jerran looked shocked, as he leaped out of the eagle throne.

"Ruan, your trusted friend, has kidnapped the queen and prince and has fled to the North. Already he has had a full day's head start. He will reach Keloran long before we can catch him. If we do not hurry, the whole North will rise up against you. But fear not my lord, I will stop him and bring your son safely home."

The king shook his head. "There must be some mistake." Jerran's paused, his anger was now replaced with confusion and sadness. *They have been gone for two days, and I hadn't noticed.* "Ruan would not harm Catriono or Horik."

"But he will, Your Majesty if he is not stopped. He will instigate a civil war. The land must be unified under a High King. It must! Only then will the prophecy be fulfilled."

"Prophecy?"

"Never mind. It is none of your concern. However, Ruan must be stopped. He is a traitor, and I plan to make an example of that one. And he has also stolen something of mine,... something that gave me pleasure, and I will have that back as well."

Jerran sat back down. "What are you talking about? There is still something wrong here, Torcull. Ruan a traitor? It's hard to believe. Ruan kidnapping my family? If I did not know you better, I would think you are hiding something from me."

"Believe me, Your majesty, he has betrayed you and betrayed the kingdom."

"It is not that I disbelieve you, Torcull, but there must be some misunderstanding. Ruan would not do this to me."

"You must believe it, Your majesty."

"No, I will not. I will not believe it until I see Ruan myself." Jerran looked down at the tiled floor. For a moment, he was silent then the king said, "I will go to Keloran myself. I will take my boat and catch up to the army. Then I will personally lead the army to the north." The king looked up, meeting the prophet's eyes. "Ruan will not fight me, and I will get to the truth."

"No! You will not! Sorry, Your majesty." Torcull gave a short bow. "I forget myself, but you cannot go to the north. You are needed here to guide the attack on Mythra. I have sent a Red Monk with five thousand of your men. That should be enough to contain Keloran. We will put an end to this traitor, and it will not slow down the attack of Mythra. The Black Army will be ready."

"You overstep yourself, Torcull. I know you mean well, but I am the king, and I will go to Keloran. Mythra can wait." Jerran started forward, slowly descending the stairs from the throne. "Call the steward. I need to prepare for my departure. If I hurry, I should be able to catch up with the army in a few days."

"No!" said Torcull with an uncharacteristic harsh tone. "The attack on Mythra cannot wait! It will not wait!"

Shocked, Jerran stopped halfway down the steps. "No? I said get the steward! Are you opposing me, Torcull?"

"If I must."

"I am your king!"

Torcull laughed, coming to a final decision. A decision he had long been waiting for, the fool king had become a liability that needed neutralizing. "You have never been a king. I am the true power. I rule all of Kambrya. You see, I no longer need you, Jerran. I need a High King to rule over Kambrya, but there are other ways. I can find a new High King. I've had enough of this; enough of you. You are becoming a nuisance to me. I do not have the time nor the desire to nursemaid you any longer! The three eyes of the Buachaille draw closer. The time is coming."

"What madness is this?"

"You are a fool. A fool that has outlived his usefulness. It is time you were put aside."

"Guards!" Jerran yelled. "Guards!"

Torcull gave a bitter laugh. "You have no guards. There is no one to hear you, except those who are loyal to me. As I said, I now rule Kambrya just as I rule this castle. I have ruled for some time, and now I will be your regent."

"You're mad! You cannot rule as regent unless I am..." A cold shiver ran down Jerran's spine. "In the name of the Three Gods, what have I done?" Jerran sank down to the steps, his head held in his shaking hands. "Ruan, forgive me. You were right."

Again, Torcull laughed. "There are no Three Gods. There is only Beli. And yes, Ruan was right. Only now that it is too late, you finally see the truth, but even now you see but a part of it. I would have made you a great king. But you are too weak for such greatness, so you will be put aside." Torcull turned to the priests. "Hold him!"

The two black cloaked priests stepped forward into the dim light and seized the king. Their grip was like cold steel. With no hesitation, they dragged the king to his feet and forced him back into the eagle throne. King Jerran struggled, but he could not break free.

"What are you doing?" He demanded. "Release me! I AM YOUR KING!"

Showing no emotions, the two priests ignored the king's orders. Jerran looked into their eyes. "Let me..!"

Horrified, he tried to recoil from them. He saw that where their eyes should have been were empty voids. Like lost souls, they stared into nothing.

Standing next to a table, Torcull lifted a silver vessel and smiled. "They serve me well. It is a shame that I cannot do the same to you. But to do so, one must give themselves freely to my master." He poured a dark red colored wine into a large pewter goblet. "I believe this was always your favorite vintage."

Slowly Torcull pulled a small leather pouch from inside of his robe, he then inserted two fingers and pulled out a pinch of fine green powder. Adding the powder to the wine, the prophet turned to face Jerran. "That should be enough. I would not be pleased if you were to die on me too soon. You still have a part to play."

Swirling the goblet, Torcull mixed in the powder, his cold blue eyes never left those of the king's. "You see, I need your death to be slow and to look natural. There are still some who are loyal to you. But your physicians will say there was nothing anyone could do. It is a shame that it must end this way. Until now, you have been ideal, but I always figured this day would come. I thought when it did, your son Horik could take your place, but Ruan has interfered with that. In the end, it will not matter. Soon I will have him back."

Taking his left hand, he grabbed hold of the dark red ruby that always hung around his neck. He held it over the goblet and spoke three strange alien sounding words. At once, the ruby began to glow and pulse like a beating heart. As the last word died on Torcull's mouth, a blood shaped teardrop fell from the ruby, and into the goblet. The wine-like concoction began to boil, as a black smoke rolled over the cup's lip.

"So, I must take other measures." Torcull smiled. "You can

understand that."

"This is madness, Torcull!" Jerran's eyes were wide with fear. "You cannot do this!"

Torcull smiled. "Of course, I can."

"I am your king!"

"You keep saying that. But I have a greater master, and he is calling me to him. He wishes to be free."

"Please, Torcull!"

"Drink it," ordered Torcull.

"I will not do any such thing!"

Torcull nodded to the priests.

Clutching a hand full of the king's hair, one of the priests yanked Jerran's head backward. The other priest held the king's nose closed. Forcing his mouth open, Torcull poured the bubbling liquid down his throat. The king coughed and sputtered, trying to spit out the liquid, yet in the end, the king drank the foul concoction.

Torcull stepped back. "It is done." The two priests let go of Jerran.

Jerran struggled to his feet, then fell back into the throne. He looked at Torcull. "Why...?" Things began to blur and spin, making his head hurt. "What have you done to me?" His throat felt sore, and his voice sounded hoarse.

Torcull smiled. "Go fetch the steward," he told one of the priests. "I fear the king has taken ill."

Jerran coughed.

"So ends Jerran, High King of Kambrya, long live King Horik." Torcull's gaze burned with triumph, "No, you are not dying, at least not yet." He replied to the horrified look upon the king's face. "However, your days of being king are over. You will soon become feverish and lose your voice completely. You will become very ill and find that you are always tired. Slowly, you will get worse until finally your heart grows too weak, then you will die. You have a month...maybe two. By then your son will be back here. For a while, and with my help, you will even be able to walk out onto the balcony." Torcull nodded at the curtains that covered the glass doors. "So, the ignorant masses can see their beloved High King. But it will be I who rules from hereon. A king as sick as you are about to be will need his rest. So, as your appointed regent, I will rule. Then when you are dead, your son will be the next High King and will take your place. But still, I will be regent, after all, your son is but a child who'll need a caring regent to watch over him and the kingdom. Once I will find the lost crown of Kambrya, it will make me a true High King. One who will set my true lord free."

Jerran coughed again. He felt like his throat was on fire.

"Run, Ruan," he whispered hoarsely. "Protect my family. Protect my son."

--

Night descended over Aonach.

Hiding in an alleyway behind several large barrels, Colin looked over his shoulder at Pallas. "Are you mad?" he whispered. "We have been avoiding patrols all night long, and now you want to walk right up to the temple's gate and say 'here we are. We would like to see the prince if you do not mind'?"

"Not in those exact words, but yes. Can you think of a better way to get inside?" Pallas nodded his head towards the Temple of the Severed Head. The iron-barred gate was no more than forty yards from their hiding place. The Grey walls of the temple stood thirty feet high, and every few minutes a silhouette of a guard could be seen walking along the parapet.

"Look at that thing," Pallas went on, pointing at the temple. "It's a bloody fortress, and guarded as if they're expecting a full out attack. We cannot afford to wait, Colin. Elwin and Aidan are in there somewhere, and they might not make it through the night. We have to try. If we walk up to the gate like we're not trying to hide anything, and tell the guards that we want to join the Black Army, well, maybe they'll let us in."

"And maybe not. This is suicide." Colin rose to his feet. "But you're right. I cannot think of a better way "

"I can."

Whirling about, Colin and Pallas saw a dark shadow. To their surprise, the ominous shadow turned out to the innkeep, Ned. Stepping out of the dark, Ned no longer looked like the owner of the Silver Thorn. His spotless white apron had vanished from around his waist. Instead, he now wore brown leather armor that appeared worn and weathered from the passage of many years. Around his waist swung a sheath and sword and strapped to each of the innkeeper's wrists was a polished bronze wrist guard.

"Ned?!" both Colin and Pallas said at the same time. "Is that you?"

"Yes," the innkeeper grumbled, "it is me, though it shouldn't be. Breaking into the temple? I must be as touched in the head as you two boys... Maybe more. I know some of what waits inside. You at least have the advantage of being ignorant."

"What are you doing here?" asked Colin. "I thought you wanted to keep clear of this. That is what you said."

"Still do, but I guess I like you boys. Stupid reason to die over, but at the moment it's the best I can come up with. Besides, if the boy in there really is Prince Elwin, well, let's just say I have to go in there."

"Where did you get that armor and sword? Are you really an innkeeper?" Pallas asked, eyeing the man up and down. "You look more like a soldier to me."

"Yes," he snapped. "I am an innkeeper. Now enough of these foolish questions. We have an ugly job ahead of us." Shaking his head, he sighed. "By the Three Gods, I thought I was done with this sort of thing."

"Can you get us past the gate?" Pallas gave the temple a quick glance. "It looks pretty formidable to me with all those guards around."

"Maybe. It is a really old castle. It's where the kings of Cluain once lived before the new castle was built, and those guards aren't really looking this way, for good reasons. They don't expect anyone to try to get in. Who would be dumb enough to break into the temple? Well, other than us that is. No, they are not there to keep us out but to keep people and other things in."

Pallas gave the temple a nervous look. "What do you mean by 'other things'?"

"I fear you will see soon enough. Let's see if my old mind remembers this remnant of the past. Follow me." With that, Ned headed off at a slow trot. Keeping low to the ground and close to the shadows, he led them around to the far side of the temple. Even this close, Colin and Pallas had trouble seeing Ned moving amongst the dark shadows. The innkeeper now turned warrior seemed like a shadow himself, moving with the soft whisper of the moonless night.

"There." Crouching low to the ground, Ned pointed at a big old tree that stood not ten feet from the base of the wall. Reaching out over the parapet, one of the tree's large branches angled up and over the wall. "That's our way in."

"Why would they leave something like that standing?"

wondered Colin out loud. "Anyone can see that it could be used to gain access to the courtyard. With a small force, the whole place could be quickly overrun."

Ned smiled, "Like I said, this is not a place to keep people out, but to keep 'em in. This is the Temple of the Severed Head, boy. Nobody in his right mind would be attempting to do what we're about to try."

Hiding in the shadows, the three waited, counting how much time elapsed between the passing of one guard and the arrival of the next.

A guard passed before underneath the tree, then vanished down the wall. "Okay," Ned ordered. "Let's go. We don't have much time."

Leading the way, Ned scampered out across the open ground to the base of the tree. Without waiting, the innkeeper leaped to the lower branches, and like a man half his age, pulled himself upwards until he was positioned above the wall.

"Okay," he whispered once the youths had caught up to him, "No more talking. We will wait here until the next guard passes. Try to keep up."

Holding their breaths, they could see the next guard coming down the wall. Like Ned had said, the man was watching the courtyard more than the outside of the wall. Passing below, the guard never saw the three sitting in the tree above him.

Once the guard had passed, Ned crawled out onto the large branch that hung over the wall, and before another guard could appear, he dropped down to the wall then to the courtyard below. A small outbuilding situated not far from the main hall stood close by. Hoping no one was watching, the three threw caution to the wind and raced across the open bailey.

With his back to the building, Ned slid his sword from its

sheath. Turning, he reached for the door, but before he could grab the handle the door unexpectedly opened. A short figure appeared before him. It's head a size too large for its short, thick, and muscular body. The face on the unusually large head was not that of a human. Its face was flat, distorted, and ugly and it had a jaundiced color to it.

Surprised, its two bulging yellow eyes shot open. With sharp jagged teeth, his mouth opened just as the hilt of Ned's sword smashed into the creature's grotesque face. The creature retreated back into the room, taking several steps before it pitched backward, crashing to the floor. Bursting into the room, Ned's sword swung into motion. Two more of the creatures leaped to their feet, their large nostrils flaring. The first was dead before it had drawn its weapon; the second died shortly after, pierced cleanly through the heart by the innkeeper's deadly blade.

Colin and Pallas had not moved. With two dead and one unconscious creature at their feet, the two youths stood frozen by what they had just seen.

"Get in here!" Ned snapped. When they did not move fast enough, the innkeeper grabbed the boys and dragged them inside, closing the door behind them.

Seeing them staring at the two dead creatures, Ned rested a hand on their shoulders. His scowl vanished from his face and was replaced with a look of understanding concern, and with a softness to his voice, he said, "It is never pretty. Now you know why I wanted you and your friends to go home and why I am now an innkeeper. The world can be an ugly place."

"I thought this was going to be a grand adventure," Pallas said, shaking his head. "I never thought..." he let his voice trail off.

"If you believe such," replied Ned. "Then take a good long

look at this and remember. War is too horrible a thing to ever think of as a glorious or grand adventure. And make no mistake boys, this is war."

Pallas leaned against the wall. "I don't think I could kill anything. Even something as ugly as that."

Ned's eyes turned hard. "You'd better! I don't want to find a knife in my back because you did not want to kill something. This is dirty, disgusting, horrifying business. Don't you ever forget that! Killing anything is a disgusting thing and should never come easily, but in this place you had better be ready to kill, and kill fast. There are worse things in here than hobgoblins, and they will kill you on sight, and love doing it."

"Hobgoblins?" asked Colin. "Hobgoblins are children's stories."

"Poppycock," replied Ned. "Do those things look like children's stories? I guess next you'll be telling me that elves aren't real either, like your friend who's somewhere in here with that young and foolish prince."

"You know that Aidan is an elf?" asked Pallas. "Few this far south even believe in elves."

"Old Ned has been around, boys," he said, answering their surprised looks. "I know an elf when I see one."

Colin looked up from the dead hobgoblins. "You're a sword master, aren't you?"

"Hobgoblins are nasty creatures. However, they are also a bit slow between the ears. It took them too long to realize what was happening." Ned replied, neither confirming nor denying Colin's question. "Now, let's wake this nice-looking fellow over here and see what he can tell us."

CHAPTER SEVENTEEN

"You're coming to bed late," exclaimed Eilidh.

"Yes, I know," answered Ruan.

It was their first night home since fleeing up the Clwyd River, and Ruan was restless and more than a bit uneasy. Ruan sat on the edge of their bed and began to undress.

"We made it up the river," stated Eilidh, "and you now need to get your rest." She rolled over, propping herself up onto an elbow. Even in the candlelight, she could see that he was worried about something. She gave a soft sigh; Ruan was always worrying about something.

"You did not sleep much on the river. But we are home now. You can rest."

"Home," he echoed the word softly as if he were unsure of its meaning. "Perhaps, but for how long? We have managed to escape Gildas, but it was a fool's run, Eilidh." He looked down at her. She looked so comfortable and warm among the fur covers. He wished that he could crawl in with her and forget all about his troubles. For a while, it would even work. However, that would

5 10

$$\begin{array}{r} \overset{2}{25} \\ \times\ \ 5 \\ \hline 125 \\ +\ \ \ 3 \\ \hline 128 \end{array}$$

not make King Jerran's army go away. Looking down at the floor, he sighed. "It may have been a mistake to come back here. I fear that we will all be taken back to Gildas and put in chains, if not something worse."

"We had to come here. We could not leave our daughter and go somewhere else."

"Yes, but now we are trapped, or soon will be. Jerran's army will be here in less than ten days at the most. I do not think I did our daughter any good. Maia would have been better off if I had stayed away."

"Ruan!" Eilidh sat up. "How can you say such a thing? She is your daughter!" The fur covers fell into her lap.

"And I have done nothing for her but put her in danger," he said, shaking his head. "You know that I love her. But you do not understand the things Torcull is capable of."

Laying back down, Eilidh shivered. She pulled the covers up over her shoulders. "I have an idea of what Torcull is capable of. I saw what he did to Conrad. King Conrad's mind is gone. Only little Horik seems able to reach him." She edged closer to Ruan. "I do not wish that on Maia or anyone else, but we are in Keloran now and behind her walls. The city is well supplied. We can withstand a siege."

Ruan pulled his nightshirt over his head. "For a while, but the Strigiol army is not like the trolls from the Drygan Mountains. This army will be well organized and well supplied. And using the river, they can resupply, while we cannot. They can wait us out, and in the end, the city will fall. And if there is a Red Robe with the army, there might not be a siege or at least not a long one. We must leave here, Eilidh. We must leave tomorrow. We will take the queen, the prince, the king, and our daughter, along with anyone else Torcull would see as a threat and we will flee."

271

"Leave?" she frowned. "We just got here."

"I know that you do not wish to go. But we have no actual army. We cannot win, Eilidh. If we stay, the city will fall, and all of our people will suffer for it. So, we must leave and we must do it before Jerran's army can trap us."

"But where will we go. Galway?"

"No. Galway would be no better than here, and Easland is out of the question. I have seen what has become of that kingdom. It is no place I want to go to again. To the Kingdom of the lakes," he mused. "But they too have lost their independence. To the west in Ceredigion and Parlan, Jerran is their puppet king. That too is no place for us."

"Then where?"

"Mythra. Somehow, we will have to reach Mythra. It was a mistake going north. Mythra is the last kingdom still holding out against Strigiol's power grab. Maybe we can help them in their fight. Maybe with King Conrad's reputation, if we can keep his mental health a secret, and along with the young Prince Horik, we can gather an army. But first, we have to get to Mythra."

"Mythra? It's so far, Ruan. Can we make it?"

He shook his head. "I don't know, but it is the last safe place in Kambrya. It will be a dangerous trip. But we have to try. First, we will have to find a way to disguise ourselves so that we can slip past any army outposts. We'll try heading West through Ceredigion where we can get a ship to take us down the coast to Mythra."

Looking up at Ruan, Eilidh felt as if she wanted to cry. "Then what?"

Ruan climbed into the bed next to her and pulled the covers over him. "We will let it be known that the prince and king are there. We will try to build an army. We will do what we can."

"Civil war?"

Ruan nodded.

"Oh, Ruan."

He rolled over and kissed his wife. Then turning the other way, he blew out the candle.

"Tomorrow we will make our plans. We will have to move fast." Without saying anything, Eilidh curled up next to him and held him close.

Cradling Eilidh's head against his chest, Ruan laid awake for several hours. Even if he could reach Mythra and manage to build an army, he had no way of stopping the Red Robes and the Black Army. What had Armies done for Easland? He looked at his sleeping wife and wondered what would become of her and their daughter. The idea was too painful to even think about. Holding Eilidh a little tighter, Ruan closed his eyes and tried to think of an answer.

--

With a start, Ruan discovered that he was staring into a gray fog. "Am I dreaming?" he asked himself. *I must have fallen asleep.* He tried to wake himself up. *Strange that I should know that this is a dream.*

The fog suddenly started to change and began to lift. Ruan found himself standing on a mountain trail. Up ahead he saw something move. Someone was coming down the trail.

Quickly, Ruan stepped off the path and into the trees.

Ruan crept deeper into the woods and hid. Through the trees, he could clearly see the trail and the figure coming towards him. Ruan swallowed. Whatever it was it had a human form, but it was clearly not human. His head was deformed and appeared like that of a black jackal. Its doglike head swung from side to side as if it was looking for something. Leaning on a crooked staff, the dog man stopped. It lifted its head and looked into the woods.

This is a dream. It's just a dream. Ruan crouched lower, hoping that the thing would not see him. Sniffing the air, the dog man looked one way, then another.

Hiding in the trees, Ruan felt his heart begin to beat faster. *This is a dream, blast it! This isn't real, calm down.* The dog man sniffed the air again, then shaking its strange head, it turned away and vanished down the trail.

After several minutes, Ruan quietly crept back out of the woods. Not sure what he should do, he headed in the opposite direction in which the dog-man had gone.

How did I get here? And where is here? He shook his head, in confusion. Nothing made any sense. *Think! I was in Keloran... I know I was.*

Ruan followed the trail up the side of a steep, sloping mountainside. Aspen and pine trees lined the steep switch-backed trail that wound its way upwards. Through the branches, he could glimpse a mountain peak. The mountain looks vaguely familiar, but he could not get a good enough look to be sure. It was as if he had seen this mountain peak before, but never from this trail or place. As he came over a rise, the ground flattened out. Before him was a small clearing. At the far side of the flower-filled meadow was a small waterfall. Running down the side of a cliff face, the falls made a gurgling, splashing sound as it flowed over mossy rocks to form a pool of cold mountain water. Above the falls was an ancient looking stone bridge, part of some long-abandoned road system. The pool, falls, and bridge made a picturesque world of tranquil harmony. Walking across the meadow, Ruan gazed above the tree line, he now had a clear view of the mountain peak, and in the not too far distance was several more mountain peaks.

I know where I am, he suddenly realized as he came up to the edge of the clear pool. *I am in the Northern Dragon Mountains.* Ruan spun around taking in the mountain ranges.

He had not recognized the mountain peak earlier because he had never seen it from this angle before. He now realized that he was far into the mountains, farther than he had ever been before. This was troll and hobgoblin country. He reached for his sword, but it was not there. Searching for dangers in the forest that surrounded him, he saw only tall trees that encircled the small clearing. It was a peaceful place. *Quiet, he thought. It's quiet here. I must be dreaming, but it feels so real.* He looked down at himself. He was dressed in his leather riding clothes.

"What kind of dream is this?" he whispered. "It feels too real." Ruan turned back to the pool. Something was different from his other dreams. Everything was so alive and vivid. All of his senses were responding to the world around him. He could even feel the cold mountain breeze on his face.

Crouching, he cupped some water in his hands and drank. It tasted cold and refreshing. *I just need to think. I know these mountains, at least the southernmost parts of them. If I head south, I will find something familiar. Then I can find my way out of the mountains and back to Keloran.*

"Eilidh!" He suddenly remembered that his wife and daughter were still in Keloran and that Jerran's army was coming. "I have to get back before it is too late!"

He lunged back to his feet. *I have to hurry!* He looked at the mountains once more. *It will take weeks to reach Keloran. I won't make it in time. Oh, Lord, I'm too late!*

"What?!" Before him, he saw the surface of the pool of water move. Taking a step back, Ruan gasped.

Something broke the surface of the water. Ruan's eyes went wide. Slowly, the top of a head rose out of the water. As Ruan backed away, a face appeared. Stumbling backward, Ruan lost his balance and fell, scraping his arm on a sharp rock. Ignoring the blood on his arm, he scrambled back to his feet. His heart raced. Connected to the head was a neck, and then a pair of shoulders emerged from the pool's cold surface.

Ruan was about to run when suddenly he recognized the face. It was the dark-haired girl that he had seen in Gildas. The one who claimed to be 'One Who Never Was,' whatever that meant. She still wore the same brown dress of a servant. Walking towards the pond's bank, the girl rose out of the water. Again, Ruan was struck by how familiar she looked. With bare feet, she stepped out of the water and onto the grassy bank of the pond. Surprised, Ruan saw that from her dark hair to her bare feet she was perfectly dry.

"You..." Ruan managed to say. "How? This is a dream."

She lifted her eyes to him. "You called me."

"I called you?" asked Ruan, forgetting his fear.

Not waiting for an answer, Ruan went on, "You should not be here. It's dangerous." Ruan scratched his head, "And where are we? Is this a dream?"

"A dream? No, and yes," the strange girl replied.

"Where is this place?"

"Don't you recognize it?" The soft-spoken girl answered the question with a question.

"Well, yes, it's the Northern Dragon Mountains, but how did I get here?"

"Sometimes when the need is great, one can reach this place.

However, it is no longer safe. It is dangerous for you to be here."

"What do you mean?"

"You have entered what is called the World of Dreams. Here everything is real and not real, but that does not matter. What is important is that you are here, and I have a message for you."

"What?" *It is only a dream,* he told himself. *It has to be a dream.*

"Do not go to Mythra."

He frowned. "How did you know about that?"

"I cannot say, but you must not go there. At least not now."

"Then where!?" he snapped angrily. "Where am I to go? I can't believe that I am arguing with a dream."

"Here," She pointed at the pond. "Your Dream Walk has already shown you. Come to this place and things will become clear."

"The mountains? I would need to bring an army. This is trolls and hobgoblins country!" he exclaimed in dismay before going on. "And there are... other things too," he added, remembering the dog-man.

She cocked her head to one side and smiled, "Come." Not waiting for Ruan to respond, she started walking along the foot of the cliff face where the ancient stone bridge stood overhead.

Ruan hesitated, then followed. He watched her, wondering why she looked so familiar. She led him to a pair of stairs that had been cut into the cliff face, leading up to the bridge and ancient road.

She pointed. "Go up."

"Why?"

"Because you need to."

Ruan shrugged his shoulders and went up the stone stairs that curved and onto the rustic bridge. Briefly, he stopped and

277

looked down at the pond and the strange girl that stood at its banks. Then with another shrug, he headed up the ancient road.

From the bridge, the road wound its way towards the north, climbing ever higher into the mountains. Eventually, the road came to an end at the foot of a steep sloping cliff face.

What a *strange road. Why would anyone build a road that goes nowhere?*

Convinced that there must be some reason for the road, Ruan began searching the cliff wall. Just as he was about to give up, he discovered another stone staircase not too far off the road. Ingeniously cut into the cliff, the stairs were created in such a way that they were hidden and camouflaged into the stonewall of the cliff. If one was not standing at its base, one would never be able to see or even know of the stairs existence.

With little choice, he began to climb. The stairs were steep and arduous. Worn by the weather, the stairs had not been used for a very long time. Twice he nearly slipped, but he went on. Breathing hard, Ruan finally reached the top where the stone stairs opened up onto a narrow landing.

The rocky shelf was no more than 20 feet wide. In the center of the cliff, that still rose above him, was a large mouth of a dark cave. Entering, he was surprised to find that he was suddenly holding a torch.

"A dream," he muttered as an explanation. "Dreams rarely make any sense."

The cave was wide but not deep. Soon Ruan found that he had cut through the mountainside and was standing on the other side and on yet another landing. He was now standing high above a valley that was surrounded by a dense forest that stretched out as far as the eye could see. He gazed over a broad valley that stretched out for many miles. Running down the center of the green valley was a meandering stream that flowed out of the mountains. But that was not all he could see. He could hardly believe it. In the center of the valley was a city.

"A city!?" Ruan rubbed his eyes, yet the city below did not vanish.

People out here? What does this mean? The city was unlike any that Ruan had ever seen. Behind the city's white stone walls, houses and buildings were painted with bright, brilliant colors. Hundreds of shimmering flags snapped briskly in the wind. It was like looking down upon a rainbow. Wanting some answers, he turned and returned the way he had come. That strange girl needs to answer some questions, however when he reached the pond, he found that the girl was gone. Ruan began searching for her, but he could not find her.

"Where are you!" he shouted. His voice echoed through trees.

"Fool!" came an answer. The voice seemed to come from a great distance and yet was crystal clear. "You are not alone here. Be quiet."

"Where are you?"

"I cannot come to you like this again," the girl's voice seemed to echo in Ruan's head.

"Remember when the High King calls, you must go. Goodbye, father."

"What? Oh, my lord! I do know you! But that can't be!" Everything faded, and the fog returned.

"No!" With a jerk, Ruan sat up in his bed. He was awake and once more in Keloran.

"Are you all right?" It was Eilidh still lying beside him. "Did you have a bad dream?"

"I saw her." He wiped the cold sweat from his forehead. His eyes grew wide.

"Saw who?"

"Our daughter!"

"Ruan, Maia is in bed across the hall." She looked at his arm. "Oh my! You're bleeding!"

Ruan looked at his arm, then back to his wife. "It was real!"

"What are you talking about?" she asked, sounding concerned. "Did you dream of Maia? Try not to worry. It was only a dream. She is fine."

Ruan shook his head. "No not Maia. I saw Rhea."

Eilidh frowned. "Ruan, it was a dream. Rhea was a stillborn. She was dead before she took her first breath. You know that."

Ruan nodded, then whispered, "One who never was."

--

Elwin opened his eyes. He could see nothing. He closed them, then opened them again. It made no difference. He could not see a thing. *I'm blind?* Shifting onto his side, he could feel a thin layer of rough straw that had been scattered across a cold stone floor.

"Are you awake?" a voice asked.

Elwin gave a startled reply. "Who's there? Aidan, is that you?"

"Yes."

"Where are we?"

Aidan, feeling his way in the dark, crawled closer. "I think we are in the Temple's dungeon."

Even with Aidan sitting right next to him, Elwin could not see him. "I cannot see, Aidan. Am I blind?"

"No, you're not. It's just very dark. I can see a little. We are in a cell of some type with a large iron gate."

Elwin sat up and leaned against a stone wall. His head began to throb. Letting the side of his face lay against the cold stones, Elwin tried not to move. The last thing he remembered was the door to their room at the Silver Thorn suddenly bursting apart, slivers of the wood had flown everywhere, then black armored men poured into the room.

"At least Pallas and Colin are safe," Elwin sighed.

Aidan nodded. Then remembering Elwin could not see him, he added, "I hope so."

"There is a light coming from somewhere." The elf hesitated. "It's coming through an archway just beyond the gate. I think someone is coming."

The light grew brighter. As the light grew, Elwin could start making out his surroundings. At first, he could only vaguely distinguish the outline of his and Aidan's cell. Then he saw the archway and a narrow door. The door was standing halfway open, allowing the light to slip in.

As the light grew brighter, Elwin started picking out more details. Between the cell and the archway was a large room. In the center of the room was a long narrow table. Seeing what was on the table, Elwin shivered. "This is a torture chamber."

Aidan did not respond. The light grew brighter. They could now hear footsteps echoing down a hallway. Elwin's heart was pounding. The door swung the rest of the way open. A black robed priest of the Severed Head stepped through the door. At his side was a small, stocky creature in tight leather armor. In one hand, the yellow-skinned creature carried an oil lamp and in its other a spear. Its yellow eyes shifted nervously from side to side and shimmered in the flickering lamplight. A hobgoblin. Elwin had never seen a hobgoblin before, but he had read enough about them to know that this had to be one of those fierce creatures of the north. *How did a hobgoblin get here from the mountains?*

"Good, you are awake." The priest had a cold voice that made Elwin cringe. His long black robe flowed as he walked across the room. His hungry and dangerous eyes locked onto Elwin's. The priest ran a hand over his shaved head. Then he looked down at the hobgoblin. "Wait outside," he ordered.

Without saying a word, the hobgoblin bowed and quickly backed away, closing the door behind him. As the hobgoblin disappeared with the lamp, a red glowing ball of light appeared above the priest's head. Making the room look more menacing than it had a moment ago, the red glowing ball bathed the room in a blood red light.

Bathed in the magical light, the priest took on a monstrous appearance, like some demon from the dark bowels of the earth, straight from Hell itself. With deliberate slowness, the priest turned towards the cell. An uncharacteristic smile touched the ends of his thin lips. "I hope you are not too uncomfortable." His voice was soft and gentle, yet it could not hide the coldness of his eyes.

Trying not to shake, Elwin came to his feet. "What do you want from us?"

"To help you, Prince Elwin." Keeping one hand inside the folds of his robe, he swung the other hand out across the room before him. "I feel that you are being mistreated. You are of royal blood after all, and one such as you deserves better than this. I would like to help you."

Elwin put his hand to his head, wishing the throbbing would stop. It was making it hard to focus. "You seem to know me." Elwin saw no point in denying who he was. "But who are you?"

"I am Gillies, a simple priest of the Severed Head." the man said as if the title were beneath him. "However, I am in a position to help you. I am more than I may appear. I am a powerful man, Prince Elwin. Stronger than anyone knows."

"Why would a Black Priest help us?" asked Aidan. He had climbed to his feet and was standing next to Elwin. Gillies smiled and looked at Aidan as if seeing him for the first time. Hungrily, his eyes sparkled. "A fair question my young elf."

"I will be honest with you. I am an ambitious man." Gillis went on. "And as I said, I am also a powerful man. However, with your assistance, I can become even more powerful. With your help, I shall soon be the High Priest of this temple and much, much more!"

"How can we help you?" asked Elwin. He found it hard to believe that this small, skinny man could be as powerful as he claimed, yet there was something about him that reminded Elwin of Faynn, and not in a good way.

"You have something I need." Gillies' smile broadened. "Help me and I shall help you. I can be very generous to my friends. I would like to be your friend, and right now you seem to be in need of one."

"What could we have to offer you?" Elwin asked, shrugging his shoulders. "We are prisoners behind these bars, and you are the jailer."

"Be careful," whispered Aidan. "Do not trust him."

From beneath his robe, Gillies pulled out a sword. Elwin's eyes widened, and he caught his breath. It was the sword of Light and Dark. It was Elwin's sword handed down to him by his father. A strange urge rose in him to reach out and hold it. To touch it. "My sword!" he gasped.

"It was. But now it's mine," said Gillies tapping the blade

283

with his free hand.

Trembling and feeling as if a part of him had been stolen, Elwin stared at the sheathed sword.

With a mixture of awe and respect, the priest placed the blade down on the table. The man looked back up. "I want to know how it works." Glistening with a mad excitement, Gillies' eyes danced between Elwin and the sword. "Torcull wants this blade. I want to know why."

With difficulty, Elwin forced himself to look away from the sword, but he too kept glancing back at it as if he needed to be reassured that it was still there.

"I have examined it carefully," Gillies went on, "and it appears to be nothing but a simple sword. I have tried many incantations. The spells should have revealed its mysteries to me, and yet there is nothing. However, it must be very powerful, or Torcull would not want it. Somehow the sword is hiding its true nature from me. I must find its secrets. Then I will be its master."

"I do not know what you mean," replied Elwin. "It is just a sword."

Gillies held out his open hand. He spoke, but a single word of an ancient language, a ball of fire materialized in the palm of his outstretched hand. Tossing the fiery ball into the air then catching it again, the priest played with the ball of fire if it were but a child's toy. With his ball of fire, Gillies appeared even more like a demon. "In truth, I am much more than a simple Priest of the Severed Head," he announced with a tone of arrogant authority. "And I can do things to you that would make your flesh crawl and make these tools on this table appear as toys." With a dramatic wave of his free hand, he gestured towards the table indicating the array of implements of torture. "Do not play games with me, my young prince. I am warning you." His eyes narrowed. "I am willing to be generous with you, I will even call you friend, but if you do not help me, I will make you cry for mercy. Now speak!"

"Speak of what?" Elwin's voice shook. "It is a sword forged of metal. It is an heirloom of my family. There is no more to tell."

With a flick of his wrist, Gillies threw the ball of fire. It all happened too fast. Unable to move out of the way, Elwin braced for the impact, but it was Aidan who yelled out. Gillies had thrown the ball at Aidan and not Elwin. Stepping back, Aidan stared down at his chest.

Without a trace, the ball had disappeared into him.

"Are you okay?" asked Elwin.

Aidan shrugged. "I don't feel anything." Then with a sudden cry of pain, his eyes rolled back into his head, and he fell to the floor.

Elwin dropped down next to him. "Aidan!"

Ignoring Aidan's screams, Gillies smiled at Elwin. "They say that your father was a proud man who did not scare easily either. They also say that he had a soft spot for his friends. A weakness I do not possess, but I think you do. In time, I could drag the truth out of you, but that would take longer than I wish to spend." He nodded at Aidan. "The fire inside your friend will slowly cook him from the inside out. A very painful death I assure you, but it should not last longer than a day or two, three at the most."

Aidan screamed and twisted in Elwin's arms.

"Stop it!" Elwin shouted.

"This spell takes a considerable amount of practice." Ignoring Elwin's pleadings, Gillies went on. "And to think Mor said that I don't have the ability to be a High Priest? Look at that elf, look at his pain. Could the High Priestess do this? I think not!

But I will show them. When the power of the sword is mine, I will show them all!" He slammed a clenched fist into his now empty palm.

Aidan thrashed out in pain. Elwin held onto him tightly. "Stop it!" Elwin repeated. "You are killing him!"

Gillies gave Elwin a confused smile. "Of course, I am. That is the whole idea. But yes, I can stop it if you want me too."

"Yes! Stop it!"

"Are you now willing to tell me what I wish to know?"

"Yes," replied Elwin. He was trying to hold Aidan still. "Just stop it! Please!" The priest waved his hand, and Aidan's body abruptly ceased thrashing, and he lay still.

"Are you okay?" asked Elwin.

Aidan nodded weakly. "Don't tell him anything."

"I can still take his life," warned Gillies. "But that will not be necessary if you cooperate." Gillies ran a finger along the sword's sheath, then he looked up from the table.

Elwin came to his feet. What could he tell the Black Priest? Elwin did not know or understand the secrets of the sword. However, if he told Gillies that, then Aidan would die.

Not sure what to say, Elwin stared silently at Gillies. "What are you waiting for?" snapped Gillies.

"I do not understand the magic myself." At least that much was true. "It just kind of happens."

Gillies mumbled something. Then he demanded, "What happens? And why did my spells fail to reveal the sword's uses?"

"Your spells." Elwin was making things up as he went along. "Failed because the sword protects itself against such magic."

"Of course. I am not a fool. I want to know *how* it does it. I want to know of its magic and how to use those powers!"

"I am not sure, it just works, or it doesn't..." Elwin stopped short. From behind Gillies, another priest stepped under the arch. The priest lifted his head, and Elwin saw that this was not a priest, but a priestess. Despite her shaved head, this black robed figure was clearly a woman.

At first glance, one might say she was beautiful. However, one soon noticed her unsettling eyes. Unblinking, she stared at Gillies' back. There was an air of power and authority about her. Like Gillies, she somehow reminded Elwin of Faynn.

"I thought I would find you here," said the priestess.

Startled, Gillies spun around, taking a step backward, his eyes grew wide. The priestess went on. "When I discovered that the sword was missing, it was easy to guess who had stolen it. It was equally easy to figure out where you would take it. You were always predictable, Gillies."

"High Priestess Mor," he stuttered, "I...I came merely to check in on our prisoners."

Mor looked at the table, then gave the priest a smirk. "With the sword?"

Gillies drew in a long breath. "I hoped to discover its secrets. We need to understand it."

"That is neither your job nor mine." Mor took a step closer to Gillies, pointing a long finger at him, she scolded at him as if he were a child. "We are to deliver both the prince and the sword to our master." Her eyes narrowed. "But you do not wish to do that, do you?"

Gillies looked down at the sword. When he looked back up, his initial shock and uncertainty were gone. His smug smile returned. "Why should we? Why should we hand such a weapon as Saran Na Grain over to Torcull? Why should we not keep it for ourselves? Think, Mor. The power could be ours. Think of the possibilities."

Mor crossed her arms across her chest. "We have spoken of this before. The Prophet will not be pleased with you, Gillies. Nor am I."

"With the sword's power, I won't care. Help me, Mor, and Torcull will serve us! Just think of it. We could rule the world!"

"You are mad, Gillies. The Dark Master will cut you down. We are his to command and to serve. To oppose him is to die a thousand deaths."

"No!" snapped Gillies shaking his head. "I will serve no more! You can grovel at his feet if you wish to, but not me. I will be my own master. I will be the master of all."

Mor frowned. "Do you think it is that easy? Do you think you can just take the sword and walk away? If you stand against the Dark Prophet, you will lose. Torcull wants the boy and sword delivered unharmed. If you must, take the elf, but leave the prince and the sword alone. Gillies. " Her voice took on a hard, commanding tone. "I order you to step aside!"

Elwin shivered at the sound of her voice. Without thinking, he stepped backward, nearly tripping over Aidan, it was almost as if Mor's voice had pushed him. Gillies only laughed. "Do not try your tricks on me, Mor. They no longer work. I've learned more than you think."

She looked at the sword.

Elwin saw a worried look cross her face. *Does she think he can use it?*

Mor looked up from the table. Her eyes still had authority in them, but now there was also doubt. "I don't believe you," she said at last. "You could not tap into the sword's powers. If you had." She nodded towards the cell. "They would be dead by now."

Gillies smiled. He moved closer to the sword. "Maybe I

have. But if you doubt me, then call my bluff. If you dare."

Feeling a tingling sensation, Elwin looked for a place to hide. The air began to spark with energy. Mor and Gillies were drawing up Earth Magic. Elwin gasped. The sword on the table began to glow.

He could feel the power of the sword. It was calling to him. Then he heard the power of Earth Magic. The magic was reaching out to him. He could hear it in his head. The magic sang a strange song to him. At first, it was a soothing tune. Strangely, the song did not have an actual beat nor a rhythm. The song was like that of a gurgling brook mixed with the sound of leaves blowing in the wind. Without words, the song sang of the grandeur of life and the mystery of creation. Held in the wonder of the song, Elwin heard it sing of towering mountains and seas without end, of forests of green thriving trees, and of life springing out of the soil. Elwin felt himself sinking into the song. He felt at peace. The world around him faded away until only the song of Earth Magic remained.

Then the song changed. It began to hurt. The song pounded in his head. Elwin tried to pull back, but he couldn't find the strength. The world suddenly went black. Those around him were gone. The song took him deeper. Terrified, Elwin struggled against the power. Helpless against the song, Elwin was taken deeper and deeper into its magic. Like a rotting animal carcass, the music had now turned dark and foul. The air became thick. It was no longer the song of life, but of death. It now sang of destruction.

Wind and rain tore down the mountains, the seas dried into vast deserts, forests became fields of dead trunks, and the land withered and died. Elwin felt a shadow rise out of the song. Within the shadow was a sense of great despair. A great hopelessness washed over him, and he felt lost within that shadow. Darkness was everywhere. The dark song pulled at him. Feeling helpless, he went down into its vast emptiness. He was alone, feeling so very lost, the song echoed in his head. All that remained was the shadow and the dark song of death. No longer able to fight the song, Elwin continued to go in deeper.

Elwin stared into the dark. Despair washed over him like a great sea. Within the shadow, there could be no hope. Then there was a light. A red spark flashed, then it was gone. Someone else was there. Elwin tried to move forward. Struggling against the shadow, he took a step towards where the light had been. It was like walking against a fast-moving river.

"Where are you?" he called out. There was no answer. Then he saw another flash of light. He struggled on. Out of the dark shadow, he saw two figures. There was another flash. This time, the light lingered for a moment before fading away. Elwin walked towards the figures.

"Can you hear me?" he called. Again, there was no answer.

A light burst out of the dark. Elwin realized that the two figures were fighting with Earth Magic. The earth was in pain as its powers were twisted into acts of violence and hatred. Elwin then recognized the two combatants as that of the priest Gilles and High Priestess Mor. Elwin moved closer. He wished these two figures had not been of the Severed Head, he wished they were there to help him escape the madness of the magic. But at least he was not alone. Then there was a thunderous crash. It was like being at the heart of a thunderstorm. A red flash of light raced towards him. Elwin could feel the light pass him by, sending a jolt of pain through him.

I'm too close! Elwin suddenly realized that Mor and Gillies were losing control of the magic. He was beginning to panic. The magic sang out to Elwin; it was a cry of warning. The prince tried to back away, but he was too late. There was another crash of thunder followed by a blinding red light. The light leaped everywhere. There was no escape. As the light touched him, Elwin screamed out in pain. The light burned. Dropping to his knees, he raised his arms over his head. Thunder and flashing light exploded all around him.

"You are no match for me," warned Mor. "Stand aside! Let go of the power."

Gillies threw back his head and laughed. "I have learned more than you think, High Priestess. Watch and see! Behold the powers that I have learned!" Blood red light sprang out of Gillies' raised hands.

Mor raised her hands, shattering the light before her. Then she sent her own waves of fiery red light towards Gillies. Gillies spread his arms wide. As the light hit him, he seemed to embrace it. For a moment the light glowed, then faded away.

Mor's eyes widened. She threw more light at Gillies, but it had no effect. Like a sponge, he absorbed any power that Mor threw against him.

Horrified, Mor's look of confidence vanished. "Gillies!" she shouted. "You must stop! What have you done?"

He smiled. "I have not yet discovered the sword's power, but I have learned other things." He pointed at her. "I tried to tell you, but you would not listen!" He threw a red ball of light at her. Mor shattered it before it could reach her, but the force made her stagger backward.

"Oh no! The great Mor could not listen to me! She would not listen to a lowly priest!" He went on with a bitter laugh. "But I am not so lowly now, am I?" Another wave of light leaped from

Gillies' outstretched hands, forcing Mor back against the wall. "And now, Mor, you must die."

She gasped. Her face became distorted with fear. She had sensed what Elwin had. Gillies was calling up too much power. "Stop!" she cried. "You can't control it! You will bring the temple down upon us!"

Gillies ignored her desperate warning. He was now beyond reasoning. "I *will* have the sword!" he howled like the raging storm that was growing inside him. "None shall stop me! None!" Above his head, he slapped his hands, and the air exploded.

Blinding light and fire went in every direction. Gillies' mouth fell open. He realized what he had done, but it was too late. Like the waters from a storm flooded river, the power poured uncontrollably out of him. At first, he struggled with the power, holding the torrents back, but soon he began losing control of the magic. There was just too much raw power. A thunderous crash resounded through the room as yet another wave of magic broke free. Shrieking, Gillies fell to his knees.

The floor buckled and the walls shook. As if waking from a nightmare, Elwin screamed and fell on top of Aidan. Trying to fend off the burning light and fire, he raised his arms over his head as a wordless song sang out to him. The wordless song sprang up from deep within the earth and raced through Elwin. For a moment, the song of Earth Magic was all there was. Prince Elwin had ceased to be. There was no room, no cell, no world. There was only the song of life and death, a song of love and hate, of endless joy and the deepest sorrow. Then there was a silence, the song ended as quickly as it had begun, and the mindless roar of the storm of unchecked power had stopped as well, Elwin let his arms drop and opened his eyes. Once more, Elwin was back in the temple, but things had changed. Both Gillies and Mor were gone, and a fire was raging everywhere. Where Gillies had stood, there was a gaping hole in the floor. The very gates of hell had opened and had taken him home. The cell room was a disaster as fire leaped from every part of the chamber. By the immensity of the power, the cell doors had been ripped free of its hinges, and now the cell's iron bars gate lay in puddles of molten metal. The cell floor and walls were burnt black. The straw that had covered the cell floor had been burned completely away except for one small circle.

Where Elwin and Aidan laid, the straw was still there, unburnt or even singed. The floor around them had not been touched by the raging power. Elwin looked down, expecting to find himself burned, but both he and Aidan appeared unhurt. With wonder in his green eyes, Aidan looked up at Elwin.

"How did you do that?" the elf breathed.

Not knowing what Aidan meant, the prince came to his feet. Part of the cell wall suddenly collapsed. "We have to get out of here." He stepped over the puddles of metal, careful not to touch them.

Aidan started for the door, but when he realized that Elwin had stopped, he turned back around. "What are you doing?"

Elwin was searching through the rubble that was scattered across the room. "My sword, I have to find it."

"It couldn't have survived," Aidan stated. There was an urgency to his voice. "The table and everything on it was destroyed. We have to leave!"

The roof above creaked. Looking up, Aidan saw that the fire was eating through the support beams. "Elwin! There's no time!" Ignoring Aidan, Elwin continued to search.

"Elwin!"

"There it is!" Elwin suddenly exclaimed.

Lying at Elwin's feet, Aidan saw the sword. The sheath had been devoured by the flames, but the sword and hilt remained. The blade glowed red hot, but the sword had survived.

Elwin bent down.

"No!" shouted Aidan. "It will burn you!"

It was too late. Elwin had already reached out and grabbed hold of the sword's hilt. To his surprise, the leather hilt was cool to his touch.

Above, the ceiling groaned and moaned. With a loud crack, one of the beams snapped in half. The two ends of the beam came crashing down to the floor, bringing a large section of the ceiling with it. Smoke and flames were everywhere.

Elwin coughed from the thick, black smoke. "Let's get out of here! This room is about to collapse."

Aidan offered no protest, and the two dashed past the archway and into a narrow hallway. With a thunderous crash, the room behind them suddenly gave way and fell. Fed by the air above, the fire leaped upwards, engulfing the upper floor.

Attempting to escape the spreading blaze, Elwin and Aidan staggered past the dead body of a hobgoblin that had been crushed by a fallen beam. Down the smoky hallway, they stumbled forward. The fire was rapidly engulfing the temple.

"Up!" cried Aidan. "We have to go up."

"Here," said Elwin, finding a pair of stairs. As fast as they could, they raced up the stairs. Three floors later, they found a closed door.

Aidan placed a hand upon a door. "It's not hot. There's no fire on the other side. At least not yet."

Pulling open the door, they hurried on, but it was not long before they discovered that the flames had outrun them, and they were forced back. They tried another hallway. The temple was like a maze, and the two wandered looking for some way out while at the same time avoiding the rapidly spreading fire.

Struggling through the winding halls of the temple, Elwin and Aidan raced against the flames. They climbed every staircase they could find, but the fire was moving faster.

More smoke filled the hallways. Below, they heard a groaning sound. Then somewhere below there was an explosion. The floor shifted, and Elwin was thrown from his feet. Aidan helped him back up, and they raced on.

"We're not going to make it," Elwin stated. "The place is burning too fast."

"We'll make it," insisted Aidan.

Aidan pulled on Elwin's arm, and they hurried on once more. Coughing, their eyes stung from the smoke. Three more times, they were forced back by the spreading fire.

Covered in soot and ashes, Elwin and Aidan rushed through a final doorway. Coughing, the two finally stepped out into a courtyard. They were outside and alive.

Elwin drank in the fresher air. There was still a lot of smoke, but it was a lot better outside the temple. "We made it!" he breathed, not quite believing their luck.

"Not yet." Aidan glanced back through the door that they had just passed through. Laying on the floor were two dead hobgoblins. "What's happening?"

Elwin stepped past him. "A battle. Look."

The grounds of the courtyard were lit by the burning temple. Ashes floated down from above. Scattered here and there were more bodies. From around the building, a small group of hobgoblins appeared. Ignoring Elwin and Aidan, the hobgoblins rushed past them. Hurrying towards the sound of men fighting, the hobgoblins were running towards the outer wall. Over the noise of shouts and the crackle of the fire, the sound of metal hitting metal could be heard.

"There." Aidan pointed.

Elwin looked. Three men were trying to fight their way to the wall. Amongst all the fighting, their faces were hard to see. A guard of the Severed Head dropped before a man in leather armor. Not far away, a hobgoblin fell before a big blond headed youth. The second teen with curly red hair broke through the guards and dashed up a ladder to the wall's walkway. His sword lashed out, and a guard screamed, toppling over the wall. The other two hurried up behind the redheaded youth. More hobgoblins and men appeared. The first hobgoblin reached the ladder and started up. With his bulging muscles, the larger of the two boys pushed the ladder away from the wall. The hobgoblin howled angrily as he crashed backward. Then the three leaped over the wall and escaped.

"Was that Pallas and Colin?" asked Aidan.

"Here in the temple?"

Aidan shook his head. "It doesn't matter. We have to escape."

"We'll never be able to fight our way across the bailey."

"Well, we can't stay here. It is only a matter of time until someone sees us."

Elwin nodded, then after a brief moment of silence, he said, "Let's make our way to the gate."

Careful not to be seen by the passing soldiers, Elwin and Aidan kept close to the shadows and the wall of the temple. Slowly, they worked towards the temple's postern gate. Hobgoblins, men, and priests rushed past, but they never gave Elwin and Aidan a second glance. They had more important things to worry about. The fire was destroying their temple.

Another explosion erupted and the ground shook. Off to the far side of the courtyard, a bucket brigade had formed to fight the fire. Avoiding the firefighters, Aidan and Elwin were forced out into the open, but again no one was paying them any attention.

Still within sight of the bucket brigade, they found the postern gate. Elwin moaned, "It's guarded." With all the confusion, Elwin had hoped that the gate would be abandoned.

The two ducked behind a wall and laid flat upon the ground. "Why so many guards?" whispered Aidan.

Beneath Elwin, the ground felt warm He nodded to the men fighting the fire. "I think they're trying to keep those people from fleeing."

Aidan looked up and saw a hobgoblin throwing a man towards the burning buildings.

"You're right. Those people are being forced to fight the fire."

Just then a black-robed priest came running out of the temple. His arms were waving over his head. "The altar room has caught on fire!" he yelled as if it were the worst possible thing to happen. Everyone stopped working and watched him run across the courtyard. The priest ran right past Elwin and Aidan, and in a mindless rush headed straight for the heavily guarded gate. Terrified, the priest ran as if the end of the world was at hand. The guards at the gate did not dare stop one of the Black Priests. As if he were being chased by a blood demon, the priest threw open the gate and vanished into the night.

"The temple is lost!" someone else screamed. "Run!"

The men that had been fighting the fire dropped their buckets and turned as one. Then, with panic in their eyes, they ran for the gate.

Chaos quickly broke out. At first, it looked as if the guards were going to be overrun. Taking advantage of the confusion, Elwin and Aidan jumped to their feet, mingling in with the panicked crowd, they ran towards the gate. Suddenly, more guards appeared. They lifted up their crossbows and leveled them at the gathering crowd. The mob stopped and stared, not sure if they should charge forward or go back, they were caught between the fear of what lay before them and behind.

An officer in black armor stepped forward. "Get back to work!" the armed man barked.

"And close that gate," he told another soldier, shoving him into action.

The crowd shifted nervously. Slowly they began to draw back, but hesitating they did not return to the fires.

"I said get back to work!"

The crowd fell further back. Reluctantly, they started heading towards the temple. Elwin and Aidan were left standing alone. "You!" cried out the officer, spotting Elwin and Aidan. "So, you are alive!" The officer pointed at Elwin. "You're the one who started this! You will pay for trying to destroy the temple!" Elwin raised his sword. He was too close to give up now. Freedom was only a dozen feet away.

The officer laughed at Elwin. "Take them, but do not kill the prince."

Upon his order, the soldiers dropped their crossbows and drew their swords. They took a step forward. Another explosion erupted. The ground shook violently. A crack in the earth opened up, and flames leaped up into the air.

"We're going to die!" someone shouted. As one the crowd turned once more. With a great cry, they surged forward. This time, they would not be stopped, dragging Elwin and Aidan along with them, they attacked the guards who were attempting to stop them.

"Get back!" shouted the officer. This time, the crowd refused to listen. The ground continued to shake. Another crack in the earth opened up, and more flames leaped toward the sky.

The guards were forced backward, but they were making the crowd pay for every step. Already, several people had died. Then another explosion erupted, and everyone stopped. Soldiers, servants, priests, and hobgoblins turned and looked. The temple began to collapse inwards. Fire surged up through the earth as large sections of the courtyard fell into a growing fiery hole in the ground, a hole that burned with a heat that no ordinary fire could produce. More cracks in the earth formed, the hole grew wider, and more fire leaped into the air.

Again, the crowd cried out. This time, the guards did not resist. The gates were thrown open, and everyone including the guards fled into the night. Elwin and Aidan were only a few blocks away from the temple when the earth violently heaved upwards. Throwing them to the ground, the trembling earth shook out of control. The ground was shaking so violently that they could not get back on their feet. Stones from buildings were shaken loose of their mortar and fell, crashing to the road. Erupting like a volcano, a tower of flame leaped from where the temple had once been. The sky turned fire red, changing the night into day.

CHAPTER EIGHTEEN

The Aonach night was as hot as the day had been. The air was still and heavy. Earlier, the skies above the city were ablaze. For hours, a great towering of flame had lit up the night. The light show was now over, yet the sky still glowed brightly over the spot where the temple had been. The mood of the city was a mixture of excitement, fear, and uncertainty.

In front of an alleyway, two boys, not much younger than Elwin, approached each other.

"Nat, did you see it?" asked one boy.

"Sure did, Trey. I was there. It was something to see, too." He held up a piece of charred rock. "Look."

"What's that?" asked Trey.

"It's part of the temple wall."

"Wow!"

"You should have seen all those people running!"

"What does it look like now?"

Nat laughed. "It's a big hole in the ground. Something is still burning deep underground, but the temple is gone. Only the outer walls are left standing, and even most of them have fallen in, too."

"I wish mother had let me go."

"Come on," said Nat. "Let's go over to Tyson's. I want to show him my rock." He smiled proudly. "I'll tell you the rest of it the way over." The boys turned and started down the street.

"Did they catch the prince yet?" asked one.

"No..." Then their voices faded away as they moved further down the street.

Checking that none of the guardsmen were about, Elwin and Aidan crept out of the alley. "Did you hear that?" asked Aidan. "I bet every guardsman in the city is looking for you."

"Great!" Elwin pointed across a small court. "Let's go over to that well. I'm thirsty, and we need to clean up." They were still covered in dirt and ash from their escape from the temple.

They had just finished washing when an elderly woman approached. She dipped her bucket into the well, but her eyes stared at the strange glowing sky.

"Boys," she asked in a raspy grandmotherly voice, "what foul thing has happened this night?"

Aidan drank some of the cold well water, then looked up. "The temple has burnt down."

"Oh, how wonderful!" the woman exclaimed. She clapped her wrinkled hands. "Who did it, the Renegades?"

"We don't know," Elwin curtly answered, wishing Aidan would keep quiet. "But I would advise against exhibiting such enthusiasm. The Severed Head is not happy, and there are spies about."

"Oh, phooey on spies! I am an old woman, young man," she pointed out the obvious, "I will not spend my last year's acting or doing as others think I should because someone might be listening in."

Hearing the conversation, a cobbler in his brown leather apron, crossed the street. "I know who started the fire. It was the outlaw, Prince Elwin. He destroyed the temple."

With a jerk of his head, Elwin looked at the man, but he quickly realized that the cobbler did not recognize him. Also realizing the same thing, Aidan asked, "The outlaw prince? Here in the city?" He was trying to hide a wry smile. Trying not to sigh, Elwin gave Aidan a nudge.

"Sure was," the cobbler answered. "Prince Elwin and an elf if you can believe it. That's what I heard at least."

"An elf?" said Aidan, not taking Elwin's hint. His long hair was pulled forward to cover his ears. His hair was also still thick with ash, so it had a darker look to it than the natural light blond hair of the wood elves of the Green. "But elves don't really exist, do they?"

Elwin inwardly signed.

Unaware of Aidan's joke, the cobbler went on as if he were a fountain of knowledge. "Maybe, and maybe not."

Others began to gather to hear the cobbler talk, and soon the cobbler had a broad audience. "I was down at one of them taverns near the temple when it all started. It was something all right. The ground was shaking so much I thought the tavern was going to come down right on top of me."

"Some places did collapse," someone added.

"I think the Old Grange was one," added another.

The cobbler nodded and went on. "Prince Elwin attacked the temple, and he did it with only a hand full of Renegades... Destroyed the whole place, too." The cobbler shoved his hands into his apron pockets. It was evident that he was enjoying all the attention he was getting. "After it was all over, I talked to one of the servants that worked in the temple." A hush fell over the crowd. "He saw the prince and this elf fellow. He said that the prince was trying to get out of the temple. Some of the temple guards tried to stop him. This servant says Prince Elwin stood right up to the officer and said to him that he better get out of his way. When the officer refused, the prince took his sword and slammed it into the earth, and that's when the temple started to explode. He used some type of magic to destroy the temple. The earth started shaking, and a fire started coming right out of the ground, it did."

Another voice spoke up. "I heard that the prince killed a priest and the High Priestess Mor." Several voices added that they had heard the same.

Enjoying himself, Aidan asked, "How do you know it was not an ordinary fire? Maybe a priest was clumsy with a lamp, or something like that."

The cobbler looked at Aidan as if the boy must be mad. "Look at that sky, boy." He pointed at the glowing dome over the temple grounds. "Is that some kind of ordinary fire? For hours, there was a tower of flames. It reached right up to the clouds, but the fire never spread past the temple walls. I was there, and I saw it. I am telling you, this prince is a wizard of some type." The cobbler mounted the lip of the well so that he could better see his audience. "There is more."He raised his arms to quiet the crowd's murmurs. "There are hobgoblins in the streets, and..."

Grabbing Aidan by the arm, Elwin dragged the elf from the growing crowd and headed down the street. Everyone was so intently listening to the cobbler that they did not notice the two leave. After a short distance, Elwin let go of Aidan's arm. "You're as bad as Pallas!"

"It was his story, not mine!"

"You encouraged him."

Aidan laughed. "By tomorrow you will be a hero."

Elwin's face turned hard. "I do not want to be a hero! And I definitely do not want to be a wizard. I just want to get out of here and find Leina."

Aidan suddenly became serious. "Okay, I 'm sorry. Let's find someplace where we can talk. Don't worry, Elwin, we'll find her."

Finding another dark alley, Elwin and Aidan were safely out of sight. Taking advantage of the moment, they sat down with their backs against the alley wall.

Aidan's mood was still serious. "How did you do that back there in the temple? Are you sure you're not a wizard?"

"You asked me that before. I didn't do anything."

"You don't remember, do you?"

"No. I had my eyes closed the whole time."

"Well," started Aidan, "when that raging fire leaped out of that priest Gillies, you raised your hands and a light came right out of you, but your light was a bluish green color, and it wrapped around us like a shield. The fire raged right past us, destroying everything except us. Inside that shield, I did not even feel warm. It was unbelievable!" Frowning, Elwin kicked at the ground.

Aidan looked at him. "You really don't remember, do you?"

"No, Aidan I don't! I don't know what is happening, but I have no powers. It could not have been me. It must have been the priestess, she didn't want us to be hurt. Remember?"

Aidan shook his head. "She could not even save herself." He then nodded at Elwin's sword where he had tucked it under his belt. "You have been carrying that sword for a long time. Maybe the druid is right. Maybe it does have some type of power, and maybe some of its magic has worn off on you. It survived the fire too."

"No!" snapped Elwin, "It wasn't me!"

"Okay," Aidan said defensively. "Just forget I said anything."

Elwin considered asking Aidan if he had heard the music too. But he knew that Aidan had not, and he did not want to accept what that might mean.

Elwin and Aidan sat without talking for some time before Elwin finally turned to Aidan. "Sorry. I didn't mean to snap at you. I am just so blasted tired and scared, but I really do not have any power. If I had some kind of magic, I would have felt something." *Did I not feel something? What about the song?* "I just want to get out of this cursed city and find Leina."

"What about Pallas and Colin?"

"We can't wait, Aidan. Soon the temple guards will reorganize and start looking for us. They've probably started already. The temple was destroyed, but I think that the Severed Head survived. They are still in control of the city, and soon they will be out looking for us on every street."

"I really think that was Pallas and Colin we saw at the temple."

Elwin nodded, "Maybe they were trying to rescue us. But we can't go about looking for them without drawing attention to ourselves. They won't be at the inn, so we have no idea where to look."

"Then we're just going to leave them behind?"

"No. With all the rumors, Pallas and Colin will be able to figure out that we have escaped, and they know that we are headed for the Tent City of Caiplich on the edge of the Aleash Grasslands. They will figure we have left Aonach, and they will then follow us. Even if they think we have died, Colin will still go on. Leina is his princess. He will try to find her, and Pallas won't let him go alone. Once we get to Caiplich, we will find them, or maybe we'll find them along the road. Maybe they'll buy some horses too. They do have all the money I gave them."

Aidan gave a quick node. "Then the next question is how we get out of the city. This late at night, the city gates are bound to be closed. And like you said, they're going to be looking for us. Even if we wait until tomorrow, we won't get past the gates."

Thinking, Elwin fell silent for a long time. Then he admitted, "I don't know what to do, but we can't stay here. Tomorrow their search will begin in earnest. We have to be gone by then."

Frustrated and feeling trapped, Elwin leaned back and tried

to think, but a soft sound invaded his head. It sounded too familiar. Fearing that it was the song of Earth Magic, he jerked his head up. The sound did not go away. "What is that noise?" he demanded.

Listening, Aidan heard a gurgling sound. "It must be the canal. One runs through the city and serves the city as a giant sewer system. The channel must run nearby this alleyway. Why?"

Relieved, Elwin sighed, happy that it was not the song of Earth Magic. "It's nothing." Then in a burst of energy, he was suddenly on his feet. "Of course! Aidan, you are a genius!"

"Well, yes that's true, but what did I do?"

"The canal is really a river, and it runs in one side of the city, then out the other."

"So?"

"We can use it to escape."

Aghast, Aidan sat forward. "You want me to swim in that? Do you know what these city folks throw in there?!"

Following the stone lined sewer canal, Elwin and Aidan quietly crossed the city, trying their best to avoid any more gatherings of people. That alone was difficult. The whole city seemed to be out on the streets talking and staring at the red glowing sky. No one appeared to be sleeping this night.

At last they reached the spot where the sewer drained out under the city walls. Away from the city's center and close to the walls, the area was deserted, dark, and quiet. Slipping into the slow-moving water, the two boys moved forward. Wading in the cold chest high water of the canal, Elwin and Aidan worked their way to where the water meets the city walls. Constructed into the city's wall was a small, flat arch that allowed the water to flow out of the city. The small opening was not guarded, but an iron gate that stretched across the canal was blocking their way.

"There has to be a way to open it." Elwin tried to lift the gate. When it would not move, he became frustrated and stepped back. "It's meant to keep people out, not in."

Hoping to find space under the gate wide enough to slip through, Elwin held his breath and dove beneath the surface of the cold water. Discovering that there was no way under it, Elwin came back to the surface, sputtering and looking like a drowned rat. Aidan pointed towards the tall wall above them to where a large platform stood out from the stone wall. "Look! There is a small building on that platform. Can you see the ropes and weights hanging out of the bottom? That must be some type of gatehouse. It's probably used to open the gate when it gets clogged up with debris."

Elwin looked up. "Sure, but how do you plan on getting up there?"

"By Climbing."

"But it is at least a thirty-foot climb straight up. We can't climb up the wall."

"There's that rope with a weight on it. It's probably part of the mechanism which operates the gate. If you give me a push, I should be able to reach it. If I am not spotted, I can make it up the rest of the way. As you said, this gate was not designed to keep people in."

Elwin looked at the wall and saw the rope Aidan was referring too. Realizing it just might work, he gave Aidan a quick nod of his head, "Okay, but be careful. The walls will be heavily patrolled."

With a push from Elwin, Aidan grabbed hold of the rope and started up. Quickly, Aidan ascended until he came up underneath the platform. He let go of the rope and swung onto one of the platform's wooden support beams. Aidan made it look easy.

Looking down at Elwin, he waved and smiled, but he did not smile back. A soldier was coming down the wall. Urgently, the prince waved and pointed. He did not dare callout. Getting Aidan's attention, the elf also saw the soldier. Then Elwin took a deep breath and ducked under the cold water. Aidan pulled himself up under the platform, clinging from the support beam.

The soldier was watching the glowing sky over the city. He stopped and glanced down at the canal. Aidan held his breath and prayed. For a moment, the guard did not move. But seeing that the gate was still in place, he finally moved on. Unable to hold his breath any longer, Elwin resurfaced. He looked for the guard, but he was gone.

Aidan had already swung up to the platform. With a quick look at Elwin, he disappeared into the small building. A moment later, the weights that controlled the gate began to move and the iron barred gate started to rise.

With the gate open, Aidan dropped back down the wall and splashed into the canal. "We will have to leave it open. There's no way to close it from the outside."

A few hours before dawn, Elwin and Aidan found themselves east of the city and heading into the Cluain countryside. It was not long before both sides of the dirt road they were traveling on was wooded, and only the sounds of the night could be heard. Not too far away an owl hooted, but they did not hear any sounds of pursuit.

"We should stop," stated Elwin. "We need to get some sleep before the sun comes up."

Aidan pointed to a tight grouping of trees. "How about over there? If we go into the woods far enough, no one will find us."

Finding shelter under a big pine tree, they settled in for what remained of the night. With no supplies or food, they laid down on a makeshift bed of pine needles. Both hungry and exhausted, they prepared to get what sleep they could.

"We should have thought about food," said Elwin, laying his sword down beside him.

"No need," answered Aidan. "We're in a woods, I'm a wood elf. I will find us food tomorrow."

Nodding his head, Elwin closed his eyes. Too tired to think of what had happened or what was going to happen, he quickly fell off to sleep. However, Aidan remained awake. Lying on his bed of pine needles he listened to the sounds of the night. Somewhere to the south, a wolf howled at the moon and an owl hooted in reply. The late rising moon could now be seen poking through the branches above. Despite everything that had happened, Aidan felt more at ease than he had in days. He was a child of nature, and as such felt at home among the trees. Aidan ran his hand through the soil, realizing just how much he missed his home in the Green. The elf wondered when he would see it again, or even if he would ever see it again. Letting the sounds of the night soothe his nerves and worries, he too closed his eyes and slowly drifted off to a dreamless sleep.

--

Pallas woke to the distant Aonach cathedral bells chiming of the 'prime'. The bells announced that morning had arrived. Usually, it was the temple bells that rang out every morning, but that was no longer possible. Now, the Church of the Three Gods once more rang in the morning, as it had before the arrival the cult.

Pallas stretched. Looking around an unfamiliar room, he sat up. The redheaded boy was in a long, narrow room lined with well-made bunks. He tried to remember what had happened and where he was. The room was filled with men getting ready for the day. They were soldiers, and they looked as if they had been up for some time. The only beds that were not already made were Pallas' and Colin's. Colin was sleeping in the cot next to Pallas'. Colin was snoring loud enough to compete with the morning bells of 'Prime'. After a brief moment, Pallas began to remember things, and he began to recognize where he was, the barracks of the city guard. The idea that he was hiding here in the barracks was somehow ironic.

Slowly, the memories of the night before came back. Pallas wished they had not. He had killed a man, and Elwin and Aidan were likely dead. Neither Pallas, Colin, nor Ned had been able to save them. Before they could reach the temples dungeons, a combination of soldiers, priests, and hobgoblins, as well as the raging fire had forced them back. Elwin and Aidan could not have survived that fire. It had been the single worst night in Pallas' young life. "We should have listened to father, and stayed home," he told himself. Trying not to think too much, he started looking for his clothes.

Unable to find them, Pallas gave up, laying back down. "Oh, Elwin," he sighed. "It was not supposed to be like this!" He wiped the tears from his eyes.

"Stop it!" he demanded of himself. "Leina still needs you. Elwin, if you can hear me, I promise you I will find her. Colin and I will not give up. I promise!"

"You two again?"

Pallas once more opened his eyes. He stared up at a tall guardsman. It took Pallas a moment to recognize the man, then it came to him. It was the sergeant that he and Colin had seen the day before. He had saved them from being killed by the man who called himself Patch. The sergeant had also told them to get out of town, or they would be arrested.

Pallas moaned.

"I guess I'm not going to arrest you after all," he said, smiling down at Pallas.

From the cot next to Pallas, Colin stopped snoring. Mumbling something about there being too much noise for him to sleep, he sat up in his cot. He rubbed the sleep from his eyes and looked up at the sergeant.

"You!" Colin looked as if he had not slept at all, and Pallas realized he probably looked about the same. Ned was right, the world was a cruel place.

Wrapping his blanket around himself to stay warm, Pallas sat back up. "Sergeant, you're a Renegade, aren't you?"

The sergeant nodded. "Yes. My name's Lud. You may call me that from now on. After all, we are now comrades of a sort." He waved towards the men in the room. "And all the guards in this particular barracks are Renegades."

"And Ned is ..."

"Our leader," finished the sergeant. "It was Kayno who organized us."

"Kayno?" questioned Colin.

"That is Ned's true name. Being an innkeeper is Kayno's cover, though I think he would prefer being an innkeeper to the Renegade leader."

"Kayno?" repeated Colin. "I think I recognize that name."

Pallas changed the subject. "Did you ever catch that fellow? What was his name?"

"Patch?" answered Colin. He doubted that he would ever

forget him.

Lud shook his head. "No...that one is as slippery as an eel dipped in hot butter."

Dressed now as a captain in the king's army, Ned appeared. He walked into the room, nodding greetings to the men he passed. Now dressed in a dark blue surcoat with the coat of arms of a single red rose, Ned had once more transformed himself. The innkeeper, who last night was a warrior, was now an officer in the service of the King of Cluain. A long red cape that matched the rose on his chest was draped over his back. In his arms, he carried two more uniforms of a Cluain man-at-arms. "Put these on. We are leaving soon."

Colin looked surprised. "Ned...I mean Kayno, I thought we were going to stay here until it was safer. That's what you said last night."

Kayno frowned at his name. "Things have changed."

"Good." Colin grabbed the clothes that Kayno offered him. "I need to get out of here." He glanced at Pallas and corrected himself. "We need to get out of here." Colin started to dress. "After you left us here last night, Pallas and I talked. We are going on ahead. Elwin gave his life for his sister, and we will see this to the end."

Pallas thought that Colin looked like he was about to cry, but with an iron will, the young Ceredigion lord would not let the tears come.

"No one's trying to stop you." Kayno looked at Lud. "You did not tell them?"

Lud shrugged his shoulders. "I haven't had the chance."

"Well, I guess I can tell them," Kayno said, addressing Lud. "Why don't you go change. I would like you to be my second in command. That is if you don't mind being promoted from a city guardsman to a Cluain officer."

"Sure, I'll come along. Getting out of this city will be a nice change. But where am I going... and do I get a pay raise?"

Ned, or Kayno, laughed softly. "Sorry, no pay raises for Renegades, and we are heading for the Tent City of Caiplich."

"Caiplich?" Pallas spoke up, surprised by the change in plans. "You're going to help us? How are you going to get us out of the city?"

Kayno smiled. "A unit of the king's men is scheduled to begin a patrol along the road to Caiplich. We will be that patrol."

"Well," said Lud. "I guess I had better change. Raise or no raise, I never thought I'd be a king's man. Do you have one of those uniforms for me?"

"I took the liberty to drop one off in your room."

"What's going on?" Pallas asked as he watched Lud leave. "What was Lud supposed to tell us?" He had a spark of hope, but he dared not believe what his heart was telling him.

"It is why I changed my plans...and why I'm going to help you reach Caiplich." Kayno stood above the two boys, his eyes shifting from Colin to Pallas and back again. "Elwin and your friend Aidan the elf, are alive."

Pallas jumped out of bed and nearly jumped out of his skin. Without thinking, he hugged Kayno. Embarrassing himself and Kayno, he stepped back. "Sorry." His blushing face turning to a bright red.

Kayno laughed. "Don't worry about it. I acted almost the same way when I heard."

"How do you know?" asked Colin, smiling from ear to ear. "How do you know that they are alive? Have you seen them? Where are they?"

"I have not seen them, but they are alive. They were in the

temple dungeon last night, but somehow they escaped."

"Where are they now?" Colin asked again as he finished dressing and sat down on the edge of his unmade bed to put his leather military boots on, but then he was quickly back on his feet. He was jittery and looked as if he were ready to run out of the room.

"I don't know for sure, but my guess is that they are headed for Caiplich. That is what I would do."

Kayno sat on the edge of the cot and put his hands on his knees. "Sit back and I'll tell you what I know."

"To start off with, I am sure that they are alive because the Severed Head is looking all over the city for them. They would not be doing that if they were dead or if they still had them."

"So they must have escaped," stated Pallas. "They might be hiding in the city."

"Then we have to find them," replied Colin. "We can't leave now!"

"Just hang on," continued Kayno. "I told you that they are headed for Caiplich. At least I think so. As I said, that is what I would be doing. Anyway, it seems the prince has made himself into somewhat of a hero. He is being talked about all over the city. The story is that Elwin and a group of Renegades attacked the temple. I guess that we are the Renegades."

"But that isn't what happened," said Pallas. "You're a Renegade, but we aren't, and Elwin was certainly not with us. He was a prisoner."

Kayno smiled. "You're close enough to a Renegade now. But there is more. Elwin apparently killed a priest, as well as the High Priestess Mor."

"Elwin?" both Pallas and Colin said at the same time.

"I know," agreed Kayno. "It is hard to believe. A skinny boy like him. But that is what they are saying, and some witnesses are saying they saw the prince bring down the temple." He shook his head. "These are strange days. Who would have thought the boy had it in him. Your prince has the Strigiol and the Black guardsmen running around like scared rats. They figure anyone who could destroy the temple and kill a High Priestess is a dangerous man. I would find it hard to argue with them."

"How?" asked Pallas. "How could he have done all that? Maybe it's just a rumor. Like us being Renegades."

"Maybe, but it does not matter. The Severed Head is searching door to door, and they would not do that if he were still a prisoner, or if he were dead. So, he must be alive."

"But that doesn't explain how you know that he is on his way to Caiplich," Colin pointed out.

"A water gate was found opened late last night, and a guard saw two men escaping through it. Since the Guardsman was one of my men, he did not sound the alarm. So, if my guess is right, the two were the prince and the elf. If that is the case and from what you have told me, Elwin will be heading for Caiplich. We will either find him along the road or meet up with him once we get to the Aleash Tent City."

"But won't the Severed Head figure out he has escaped?" asked Pallas.

"Not for a while," explained Kayno. "As I said, the guard that spotted them was one of my men. He closed the gate and told no one but me. With any luck, it will be days before the dark cult figures it out that Prince Elwin is no longer in the city, and they shouldn't know where his going. That gives us a good head start."

"And if you're wrong, and Elwin is still in the city?" asked Colin.

"The Renegades are already in the streets looking. It is the best we can do, Colin. And if he is discovered by the Temple, the Renegades will send a fast horse and rider to let us know."

--

Mounted upon a gray stallion, Pallas held the reins tight. He was having trouble keeping the restless horse still. The horse snickered and pawed the ground. "Come on, Willow, try to behave."

Colin fell into line beside Pallas. "Willow?"

"Lord Rodan told me that one should always have a name for his horse."

"But why 'Willow'?"

"Because of his mane." Pallas fluffed up the horse's long, thick mane. "It reminds me of the branches of a willow tree."

Thirty soldiers of King Lyon's army maneuvered their mounts into two columns of fifteen men each. At the head of the columns, Kayno and Lud watched as the men fell into order.

"Do you think this is going to work?" asked Pallas. "Even in these helmets, we still look too young to be king's men."

Colin looked at the soldiers in front of him and shrugged his shoulders. "I don't know. But we will find out soon enough."

Once things had calmed down, Kayno raised his hand and signaled for the men to move out. A trumpet sounded, giving the order to march. The columns slowly progressed through the city streets. People stepped out of their way, with curious eyes watching them pass, yet no one cheered as they once would have done. King Lyon had surrendered to Strigiol and without even a fight. Now the king was held up in his castle, and he rarely made any appearances. The people of Cluain blamed the king and his army for the loss of their independence. They were now a conquered people, who had surrendered their freedom without their king lifting a finger. The looks they gave the patrol were a mixture of anger and shame.

"It seems that the king's men are little loved," noted Colin.

The soldier in front of him turned his head. "And for good reason. The king let Strigiol take Cluain without a fight. We just stood aside and watched. Your Prince Elwin is already more of a king than ours ever was." The soldier sounded as embarrassed and angry as the crowds of onlookers. And yet there was a note of pride in his voice when he spoke of Elwin, who was now being referred to as the Outlaw Prince of Kambrya. In this Cluain city, Elwin was becoming a folk hero.

Like Kayno had said, the city guards did not try to stop them. As the patrol approached the city's east gate, the drawbridge was lowered. Standing on either side of the gate were two city guardsmen. They snapped to attention and saluted Kayno. Kayno gave each a simple nod as his road by.

Are they Renegades? Wondered Pallas. He kept his head low, trying to hide his face. Pallas sighed in relief as the last man rode past the gates and the drawbridge was raised back up. Once more the trumpet sounded, and the patrol picked up their pace to a canter. They quickly left the city behind them.

Pallas looked over his shoulder at the receding city. A thick column of smoke rose above the skyline. The smoldering ashes of the temple would take weeks, if not longer to die out.

Smiling, Pallas turned back. "We made it!"

The road to Caiplich was one of the busiest roads in all of Kambrya, and as such was a large wide road. Yet it showed signs of decay and neglect.

"They have let the road go to ruin," complained the soldier

in front of Colin. "If it's not taken care of soon, next year you won't be able to get a wagon down it."

"Maybe that is what King Jerran wants," said the man next to him. "If you ask me, the king is trying to discourage people from using the roads. He intends to stop all traffic going to free lands like Aleash and Mythra."

"Huh!" grunted the other soldier.

Pallas turned to Colin. "Do you think that Elwin and Aidan came this way?"

Colin looked down at the road. "It is hard to tell. If they did, there is no sign that I can see, but I'm not a scout."

A few short miles beyond the gates of Aonach, the road entered a woodland. The city and ocean vanished from view. Here and there, the woods were broken by a few farmhouses. Farmers had cleared away the trees to make room for their fields. However, as the day wore on the farms grew fewer and farther apart, and the woods grew thicker. By noon, they had passed the last farmhouse, and the dark shadows of the forest closed in on the roadside, and the smell of pine was thick. Hours slipped past before Kayno called for a stop and made camp in a small clearing next to the road.

The days and nights that followed soon became routine. The company would rise with the sun, and after a quick breakfast, the men would saddle their horses and ride on. Every few days they would come across a village, and the company would stop while Kayno and Lud checked in at the manor house to resupply. Due to Pallas' foreign looks, they never stayed in the villages any longer than what was absolutely necessary, and he never got to visit any of the taverns that they passed. Preferring to avoid the townspeople, Kayno always had the company camp in the countryside away from any possible spies. By mid-afternoon, the company usually stopped for the night. Progress toward Caiplich was slow, and for the most part, the road was quiet; too quiet. The once busy road now saw few travelers. Most people, including merchants, were not willing to venture far from home.

So far, they had not seen nor heard anything of Elwin and Aidan. The weeks passed, and they still had not found any sign of Aidan and Elwin. Fearing that they had passed them up, Colin wanted to stop, but Kayno said no. Shaking his big head, the ex-innkeeper assured Colin that the prince had to be traveling this way.

"It is true we may now be ahead of them. More likely they left the road for the shelter of the trees, but don't worry. Elwin and his friend will be able to keep up. Even on foot, they should not be too far behind. We have been going very slowly. If my guess is correct, we won't be in Caiplich more than a week before they show up."

Kayno smiled. "How about a little sword practice. It will keep your mind off your friends."

"How much further to Caiplich?" asked Pallas.

Sitting on a log next to Pallas, Lud stretched out his feet. "Not too much longer. A few days, maybe a week."

"What is Aleash like?"

Lud shrugged. "How should I know? I have only been to Caiplich, and Caiplich is not really a part of the great plains. The Aleash do not like us Kambryan folk on their land."

"But Aleash is part of Kambrya isn't it?"

"If you mean does it lie within the Dragon Mountains, then yes, I guess it is. However, that is where their ties to Kambrya end. The Aleash are a different race than us Kambryians. They speak a different language and have a different religion and culture. As far as I know, no Kambryan has ever ruled in Aleash.

Not even the old High Kings."

Camp had been set, and the sun was still well above the horizon. This was the time that the soldiers relaxed. Not far away, Lud and Pallas watched Kayno and Colin, who were sparring once more. Seeing Colin's potential as a swordsman, Kayno decided to start training him, and every evening the two entertained the men with their practicing.

Feigning one way, Kayno dipped his sword in the opposite direction, and then with a quick burst of speed, brought it straight up. With the tip of his practice sword, he gently touched Colin on the chin. "You're dead."

In all their sparring, Colin had yet to make a kill, however in the last few nights he had scored once or twice. The audience of soldiers cheered enthusiastically every time Colin showed improvement.

"The sword master never taught us that one," said Colin, feeling his chin.

"Lord Comyn is a good and talented man, but there are many things he does not know, and he tends to teach according to the rules of the courtly world and not of the real world. In true combat, rules don't matter. All the same, do not worry, Colin, you have a natural talent and amazing balance and speed. You are learning faster than you think."

So, intent on learning, Colin did not notice that Kayno had called the Ceredigion Swordmaster by his name, but Pallas had. "He knows Lord Comyn, the Ceredigion Swordmaster?"

Lud frowned at Pallas. "What does it matter?"

"It's just strange that he should know Lord Comyn," Pallas replied with a shrug. "Lord Comyn is not well known outside of Ceredigion."

"Stop prying," warned Lud, "a man's past is his own

business."

--

The day after Elwin's and Aidan's escape from Aonach, Elwin woke beneath a large pine tree. With a creak in his back, he rolled over and off the root he had been sleeping on.

Through the branches overhead, he looked up at the blue sky. "It's almost noon!"

Coming to his feet, Elwin found Aidan nearby sitting on a large boulder. Sitting on the rock surrounded by trees, Aidan looked like the king of the forest sitting upon his throne. He was now in his natural element.

"Why did you let me sleep so late?" Elwin asked.

Aidan looked up from polishing a wooden long bow. "I had things to do." He nodded at the bow and wooden arrows that lay next to him. "I wanted to make these before we started off. It's not the best bow I have ever made, and the arrows are a bit crude, with only stone carved tips, but it is the best I can do for now. But it should do. Luckily there is a lot of snake plant growing around here."

"What is a snake plant? Does it bite?"

Aidan laughed softly, "No it doesn't bite, nor is it poisonous. In fact, it can be used to relieve a stomachache. It is called snake plant because of its stiff sword-like leaves, which kind of makes it look like a bunch of green snakes rising out of the ground. With some snake plant, you can make a pretty good bowstring. Because of this, it's also sometimes called viper's bowstring hemp."

"I also gathered us some supplies." At the foot of the boulder was Aidan's green cloak. Spread out over the cloth was an assortment of nuts, roots, berries, and a few mushrooms. "That should hold us through the day, and if we are lucky we might see some small game along the road."

Elwin picked up some berries and a couple of nuts. "How do you know that these are safe to eat?"

Aidan laughed. "I am an elf, remember? Woodcraft is our life. Actually, this is the first time I've felt relaxed in a long time. I miss being among trees."

"I should learn some of that...woodcraft. It might come in handy."

Aidan shrugged. "It is a long way to Caiplich. I'll teach you what I can. It will pass the time if nothing else. However, humans are not very good at it. They prefer to dominate nature rather than work and live with it."

Elwin smiled. "I think that is man's greatest fault. Shall we get going? Caiplich and the tent city isn't getting any closer."

"Another human fault is always being in a hurry," Aidan said, climbing to his feet from his boulder throne. Using his cape as a pack, he rolled up their supplies and swung it over his shoulder. "Let's not move too fast, not too long ago a patrol of soldiers passed. I think we should let them stay ahead of us."

Elwin looked in the direction of the road, but he could not see it through the trees. "Do you think they were looking for us?"

"I am not sure. They did not appear to be searching the woods, but they were moving slowly. I followed them for a little while, but they just kept going east."

"You followed them? What if they saw you?"

Aidan smiled. "See an elf in the woods? Even in woods as tainted by humans as this one is, that is not very likely. Besides, I did not get very close, and stayed among the trees."

CHAPTER NINETEEN

A morning mist clung to the trees, making the road to Caiplich look like a path among the clouds, it was the first chilly day that Elwin and Aidan had experienced since escaping Aonach. However, the misty morning had more of a calming effect on Aidan then it did on Elwin. The past two weeks had been tense, and for the first few days they could see a column of smoke rising high above the trees. The fire that had consumed the temple grounds was still smoldering. Even after they could no longer see the smoke, Elwin felt uneasy. He was always looking over his shoulder, but no one was ever there. Elwin's nights were even worse than his days. His dreams were filled with red-robed figures, Torcull, and the crown that could not be touched, that he dreamed of before. Lately, Elwin dreamed that the crown rested on the side of a high mountain. In a thunderstorm, he would try to climb up the mountainside, but it was treacherous and slippery, and he could never quite find a way to reach the elusive crown.

Adjusting the bow that Aidan taught him to make, Elwin stopped for a moment. "Is this how you are supposed to wear it?"

Aidan looked. The bow string ran across Elwin's chest, with the bow itself resting against his back. "Pretty much. The main thing is to be able to retrieve it quickly."

Around the next bend, the road started to climb. Through the thinning mist, they could make out the dim outlines of rolling hills and large boulders that lined the road. Coming upon a meadow, they stopped. Covered in the silvery mist, green grass and flowers shimmered in the morning light. As they paused to take in the view, the morning sun broke through the clouds. Staring, Elwin and Aidan became lost in their own thoughts. Doing as Aidan had taught him, Elwin listened. He could hear a soft wind rising out of the surrounding hills and the call of a bird.

"There's a deer in those trees," whispered Aidan, pointing past the meadow.

Elwin tried to see it, but he could not find it within the woods and mist.

"Don't look with your eyes," said Aidan. "Smell and listen."

Elwin closed his eyes. Carried on the light breeze, he did smell something, and he heard a tree limb snap. "Should we go after it?"

Aidan shook his head. "It knows we are here. If we get too close, it will flee. We could track it, but I don't think we should take the time. Besides, we could not carry all that meat."

Elwin nodded. Standing there, he felt as if he were a part of the world around him. Despite his nagging fears and worries, Elwin found the woods a peaceful place. The misty forest seemed to be hiding him from the dangers that Elwin faced beyond the trees. Elwin shrugged his shoulders. *Maybe Aidan's love of forests is rubbing off on me.* Whatever the reason, Elwin did find a type of tranquility in the quiet simplicity and rhythm of the woods. The more days that passed without any adventures or dangers, the more at ease Elwin was slowly becoming. If it had not been for the dreams, he might even say he was happy here. Standing there among the towering pines and the ever-soft sound of the aspen leaves quaking in the growing morning breeze, Elwin took in the smells and softly smiled. The forest was having a positive effect on the young prince, and with Aidan's wood lore and bowman ship, they were never short of food.

After a moment, Aidan nodded and started down the road once more. With a soft sigh of regret, Elwin followed. Walking once more towards the world he did not want to face, but he could not hide from forever.

As the day wore on, the mist burned off, giving way to another bright sunny day. "It's hot again!" moaned Aidan. "I thought it might be cooler in these hills."

Elwin came to a sudden stop. "Quiet," he breathed. Sliding his bow from his back, Elwin notched an arrow onto the string. He pulled the arrow back until its feathers touch his check.

Looking down the road, Aidan saw the rabbit that Elwin was aiming at. It was sitting in the shade of a big old maple tree. "You learn to make a bow one day, and the next you think you can hit a rabbit at over hundred paces?"

"Shhh! You'll spook him."

Aidan smiled. Elwin would never be able to make that shot. Even the best elven archers would find it difficult. With his bow string held tightly to his cheek, as Aidan had taught him to, Elwin tried to find the meditative state that Aidan called the 'atman,' the center of one's being. Aidan said that all living things have an atman. For the past few days, Elwin had been trying to find his atman, but he had repeatedly failed.

Despite Aidan's assuring him that he had one, Elwin was beginning to believe that only elves could find it. So, when Elwin felt the meditative state of his center wash over him, the shock of it nearly brought him right out of the meditative state. Relaxing, he held onto his center and let himself sink back into it. The world around him began to slow down. Holding onto his center, he could feel and hear his heart beginning to beat slower. Everything around him became crisp and clear. He focused on the rabbit. As if it were a living thing, the wind whispered through the trees. He could see the rabbit. It appeared so close. Then everything suddenly changed. With no warning, a song filled Elwin's head. Once again, the song of Earth Magic touched him. Not realizing what he was doing, he let the song of life flow into him. It was exhilarating. He embraced it, the song was of power and nature of mighty mountains and swift rivers. It was as if the earth itself was whispering within the rhythm of the song. Letting the mystical song lead him, Elwin held his breath and released the arrow. Slowly, the arrow arched into the air. The rabbit jumped. Then it lay still.

Stunned, Aidan stared at Elwin. "So, you found your atman?" It was the only way that someone could have made such a shot. Even then it was unbelievable.

As the meditative state slipped away, so did the song, and the world returned to normal time. Suddenly Elwin became aware of what he had done.

"What's wrong?" Aidan saw the look of horror on Elwin's face.

"Nothing. I don't want to talk about it."

"What happened? Are you okay?"

"Yes, I am fine. Please Aidan, let it be."

--

The days that followed were warm and sunny. Elwin tried to forget what had happened. He promised himself that he would never let it happen again. He would never touch Earth Magic again. The power of the earth song was exhilarating, but it was also terrifying. For someone who had always been taught that magic was evil, the beauty of the song of earth felt to Elwin like he had committed a sin.

Finding that the woods were full of small game, Aidan had no problem providing Elwin and himself with fresh meat. Refusing to explain, Elwin would no longer hunt, or even practice with his bow. Sensing that something had happened when Elwin touched his atman, Aidan did not press the issue. Instead, Aidan passed the time by explaining the ways of the elvish people—their life, religion, and wood lore.

As they walked, Aidan pointed out the various plants, explaining which were edible, which were poisonous, and which had medicinal qualities. Not having to think about his atman or Earth Magic, Elwin was grateful for the distraction. The prince eagerly listened to everything Aidan had to tell him. Along with learning about the elvish people and their culture, Elwin memorized the elvish names and was learning the rudiments of the language. Soon the days turned into weeks, then the weeks into a month. Gradually, the road to Caiplich climbed higher. The woods became dominated by tall pine and ash trees. The hills grew steeper and over the treetops they could see the peaks of the Gobhair Mountains, which were not as tall as the Drygan mountains, yet they were majestic with their tall peaks and craggy pine-covered slopes.

Picking a few bluish green berries that grew from a short, stubby bush, Aidan shoved them into the cloak that served as their pack and started back down the road. "That plant is called azan, and its berries will stay fresh for a very long time. It grows only in mountainous regions. If chewed, it will cure headaches, but do not swallow it, or you will get a painful stomachache, which can last for hours, thankfully it isn't fatal."

Looking at the red sky that was quickly turning into a dark azure color, Elwin said, "It will be night soon. We should find a place to camp for the..."

Abruptly, Aidan came to a stop. Holding up his hand, he cut Elwin off. "Someone is coming," he murmured.

Elwin listened. At first, he could hear nothing but the chirping of crickets. Then the crickets fell silent. He heard the soft clopping of hooves. A rider, hidden by a curve in the road was coming up from behind them. "It's probably just a merchant," said Elwin, "or a farmer from that village that we passed through this morning."

Aidan nodded in agreement, but he looked concerned. "You are probably right, but it is late for a rider to be out. Would it hurt us to be on the safe side?"

"Okay," agreed Elwin. "Let's move off into the woods and let him pass."

Not having much time, the two hurried into the woods and crawled beneath the trunk of a fallen tree. Laying on the ground, they waited. Through the thick underbrush of the forest floor, the two peered back towards the road.

The woods became quiet. Even the wind fell silent. Feeling a cold finger run down his spine, Elwin wished that they had gone deeper into the woods.

An ebony-colored horse appeared. Its nostrils flared. Upon the horse was a tall figure in a blood red robe. Elwin's heart nearly stopped.

The Red Robe reined in the black mount, and the horse nickered and pawed the earth.

Elwin's throat felt dry. A memory of a dream flashed in his head. In the dream, he was running through the woods and being chased by the monk. An urge rose in him. *Run!!* The face of the Red Robe lay hidden within the midnight blackness of its hood. He dropped his head and looked down at the road.

At first, Elwin could not make out what the monk was looking at. Then a dark form moved. From behind the horse, something inhuman emerged. It was chained and collared. It was humanoid in form, and yet no one would mistake it for a man. Like a primate, the creature had long forearms which it used to walk. The skin of its thin upper arms was deathly pale. Below the elbow, the white flesh of the upper arms turned to a raw red color where living flesh became fused to long metal shafts that ended in deadly looking claws. Its metal claws reflected the dim light. Turning its head up to its master, the thing rocked back and forth. As it looked up, Elwin saw that it was wearing a black iron mask. A black mask that had a nose guard and a hole for its mouth, but nothing for eyes. *It's blind!* As if it were a dog on the trail of a fox, the creature lowered its head and began to sniff the ground. Slowly it moved towards the edge of the road where Elwin and Aidan had gone into the trees. At the side of the road, it raised its eyeless mask. With a sightless stare, it gazed into the trees.

The monk dropped off the horse's back.

Run! Elwin's mind screamed. *Run before it's too late!!* Whimpering, the creature clawed at the dirt. The monk came up next to it. Hesitating, the masked creature tilted its head to one side then to the other. It swung its unseeing gaze from the woods to the monk, then back again.

Terrified, Elwin's heart began to beat louder. He was sure that the sound was going to give them away.

Still whimpering, the creature shifted from one foot to the other. Then it turned its back to the woods and returned to the side of the ebony horse. Curling into a ball, like some strange dog, it laid on the ground.

The monk did not move. Rock still, the Red Robe stared into the trees. It was as if he was waiting for something to happen. Trembling, Elwin could feel the monk's eyes pass over him. *Run! You must run!* The urge was almost too much to resist. Elwin felt something pulling at him. Unable to take his eyes off the monk, Elwin felt his muscles tense up. *Run!* a voice in his head told him. *I am here. Run and I will follow. Run.* Elwin trembled. *I have to try and escape,* he told himself. Yet something else told him that was what the monk wanted. It did not matter. Elwin had to run.

Then slowly the Red Robe turned away. Elwin still trembled, but the urge to run slipped away.

The Red Robe remounted the ebony horse. With one more look into the woods, he turned and started down the road. Coming to its feet, the masked creature hurried after him. Just before they disappeared from sight, the creature turned its head, and Elwin was sure that it knew he was there. Then they were gone. For a long time, neither Elwin nor Aidan moved or made a noise. Slowly, the sounds of the woods returned. "That was close," whispered Aidan, breaking the silence at last.

Elwin moaned, "He's following me!"

"If it is the same one," whispered Aidan. His voice was trembling. "I heard Faynn say that there are more than one of these Red Monks. What if they are all hunting us? Where can we hide!?"

Elwin did not have an answer, but he knew that the monks were not after Aidan, but himself and the sword that was tied to his back.

Aidan crawled out from under the fallen tree. "What was that thing with the monk? It's hard to explain, but I have a strange feeling that it is even more horrible than the Red Robe."

Reluctantly, Elwin also climbed out of their hiding place. After catching his breath and calming his heart, he said. "What are we going to do now, Aidan?" The fear was still in his voice.

"Go on," responded Aidan. "What other choice is there?"

"But what if he returns? Or what if there is more than one?" He glanced nervously at the road.

Understanding, Aidan nodded. "You are right. We cannot go back to the road. We will have to cut across the country. If we move up into the mountains, we can turn east and make our way to Caiplich. Caiplich is just beyond these mountains in the plains. It cannot be that hard to find."

"But can you find your way through the mountains?"

Aidan shrugged. "I can tell which way is east, but I don't know these mountains. We might make a few wrong turns, but eventually, we'll get through. And if Pallas and Colin make it to Caiplich, they will be looking for us. We should not take too long getting there. The only other choice is to return to the road."

That settled it for Elwin. He was not going back to the road. The Red Monk and his nightmarish pet might come back down the road, or he might be waiting somewhere up ahead hiding in the trees. Waiting. There could also be more monks around. Just the thought was enough to start Elwin shaking all over again.

--

Climbing into the foothills of the Gobhair mountains was not very difficult. However, when they tried to go east, the mountains suddenly became steeper and more challenging, and the easy paths always seemed to be taking them to the north and deeper into the mountains.

Soon the hot days were replaced by the cooler mountain air.

Night settled over the land, and the woods became a dark, foreboding place as Elwin's imagination started playing tricks on him. He began seeing dark, red-robed figures lurking behind every tree and rock. The air had turned cold, and for the first time in days it started to rain. Any thought of making a campfire ended when a bone-chilling cry in the west broke the night's silence and was answered by another scream that called out from the south.

"What was that?" asked Aidan.

"Red Robes," Elwin answered in a deeply serious tone. "They're out there somewhere."

He nodded his head towards the night. "And they know that I am close."

Not asking Elwin how he knew, Aidan looked at the prince. *He is changing...* Aidan was not sure if that realization should be reassuring or not.

Dragging their sore, tired feet, the two stumbled on into the night. Too exhausted to go on, they at last made camp. Huddled on the side of a cliff face, the two ate a cold meal of nuts, berries, and a little dried rabbit jerky. Once their meal was completed, they silently settled in for yet another cold night. Along the cliff face and out of the rain and wind, Elwin drifted off to sleep.

--

Elwin opened his eyes. He was standing before a mountain. Halfway up the mountain, he could see a crown. Balanced upon a pointed rock, the silver crown was almost daring Elwin to try and touch it.

"This time, I will have you!" Struggling, Elwin started to climb up the mountain face. To Elwin, the crown had become a living thing. It was a thing, he needed to have, yet at the same time he knew he did not want it. Above the mountain, thunder cracked, and the night sky flashed. Rain pelted down upon his face.

Slipping, Elwin began sliding back down the mountain. Digging in his fingers, he stopped himself. "Not this time!" he shouted angrily. "You call out to me, but never let me close. This time, I will not fail."

Determined, he slowly started to climb once more, carefully choosing his footing. In his dreams, Elwin had climbed this

332

mountain so many times that he knew where to find the best places to hold onto.

Slowly, he climbed. The storm grew stronger, but Elwin would not give up. He reached out, but he could not quite touch the silver crown. *Just a few more feet...* He reached out again. *Almost there!* The crown was perched just above him, but there did not seem to be a way to get any closer. He searched and searched, but he could not find a place to hold onto.

"No! I will not give up." Elwin pulled out his sword, reaching out for the crown. The silver blade touched the crown. He smiled. This time, he would succeed. Somehow, Elwin knew that this was only a dream, yet that no longer mattered. Reaching the crown was what counted. It was all that mattered. He was obsessed with it. Without the crown, Elwin felt as if he would die. He nudged the crown. It rolled over the tip of his sword, then at the last moment, it skittered away. Slipping off to one side, the crown rolled off its perch.

In a panic, Elwin saw the crown sliding past him. Dropping his sword, he grasped out for the crown. Eluding his grasp, both the crown and the sword fell tumbling down the mountain. Panicking, Elwin hurried after. Bouncing down the side of the mountain, Elwin hit the ground with a loud thud. Finding himself bruised but not broken, he came to his feet.

"Torcull!" he gasped.

Torcull smiled. In his hand, he held the sword. At his feet rested the crown. "The mountain and those who call it home cannot help you, Elwin." Torcull handed him back the sword. "You see, I am not the enemy. I can help you, Elwin."

Elwin took the sword. *Why would he give it back? A trick?* "And the crown?" Elwin stared at it as it rested at the Prophets feet. He could feel it pulling at him.

Torcull shook his head. "You do not actually want it, do you?"

Elwin did not want it, and yet he did. "Leave me alone! Get out of my dreams!"

Torcull stepped over the crown, putting himself between Elwin and the crown. "Let me help you."

"No!"

He took another step. "Why do you fight me? I am your friend."

"You lie!" Elwin raised his sword. "Get back!"

"There is so much I could teach you."

"Go away! I don't want your help."

"You are growing stronger in both mind and spirit. That is good, but there is much you must learn. If you do not let me help you, the sword will destroy you. It is a thing of madness, Elwin. It is dangerous! Free my master. He alone can save you."

"Never!!" Elwin sat up with a jerk.

"What's wrong?" Aidan asked, awakening at Elwin's cry. Elwin looked down at the bruises on his arms. "Just a bad dream."

The next day they moved on. The rains had stopped, but by midday it started to come down again. Three times that day, mountain passes that Aidan had thought would take them through ended in boxed canyons, forcing them back. To the south, Elwin feared that the Red Robes were hunting for him. So, they went northwards and higher into the mountains.

Several more days passed, and they still could not find a way east and out of the mountains.

"We're going north again, aren't we?" asked Elwin. The

mountains around them grew steeper, and the peaks have now appeared much closer.

"Yes," admitted Aidan. "All the passes seem to run to the north. Every time we go east, it ends up being another boxed canyon, or it turns to the north. It is like the mountains are leading us deeper into them. Every time I try to go another way, we still end up going north."

"Are we lost?"

Aidan was silent. He stopped walking, and his head dropped. "Yes. I don't know how it happened. It shouldn't have happened. I am an elf! But I guess I am not a very good one. My parents would be ashamed. I'm sorry, Elwin. I've let you down."

Elwin put a hand on his friend's shoulder. "It's okay. You will find us a way out. And this is still better than running into a Red Robe."

But how long until they find us? thought Aidan. *Every night we hear them calling out to each other. They're hunting us like wild animals!*

Elwin pointed down a narrow pass. "Let's try that way."

Aidan looked. "It goes north."

Elwin laughed. "They all go north."

Once more, night settled over the mountains. Elwin and Aidan were no better off than they were the night before or the one before that. They were still lost, and the rain kept coming down. It seemed as if it would never stop raining. From the south, a scream like cry echoed through the trees. Elwin's blood went cold. Then another cry answered farther to the west.

Elwin looked into the darkness.

"They won't find us." Aidan tried to sound cheerful and reassuring. "We cannot even find ourselves!"

Elwin smiled weakly. "You know that it is me they want."

"If you are suggesting that I should leave you here, you can forget it. It is bad enough that I have gotten us lost."

Elwin smiled again. This time, it came a little easier. "Let's not stop yet."

Aidan nodded. He too wanted to keep far away from the monks. A few more hours passed when Elwin came to a sudden stop.

"What is that?" he asked pointing up ahead.

With a startled jump, Aidan looked up. His eyes narrowed, trying to pierce the rain and the dark. "It looks like some type of building or house."

"Do you think someone lives out here?"

Aidan did not have an answer.

Casually, they moved closer. The idea of a warm house with a fire was too much to pass up. In front of the house was a small stream and what remained of a bridge. The bridge looked worn, old, and unsafe, so they waded across the cold, gurgling stream.

The house's windows were dark. It appeared as if no one was home. Once closer, they saw that the door was hanging from its hinges and part of the roof had collapsed inwards.

"It's a ruin," Aidan announced feeling disheartened. "No one has lived here for a very long time."

Just past the ruined house were more buildings, all of which looked abandoned and ancient.

"This was once a small village," Elwin pointed out. "Isn't that a street?"

"It looks like it was paved at one time," added Aidan.

They came up to another house. One side of the stone wall had fallen in. Elwin pushed open the door. It came off its hinges, crashing to the floor. "Deserted. This whole village is deserted and has been for a very long time."

"I wonder who lived here?" Aidan gazed through an empty window. "I think it was more than a village, this town appears fairly big. The streets and buildings just keep going. It looks more like a city."

Elwin nodded in agreement, "But where are the walls? What kind of city would not have any walls? And why would anyone build a city so deep into the mountains?"

Aidan sat down on the remains of a stone wall. "I don't know, but I think we better stop for the night." Glancing over his shoulder, Elwin looked back down the dark street they had just come up. He was always afraid that a nightling was just behind them. A part of him wanted to push on, yet another part wanted to get out of the rain. "Okay, we'll stay."

Aidan led the way deeper into the ruined city until he picked out a house that still had most of its roof and all of its walls. "This one looks promising."

The doors and windows were gone, but inside it was reasonably dry. Feeling the comfort of being inside, Elwin leaned up against the stone wall. "I'll take the first watch."

Without arguing, Aidan curled up in a corner and closed his eyes. "Will you be okay?"

Elwin nodded, "Yes, I am fine, Aidan. I can't sleep anyway. At least not yet."

"You are still having those dreams?"

"Yes." Elwin had awakened several times during the last few nights, crying out. Torcull would not leave him alone. *There has to be a way to keep him out of my dreams. Maybe Faynn could teach me some way to stop him.* Elwin knew if Faynn did have a way, it would mean using magic. Yet, even if it did mean using magic, Elwin knew he would try it. He would try anything to keep the Dark Prophet out of his dreams.

Aidan laid back. "Just wake me if you need anything."

"I will."

Closing his eyes, Aidan fell quickly asleep. Alone, Elwin felt the night close in. Hugging his knees, he listened to the wind whispering through the empty streets of the dead city and the rain gently falling on the ceiling above him.

Aidan sat up. He looked around. The elf was no longer in the house, but outside among the ruins of the city, and Elwin was nowhere to be seen. "Elwin!" he called out. His voice echoed through the city, but no one answered. Rising above the rooftops was a full moon. Big, round and bright, the moon lit up the night. Aidan looked up. "That is strange," he said to himself. "There should not be a full moon for another two weeks. I must be dreaming."

Aidan climbed to his feet and started walking. "Maybe I can find Elwin. I'm sure the house was around here somewhere." The streets were deathly quiet. *This must have been a beautiful place to live at one time*, Aidan thought as he walked. But now it is just a place for the ghosts of a forgotten time. Even the surrounding woods and mountains seemed strangely quiet as if the silence came out of respect for the now dead city. Aidan turned a corner and walked on. In the moonlight, he could see patches of brightly colored paint on a few of the buildings. *Once this city was full of color and life. That must have been a long time ago.* It seemed sad now. Along the wide streets, he could see places where marble slabs were sticking up through the earth. *Streets of marble? I wonder what could have happened to all the people.* He could not see any signs of a battle or any other catastrophe. It was as if the people had just vanished.

"Hello, child of nature."

Startled, Aidan jumped. A child stepped out of a building. "I have been waiting for you," she said.

Aidan stepped backward. Then seeing it was only a child, he asked, "Who are you? Where are your parents? Do you live here?"

The girl smiled and pulled back her long black hair. "I am one who never was, Aidan."

"'One who never was'? How do you know my name?" There was something different about this child. Aidan suddenly felt uncomfortable and exposed.

"I know many things." A sad smile appeared across her soft childlike features. "And I knew you would come here, so I have been waiting."

"How? We did not even know that we would be here. We're lost, and if it were not for that Red Monk, we would not have come here at all." He looked around. "Where is Elwin?"

"He is safe. At least for now." With large black eyes, she looked up at him. "Even the darkness plays a role in the universe, Aidan. But once they have let the arrow loose, who may say where it will fall."

"What are you talking about?"

"The three eyes of the Buachaille grow nearer. The time of Sian is at hand," she said, ignoring his question. "The path before you grows narrow, and I cannot always be here to guide you and your friends. The three will change, or all will die. But how will they change, and into what?"

"You're not making any sense."

"I have come here to help you find that which you need—to find that which you have lost. You have been brought here for a reason, Aidan JaRe of the Hawk. You and your people have been without their wings for too long."

Aidan's face became pale, and then he turned angry. "How do you know my spiritual name!? Only the wise ones know it! Answer me!"

The girl turned and started down the street. "Come with me, Aidan JaRe. Time is something we have little of."

Frustrated, angry, and confused, Aidan followed.

"There," she said, pointing at a round house. "In there you will find what you need."

Aidan looked at the house. Amazingly, it was in perfect condition. It was as if time had not touched it. All around it were remains of the long-abandoned structures, but the roundhouse stood as if it had been built just yesterday. Painted a brilliant yellow with a bright red door, the house stood out against all the grayness around it. Encircling the house was a well-kept garden of brightly colored flowers. A large porch stood before the rounded doorway.

"Is this where you live?"

When the girl did not answer, Aidan turned around. "What is this...?" the words froze upon his lips. The girl was gone. Taking a deep breath, he placed a foot upon the first step of the porch. On either side of the porch stood white marble statues of tall warriors. Aidan had to look up to see their faces. The stone statues stared off into the dark ruins of the city as if they were looking for something.

Trying to ignore the statues, Aidan placed a hand upon the red door, pushing the door gently, it silently swung open. Inside was a large room. The room had the feeling of a living thing, a thing of immense age. There was also a sense of waiting. *The house had been waiting for something. For me?* It made no sense, but Aidan felt as if the house had been waiting centuries for him.

Don't be foolish.

He stepped inside. At the center of the room was a stone altar, with a single white candle. Its flame gave off a golden light. A soft breeze blew in through the door, making the flam flicker, and light danced across the walls. Apprehensively, Aidan approached the table.

Nervously, he glanced around. Except for the altar, the room was empty.

Like a living thing, the house moaned. Aidan could feel it breathing. *I should not be here.*

Lying beside the candle was a silver chain. Attached to the chain was a hawk feather that had been cast in silver. Almost without thinking, he reached down and touched the chain. A cold chill ran up his arm. A gust of wind rushed in through the door. Feeling dizzy, Aidan steadied himself against the altar.

The house seemed to sigh, "Free."

The wind grew louder. Without trying, he felt himself sinking into the meditative state of his atman. As if carried on the wind, he went deep into his center. Never had he been so far into his center, and still he went deeper. The wind changed. There were voices in the wind. No, not voices, sounds. The cries of a thousand hawks filled his head. The room around began to spin faster and faster.

"No!" he cried, trying to escape his own center, but he could not. Like a hand holding him, the wind pulled him deeper and deeper. The hawk's cries grew louder. Then suddenly both the wind and the sounds were gone. He was no longer in the room but outside. He blinked. The city had changed, no longer was it in ruins. Under a hot sun, marble streets stretched out in several directions. Aidan was standing at the cross section of a great city. Beside him was a fountain of green marble carved in the shape of a great bird. From the bird's open mouth, water sprayed into the air. Along the white streets, brightly painted buildings and homes stood tall and straight.

"Where am I?"

People with sun-darkened faces and straight black hair started to gather around him. He did not know who or what they were, but he was aware that they were not any race that he had ever seen before. Their eyes were large and black. *Why are they staring at me? What do they want?* A man came up close. He did not look like the rest. He was a human, but there was madness in his eyes. In his hands, he carried a crystal harp. He pointed at Aidan and started to say something.

"What?" asked Aidan. He could see the man's mouth moving and his wild gesturing, but there was no sound.

"What is happening?"

More of the strange beings started to gather around him. "Why can't I hear you?"

Still talking, the man with the harp pointed towards the north. The people turned away and started walking back into the city. There was a hint of sadness in their eyes that had not been there before. *What did he say to them?*

For a moment, the city became blurred, and then it was back again. It looked the same, but now everyone was gone. The fountain was dry and leaves blew across empty streets.

The city had been abandoned.

Why did they leave? What happened?

Again, the city became blurred, and now Aidan was back in the ruins. He looked into a bright blue sky. It was the bluest and clearest sky that Aidan had ever seen.

At his back were the remains of a fountain. A large stone bird lay off to one side. Its wings were broken off, and its beak was cracked from years of neglect.

High above the treetops, in the clear blue sky, circled a hawk. It cried out, and Aidan felt the cry echoing through his head. "No!" he shouted.

As if answering Aidan, the bird of prey cried out again. Growing dizzy, the world around Aidan began to spin. The sky rushed towards him, and the wind howled in his ears. Aidan blinked and suddenly he was Aidan no longer. With an amazingly sharp eye, he gazed down at the world below. Tucked up against the Gobhair Mountain, he saw the ruins of a city. It had been a large city once.

Among the remains of the city, he could see an elf standing beside a fountain. A silver feather was clutched in his hand. Strangely, the hawk thought that the elf looked familiar, but that was impossible since he was a hawk and the other was an elf. As a hawk, he had nothing to do with such creatures. With strokes of his strong wings, he left the elf and the ruins behind. Racing over the treetops, he followed a narrow stream until he came upon a valley. There the stream joined with a river. Turning east the hawk followed the river. Meandering along the valley floor, the river cut its way through fields of flowers and deep, green grasses. Spotting a mouse scampering for cover, the hawk was filled with an urge to fill his empty stomach. Swooping down, he aimed at his prey, then at the last moment, he rose back into the air. For some strange reason, he felt as if he were not truly a hawk.

He soared through the valley. Below, the river was a silver blue line that shimmered in the sunlight. Then the valley came to a sudden end. The river turned into a lake, and the valley floor rose steeply until it met a tall cliff face. A boxed canyon. Not stopping, he flew up towards the cliff and then along its base, until he saw a narrow cut in the side of the cliff. It was no more than six feet wide. The hawk knew that they canyon was important. *But why should I care,* it thought as towering walls of stone cliffs raced past him. Moments later, he emerged on the far side of the cliff where he discovered a steep sloping meadow that angled away from the cliff. At the foot of the meadow was a winding road that led up to a city of man things—a city of tents. The hawk could not understand why the man things lived in such small confining places. Beyond the tent city was an immense grassland as flat and as wide as the sea. It was a place where one could soar, yet there was no place for one to perch or build a nest. Not understanding what it was that he had discovered, yet at the same time knowing he had found what he was looking for, the hawk turned and flew back into the canyon. Racing now with the joy of freedom beating in his heart, he flew faster and higher. Then far below he saw the ruins of the deserted city once more. At first, he ignored it. But something pulled at him.

Aidan sat up with a jerk. Not far away, he saw Elwin leaning against a wall. Elwin had fallen asleep during his watch. Outside, it was already late morning. Leaning back, Aidan sighed, "It was only a dream."

"Huh?" said Elwin, waking up. "Oh, I must have fallen asleep." He glanced at Aidan. "What was the dream?"

Aidan shook his head and said, "It doesn't matter now." Aidan stood up and stretched. Then his calm green eyes suddenly went suddenly wide. Tightly clutched in his hand was a silver chain and a hawk feather cast in white silver. "No!" he shouted. "It cannot be!"

Suddenly Elwin was wide awake. He leaped to his feet and his sword appeared in his hands. "What is it?" He had not seen the feather and so he thought Aidan's cry was a warning of some approaching danger. Crouching, he stared outside. The rains had finally come to an end and a blue cloudless morning sky stretched out above the treetops.

"I don't see..."

Aidan raced past him and out of the house. Surprised, Elwin chased after him. "Wait!" he called.

Aidan didn't stop. He ran through the streets of the city as if he knew them by heart. The blond youth ran past a fountain and turned down a street that had once been paved in marble. He did not stop until he came to a burned-out ruin. One side of the round shaped house had been partially destroyed when a tree had fallen onto it. The timbered roof was gone, eaten away by the passing of time. The once red door was bleached gray by the sun. A garden that had once been well tended was also gone, in its place were weeds and wildflowers growing out of control. Aidan stepped onto the porch and up to the doorway where the once red door stood open, hanging from a single rusty hinge. Lying among the weeds and flowers were two statues that had fallen off the porch. He stepped inside. The room was silent and cold. He shivered. The house felt like a tomb or a monument to the dead. In the center of the room stood an altar, a pile of leaves had gathered around the altar's base, and upon its top was a puddle of wax.

Panting, Elwin entered the room. "Aidan? Are you okay?" Silently, Aidan stood staring down at the altar. Looking about the ruined room, Elwin also sensed the strangeness of the place. He felt as if he were violating sacred grounds. Before speaking again, Elwin, in respect of the place, sheathed his sword into his belt. "Aidan, what's going on? What is this place?"

Slipping the chain over his neck, Aidan tucked the feather under his shirt. "I don't know."

"What were you running from?"

"Dreams," the elf said in a voice just above a whisper. "Only dreams." *What did that girl do to me?* he asked silently. Aidan looked the room over one last time, and then said, "Let's go."

CHAPTER TWENTY

Like a whisper, a dry wind rolled out of the Gobhair Mountains. The whispering wind passed through the empty streets of the long-deserted city. As if voices of lost souls were being carried upon that dry wind, the whispering wind echoed and moaned. The voices carried upon that strange wind urged Elwin and Aidan to leave them and their dead city in peace.

Elwin hesitated. Within the wind, he heard the distant whispering voice of the Earth Song. It now sang of faceless sorrows, and broken dreams, of lives lost and paths not taken. The haunting song filled him with emotions that were not entirely his own and this time Elwin did not recoil in fear; this time, the song was not so overpowering, but simply sad. The song did not threaten, it only moaned with sorrow, a deep sadness that longed to be shared, and yet too deep to be truly spoken. It was as if the earth itself had absorbed all the stories, hopes, and dreams of those who had once lived here. Elwin stood silently as the city shared its loss and loneliness. Then, at last, the city's sadness had been fully shared. The ghosts of the past were satisfied, and now the city wished only to be left alone.

"We don't belong here," Elwin sighed softly.

Stepping off the porch of the round house, Elwin looked down the deserted streets of the ancient city. Above, the sky was clear and blue, and the sun felt warm. For the first time in days, the rainy weather had finally come to an end. Despite the improved weather, Elwin felt a heaviness around him. All that remained of the past days of rain were a few puddles lying along the crumbling streets.

Remembering the things that he had seen, Aidan only nodded. He, too, was heavy of heart. He was ready to leave the city and give it back to the silence of the past.

Glancing at Aidan, Elwin saw a distant and haunted look on his friend's face, a look that he had never been there before. Elwin suspected his own face did not look all that different. Aidan was always lighthearted and carefree, but now he looked as if his world was coming to an end.

Elwin looked up at the sky. "At least it doesn't look like it's going to rain today. That will be a welcome change."

Again, Aidan nodded.

In a hurry to put the ruins behind them, Elwin and Aidan quickly started back across the city and to the house where they had left their supplies. From above, empty windows stared down at them. Looking up, Elwin tried to imagine the faces that had once stared out of them. The only sound was the whispering song, reminding him that he was an intruder here. Once this place was the home to thousands, but no more. Now it belongs to the dead. Elwin walked a little faster.

Quickly and quietly they gathered their belongings. Leading the way, Aidan returned to the bridge. In the daylight, the bridge looked even older than it had the night before. It sagged and leaned off to one side.

"Why are we going this way?" asked Elwin.

"If we follow the stream," said Aidan in a soft voice, "it will lead us to a river valley. The valley cuts through the mountains and will take us to the plains, from there it won't take us long to reach Caiplich."

Hanging his bow across his back in the manner of the elves, Elwin asked, "How do you know that?" He looked at the stream. It was narrow and shallow, and he could see nothing about it to suggest that it would take them anywhere.

Looking uncomfortable, Aidan rested a hand on his chest.

Beneath his shirt, he could feel the silver feather. "Elwin," he said after a long hesitation. Elwin saw the pleading look in his eyes. Aidan was scared. Without meeting Elwin's eyes, Aidan went on, "Please don't ask me that. I just know. Let that be enough for now."

Elwin answered with a nod. "I won't ask." *What is he scared of?* "If you say this is the way out of the mountains, then it is the way we well go. Lead on my friend." In the distance, a hawk cried out.

Following the stream, Elwin and Aidan found themselves descending gently towards the southeast. That night they again heard the cries that haunted the woods, but they seemed distant now. Elwin hoped that meant the Red Robes had lost their trail.

It took them the rest of that day and a good part of the next to reach the valley Aidan had spoken of. In the center of the valley was a large river that meandered off towards the west. The river basin had steep sloping walls, giving the lush green valley a wide U-shape. Making his way to the banks of the peaceful river, Elwin cupped his hands and took a long drink.

Aidan kneeled beside him. The water was cold and refreshing after the long day's walk.

Standing up, Elwin looked around. Flowers and tall grasses grew to either side of the river. The valley was as peaceful as it was beautiful. Elwin stretched out his arms, letting out a long yawn. "Let's camp here tonight. I think we have lost the monks."

Aidan shrugged his shoulders. Ever since leaving the ruins, Aidan had been quiet and withdrawn.

High in the blue sky, a hawk slowly circled. As if sensing that the day's journey was at an end, the proud bird descended slowly to a small grove of trees. Among the trees, the hawk vanished from view.

To Elwin's relief, that night they did not hear the cries of the monks. Under a canopy of a starry night, Elwin slept a dreamless night. He woke the next morning feeling rested and ready for an early start. Looking toward the northern rim of the valley, Elwin could just make out the peaks of the Gobhair mountains. He knew that the road had to be somewhere to the south beyond the valley.

For three more days, they walked beside the river. Its water was cold and clear, and life of all kinds gathered along its banks. The river was the heart and soul of the valley, providing both water and food to the animals that made their home there. With the skills that Aidan taught him over the last month, Elwin managed to catch a few fish. Slipping into a moody depression, Aidan left their food gathering needs to Elwin. So, Elwin did the best he could. Still refusing to use his bow, he fed them on a diet of fish and edible plants. At night they would lie upon a bed of wild grasses and let the river sing them to sleep. The valley was a beautiful oasis, a place untouched and unspoiled by man. With each passing day, Aidan drew deeper into himself, and Elwin was left to reflect upon his own troubles. He was always listening for the cries of the monks to return and break the silence of the nights. The waiting was almost worse than the cries themselves. But sleeping was even worse. In his dreams, Torcull was always there waiting for him, while above a hawk circled as if following them down the river basin.

The morning was crisp and clear and promised of yet another beautiful day in the long river valley. Elwin leaned back and watched the water flowing by. Coming to a decision, he nodded to himself. *When I find Leina, it will be over. I am going to leave the sword with the Guardians of Light. If they have half the powers they appear to, then surely they could protect it from*

350

Torcull, and do so far better than I can.

Elwin lay back in the grass. For the first time in over a month, he felt at ease. It felt good to have made a decision. He let the world around him sink in, but as he relaxed, the gurgling music of the river rose up to him. The sound of the river reminded him of the song of Earth Magic, and Elwin felt his heart beat faster and had a desire to embrace the song of power. Shocked and terrified at his own feelings, Elwin once more shut out the world.

"Cursed blade!" he swore. Elwin could feel the weight of the sword at his side. It was always there, dragging him down. *I will not let you change me! Let the Guardians have you!*

--

The day dragged on and despite his misgivings, Elwin was in a much better mood. He had made his choice to give his sword to the Guardians of Light. Once rid of the sword, he hoped it would also bring an end to the dreams as well as the seducing call of the Earth Song. However, by mid-afternoon, Elwin found himself feeling frustrated. Throughout the day, the valley had slowly narrowed and had transformed itself into a canyon that cut between two snowcapped mountains. The once calm river that ran through the middle canyon now leaped and danced over the large boulders as the water attacked everything in its way. Picking their way up the canyon floor had been slow and tiring. As they went further up the canyon, the canyon floor became steeper and steeper, and with larger and larger boulders that had to be navigated around; the going was slow and hard. Higher and higher, they climbed. Then, at last, the canyon opened up onto an emerald green mountain lake. Elwin frowned as he stood staring over the small lake. From across the green surfaced lake, he could feel a cool mountain breeze blowing against his face. Sighing to himself, he looked at what lay on the far banks of the lake. From the far edge of the glacier-fed lake rose a steeply sloping hill that was littered with stones, boulders, and large sheets of snow and ice. Above the rock and icy slope was a towering cliff of a mountain.

"Another boxed canyon," he moaned, shaking his head. "It took us three days to get here, and now we have to turn back."

"No, we won't. There is a way through," stated Aidan.

"Through that?" Elwin pointed up at the craggy looking cliff. "Maybe if you were a bird you could fly over it. We cannot climb over it. It's too big, Aidan. We have to go back."

Aidan cringed and looked away from Elwin. "There is a way. We cannot see it from here, but there is a narrow slit in the cliff wall that opens up into a very narrow canyon. The canyon cuts right through the mountain and will take us to the other side."

Elwin's frown deepened as he stared at Aidan's back, but remembering his promise not to ask, he held back his questions. *Well, if he is wrong, we can still go back down the valley.*

"Should we try, then?" he finally said out loud.

"Tomorrow," Aidan replied. "It will be a hard climb to reach the pass. We should wait until the morning. We will make camp here at the lake's edge."

They had no more than set up camp when Aidan turned around. "I'm going to take a walk. I need some time to think."

"Are you okay?"

Aidan nodded and walked back down the canyon and away from Elwin.

Elwin watched him for a moment. Then shrugging his shoulders, he turned towards the small gem colored lake as it reflected and shimmered in the afternoon sun.

Elwin walked along the banks of the lake until he found what he was searching for. A large flat boulder reached out into the lake. Climbing out onto the wide flat boulder that stretched several feet from the banks, he approached its farthest edge. There the rocky surface of the stone slipped under the smooth surface of the lake. Elwin, finding a place to sit, settled in close to the water's edge. Sitting on the edge of the boulder, he stared down into the depths of the crystal-clear water. Patiently, he waited. Just below the lake's surface, a large brown trout circled. Slowly, Elwin lowered his hand into the icy water. The fish shifted, but it did not swim away. Carefully, he began to caress the belly of the fish. The fish became sluggish and stopped circling. In a sudden motion, Elwin cupped the fish in his hand and jerked upwards. The fish flew over his head and landed on the rocky bank of the lake. Elwin smiled at himself and returned to watching the water. Soon another fish appeared. By the time Aidan had returned, Elwin had a fire going and three cooked trout that were laid out neatly on a rock next to the fire to keep them warm. As Aidan approached, Elwin was slowly turning one more trout over the fire.

After dinner, the two lay next to the fire and fell off to sleep.

--

"Why are you running?" called out a dark voice.

Panting, Elwin ran through a dark forest. The branches of the black trees slapped at his face. Among the trees, Elwin could feel the evil, hungry eyes staring out at him. He ran faster. Suddenly Torcull was right in front of him. "Come to me."

Elwin turned and fled in another direction. Again, Torcull

was before him. He stepped out of the darkness. "You cannot run from me. I have touched your soul, Elwin. The druid tried to keep me from your dreams, but where is he now? He is gone, but I am still here. I am your true friend. I will never leave you."

Finally, too tired to run, Elwin fell to his knees.

"I am here to help you. My master wishes to help you. Do not listen to the druid's lies. He hides the truth from you. You know it to be true. The druid knows that only by freeing my master can you free yourself of the sword." Suddenly the priest of the severed head stood over Elwin. His blue eyes taking in the form of the prince.

Elwin stared up weakly. *How long have I been running?* "I don't need you or Faynn!" he shouted at the priest.

Torcull smiled and shook his head. "The Guardians of Light? You do not need them either. They will try to take the sword from you, Elwin."

"They won't have to!" he snapped. "I am going to give it to them."

For a brief moment, Torcull's eyes widened, then he quickly composed himself again. His smile returned. "You still have much to learn. Search yourself, Elwin. The truth is inside of you. You cannot give up the sword, and you know it. Its hold on you is already too strong. Only my master can set you free. You cannot fight your destiny."

Elwin woke with a start. He rolled over. The fire was almost out. Not far away, Aidan was sitting on a fallen tree. With his back to Elwin, he sat with his legs folded up under him and he was looking up at a silvery moon.

Sitting up, Elwin pulled his cloak around him. For a long moment, he sat there and said nothing. Silhouetted in the moonlight, Aidan's hair looked as silver as the moon. *He's like a mythical tree spirit.* Elwin came to his feet. *A tree spirit that has just watched his forest burnt to the ground.* Breaking the silence, he remarked to Aidan, "The moon is almost full."

Startled, Aidan shoved something under his shirt. In the moonlight, Elwin thought it looked like a feather. Trying not to stare, Elwin climbed to his feet. He turned his gaze up towards the sky, he walked over to the tree and took a seat next to his friend. "Even with a bright moon, there are so many stars."

"I guess," Aidan replied dryly and looked away.

Elwin frowned. *How long are you going to keep brooding?* Then out loud Elwin said, "Why don't you get some sleep. I can take the rest of the watch." *Is this how I have been acting? If so, it's time I should stop.*

"I don't want to sleep."

Elwin could sympathize with that. He leaned up against a large boulder. Staring up at the sky, he and Aidan became quiet. Silently they watched the stars and listened to the sounds of the night.

After a while, Aidan turned his head. "Thank you."

"For what?"

"For not asking about the canyon and how I know where to go. I know that I have not been the best of traveling companions. Colin or Pallas would have been better."

Elwin sighed. Then he said, "When you are ready, I will be here. Until then, you do what you have too. I also have been a poor friend. I've been lost in my own problems. I think we have a lot in common, Aidan, and that make us the best of traveling companions."

Aidan looked at Elwin's sword. In the last few days, he was never far from the blade. Even to get a drink from the river, the prince would take the sword with him. Then Aidan glanced up at the prince's face. Elwin's face had changed in the last few months. The innocent youth with the thin sickly-looking body was changing. His face was now tanned from the sun, and there was a harder edge to it. He had also put on some muscle from the long hard days of walking, hunting, and fishing. Elwin's outer body was changing and becoming fit and healthy, but he was also changing on the inside. There was no hiding the worries he tried to keep inside, yet at the same time, Elwin was growing more confident in himself.

"It feels like I have been wounded," Aidan said at last. "It's like I have been fighting some great battle that can't be won."

Elwin smiled. "They say that time heals all wounds, but I don't know if that is true." With heavy eyes, he looked at Aidan. "I think that some things can never be truly healed." He shook his head sadly. "I don't know. I don't know what is happening to us, or why, but I have a plan. I cannot change what has happened, but I can still control my future. I do not believe in destiny."

He is a lot like his father, thought Aidan. *Always needing to be in control, at least when it comes to himself.*

Elwin went on. "Maybe you were right about the sword. It is too dangerous of a thing. I have to get rid of it. I can feel its pull on me."

"What about Torcull? Faynn said that Torcull would find it and use it to free the dark god."

It's me you should fear. Torcull wants me to release Beli. Did Faynn know that was what Torcull wanted? Is that what he tried to hide from me? That I am the one who will bring back the darkness and destroy the world? "I don't know if I can completely trust Faynn."

"He saved your life."

"But why did he do it? The druids have never helped us Kambryians before. Why now? And why me? He wants something. He wants something from me, or maybe to keep me from doing something. Whatever it is, I am not going to give it to him."

"What are you going to do?"

Elwin shrugged his shoulders. "Don't tell anyone, but I am going to give the Guardians of Light my sword. Let them protect it. If I get rid of it, maybe I can return to who I once was. Without the cursed thing, perhaps I can stop..." Elwin looked at Aidan's shirt. "Aidan, maybe they can take whatever you might wish to give them as well."

A spark of hope flashed in Aidan's eyes. "Do you really think so?"

Again, Elwin shrugged. "There is only one way to find out. But first we have to find the Karr al-Isma and the sacred mountain that lies in the heart of Aleash, beyond the city of Caiplich. When we find it and the Guardians, we can ask. What's the worst that can happen? We cannot be any worse off than we are now."

Aidan nodded his head. "You are right. It is worth the chance. It can't hurt to ask."

For a long time, they were quiet, then Aidan stood up. "I think I'll try to sleep. Thank you, Elwin. You have given me something to think about."

--

The next day the two attacked the sloping hill on the far side of the lake. Catching his breath, Elwin started up at the eastern rim of the valley. The rocky slope that he was trying to climb was much steeper than it had looked from the bottom and stones rolled under their feet as they tried to climb. Like Aidan had said, the going was slow, challenging, and tiring. Looking up the steep hill, Elwin could see little chance of things improving. Once they reached the top, they would still have to find the opening in the cliff face, and so far, he could not see any narrow canyon. Glancing upwards, Elwin noticed the ever-present hawk circling above the cliff face.

From below, Elwin had thought that the cliff looked impassable, and now that he was closer to it, he was sure that it was. Elwin looked back over his shoulder. Below, he could see the green lake and the river that flowed out of it and down the lower canyon. He turned back facing once more upwards and towards the cliff face.

Elwin wiped the sweat off his face. "I need to rest," he admitted.

Sitting on the edge of a large boulder that many years ago had broken free of the towering cliff above. It had tumbled down until it found a resting place halfway down the sloping hillside. There on the sun warmed boulder, they stopped to have a small lunch of leftover fish and nuts. With satisfied stomachs and a little rest, they once more started to climb.

Finally, they reached the top of the slope. Panting, Elwin leaned up against the cliff's face that towered over them. "Are you sure that there is a way through?" He slapped the rock surface. "I can't see any way past this."

Aidan nodded. He seemed to be in a better mood today, but he still had the look of someone who was reliving a nightmare. "It is here," Aidan assured him for what must have been the hundredth time. "All we have to do is follow the cliff, and we will find it."

Doubtfully, Elwin looked up ahead. All he could see were a

few shrubs, giant boulders, a few short stubby pine trees, and the towering cliff. "Well," he said at last, "let's keep moving, then."

Another hour passed. Walking along the base of the cliff was easier than the climb had been. However, it appeared to Elwin as if they were going nowhere. The cliff showed no sign of any canyon. Elwin was about to demand that they turn back when Aidan pointed, exclaiming, "There!"

Elwin looked. There was indeed a narrow cut in the wall which was partly covered and hidden by a stubby pine tree. The twisted pine tree leaned out away from the cut where it had managed to find just enough room for its roots to take a grip in this harsh high-altitude environment. The cut itself was not much wider than the weather-worn tree that grew out of it.

"That's it? That's your canyon? It is too narrow. It cannot go all the way through."

Aidan only smiled and squeezed past the twisted tree. Elwin shrugged his shoulders and followed.

Aidan's canyon seemed to be no more than a notch in the cliff face. Ahead of the prince, Aidan squeezed between the stone walls, and Elwin quietly followed. It was a difficult process to squeeze in-between the walls and climb over the boulders that had fallen from above. Then, to Elwin's surprise, the canyon did not come to an end. After several yards, the narrow canyon widened up enough to allow the two to walk side by side, and the canyon floor was level with almost no boulders blocking their way. The canyon, which curved and twisted deeper into the cliff, appeared to have been created by the raging waters of an ancient glacier that fed the river. Above their heads, they could see a narrow band of blue sky between the towering cliff walls. Within the walls of the canyon, the air was cool, shady, and damp. Moving deeper and deeper into the canyon pass, Elwin kept expecting it to come to an abrupt end, but it didn't. In some places, the canyon would narrow so much that they were barely able to squeeze through, but it always widened up on the other side. However, it was never wider than ten or twelve feet.

Stepping under a stone arch that formed a natural bridge that stretched from one side of the canyon to the other, the two suddenly stopped. Awestruck, the two boys gazed upon a vast valley. Hemmed in by towering cliff walls which encircled the entire valley basin, the view was breathtaking. To the north, a towering waterfall flowed down the cliff face that fed a small crystal-clear lake. Above, white birds circled, hunting for fish. The rocky canyon floor had given way to rich fertile soil that fed several groves of pine and aspen trees. Between the groves of trees were open fields of tall grass that waved gently in the mountain breeze. Spooked by the arrival of two travelers to their private home, several deer fled, disappearing into the shelter of the trees.

"Wow!" breathed Elwin. "This valley must be two miles wide. Who would have thought something like this was here!"

Aidan pointed off to the north face of the valley. "Look! There are caves along that cliff wall. Let's take a closer look."

Aidan was not surprised by the valley. After all, he had seen it as a hawk. However, he had not noticed the caves. "They could provide some nice shelter for the night. It's been a long time since we had any real shelter." *And I won't be able to see that hawk from the inside of a cave.*

As soon as they reached the north cliff face, Elwin started gazing into a string of several cave mouths. The whole north side of the valley wall was honeycombed with caves. "These are strange. All the entrances have triangular openings."

Aidan nodded in agreement. "They are not natural. They

have been carved to look like tent flaps."

Elwin agreed with a quick nod. "But who would create such things out here in the middle of nowhere?"

As they explored the caves, they soon discovered that once inside, all the caves appeared the same and were rather small, they did not go back far into the cliff face but were carved into a single round shaped room. The now empty caves actually did feel like being inside a tall tent. Each one had a round, smooth stone floor and short walls. Above, the ceiling came to a peak in the exact center of the stone tent. As if the caves were made of cloth, standing in the center of each room was a stone post, similar to a tent post, but made of stone. Flakes of ivory colored paint could still be seen on the walls, adding to the sensation of being in a cloth tent.

"Elwin! Come out here," Aidan called.

Elwin came out of a cave he was exploring to see what Aidan had found. Finding Aidan standing in front of the largest cave they had yet seen, Elwin looked up. He suddenly found himself staring up at a pair of giant statues. Carved into the hard granite walls of the cliff, the statues flanked the cave opening. In outstretched arms, one statue held a sword and the other a crown.

"They look like gods, or maybe a king's guards," commented Elwin.

"Strange," stated Aidan, still staring up at the statues. "They have no faces."

"I think they once had faces, but someone destroyed them." Elwin pointed up to their strange faceless heads. "Where faces should have been, the stone appeared to have been chipped away."

"Who do you think carved them?"

"Maybe the Aleash," Elwin replied. "I read once that during

one of the tribal wars, one of the clans refused to surrender to the new Caliph and took to hiding in the mountains. This must be where they lived."

"Did they ever return to the plains?"

Elwin shook his head. "No. They lived here for years. But in the end, the Caliph found them. He sent an army into the mountains after them. There was no hope. A single clan could not win against the Caliph's army. Years before, the Aleash had fought a bloody civil war known as the "Aleash Wars of Unifications." After years of warfare, a single Caliph had united fourteen of the fifteen clans into a federation of clans. However, one clan had still not been defeated, nor were they willing to join the Caliph's new alliance. Militarily, that one clan was totally outnumbered, they had no chance. Still, they refused to join with the unification under one single Caliph. The Caliph was furious, as he wanted total unification.

So, in desperation, that one rebellious clan which had refused to submit fled the grassland and tried to make a new life in these mountains. According to the histories I've read, the Caliph never relented in his search for the missing clan. When he finally discovered their new home hidden here in these mountains, the Caliph attacked with overwhelming force. Of that one last independent clan, there were no survivors. The Caliph's army destroyed them all. The Aleash are a hard people."

"I cannot imagine the elves being at war with one another... Humans are hard to understand. Let's go on. This is too sad of a place."

Instead of using the caves as a shelter for the night, the two walked to the far side of the valley. Like on the far western side of the valley, the eastern side was another narrow canyon that was cut into the cliff face. Once more, the steep walls of a narrow canyon closed in on them. Walking just behind Aidan, Elwin looked up. Between the walls, he could see the thin line of the blue sky of the fading day. Another day was quickly coming to an end and the thin line of blue sky was beginning to darken. Soon the night was upon them.

Lying on his back, Aidan stared up at the few stars he could see through the canyon roof.

"That Aleash clan picked a good place to defend themselves," he mused out loud.

Elwin nodded. "But they were greatly outnumbered. What I don't understand is why they did not escape through the western canyon. They should have retreated to the river valley. They did not have to stay and fight. They had already fled once, why not again?"

"Why do humans hate each other so much? Why would the Aleash want to kill their own brothers and sisters?"

Elwin was silent; he did not have an answer.

"It must have been horrible," Aidan went on. "Were there children?"

"Yes." Rolling over, Elwin closed his eyes. That night he did not dream of Torcull, nightlings, or of the crown, perhaps the canyon somehow protected Elwin from the Prophet probing into his dreams. Instead, he dreamed of the Aleash clan that had lived in the hidden valley.

The dream came with the soft murmuring of the Earth Song that Elwin was becoming all too familiar with. He recognized the valley as the same one Aidan and himself had passed through only the day before. However, it was different. All around the northern rim were the sounds of a small village. A village of caves. Children ran after one another, laughing and playing games. Within the valley floor, men tended their flocks of sheep and horses, while women worked in a large community field that sat in the center of the valley. It seemed a peaceful place, except for the faces of the men and women. There was a tension in the air.

"Are they coming?"

Elwin turned to see who had spoken. It was a tall, dark-haired Aleash woman. The man that she was talking to was an Aleash as well. "Yes."

The two Aleash seemed totally unaware of Elwin standing right next to them. Like a ghost, he listened in on their worried conversation.

"Abir, are we doing the right thing?" the woman asked.

Abir nodded. "Yes, my love. He will come, and as it was foretold, the Caliph will try, but he cannot stop it. No one can kill the prophecy. When the prophesied one comes, it is foretold he will bring both death and peace. Yet, who will proclaim him if the Al-Elche do not stay true?"

"But will he come in time?"

Abir shrugged. "For us? I do not think so, Alma. Our time is coming to an end, as it was written. But we are not doing this for us, but for our children and for our children's children."

From across the valley, a man came running towards them, his hands and arms waving madly over his head. "They're coming!" he shouted, "They're coming!"

Abir turned his head, "It is time."

Alma looked at him. There were tears in her eyes. "I don't know if I can do this."

Abir looked carefully at her. "You must. I do not matter. It is the destiny of the Al-Elche that matters now. Our people must be ready when the time comes."

Elwin looked around. He felt invisible. The laughter was

gone from the valley. Now the Aleash of the Al-Elche were rushing around like angry ants. The men grabbed their weapons and formed into ranks. The women and a handful of men hurried the children to the western end of the valley. Alma shouted out orders. She was hurrying about and trying not to look back at Abir and the other men.

At the far eastern side of the valley, the Caliph's army suddenly appeared, coming out of the canyon and into the valley. A tall man wearing a blue turban raised his hand. The army halted, and the blue turbaned man stepped forward. "We do not want a war, Abir. Return and all will be forgiven." Abir climbed onto a rock so that he could be seen better. "Zuriel, is that you? Why did they send you?" He stared down at the opposing commander.

"Yes. It is me. And you know why I was sent. Don't be a fool, and the Caliph will take you back."

"I cannot return, Zuriel."

"And I cannot leave you here."

"I know."

"Abir, listen to me. I am your friend, or at least I was once. Do not do this."

"What other choice is there?"

"The Caliph will forgive you. He will take you back, Abir. You and your clan can leave in peace."

"Peace!" Abir almost laughed. "Will the Caliph truly let us be? Will he listen to the words? Will he let us keep our beliefs?"

"You know he cannot."

"Then you know my answer."

"Abir..."

"There is no point in arguing, Zuriel. Do what you are here to do." Abir climbed off the rock. He turned to his men. "When they come, fall back to the western canyon. Our blood will buy time for the future."

"Abir!" Zuriel shouted.

Abir did not answer. He stood with his men watching and waiting.

"Curse you, Abir!"

The Caliph's army slowly moved forward. The Al-Elche retreated back to the western canyon, there they turned and held their ground.

"No!" shouted Elwin, who had followed them into the canyon. "The river valley is that way." He pointed, but no one moved or heard him.

Then the fighting began. It was fierce, and men from both sides fell. The narrow canyon made it hard for the larger Aleash army to bring its whole force against the Al-Elche. However, the men of the Al-Elche were few, and they were outnumbered. Slowly they began giving up ground, and more men began to fall.

Suddenly Zuriel and Abir faced each other. "Please!" pleaded Zuriel. "You've lost! Surrender!"

"Lost?" Abir smiled. "Today maybe, but there will be other days."

Thrusting his sword at Zuriel, Abir attacked. Zuriel parried and returned with an assault of his own. Their long curved swords crashed together. With mad fury, they threw themselves at each other. Back and forth they fought across the canyon floor. Soon both men were sweating in the summer heat. The sound of their swords echoing down the canyon. Time seemed to slow as the two fought on. Then suddenly, Abir dropped his guard. Zuriel could not stop his blow in time, and Abir fell to his knees.

"No!" howled Zuriel. He dropped to the ground next to Abir. Replacing the sound of the swords, his anguished voice now echoed down the narrow canyon.

Abir looked down at his wounded side.

"Why, Abir? Why!?"

Cringing, Abir looked up. "It had to be, Zuriel. The Al-Elche can now fulfill their destiny."

Zuriel shook his head as if he were watching a madman. "There is no Al-Elche. Not after today."

Abir coughed up some blood and slumped against Zuriel, then he was still. Shivering in his own sweat, Elwin sat up with a start. The Earth Song came to an abrupt stop, only the whispering wind sighed through the canyon. Lying back down, Elwin wrapped his cloak about himself, but he could not go back to sleep.

The following morning, Elwin and Aidan emerged out of the canyon's far side. Standing on the northeastern edge of the foothills, Elwin stared out over the rolling landscape that quickly descended down to the flat lands below. The great mountains now lay behind him and Aidan. Below and beyond the green rolling hills was a vast grassland that stretched out as far as the eye could see. Swaying in the hot, dry wind, the tall silvery grasses looked like waves rolling across a vast sea. Elwin caught his breath. He had never seen such an immense, empty land. "So, this is the high plains of Aleash," he uttered, knowing that out there somewhere in that vast emptiness, was his sister.

The going was easier now that they were beyond the high mountains and canyon lands, and soon they reached the edge of the foothills. The two weary travelers quickly crossed the foothills of the Gobhair mountains. Cresting the last hill, Elwin saw the Tent City of Caiplich, as well as the blue-gray walls of a small inner city. Even from this height, he could see a white flag hung at the city's gate. He did not need a closer look to know that on the flag would be the black eagle of Strigiol.

"I thought Aleash was still a free land," said Aidan, seeing the flag.

"Rodan once told me that Caiplich is not really a part of Aleash, at least not the inner walled city," explained Elwin. "He told me that the city used to be a free, independent city that belonged to no nation. The inner city of Caiplich is mostly made up of Kambryians, and the Aleash rarely enter the walled city, which is really just a trading fort ruled by a guild of wealthy elite. The Aleash do not like walls. The actual Aleash city of Caiplich is the tent city that surrounds the walled center, and most Aleash only come here to trade and sell their horses to the Kambrya businessmen of the inner city. I guess King Jerran thought that Caiplich was too important of a place to be left free. It is the gateway to grasslands and the horses that the Aleash breed. It's small but a very wealthy city."

"And the Aleash don't care?"

Elwin shrugged. "According to Rodan, the Aleash believe one Kambryan is as bad as another. I don't think they care who rules in the inner city, as long as they continue to trade with them."

Elwin pointed at the clusters of tents that stood around the city walls. Some of the clusters were made up of several dozen tents, while others had only a few in them. Yet each looked tiny compared to their herds of horses that grazed around them. "In the spring and summer, the clans roundup their horses and bring them here. In the Aleash language, Caiplich means 'place of wild horses'. It makes sense. When the clans have sold or traded the last of their horses, they will pack their tents and go home. For now, Caiplich is a city of tents, yet in the fall and winter there is only the inner city." Elwin nodded towards the plains. "Out there is the real Aleash."

"The city looked smaller before," sighed Aidan. *From the air, everything looks smaller.*

Elwin stopped and stared at Aidan. "You have been here before?"

Feeling Elwin's eyes upon him, Aidan looked away. "Come. The road is this way."

CHAPTER TWENTY-ONE

There it was. Caiplich, the city of horses. Surrounding its gray-blue stone walls of the inner town was the tent city. It was an impressive view of the city rising out of the plains, dominating the green and silvery grasslands that stretched out behind it. Elwin smiled to himself; he had made it to Aleash. He looked up the dirt road. The dusty road ran directly towards the city. *But now what? I have no money and no idea where Pallas and Colin could be. They might not even be here yet. We could be the first to arrive. It's also possible that they're not coming. What if Colin and Pallas were captured back in Aonach?* Elwin shook his head. There was too much to worry about.

"Now what?" asked Aidan, as if he had read Elwin's mind.

Why ask me? He thought. "I'm not really sure," Elwin admitted. "We need to find Pallas and Colin, but I don't know where to start. And what if they are not here yet? They could be days behind us." He refused to accept that they were not coming.

"We could find some jobs," offered Aidan. "And search for them when we're not working."

Elwin shook his head and laughed, "Us? The son of a king and an elf from the Green. What would we do? Neither one of us has been trained in anything practical. I don't think your wood lore will be a big seller in the high plains. There aren't too many trees around. Horsemen find jobs here, and neither of us have great skills in that area."

"We can't just live off the streets!" exclaimed Aidan. "Are we to be homeless beggars?"

Elwin frowned. "Street people are invisible to most. It could be an excellent cover. We could hide right under Strigiol's eyes, and they would never see us. However, I don't think it will come to that. We will just have to do the best we can. We can start by searching the inns one by one. If Colin and Pallas have not spent all that money I gave them, then they should be able to afford a room. They will be searching for us too, which should make things easier. But we will have to be careful. Like Aonach, this is an occupied city, and we do not want to end up in the temple again."

"Right. But what if we can't find them? I really don't want to be sleeping in some alleyway."

Elwin sighed. "If we have not found them by sunset, we will leave the city and spend the night back in the foothills, then we will try again tomorrow."

Aidan smiled. He preferred being outdoors rather than the crowded streets of the city. It was the first time in days that Elwin could remember seeing Aidan smile. It was a welcome change.

To reach the inner city gates, they would first have to pass through the city of tents that surrounded the Kambryan part of the city. As they approached the tent city, the smell of horses became intense, and the dirt road became muddy and branched off in different directions. The tents themselves were divided into groups or clusters. Elwin knew from his readings that each cluster was an Aleash clan. In between the tribal tents were the large herds of horses.

It was almost noon, so the day was getting hot. It was the time of day that the Aleash went into their tents to stay out of the intense heat that blew in off the grasslands. Few people were out on the road, and those who were had dark olive skin and even darker eyes.

Suspiciously, the few Aleash outside watched Aidan and Elwin walk past.

Aidan turned his nose at the smell of so many horses in one

place. "How can they stand that smell?"

"Be careful," warned Elwin. "These are Aleash, and they probably like the smell. And I don't think they like strangers much...What?"

"Excuse me." an Aleash approached them from a nearby tent. He was a tall, thin man with an oily mustache that matched his dark oily hair. Stepping out in front of Elwin and Aidan, he forced them to stop. "You seem lost." In one hand, he held the hem of his white robe, keeping it out of the muddy road. With his other hand, he gestured dramatically as he talked. "The tents can be confusing. Some say it is like a maze. May I be of some assistance? Help you find your way?"

"No, thank you," Elwin returned. "We are fine." He tried to get around the man, but the Aleash would not let them pass.

"Please," he said with a thick accent. "Let me be of help. You are strangers to this place, no? Have you come from the west?"

"Thank you again." Elwin tried to keep his voice steady. "But we are fine."

"I am called Inan. I have friends. They can help too."

"No thank you!" Elwin pushed past him. Finally stepping aside, Inan let them go.

"What was that all about?" asked Aidan.

"I don't know. Maybe he was trying to help us, or maybe he hoped to rob us. Either way, I don't trust him. Let's keep moving." Elwin looked over his shoulder. Inan had vanished between two tents.

The tent city was a maze, and the two were slowing, picking their way towards the inner city.

Aidan pointed down the road. "Look! It's that fellow Inan again. And he is not alone."

Somehow the Aleash had gotten in front of them and now there were a half dozen men with the dark skinned Inan. In a threatening pose, they stood before them blocking their path, each of the Aleash men was dressed all in long white robes and holding long curved swords.

Elwin and Aidan stepped back and turned to run, but close behind them were another six men holding the same long curved blades. The Aleash quickly encircled them, giving Elwin and Aidan no chance to escape.

Inan stepped forward. "Now come, please." It was not a request.

"Where are you taking us?!" demanded Elwin.

"Move," Inan said and gave Elwin a push with the point of his sword. "You will see."

Not having many choices, Elwin let Inan and his men guide them into the tents and away from the road and away from the inner city walls.

Elwin thought they were thieves, but Inan made no attempt to rob them. Instead, the Aleash took them to a large compound of tents that were well removed from the others.

"In." he said, pointing at a small tent.

"What do you want from me?" asked Elwin. "We don't have any money."

Two men grabbed Elwin and tossed him inside. Inan poked his head inside the tent. "You will stay here until you are sent for," he ordered. "Do not try to leave. There will be guards outside."

Once Inan was gone, Elwin decided to look outside, but a guard shoved him back inside.

An hour passed.

The tent was small but comfortable. There was no furniture.

However, there were a few large silk pillows to sit on and a richly carpeted floor. It was a pleasant space, at least for a prison cell. In the center was even a large bowl of fruit. *Why did they let us keep our weapons?* Elwin wondered, sitting among some of the pillows. *I was a fool to think that the temple would not have sent someone to look for us.* He now suspected these men knew who Elwin and Aidan were and were probably hoping to collect a reward.

Several more minutes had passed before someone arrived. Turning, Elwin saw the tent flap being pulled back as two men ducked into the tent. Elwin jumped to his feet and grabbed his sword hilt. One had dark hair and had the traditional look of an Aleash. However, he was dressed from head to foot in black riding leathers instead of the traditional white robes of the plainsmen. The other man wore a long brown robe and carried a long staff.

Elwin gasped. "Lord Rodan, Faynn?!"

"So, it is you," Rodan Macay said as he fully stepped into the tent. He sounded angry and more than a little relieved. "We were beginning to wonder if something had happened."

"How did you get here? Are we prisoners?"

Rodan shook his head. "No, you are not a prisoner. But you are very lucky you are not. There are Strigiol men all over the city.

What were you thinking? Running off and leaving Reidh like that! You're still a boy, and a foolish one at that. You could have been killed! It is lucky that we found you before you tried to enter the walled city. It is full of black soldiers and spies."

"But how did you get here?"

Rodan placed his hands on his hips and scowled. "Lord Dovan sent us. We have been here for five days now, waiting for you. It did not take much thought to figure out where you would go. You were going to try to cross the high plains, weren't you?" Rodan went on without waiting for an answer. "What were you thinking? You would die out there! The grasslands are no place for a Ceredigion boy."

"I am not a boy, and I was not going to go alone. I planned to get a guide to take me."

"To the Karr al-Isma?!" exclaimed Rodan. "No one would ever take a non-Aleash to the sacred mountain!"

Elwin sighed. "Okay, what happens now?"

"I am going to take you to Mythra. You will be safe there."

We'll see about that! thought Elwin. "How did you get here before us?" Looking down at Elwin as if he were seeing the youth for the first time, Faynn hesitated, and then said, "We must have passed you along the road. We arrived in Aonach a few days after you. It did not take long to discover that you had been there. You left a strong impression on that city. My guess was that after you escaped from Aonach, the two of you went off into the mountains. That is probably what saved you. The roads are no longer safe." He glanced at Aidan for a brief moment and then turned back to Elwin. "What I do not understand is how you managed to find your way through the hills. The foothills of the Gobhair Mountains are known for their dead-end valleys and boxed canyons. Even with an elf as a guide, it should have taken you weeks to find a pass."

Sensing Aidan tense up, Elwin replied, "We found our way. We stayed close to the road, and we tried not to wander too far into the hills." It was a lie, but Elwin did not care. He was not going to tell them the truth. Elwin wasn't even sure what the truth was, though he had guessed it had something to do with the silver feather that Aidan wore around his neck.

With doubt in his voice, Faynn simply said, "Interesting... You are becoming a fascinating young man, Prince Elwin."

Rodan's dark eyes narrowed. He did not care how they got here, only that they had, and that they had disobeyed Count Murray's orders. "Did you have to destroy the temple?" the dark-haired lord asked harshly. "It's all that the Aonach people will talk about—the Ceredigion prince that burned down the temple and killed the High Priestess. In the name of the Three Gods! What were you thinking?"

"But I..."

Angrily, Rodan Macay cut Elwin off. "Unlike the druid here, I do not care how you did it. No doubt it was an accident, but destroying the temple was the stupidest thing you could have done. Getting you to Mythra will be just that much harder. The roads for a hundred miles, as well as this city, are crawling with the Strigiol soldiers, the Black Army, and the Severed Head. They're all looking for you. You have been named an outlaw! There is even a price on your head."

"They are calling you the Renegade Prince," added Faynn, with a thin smile. His calm voice sharply contrasted with Rodan's anger. "You are somewhat of a legend."

"A legend!" spate Rodan, as if that were the worst possible thing. "What did you think you were doing? The temple? Are you mad? You have made yourself the most wanted man in all of Kambrya! After what you did in Aonach, the King of Strigiol himself will be out looking for you!"

"But I did not..."

"This is not the place to talk." Rodan cut Elwin off once more.

"What about Pallas and Colin?" asked Aidan, speaking up for the first time. "Has anyone heard from them?"

Rodan lowered his voice and let out a long sigh. "They are here too. And luckily, they are safe as well. As soon as I can make arrangements, all four of you will soon be on your way to Mythra. Once safely there, we can figure out what comes next. Most likely it will be another war."

"Who were those men that brought us here?" asked Elwin, finally getting to complete a sentence.

"Friends of a friend," Rodan stated. "Now come with me, before you can cause any more trouble."

Outside they saw more Aleash, most stopped and stared, saying nothing as they followed them with angry, accusing eyes, as if the mere presence of outsiders was a great insult. Moving deeper into the compound, the group of outsiders passed the tall white tents topped with bright red flags. There did not seem to be any logic to where the tents were placed, making it hard to tell exactly where they were headed. Finally, they came to a small clearing of trampled grass. At the center of the clearing stood the largest and grandest tent in the compound. Unlike the others, it was not white, but dyed sky blue and lined with a gold fringe. At the top of the tent, a red flag triangular fluttered in the hot breeze. Among the sea of tents, this was a palace.

Two guards stood before the large tent flap. In their black robes and matching turbans, they looked like statues. Around their waist, they wore a silken sky-blue belt and a large red buckle. Armed with long curving swords and spears, the guards watched the four outsiders approach with cold hard eyes.

As the outsiders entered the clearing, one of the Aleash guards lifted his spear in a threatening manner and pointed its silver tip at them. "Who approaches?" He spoke in Aleash. Elwin, who had studied the language, recognized it as a northern Aleash dialect.

Rodan stopped, and with a raised hand he brought the others to a stop as well. Still a good dozen paces away from the tent, Lord Macay met the Aleash's cold stare with his own hard gaze. "I am Jarbi of the house of the Al-Amin. I have come as I was asked." Rodan too was speaking in the Aleash tong. tongue

"Stay where you are." The guard who had spoken lowered his spear and disappeared into the tent, while the other guard stood his ground, arms stiffly crossed across his broad chest. The space between the outsiders felt awkward and packed with tension. Elwin shifted from one foot to the other as he silently waited. It was only a moment, but with all the hostile tension of the black robed guard, it felt longer. The tent flap reopened. Stepping to one side, the first guard held open the tent flap as a third man appeared in the entranceway. He was a tall, thin man wearing loose fitting white silk robes. Around his head was a turban as white as his robes. A red sash was tied around his waist with a sheathed jewel handled dagger. Dominating the man's narrow face was a black beard streaked with gray. He wore no emblem, yet he had the looks and manner of a high ranking noble. A step behind him were three more of the black robed guards. They too had the sharp angry eyes that the other guards had shown them. However, the white robed nobleman's eyes were softer. *A clan chief* thought Elwin.

"This is the sheik of the Al-Amin clan," whispered Rodan. "He honors us by coming out to greet us. Everyone except Elwin is to kneel. Elwin, you are to bow to him, but not until he bows to you first, and do not speak unless you are spoken to."

As the sheik approached, Rodan dropped to one knee and bowed low, placing one hand onto the ground. Faynn and Aidan followed his example. Elwin watched and waited. The sheik walked across the trampled grass. His dark eyes met the brown eyes of Elwin. Elwin felt as if he were being judged, yet not as harshly as the others had. There was a sense of curiosity and fascination in the tall man's serious gaze.

"Rise. You are my guests," the sheik said in the Kambryan language. "Jarbi, I take it these are your other strays?" Coming to his feet, Rodan bowed. "Yes, Zafra Pasha. You have already met Faynn Catach."

Zafra nodded to Faynn. "The druid. Yes. It is a pleasure to see you again. I hope you are finding your stay pleasant?"

Faynn returned the node. "Yes, Zafra Pasha. It was kind of you to let me use your collection of books and scrolls."

Once more, Zafra nodded to the druid as Rodan turned next to Aidan. "Zafra Pasha, this is Aidan JaRe of the Green."

"Welcome, young JaRe. Few of your people have ever honored us with a visit. You are welcome in my home."

"Thank you, Zafra Pasha. But it is you who honor us." Aidan was quick with his judgment of the proper protocol.

Zafra smiled and gave Aidan a short node.

"And this is His Highness," Rodan introduced, "Elwin ap Gruffydd, Prince of Ceredigion and heir to the throne."

As Rodan introduced Elwin, Zafra gave him a short but respectful bow. Throughout the bow, his dark eyes remained locked onto Elwin's. Bowing likewise, Elwin was careful not to bow deeper nor less than the sheik had done. The sheik gave a half nod of approval.

"So," the sheik said, a smile coming to his slightly wrinkled face, "you are the renegade prince who burned down the temple. I did not really expect a boy, despite what Jarbi has told me about you. And yet you are more of a man then Jarbi has let on."

"Prince Elwin," Rodan went on, "this is Zafra Ibn Ridwan, Sheik of the Al-Amin."

Elwin bowed again, and in the Aleash language said, "I am honored, Zafra Pasha. May the waters of K-rrWa give joy and life to the people of the Al-Amin."

The sheik's smile turned into a broad grin as he returned Elwin's bow. "You honor me and my clan. You speak well for an outsider. So, few take the time to learn our language and ways. It is a great pleasure to know that not all foreigners are alike." Zafra spread his arms out wide. "Elwin, you are welcome among the Al-Amin. May the K-rrWa waters be abundant to the people of Ceredigion and give you long life and happiness. But enough formalities. Please, come. You must be tired from your journey and are anxious to see your friends, and there is much to be discussed."

Using some type of sign language, the sheik dismissed the guards. Elwin noticed the guards tense up, but they did not attempt to stop Zafra from leading the outsiders into his tent. Ducking into the tent, Elwin wondered why the people of Aleash seemed to dislike them so much, or why this sheik took them into his tent so freely. Through his studies and readings, Elwin knew enough of Aleash customs to know that being asked into an Aleash tent was a great honor. Zafra, by inviting them into his home, had just announced that these outsiders were his guests and under his personal protection, and if any harm was done to them, the sheik would take it as a personal insult. The Aleash were protective of their personal honor. Blood feuds and wars could be fought for generations over a mere insult.

Inside the tent, Elwin was pleased to find Pallas and Colin, and he was surprised to discover that the innkeeper, Ned, was there as well. Even more surprisingly, Ned no longer looked like the innkeeper he had met in Aonach. Instead, the man looked like a hardened mercenary in brown leather armor. Now that Ned was outside of the Cluain Kingdom, he had reverted back to his preferred brown leather armor.

Seating among an array of colorful pillows, the group joined by Zafra, told of their journeys to the tent city of Caiplich. As their stories unfolded, Elwin was further surprised to find out that Ned, now Kayno, along with Pallas and Colin, had disguised themselves as Royal Cluain Soldiers and had marched right out of Aonach's gate. More surprising was that Aidan had actually seen them as they had passed through the woodlands outside of Aonach. Aidan had even followed them a short distance, not realizing that Colin and Pallas were among the soldiers. Kayno found it hard to believe that Aidan could have followed them without him knowing it. Yet, Aidan assured him that it was true, and his description of the patrol left no doubt. To top things off, Elwin thought that Ned's actual name, Kayno, sounded familiar. He was sure that the mercenary expected him to recognize him but appeared relieved when he did not.

"No," said Elwin, "I cannot go to Mythra. I must find my sister."

Angrily, Rodan shook his head. "You have grown bold and have put on some muscles since you ran away, but you are still just a boy and will do as I say. Count Murray wants you in Mythra, and I am going to take you there, and that's all there is to it. From there we will build a resistance and take back what Strigiol has stolen.

Once the word is sent out that you are there, knights from all over Kambrya will have a place to rally too. You are needed in Mythra. The queen of Mythra now stands alone against Strigiol. She needs all the help she can get."

Elwin adjusted the silk pillow beneath him. "I do not have to obey the Count anymore. I respect the Count, but I refuse to go. I am not in Cluain any longer, nor do I owe any lord in Cluain my allegiance. I am the Prince of Ceredigion, and as such can do as I please." Elwin turned and bowed to the sheik. "With Zafra Pasha's permission, of course, I will go into the Great Plains." Elwin knew much of what would happen next depended on the sheik, and Rodan had the advantage. Through Elwin's love of studying and reading, he was aware of many of the customs, history, and language of the Aleash people, but Lord Rodan was half-Aleash and had lived several years in this land. He knew the laws and customs far better than Elwin. It was also apparent that the sheik looked fondly upon Rodan and considered him a close friend, maybe even family. Rodan was indeed a member of Zafra's clan. That alone created a strong bond.

Zafra bowed to Elwin in turn. "Rodan has told me that you wish to go to the Karr al-Isma. You know that no one other than an Aleash has ever been allowed near the holy mountain?"

"Yes, Zafra Pasha. But I have reason to believe that my sister is there."

"What you are asking is a great thing. If the caliph found out that I helped you across the plains, he would make war against the Al-Amin. Yet I hold no love for our caliph. And there are no laws that state that you cannot go, though many think there is. It is simply a tradition that says only an Aleash may look upon the sacred mountain. There is a legend, Elwin Pasha, that your great ancestor Coinneach came here after the wars to pray to the Great Mountain. Certainly, he was not Aleash. Yet it is a strong belief among my people that the mountain is for the Aleash alone. The caliph is of that thought, and he would certainly not approve. The caliph is a dangerous man who should not be taken lightly. For his own reasons, which I need not go into, the caliph would see such an act as treason."

"I do not want to put your people in any danger," Elwin replied. "If I could have but one guide, no one would ever have to know that it was you who let me enter the plains. And as the Prince of Ceredigion, I would be in your debt." *Let Rodan match that. I can give Zafra a powerful ally, at least once I am on the throne.*

"I am caught, Elwin Pasha. You are a prince among your people, and you have shown to have much courage and respect for one so young. I am half inclined to let you go to the mountain. It could be very interesting, very interesting, indeed." He rubbed his graying beard and smiled, "Yes, I would like to see the caliph's reaction to that." Relieved, Elwin sighed. He seemed to be winning the sheik over.

"Yet, as an Aleash," the sheik went on, "I am also inclined to do as Jarbi wishes. He is of my blood, and he is Al-Amin, while you are not. So, it must be the laws of my people that govern my choosing. I will hear arguments for and against your going on to Thunder Mountain. I will rule according to our laws. I hope you understand as a leader, I am bound to these laws."

Resigned to the fight ahead, Elwin nodded. He had not truly expected it to be that easy anyway. At least the sheik was keeping an open mind, and Elwin did have some knowledge of Aleash laws. "First, I would state that Lord Rodan, who you know as Jarbi has no authority over me. He is sworn to Count Murray of the Cluain kingdom, which has no authority here in the plains." Elwin nodded to Rodan. "He is a friend, but I am no longer in Cluain."

"I am a bound lord," interrupted Rodan. "A bound lord's duty does not stop at any border."

Kayno suddenly stood up from his bellow seat and bowed respectfully to the Sheik. "May I speak?"

Zafra nodded, "We will hear from all who would like to speak."

Before speaking, Kayno looked over at Elwin, and the prince was sure that he knew him from somewhere. The mercenary quickly looked away.

"Lord Zafra—I mean Zafra Pasha," Kayno stumbled over the proper titles, "the prince speaks the truth. This is Aleash and Lord Rodan has no authority outside of Reidh. Kambryan law is very clear on that. A lord's duty is not the same as the law. If a lord is sent into another kingdom in order to fulfill an oath, he is bound to do so. However, if that same oath violates another's laws or rights, the oath holds no precedent. If not, it would be acceptable for a lord to murder a king if he had sworn to do so. If the free kingdoms of Kambrya are to live peacefully, we must respect each other's laws and customs." Finishing, Kayno awkwardly sat back down.

Elwin frowned. *Why is Kayno here? What does he want from me? Does he expect a reward for helping a prince? And how does an innkeeper know about international laws?* The more Elwin learned of Kayno, the more of a mystery he became.

"You are right. However, this is not Kambrya. We have our own laws." Zafra politely pointed out. He ran a hand along his beard, then he added, "Tell me, Kayno. Why do you care if I let the prince go on his way or turn him over to Jarbi?" Elwin was interested in his answer as well. "Certainly," Zafra went on, "the prince would be safer in Mythra than trying to cross Aleash. The Karr al-Isma is a holy place, and many would rather see him dead than be allowed anywhere near the sacred woods or the Great Mountain."

As if facing a dilemma, Kayno hesitated, and then answered by saying, "I believe a man, even one as young as his Highness, has a responsibility to his family. The prince says that his sister is in this 'Woods of the Mist.' I believe he should be allowed to make the journey, no matter how dangerous it might be. A man has a responsibility to his family that comes before all other responsibilities."

"There is truth in what you say, Kayno," Zafra responded with a quick nod. "The Aleash, too, holds the family in high regard."

Rodan straightened his back. "Zafra Pasha, I know you do not wish to offend the prince or his people, but there are duties other than to one's family. There is a duty to one's lord, to one's kingdom, and to one's people. As sheik of the Al-Amin, you know these responsibilities well. Prince Elwin is important in the struggle against Strigiol's ambitions, and he is still too young to be allowed to make decisions of this scale. You know he cannot enter the Karr al-Isma and live. To allow him to try is to let him die, and to take with him our last hope of stopping Strigiol. We need him in Mythra, only there can Kambrya rally behind his banner. This foolish quest cannot be allowed. The prince is simply too important to lose."

Zafra frowned as he listened. "You, too, speak wisely, Jarbi, yet a few months ago I would have said the same of his Highnesses chances to destroy the temple of Aonach. Now that the temple has been reduced to smoking rubble, I am wondering if I am the best judge of what is, or is not possible. Perhaps our world is changing."

As if he had just come to a hard realization, Faynn, with his cloudy gray eyes, gazed up from the floor. "Zafra Pasha, you are as wise as men say you are. The world is indeed changing, faster than I would like to admit, and as yet, none can say if the change is for the good or for the bad. I am an old man, and as the old do so often, I have resisted that change. I have been a fool who has refused to see. And though I now admit that I cannot see, still I am blind to the truth. Perhaps that is the way it must be. However, I do know that all of Kambrya is at risk, including Aleash. As Lord Rodan says, Prince Elwin is at the heart of our salvation. I too wanted to take the prince to Mythra, but I was wrong. I do not know why, but I now see that the prince must be allowed to reach the Woods of the Mist, the Karr al-Isma. I believe it is his destiny. I also can't say why, but I believe it would be disastrous if he were stopped short of fulfilling his destiny."

Elwin was taken aback. Here was an ally he had not expected, and by the look of Lord Rodan, he too was taken aback by this change in the druid. *That leaves only you, Lord Rodan. Perhaps I still have a chance.*

"I still have reservations," Faynn went on, "but forces beyond my understanding have taken a hand in events. The river of time runs strong and swift. Who can swim against such a fierce current? The river has many bends and curves, and I do not know where the current will take us. That is for others to foretell, but for better or for worse, we must accept that the river has the power and not us. To fight the river is futile, even dangerous. Prince Elwin must be allowed to swim. We are left only to follow."

Angry, Rodan nearly leaped up from his pillow, but he restrained himself, knowing that such an action would be an insult to the sheik. With difficulty, he turned his hard eyes away from Faynn. "Zafra Pasha," he said as calmly as he could, "I demand my rights to obey my lord's orders. Neither Cluain nor Ceredigion has any authority in Aleash. It is true that here, I am not a lord. However, the prince is still but a boy, and I am Aleash. I have sworn an oath. I have a right as an Aleash to keep my oath. The Fijah demands it."

"A count has no authority over a prince," pointed out Pallas. "Even if he was my father's friend."

Rodan shot Pallas a razor-sharp gaze, and Pallas tried to sink into the floor.

"Ah, but Jarbi is right," Zafra began. "As I have said, the Aleash have their own laws. Jarbi, or Lord Rodan as you call him, is half Aleash. As an Aleash, he must fulfill his oath or be shamed. No Aleash, including myself, has the authority to stop him as long as his oath does not endanger the Aleash or my clan and does not violate any laws. And you, Elwin Pasha, are still a minor according to our laws. Jarbi is acting as your guardian. You must do as he says and go to Mythra."

"Then it is settled," Rodan said, pressing his advantage. "We will leave for Mythra in the morning. Zafra Pasha, it would be of great help if you could lend us some horses. We appear to be two short."

"Of course," the sheik replied. "Horses are never a problem. You shall have the best I have to offer."

"I am sorry," the Sheik added, turning his eyes towards Elwin. "But I must respect the laws of my land."

"No!" exclaimed Elwin. "They have no right! I will not go. I'm not a child to be told what he may or may not do! I do not know all the laws of Aleash as you do, but I will not be taken against my will."

Zafra frowned. "At the moment, Elwin Pasha, you are acting like a child. The Fijah is the law of the land and must be obeyed."

"What of my duty to my sister?" asked Elwin. "I have sworn an oath to save her. Does my oath count for nothing!?"

"The Fijah does not recognize an oath to oneself," pointed out Zafra. "Such oaths are too easily made and too easily broken. Besides you are a minor, and a minor cannot take a binding oath.

You are still a year away from adulthood."

"And what of Colin's oath?" interrupted Faynn. All eyes turned on the druid.

"What do you mean?" snapped Rodan.

"Does the Fijah not say that all men of honor have a responsibility to their oaths? I have been reading the law codes, and I have not seen where it says that the laws are only for the Aleash people, rather it says that it applies to all honor bound individuals."

"I don't understand," said Colin.

"Is Elwin not your lord?" Faynn said, answering Colin's question with a question. "And have you not sworn an oath to serve him? Protect him? To help him rescue the princess?"

"I have," admitted Colin.

Turning to the sheik, Faynn went on. "If I am not mistaken, Colin has the right and obligation to obey and support Elwin's wishes. As his vassal, Colin has sworn an oath to help the prince reach the Karr al-Isma, as Lord Macay has sworn to take the prince to the Island Kingdom of Mythra."

"I see," said Zafra, nodding his head. "We have a conflict of oaths."

"Colin is not Aleash," demanded Rodan. "He does not have the right!"

"He has sworn an oath, Jarbi. You know that it does not matter if he is Aleash or not. The druid is correct. This young man has the right to serve his Pasha."

Rodan shook his head angrily. "Colin is a minor like Elwin. He cannot be held to that oath."

"How old are you?" Zafra asked Colin.

"I turned eighteen last week."

Zafra nodded his head again. "In the eyes of Aleash, you are no longer a minor. So we have a conflict of oaths. There is only one way to settle this."

"No!" cried Rodan, "I will not fight him."

Colin's eyes went wide, "Fight!?"

Zafra nodded. "Yes. It is the law of the Fijah. If two oaths are in conflict, and cannot be reconciled, then they must be settled through a test of arms. The survivor's oath is deemed the stronger and purer oath. Do you, Colin, claim your rights to battle for your lord?"

The moment was tense. Colin's nervous gaze danced from Prince Elwin to Rodan, then back to the sheik. "I...I do not know...I do not wish to fight, but I will not let him take my lord against his wishes."

"The law is the law," Zafra sighed. "The Fijah is not always easy, but it must be obeyed. If you wish to keep your oath and help the prince to reach the Karr al-Isma, you must fight."

"Zafra Pasha, that would not be a fair fight. He is only a boy!"

"Oh," murmured Kayno under his breath. "If I were you, I would not be too sure of winning."

"Perhaps there is another way," Elwin spoke up.

"Speak," commanded Zafra. "If we can avoid bloodshed, I will be in your debt."

Elwin went on. "The two oaths are not necessarily in conflict. If Rodan would allow me to find my sister first, I will promise that I will then to go Mythra. Both oaths would be upheld and honored."

Zafra nodded. "Elwin Pasha, you are wise. You continue to amaze me. You would make a great sheik or even a caliph."

"You honor me," replied Elwin with a short bow of his head. "But I am of Kambryan blood. Forgive me for saying so, but I do not believe that the Aleash would accept me."

"You are no doubt right. It is a shame, though." The sheik turned to Colin. "Will this comply with your oath?"

"Yes," Colin replied hurriedly.

"And you, Jarbi? Will you accept this compromise? Will you avoid the spilling of blood by letting your oath wait?"

Zafra waved off Kayno who was about to say something. "You must choose, Jarbi."

For a painfully long moment, Rodan was silent. Elwin feared that he was going to refuse. Then Rodan gave the sheik a tight nod. "Though it means we shall all die, yes, Zafra Pasha, I will agree. I would rather die a thousand deaths than kill the young friend of Pallas and Elwin."

"Then let us drink." Zafra clapped his hands, and a young servant appeared from an adjoining room. "We drink for the life saved and to new friendships."

The servant dropped to the floor, bowing low to the Sheik. "How may I serve you, Pasha?"

"We will have Kumiss."

Moments later, the servant returned carrying a tray with several large silver goblets and a large glass pitcher. The pitcher was amazingly crafted with colored glass in the shades of red, sky blue, and green. While the glass vessel shimmered in the light of the tent's lamps, the goblets were of equally impressive quality. Each of the goblets had been created out of pure silver and engraved with elegant and detailed geometric patterns. In a smooth, graceful motion, the boy balanced the tray with one hand and poured with the other, never spilling a drop of the Kumiss.

Taking the goblet, he was offered, Pallas stared down into the silver cup. Swirling the white liquid around he looked down in confusion. "What is it?"

Trying to keep his voice level, Rodan replied, "It is a type of sour beer made of fermented mare's milk. Drink it."

"Horse milk!" Pallas exclaimed. "I can't drink horse milk!"

"Do not be a fool!" snapped Rodan between clenched teeth. "The Sheik honors you. Do not insult him or me by refusing."

Grumbling, Pallas held his breath and sipped the beer. Finding that it was not as bad as he feared, he discovered that he kind of liked it, though he would never admit that to Rodan.

Zafra smiled and laughed. "This is a fitting end. Or perhaps it is a beginning." The sheik held up his goblet above his turbaned head. "Elwin Pasha, I hope you can pull off the impossible, and that we meet again. You are a man of great courage. In my heart, I believe you will return, and then we will see what happens. Yes, indeed. We shall then see what happens."

Elwin smiled. "I am honored. I too hope to meet you again. Perhaps on my return from the sacred mountain and I can introduce you to my sister."

Zafra laughed and had his goblet refilled. "I would be honored. If she is half the woman that you are a man, she would indeed be a marvel to behold."

Again, the sheik held up his drink. "Tomorrow we may die, but today we celebrate." He then drained his goblet and called for more.

After more toasts and drinks, the group turned back to the business at hand. The first order was to decide who should accompany the prince across the Great Plains. It was quickly determined that everyone in the tent, except for the sheik himself, would accompany Elwin. Again, Elwin wondered why Kayno was joining their little party. Everyone else had reasons; Rodan had given his word and oath. Pallas, Aidan, and Colin were Elwin's closest friends, and Faynn wanted to protect the sword from falling into the hands of Torcull, but Kayno's reasons remained a great mystery, as did the man himself.

Promising to supply them with horses, provisions, and a fifty man escort, Zafra toasted the exhibition and returned to his celebrating. It did not seem to take much to give this plainsman cause to celebrate.

Interrupting his merrymaking, the sheik noticed Rodan's sullen mood. "Jarbi, it is unlike you to hold a grudge. A life was saved today. And by the way this youth carries his sword; I am not too sure that it was not your life that was spared. This 'Colin', young as he is, has the look of a man who was born with steel in his hand. Do not be glum, my friend, think on the bright side. Remember that by going into the Great Plains, you will no longer be hunted by the forces of Strigiol. Even the Black Army will not enter the plains and risk war with Aleash."

Listening, Colin asked, "Why won't they enter the plains? I mean no offense, Zafra Pasha, but Aleash is a conquered nation. Is it not?"

Elwin held his breath thinking the Sheik would be angered and insulted by Colin's question. However, Zafra only shook his head and laughed, something he was doing more frequently as he continued to consume more Kumiss. "Aleash conquered? Hardly. This is not the Aleash, Colin. This is Caiplich. Technically, Caiplich is a part of Aleash, yet it is populated and ruled by traders from around Kambrya. The Aleash come to the city to trade their horses and buy goods, but they do not live here." The Sheik stopped momentarily to let the servant refill his goblet. "No true Aleash would ever stay here longer than necessary. We come here to trade our horses for outside goods, and no more. Caiplich is really a city-state. It is a country in its own right. The city has only symbolic ties to the Caliph of Aleash. If Strigiol's king thinks that he has taken Aleash by conquering Caiplich, he is wrong." Zafra nodded his head to the east. "Out there, beyond the walls of the city, beyond the tents that surround it, is the true Aleash. That is my home." His dark eyes sparkled as he spoke of his beloved grasslands. "The home of Al-Amin and all of our ancestors who came before us."

Rodan sighed. Setting his drink down, he looked to the east as if he could see through the canvas walls of the tent and out over the plains. "Aleash," he whispered as if to himself, "I swore I would never return." After a long moment of uninterrupted silence, the Reidh lord looked back into the tent and his dark eyes settled onto Elwin. "Your Highness, I believe this is madness, and I believe that we are going to die, but that is not what is bothering me. As an Aleash, I accept that death waits for us all. But there is something you need to know. There is a price upon my head. My presence could make things more complicated than they need to be." Again, the lord sighed as if every word came at a great personal loss. "Zafra Pasha knows this, but he is too great a man to mention it. Zafra Pasha has risked much in bringing me into his tent. You see, Zafra Pasha is my uncle, the brother of my mother. What he already knows, you too must know before we head into the east. In the Great Plains, Zafra Pasha cannot protect you or me. Even his generous escort of fifty men will be helpless if the Caliph decides to have me arrested, which he is very likely to do if he discovers I am here. If that happens, I will be executed, and those with me will be put in danger."

"Why would the Caliph have you arrested?" asked Elwin. "What have you done to him?"

"As you know, I am half Aleash. What you do not know is why my father, mother, and my wife died all those years ago. It is something only the count, the Sheik, and I know, and none of us care to speak of it."

Rodan swallowed hard as he continued. He looked down at the floor and went on. "My wife, Teba, did not have her family's approval to marry, I had asked but was refused. We were young, foolish, and very much in love. As the young tend to do, we did not care, so we married anyway. According to the Fijah, the law of Aleash, it is a crime to marry without the family's blessing. I brought great shame upon Teba's family. The Fijah says that such an offense is punishable by death, but the caliph who ruled at that time was a kind man. Knowing that I was an outsider and did not know or truly understand their laws, the caliph took pity upon me. He was a man who understood love. Still, he could not let such an offense go unpunished. Teba's clan, the Ibn Jallab, were and still are a powerful clan, and they demanded retribution. The caliph decided upon a compromise. He exiled Teba and myself, banning us to never return to Aleash. So we left the high plains, hoping to make a home in Reidh. Reidh was the land of my father. And for a while, we were happy there. As a favor to the caliph and my Reidhen father, Pallas' father, Count Murray, gave me land and a place I could call home. But Teba's family could not or would not accept the caliph's compromise. They wanted the letter of the law followed. They wanted their daughter back so that she could be given a ceremonial execution for bringing such shame upon their name."

Aidan gasped, "They would kill their own daughter?"

"Yes." Rodan closed his eyes as if he were holding back tears. "The caliph was an old man, and he died soon after we had left. Following the death of the caliph, there was a short war of succession and the Ibn Jallab family rose to a new position of greater power. Teba's cousin, Adra, married Banu Abu Ishaq, who becoming the next caliph of the united clans of Aleash. Caliph

Banu, mostly for reasons of his own, requested that Count Murray return Teba to her clan. Knowing what would happen, the count refused, but the Ibn Jallab family would not give up. With the new caliph's unofficial permission, Teba's clan sent a small raiding party across the mountains and into Reidh.

Their plan was to kidnap Teba and to bring her back to Aleash. At the time, I was in Port Murray, far from my home in Northdall. The Aleash party came as a surprise, and they were successful. They murdered my mother, Zafra's sister and took Teba." Rodan looked up at the Sheik. His cheeks were wet with tears. Never before had Elwin seen the stoic lord cry.

Zafra nodded as if telling Rodan to go on.

"Returning from the fields, my father found out what had happened and went after the Aleash raiders, who were now attempting to escape back over the mountains. There came a late snowstorm. In the mountains, such storms are often fierce. There were no survivors. One of the Aleash raiders was the caliph's youngest brother. He now holds me personally responsible for his death."

Elwin hesitated, before saying, "I am sorry for your pain. And yours, Zafra Pasha. I have heard that your sister was as kind as she was beautiful."

Rodan nodded. "My mother was both. And though it happened a long time ago, the memories remain. If my love had not been so blind, Teba would still be alive, and so would my father and mother. For that matter, Banu's brother would be alive as well."

Zafra half rose in protest to what Rodan was now saying, but Rodan waved him off. "No, Zafra Pasha. You are kind, but what I am saying is no more than the truth. Through blind love, I killed those that I loved most. But that does not matter now."

Rodan lifted his head to Elwin. "Now you see why I am a liability to your chances of ever reaching the Karr al-Isma."

Elwin cleared his throat. "I appreciate your honesty, Lord Macay, but we are in this together. I am no less a hunted man than you. And if we are lucky, we'll be in and out of Aleash before either the caliph or the Ibn Jallab knows we have been in the high plains."

Rodan shook his head. "The caliph's clan already knows. The Abu Ishaq has spies everywhere."

"They are here in Caiplich?" asked Elwin.

Zafra nodded. "Yes. This is the time when all the clans bring their horses to the city. All the clans are represented here. The caliph himself is not here, but one of his brothers is. His name is Khalu Abu Ishaq. Khalu is the heir to Caliph Banu and may one day rule the Grasslands of Aleash. He is a cruel and ambitious man."

"Then why have they not come for you?" Elwin asked Rodan.

"They wait, Elwin Pasha." It was Zafra who answered. "They will wait to see why my nephew has returned. For a long time, the caliph has feared that I have been plotting to overthrow him and avenge the death of my sister. But I grow tired of the bloody wars. It is not something that my sister would have wished. Yet Khalu will think that Jarbi has returned to help me in some grand plot. Khalu is as paranoid as he is powerful. He will believe that I am trying to make an alliance with the Count of Reidh. And while it is true I have close ties with Count Murray, I would never lead our people into a civil war over personal feelings."

Deep in thought, Elwin considered the situation. Then with a nod of his head, he said, "Maybe you are less of a liability than you think, Lord Rodan."

Rodan raised his eyebrows. "How so?"

"The Aleash, from what I know of them and what I have gathered from our conversation here do not usually allow nor like foreigners to cross their lands. They especially don't approve of outsiders traveling to the Karr al-Isma."

"That is true," said Zafra. "Foreigners who try to cross our land without the caliph's consent are treated harshly. It is important that you are not seen. You will have to travel by night until you are in the deep plains. It will be slow going, but otherwise, you are sure to be captured."

"That is why Lord Rodan is a blessing in disguise." smiled Elwin.

Confused, Rodan stared at the prince. "What do you mean?"

"Tell me, Zafra Pasha," Elwin began, "will Khalu know when we have left and headed out into the plains?"

"He has many spies. However, if we are careful, we should be able to fool them for a short time," said Zafra. "With luck, it could be several days before the Abu Ishaq spies learn of it. Then yes, Khalu will follow. We can make this difficult, but they are not fools."

"Then let us not be too careful." Elwin's smile grew wider. "Zafra Pasha, can you arrange it so that the spies know that we are going into the plains? And can it be done so Khalu will not suspect we want him to know?"

"Yes. I know the identities of several spies, and they do not suspect that I know they are of the Abu Ishaq clan. But why should I do such a thing?"

"With Rodan with me, what will they do?"

"They will be suspicious and curious. Most likely, Abu Ishaq will follow you all the way across the plains, hoping to figure out what is going on."

"Exactly." Elwin hesitated as he took a sip of his Kumiss. The prince had been drinking very slowly and was still working on his first cup. He needed to keep his mind and wits sharp. "The Abu Ishaq will be my escort to the Karr al-Isma."

Confused, the Sheik frowned at first, then his eyes slowly brightened. As he grew to understand Elwin's plan, Zafra threw back his head and laughed. "Clever! We will make a clansman of you yet!"

"I don't understand," admitted Pallas. "Why is that clever?"

"Your Highness has matured since we were last together," stated Faynn, ignoring Pallas' question. The druid's eyes sparked with interest. "You are learning to see the world through your enemy's eyes. It makes things much easier when you know how they think. However, what you propose is risky, but it might just work, and it would save much time. I am impressed. To turn a threat into an advantage and to do it without the edge of a sword. You have found the enlightened way to solve one's problems. To seek solutions without the use of force is the way of the druids. You have great promise, my young friend."

"What is risky!?" exclaimed Pallas, still not understanding. "Won't somebody tell me?"

Elwin smiled at Pallas. Elwin was actually enjoying this part of his adventure, and it was about time something was fun. "We will use the Abu Ishaq's paranoid fear of Zafra Pasha to our advantage. As long as we can keep Khalu guessing and thinking that Lord Rodan and Zafra Pasha are conspiring against his brother, we will be able to move freely. To discover what Lord Rodan and Zafra Pasha are up to, Khalu and the Abu Ishaq will follow us across the plains, but they will not stop us. With a little help of some misinformation, they might even think other clans are involved in this imaginary plot against them. We can lead them to believe there is to be some type of clan meeting deep within the grasslands. A meeting to overthrow the Caliph. Khalu and Caliph Banu will want to find out who are their enemies, and to discover what we are up to. They will keep everyone else from stopping us as well, including the Ibn Jallab. The Caliph and his brothers' unfounded fear will be our passport to the Woods of the Mist. Unknowingly they will be our guards as we cross the grasslands."

"But be careful, Elwin Pasha." Zafra's smile turned into a deep frown, as he became serious. "If Khalu discovers that you plan to enter the Karr al-Isma, he will do everything he can to stop you. I will drop information that you are meeting other clan leaders near the woods. It is not an unusual meeting place among our people. But none enter the forest, not even the Aleash. That is something you can never speak of until the time arrives. And I hope no one ever speaks of my knowledge of you entering the woods. Even among my own people, that could be dangerous for me."

"Understood," replied Elwin. "Tomorrow we will head east."

Elwin was finding it hard to sleep. He leaned back among the silken sheets and pillows of his large bed. With only the finest furniture and luxury items, the Sheik had provided for Elwin with a truly princely tent. Everywhere he looked there was silver, gold, and silk. The bed alone could sleep five adults without them ever touching. After days in the mountains and sleeping on the cold hard ground, the softness seemed strange. Yet that was not the reason for his sleeplessness, nor was it the journey ahead. It was fear. Elwin feared to go to sleep. He knew what was waiting for him in his dreams. He dreaded that Torcull would once more be waiting in his dreams as he was most nights.

From outside Elwin's tent flap opened and Faynn tucked his head in. "You requested to see me?"

Elwin nodded and gestured, indicating the druid should join him. "Please come in." Elwin could hardly believe he was asking Faynn for help, but he was growing desperate. He was only getting a few hours rest each night. If the sleepless nights continued, Elwin's physical health would soon start to deteriorate.

Dressed in the soft silken robes of the Aleash, Elwin rose from his bed. "Thank you for coming. I know it's late."

Faynn smiled. "It is fine. What can I do for you?"

Elwin led Faynn to the central bronze oil heater. Even in the heart of summer, the nights in Aleash could be as cold as the days were hot. Taking a seat on one of the many silken seats, Elwin leaned forward, turning up the flame as he invited Faynn to join him.

Once Faynn had taken his place on a collection of large pillows, Elwin started to explain the past dreams. "They come almost every night. Torcull is haunting me. Sometimes he chases me, while at other times, the prophet tries to convince me that he is my friend, he wants to help me. I never believe him, but I fear going to sleep. If I sleep more than a few hours, he is always there. The only way I can keep him out is to sleep a few hours at a time, but that is slowly wearing me down. I don't know how much more I can take."

Faynn listened silently nodding his head in understanding. He could hear the desperation in the prince's voice. He was aware of the torment one can cause through invading another's dreams. For the order of druids, it was considered a violation to force oneself into someone's dreams. Torcull would make the prince

400

insane or break down his will to resist. Torcull was slowly torturing the vulnerable young price. Elwin had neither the knowledge or training to protect his dreams.

When Elwin had finished, the druid was silent for a moment longer, then asked. "Are you requesting my assistance?"

"Yes, can you help me?"

Looking at Elwin from across the heater, Faynn noticed the sword lying next to the prince. Elwin was never far from the ancient blade. The sword was now sheathed in a new scabbard of finely polished leather which was painted sky blue with detailed red abstract images of the Al-Amin. Connected to the sheath was a black leather shoulder belt studded with silver griffins of the Altair family crest. It was a gift from Zafra to Elwin that was meant to illustrate the newly formed friendship between their two families as well as to replace the sheath that had been destroyed in the temple fire. It also served to create suspicion in the Khalu. Spies were sure to note the prince's new sheath. They would understand what the decorations indicated. It would help convince Khalu that the two were plotting against the Caliph, and Khalu would be determined to find out what the two were planning. However, it was not the sheath that concerned Faynn, but the sword inside it and how it was changing Elwin. Then the druid brought his eyes back to Elwin. "Have you started to hear the songs of the Earth Magic?"

Elwin was reluctant to tell Faynn of the Earth Song. He still did not trust Faynn completely and he suspected things were being kept from him. Yet another part told him Faynn was a friend. Elwin was not sure which emotions he should trust. In the end, it was his hope of driving Torcull out of his dreams the led him to at last to say, "Yes, I have begun to hear the song. It's sometimes the voice of nature but not always. Sometimes it sings of the past, and at other times it's a song of life and death and of power."

Faynn nodded, "Earth Magic is all those things and more. The sword is starting to have an effect on you. It is opening in you the power that is all around us. There is magic in everything that is connected to the earth."

"Will it harm me?" there was a new fear in Elwin's eyes.

"I won't lie to you, Elwin. Power is always dangerous, but ignorance is an even greater danger. Within the earth, there is great, unbelievable power. Life could not exist if that were not true. And yet this earth power, or more commonly called Earth Magic, does not hurt or help, it simply is. A trained individual like myself or Aidan, who was born to it, can, and to a limited way, direct its power. Yet with such abilities comes great responsibilities. It is the wielder of that power that can lead it to good or ill. The sword is only a key that is opening up a new world to you.

For most magic users, it takes years to learn the ways of Earth Magic, but with you, it's happening fast. This is different than what I experience; the song is louder and stronger within you. For me, the song is never more than a whisper, like the sound of leaves blowing in the wind. The earth is calling to you, and within you, Earth Magic is growing. The power of the earth is connecting with you in an almost intimate way. It is such a different relationship than what I experience that I can't truly say I fully understand what is happening to you, or what it all means. No one has had such a close relationship to the powers of earth in a very long time, Elwin. You are learning the ways of the earth in a way no living person has ever done. Even your father never heard the songs of the earth. For whatever reason, the earth has chosen you."

"Magic is not something I wish to know more about," Elwin stated honestly.

Faynn shrugged, "And yet I doubt you can stop it. You are becoming a user of Earth Magic. True, Earth Magic is not something you would have chosen, but you are not the one choosing, it is the earth who has chosen you."

Elwin felt his fear rising. He had always been taught that magic was evil, and now he was being told he had no choice. "I don't want this Earth Magic."

"You have to accept it, Elwin. No matter what happens, the power will grow in you. If you do not learn to control it, it can become very dangerous. Uncontrolled, Earth Magic can quickly spiral out of control."

Elwin thought back to the Temple of the Severed Head, where he had felt the power rage through him. He also remembered how the priest lost his control over the magic, which had led to the total destruction of the temple. *But can I ever accept the use of magic? I'm not like Aidan.*

"It does have an upside," Faynn continued. "If used wisely, the Earth Song will guide you. It can become a tool for good. The earth is in pain, Elwin. But you can use the magic to heal the wounds that the Severed Head are causing. If you let me, I will help you where I can and teach you how it can be used to keep Torcull out of your dreams. As long as I am close, I will set wards around your tent which will keep the prophet out of your dreams, but I won't t always be close.

If you would like, I can stay here tonight so you can sleep in peace. Nevertheless, you will need to start understanding the powers that are growing inside you. I can start by teaching you what you need to know for you to keep Torcull away and out of your dreams. It will also help you learn how to control the magic."

Elwin suspected this was what Faynn had always wanted, to turn Elwin into some type of champion to fight Torcull. At the moment, Elwin did not care; he was tired and wanted to sleep in peace. If the price of that peace was the use of magic, Elwin would pay it. At least he would pay it until he reached the Guardians of Light and gave them the sword. That was one thing he was not going to tell Faynn. The druid did not seem to think anyone but Elwin should even touch the sword. The prince suspected that Faynn would not be pleased with the idea of him giving the sword to the Guardians of Light. That was one secret he would keep from Faynn. Faynn said he had no choice, but he did. He could give it away.

"What do I have to do to keep the Prophet away from my dreams?"

Faynn almost seemed to smile, "For one, stop fearing the Earth Song. It can help you if you learn its ways."

"Can it actually keep him out of my dreams?"

"Yes, but I will not lie to you; all things come at a price, Elwin. The Earth Song will protect you, but it will likely begin to show you other things in your dreams. Once you learn a few things, you should be more or less in control of most of your dreams, and they will not be something to fear."

Giving into the inevitable, Elwin nodded, "What do I do."

Faynn pulled out his pipe, stuffed it with tobacco and lit it. Aromatic smoke soon drifted through the tent. "Each night, before you go to sleep, you must call up the Song. Let the song enter you, let it wrap about you just as you would a blanket. Visualize it as a buffer or a shield as you sleep. It is very easy, but it will take practice to master. Once you have it, it will protect you from anyone trying to enter your dreams. In the meantime, I will sleep in your tent with you. I can monitor you progress. Once you have called up the Earth Song, I will show you the way. You do not have to learn this alone."

"How long will it take me to learn this?" Elwin still feared the idea of willing up the Earth Song, yet he feared Torcull more.

"Hard to say." Faynn let out another puff of smoke. "Days, weeks, or months. It depends mostly on your willingness to trust the power."

Elwin nodded. "Thank you, Faynn."

That night Elwin slept in peace knowing Faynn hid him from Torcull. He also felt a bond forming with Faynn, that might even be called friendship, and yet the suspicions remained.

CHAPTER TWENTY-TWO

There was a damp chill in the air. The pre-dawn light spilled in through the forest of pine trees, creating dark shadowy images. Wrapped tightly in his cloak, Ruan Deuchar leaned up against a large gray boulder. His eyes drifted across the dark silhouette of trees. Somehow, the towering trees managed to find enough soil in the rocky earth to send down their roots. Rubbing his hands together, Ruan waited for the coming of dawn. Soon the sun would rise and chase away the night and the cold, but the sun could not chase away the shadows that haunted the count.

Like most nights, Ruan could not sleep. Finally giving up, he tossed aside his blankets and got up. Taking over the last few hours of the watch, Ruan sent a tired soldier off to bed next to the warmth of the campfire. Fighting off the chilly mountain air, he held his cloak tighter. Lately, the nights seemed to be getting colder. In most of Kambrya, summer had already started. However, here in these northern mountains, nights could still be bitterly cold. Last night the temperatures had dropped below freezing, and Ruan had awakened to find that a light dusting of snow was covering the campsite. For the first time in his life, Ruan was deep in the northern Drygan Mountains. As far as Ruan knew, he was the first Kambryan to have ever ventured this far north.

Fool! he said to himself. *You had to chase a dream. But you haven't found it, have you? A city? Here? What were you thinking of? You have led your men and family here to die because of a dream!* It had been just short a month since he had fled his city of Keloran. An ironic smile crossed his hardened face. So much had changed in the past month.

Trying to pierce the darkness that clung to the woods,

Ruan's eyes narrowed. He was looking for any threat that might be out there, hiding in the dark. This was troll and hobgoblin country. Too many times, a troll or a handful of howling hobgoblins had come crashing out of the trees. Ruan and his men were always able to push them back, but not before the half-human creatures of the mountains succeeded in wounding or killing one of Ruan's men.

"Has it really been just over a month since I was with the king?" Ruan murmured to himself. Sadly, he shook his head, remembering that Jerran was not the true king, but a pretender. He glanced at the frail old man lying near the fire. Wrapped in a blanket, the old man shivered in the cold. *That's the true King of Strigiol*, Ruan reminded himself. As broken as the old man was, he was still the true king.

Ruan worried about the aged king. Conrad was too old and weak to be in this strange and unforgiving land. Ruan feared that if the savage races did not kill him, then the cold, wet nights would. Yet, like Ruan, King Conrad was a fugitive, forced to wander the harsh wilderness of the north. If he had stayed behind in Keloran, he would be dead, or worse. In the last month, King Conrad's sanity had improved, if only slightly. At times the king remembered who and where he was, but then just as suddenly, he would slip back into his madness. The tortures of Torcull had left their scars upon the man's spirit, but those torments paled in comparison to a deeper pain. When he was lucid, the king had come to believe that his son, Jerran, had betrayed him. Above all else, that torture ate at the aging man's soul. The perceived betrayal of his son was more painful than the torture that Torcull had inflicted upon him.

No, Ruan realized sadly, *King Conrad will never again be fit enough to rule as the king of Strigiol. He would never be the man he once was.*

On the far side of the fire was a boy, not even seven, who was also sleeping close to the warmth. The small and fragile boy was curled up into a tight ball. It was unfair, but Horik's life would be a hard one. Like so many around him, the small prince had no real choice. If they somehow survived this harsh land, Ruan knew that he would use the child to try to raise an army. Ruan needed an army to fight a civil war against the prince's father. There was little chance that he would win such a war, yet Ruan realized that he had to try. And if somehow Ruan did win, he would place Horik upon the throne. Ruan felt guilty and ashamed of himself, knowing it was unfair to the child, yet he knew he would do it all the same. As Ruan had learned, life was rarely fair. He sighed. At least the child would not be alone. The prince was still a boy and far too young to rule on his own. The true ruler, if they somehow succeeded, would be his mother, Queen Catriono.

The queen lay near her son, her slender white arm draped protectively over the prince. Catriono had been raised in the luxurious pampered south, educated in the refined courtly ways of southern Strigiol, she of all the people was the least prepared for this northern land. Ruan frowned. This was no place for a lady like Catriono. Yet he had to admit that she had carried herself well, never once letting on that she was scared or tired. Ruan could see another story in her eyes; her eyes gave her true feelings away. She was always looking over her shoulder and always kept her son close. The queen was a strong woman. She has stood up to so many fears and never once complained or requested a break from the endless march into these mountains. Along with the royal family, Ruan had brought his wife, daughter, and two dozen soldiers. He sighed. *By now the Black Army has occupied*

Keloran. Will they follow us? Unlikely, but with luck, they have given us up as dead.

While Ruan had never been this far into the mountain pass, he had often been in the southern end of this pass. It was said that the pass cut straight through the Drygan Mountains and into the White Forest. The White Forest was said to be a cold and harsh land filled with strange creatures and wild beasts, or so the stories and folklore would lead one to believe. The only creatures that Ruan knew for sure who lived in the mountains were trolls and hobgoblins, and it took everything the south could do to keep them there. Ruan had been into the southern pass several times to fight back a hobgoblin or troll invasion. But as far as he knew, no one had ever ventured this far north.

His frown deepened. In the last month, he had seen six good men killed, and two others wounded. At first, the pass had been strangely quiet, but that had quickly changed. As the days turned into weeks, they began to encounter trolls and hobgoblins. Usually, the trolls attacked one at a time, but the hobgoblins would come at them in groups of three or four.

A twig snapped. Ruan looked up with a start. A black shape moved among the trees. He drew his sword, and then with a sigh, he let it drop back into its sheath. It was only Imrich returning from scouting the pass ahead.

Ruan saw the tension written across Imrich's face. Something was wrong.

"What is it?" Ruan asked as the river captain approached.

Nervously, Imrich looked over his shoulder and into the dark line of trees. "You have to see it," he breathed. "I saw it, and I still don't believe it."

Ruan jumped to his feet. "Did you find the city or the waterfalls?"

"What? Your dream? No. It is something else. Something much worse. Come, I will show you." With that Imrich stood and led his Ruan into the woods.

After covering a few miles of thick woodland, Imrich abruptly stopped. A pre-dawn light was beginning to chase away the night. "It is just over that hill," he whispered, pointing up ahead. Coming over a ridge, Imrich dropped to his stomach. Ruan followed him, dropping to the ground as well. They slowly climbed up the hill until they could see over the ridge and into the mountain pass beyond.

Imrich pointed. Below the two men were at least a thousand campfires. Like a swarm of fireflies, the fires covered the pass from one side to the other. In the early morning light, Ruan could make out large bulky creatures warming themselves by the heat of the fires. "Oh, my lord!" he breathed. "It's an army!"

"An army of hobgoblins and trolls," added Imrich. "There must be over ten thousand."

"How can there be so many? We have never seen more than a few hundred gathered together before. Where did they come from?"

Imrich shrugged. "I do not know. Nevertheless, they are here, and they seem to be working together. I have never heard of hobgoblins and trolls getting along. These are indeed strange times, and getting stranger all the time."

"You're right," agreed Ruan. "Trolls and hobgoblins don't get along. They are at war with each other more often than they are with Kambrya. Trolls generally won't live with more than a few others of their own kind, much less than thousands of hobgoblins."

"Well," whispered Imrich, "they seem to have solved their differences and have formed themselves into an army."

A look of horror crossed Ruan's face. "Oh, lord. They are coming down the pass. They're marching for Strigiol aren't they?"

"That would be my guess," answered Imrich with a quick nod of his head.

Ruan crawled back off the ridge. His eyes still were wide with shock. "I have to return to Keloran."

Imrich's eyes narrowed as he sat down next to the lord. "What are you talking about?" "Imrich, that army is marching for Strigiol! Jerran is gathering the Strigiol army in the south to invade Mythra. There is no one between Gildas and us. Other than Keloran and maybe a thousand men of the Black Army, there is no one to stop them, and that will never be enough to stop this army. They have to be warned."

"By you? They won't listen to you. They'll kill you before you can get two words out of your mouth. Besides, who would believe that a troll and hobgoblin army is invading Kambrya."

"They have to! Imrich, if I can get them to believe me, something might be done. As it is, Keloran is already lost. There is nothing that can be done to save our city. However, if those thousand Black soldiers in Keloran are prepared, they may be able to slow down the invasion. Word can be sent to the king, and he can recall the army from the south. If I do nothing, the Black Army will be trapped inside Keloran. Half of Strigiol could fall before the end of summer."

"They will not believe you and even if they do, you will still be as good as dead. Once they get their hands on you, they're not going to let go."

"I know, but I have to go. This army has to be stopped. I cannot imagine the horrors that will happen if they are not. An army of trolls and hobgoblins set loose in Strigiol? It will be a nightmare!"

"Send me... I can tell them as well as you."

Ruan shook his head. "I will do it. We all have to start back anyway. That army will be marching this way. There is no way around them. And I need you to protect the others. Once we're out of the mountains, try to slip past Keloran and get everyone to Mythra. The Queen of Mythra will protect them."

"Even if we can make it back, Mythra is a long way. There are not many of us left, Ruan. We might not make it."

"I know, but there is no other place of safety. Please, Imrich, promise me you will protect my family."

"I'll try. But what about your dream of the city? I never really believed it could be here, but are you willing to give it up?"

"I can't find it, Imrich," Ruan sighed. "We have been searching everywhere. If I can't find the waterfalls, I don't think we will ever find the city. I don't know, maybe you're right. Maybe it was just a dream. What I do know is that army is real and if I don't do something, half of Strigiol will be destroyed. I still love my country, Imrich. I can't stand by and do nothing."

The sun was just coming up when Ruan and Imrich returned to camp. Ruan had expected to find most of his party still asleep. Yet everyone, even the young prince, was up. Gathered around the fire, everyone stared down at something. An eerie silence filled the camp.

Hesitantly, Ruan stepped forward. He felt his chest tighten. He knew this silence too well. Off to one side laid the body of a troll. Another attack and another one of his men injured. He approached the circle, pushing his way through, he found Catriono kneeling over a bloodied body. She was administering first aid. A lump formed in Ruan's throat. He stopped short and tried to swallow. *So much blood.* Ruan's stomach sank. Another of his men was dying. He wanted to cry out, yet he did not, knowing that he had to keep up an image for the rest of the party. Responsibility. The word felt like a curse. He could feel eyes on him . . .waiting . . . hoping and believing that somehow Ruan would lead them out of this nightmare. It was what kept these men going.

"Is he...?" The word dead stuck in his throat.

"No," replied the queen. She looked up over her shoulder. "He will live. He has a broken arm, but nothing more, in time he will heal. The blood is not his own, but that of the troll. He is a very brave man."

Ruan nodded and silently gave a thankful prayer. The man would live. That was something.

Catriono shifted, and Ruan saw the man's face. He gasped. Stepping back, he half drew his sword. "A black elf! A Yorn!" This was not one of his men, but a Yorn.

In a flash, Catriono was on her feet. Squaring her shoulders, her dark eyes bore into Ruan's. She looked like a mother bear protecting her cub. "Stop that!" she snapped. "Can't you see he is wounded?!"

"Catriono, he is a black elf!"

"I don't care what he is," she snapped angrily. "This man saved my life. The troll he killed would have killed me! Me, Ruan! That thing acted as if it knew who I was." She pointed at the dead troll. "It was about to club me to death. No one even saw the troll until it was standing over me." She pointed towards the wounded man. "If he had not appeared when he did, I would be ..." She left the rest unspoken, but it was clearly understood. "Do you hear me, Ruan? You will not hurt this man! I am still your queen."

Ruan did not answer. He could only stare down at the face of the man, if one could indeed call him a man. He had the ears and features of an elf, but rather than green eyes and blond hair of the Woodland Elves of the Green, he had dark features. From a life spent in the sun, his skin was a golden bronze color, and his narrow eyes were as dark as his long black hair. Ruan's own eyes were wide open. He could not believe what he was seeing, and it was more than just facing a legendary black elf stepping right out of myths and into the world. Ruan had seen this face before. In Gildas, he had seen those dark eyes staring up out of Torcull's strange magical well. Even with the man lying before him, Ruan found it hard to believe. The mountain elves were nothing more than legends and myths. They were said to be creatures born of magic. Creatures that were nothing more than tall tales spoken on cold dark winter nights.

"A mountain elf," he mumbled in amazed disbelief. It was impossible.

The elf blinked. Slowly he sat up carefully cradling his broken arm in the sling the queen had made from her torn dress. Cringing in pain, the elf looked up at Ruan. "Rathad!" he exclaimed. The black elf had a strange accent, but he spoke in the Kambryan language. "You have come. I am the last of the searchers, and at last, I have found you."

"What gibberish is this?" asked Ruan, sounding angry. "His mind is rattled."

"At last, you have come," the black elf went on as if he had not heard Ruan at all. "Now that it is too late. The army has cut you off from the city. It is too late. Even you, Rathad, cannot save us."

"You say you have been looking for me..." Ruan stopped in mid-sentence and dropped to his knees. "Did you say a city? A city with great stone walls!? A city of elves? By the Three Gods, did you say a city?!"

The elf nodded. "Yes. It is my home, Cearcall."

Ruan grabbed him by the shoulders. "And a waterfall... Is there a waterfall nearby? One with a small pond, a cliff, and an ancient stone bridge and road?"

"Ruan!" snapped Catriono. "Stop it! You're hurting him." Ruan ignored her protest.

"Yes," the Elf answered at last. "There is a small fall not far from here, but it is on this side of a great cliff. It will not help us reach the city. The Satrie knew you would come, and he has blocked the pass."

"Satrie?" Ruan shook his head. Half of what the man said made no sense, but maybe the dream was real after all. If so, perhaps he could find a place where there was safety. Then he could return to Keloran without having to worry about the others. "The waterfalls! Where is it?" he urged in a desperate voice.

The elf shook his head. "There is no way past the Great Cliff. The road you speak of lies at the end of a boxed canyon. Once there we will be trapped. From the bridge, the road runs in two directions, east and west along this side of the Great Cliff. To the west, the road will take you all the way to the Iar Sea and dead ends high above the cliffs overlooking the sea. To the east, it will not bring you beyond the great cliff, but just into a boxed canyon. No one understands why such a useless road was ever built. It is far older than the Yorn's histories and remains a great mystery."

"There is a way past the cliff, it lies above the bridge and the road to the east," insisted Ruan. "Just tell me where the canyon is. There is a way. I have seen it."

The elf's eyes widened. "You are Rathad, the Pathfinder, and so it must be. I will show you."

CHAPTER TWENTY-THREE

The Great Plains of Aleash was a vast, silent land. The Aleash called the Great Plains home, yet to Elwin, it was a lonely place. He could only imagine how Aidan must feel. Aidan had been raised in the wooded forest of the Green. The Green teamed with all types of life, so here among the silence of the high plains, Aidan felt lost. Jokingly, Aidan had begun calling the plains, "a prison without bars." The Aleash, however, did not find it funny. Flat, barren, and dry, Aleash was a harsh place, yet Elwin had to admit this land was not without its beauty. In its vast open plains, one had the space to be free.

For the first time since leaving Reidh County, Elwin did not fear that a Red Robe was sneaking up behind him. In Aleash, there was no place for them to hide. Elwin was also sleeping better. He had still not completely mastered the magic that would protect his dreams, so Faynn continued to share his tent at night, keeping the profit and his Red Robes away from his dreams. However, he was slowly learning the ways of Earth Magic, and the time spent with the druid was slowly bringing the two together.

Elwin licked his dry lips. Under the relentless heat of the sun, he always seemed to be thirsty. Taking up the leather water bag that hung from his saddle horn, he wet his lips and took a small sip. He held the sweet tasting water in his mouth a short time before swallowing. In this dry land, water was a rarity and had to be used sparingly. Carefully re-corking the water bag, he put it slowly back down.

Yes, the prince thought to himself. *This is a vast and lonely land, yet it is here I have found peace.* In this starkly beautiful land, Elwin breathed in the dry air and smiled. It was here, for the first time in many weeks, Elwin was not haunted by his dreams nor chased by nightlings.

For that peace, Elwin would always appreciate the vastness of the plains.

It had been nearly a week since they had last seen a watering hole, and Faraj, the leader of the Aleash escort, said they would see no more water until they reached the Karr al-Isma. They were now in what the Aleash called the Deep Plains. Here, life was extremely hard and harsh. Few animals could survive, and it virtually never rained.

"How do the grasses manage to survive?" Elwin wondered out loud.

"What?" asked Colin, riding, as always, next to Elwin. Colin, Elwin's self-appointed bodyguard, was never far from the prince's side.

"The grasses. They are browner out here in the Deep Plains, yet they are still alive. How can it survive with no rain?"

"I don't know. Maybe you should ask Faraj."

"Ha!" retorted Elwin. "I would rather ask a nightling."

Colin smiled. "Faraj is indeed an unhappy man."

"With a hot temper," added Elwin. "He is always complaining that we outsiders are drinking more than our fair share of the water. It's not true."

"I could say something to him."

"No. We need the Aleash. We won't make it to the Karr al-Isma without them."

Staring up ahead, Elwin watched Faraj. Mounted upon his tall, noble gray horse, Faraj was leading the party across the plains. He was always up in front, leading the way. It was one of the reasons Elwin stayed near the rear. The dark-skinned leader of their party had a face as dry and as hard as the plains, and the personality to match. His black eyes, which appeared to be too closely placed together, were separated by a large hooked shaped nose, making him look like a bird of prey that had just discovered a snake hiding in its nest. Faraj spent most of his time scowling, and he had even less of a sense of humor than Lord Rodan, if that was possible.

"I do not like the way he treats Lord Rodan," stated Colin. "It's not right."

Elwin nodded in agreement. "The Aleash do not hide their feelings well, and Faraj is no exception."

"He does not like us much, but he downright hates Lord Rodan. You are the only one he will even talk to."

"It's only because he has to talk to me, but I know what you mean. He won't even look at Rodan. Faraj acts as if he does not exist. Whenever Rodan asks him something, Faraj will answer to me, as if it was I who had spoken."

"Why is that?"

Unsure, Elwin shrugged. "We are outsiders. I think that is enough of a reason for Faraj."

Rodan isn't. He's half Aleash."

"True, but Lord Rodan has a reputation. He is an outcast of sorts."

"I still do not like it. It's not right."

"Nor do I. The truth is, I do not care if Faraj likes me or not, but it angers me the way Rodan's own people are treating him. The Aleash entirely ignore him. In camp, they even go so far as to turn their backs on him when he passes. Though at times, I have noticed that some of the Aleash turn away a little slower than others. I am not sure what that might mean. I've talked to Rodan about it. I even told him I was going to speak to Faraj and tell him to knock it off and tell his men to stop behaving like children. I would've if Lord Rodan had not stopped me."

"What did, Lord Rodan say?"

"He told me it would do no good. He stated that he was Isham. If I understand the word right, Isham means 'one who is shunned.' Anyway, Lord Rodan said that I cannot afford to anger or offend Faraj. Zafra Pasha is far from here, and he cannot help us now. We need the Faraj."

Colin shook his head. "Some of these people are Lord Rodan's' relatives, and they openly insult him and he does nothing. It's as if it doesn't matter to him."

Elwin shook his head. "Don't be fooled. It matters. I have known Lord Rodan for a long time. He might not say so, but it bothers him. The lord lives by a unique set of rules and codes of honor. It must be complicated to be half Aleash and half Kambryan."

"It is especially hard for Pallas."

"I know," agreed Elwin. "Rodan is like one of Pallas' older brothers. Pallas finds it hard to just stand by and watch."

Colin laughed. "He's not standing by. He has already gotten into a few fights. It's becoming hard to keep his hot head out of trouble."

Sitting upon the silvery-black back of his stallion, Elwin stared out across the flat plains. Gently, he stroked the horse's thick dark main. The horse had been a gift from Zafra, and it had been the pride of the Sheik's corral. Elwin realized that the gift of this proud horse was a great honor. To honor his host, he had chosen an Aleash name, Sah-Ib. Sah-Ib in Aleash meant Black Wind. Pleased by the name Elwin had chosen, Zafra had slapped the prince on the back and said it was a noble name.

"What are you thinking?" asked Colin.

Elwin smiled. "Zafra Pasha. I wish he were here."

Colin always became concerned when Elwin became quiet. Nowadays, Colin rarely left his side for any length of time, only to continue his lessons in swordsmanship from Kayno. Colin was not a complicated person. He lived a life that was organized by a strict code of ethics. Elwin admired his friend and the way he saw the world. To Colin, the world was divided into two types of people, good and evil, things were black and white; it made life easier. Kayno, on the other hand, was anything but simple, and he remained a mystery to Elwin. There was no reason for him to be here. A Cluain out tramping across the dry plains of Aleash. It made no sense.

"I wish he could be here, too," admitted Colin. "Zafra Pasha would put Faraj in his place."

Twisting in his saddle, Elwin found Kayno. Like Colin, Kayno was never too far off, yet he never came very close to the prince either. "Yes, he would," the price mumbled as he thought about Kayno.

Kayno looked like a mercenary. He sat up straight in his saddle refusing to remove his worn leather armor despite that it had to be terribly uncomfortable in this unforgiving heat. He always looked nervous. He was constantly looking over his shoulder, watching for the Caliph's men who had been following them since leaving Caiplich. Absentmindedly, the mercenary ran a hand along the hilt of his sword. The long narrow blade hung over his saddle horn where he could easily reach it if needed.

"You don't trust him?" asked Colin, seeing where Elwin was looking.

"Who? Ned? I mean Kayno?"

The mercenary looked over his shoulder again. He acted like a man just before a battle. Nervous. It was obvious he did not like being shadowed by a potential enemy. Elwin had wanted the

Caliph's men to follow him across the plains. Still, Kayno did not like having enemies this close. They outnumbered them three to one, and in the plains, there was no place to hide. It made Kayno feel like a dog on a long leash. He was always waiting for them to pull on the leash and stop them in their tracks.

"Yes. Why don't you trust him?" asked Colin.

"I know you and Pallas like him, and you probably have good reasons to. Yet there is something about him. He's hiding something. I can feel it." Elwin still found it strange that this sword master had been an innkeeper in Aonach. A mercenary, yes, but an innkeeper? "I'm also sure I have met Kayno before, but where? And How? I still can't remember."

Kayno's eyes met Elwin's. Elwin shifted in his saddle. The ex-innkeeper's eyes were dark and hard, and there was a secret hidden behind that iron-like face. Elwin looked away, pretending to adjust the black band that held the white scarf, called a keffiyeh, over his head. Even with the protection of white keffiyeh of the plains people, Elwin could still feel the effects of the intense heat. The land seemed to be completely without wind or shade.

"I don't see how you could know him," Colin stated.

"I don't either. But still, I feel I should, and I am sure he remembers me. I think he is hoping I won't remember."

The powerful black stallion swayed slowly under Elwin. Sah-Ib was also feeling the effects of unrelenting summer heat. It was said that if one was not careful, the sun in the Great Plains could burn the skin off a man in the day. Elwin did not think it would take that long. For a full month, he had been crossing the grasslands, and he was just beginning to adjust to the heat. His skin had lost all its whiteness, becoming a golden-brown color. With his dark skin and wearing a keffiyeh over his head, he almost looked like an Aleash. Almost. However, his long wavy brown hair gave him away as an outsider, and according to Aleash customs, outsiders were not allowed this far into the Great Plains. A fact Faraj never let him forget.

The cold Aleash leader would protect and guide Elwin across the plains because Zafra had ordered him to do so, but he did not have to like it, or even to pretend to. For Elwin, that was good enough. As long as Faraj got him to the Woods of the Mist, the Aleash man could hate him all he wanted to.

Trying not to look at Kayno, Elwin forced himself to stare out over the now all too familiar horizon. Never had he seen a land so big and flat. From one horizon to the other, there seemed to be nothing. Out here one could see forever. It was like being on a sea of grass. The tall waving grasses of the high plains seemed to be the only thing that could live out here. Only at watering holes had there been any trees, and then only a few at that. It had now been over a week since they had seen their last watering hole. Twice since leaving Caiplich, they had seen herds of wild horses. The grasslands of Aleash were famous for their wild horses, but like the watering holes, they had not seen a wild horse in a long time. This was the deepest part of the plains, and even the wild horses never came so far into this hostile, unforgiving land. Overhead vultures could be seen circling, looking for unfortunate animals that had wandered too far out into the plains. Elwin refused to admit it, but Lord Rodan had been right; alone, he would have been lost out here and dead within a few days. There was nothing but the sun and the stars to keep one from going in circles, and to be lost out here was to die.

Seating high in the pale blue sky, the fearfully hot sun burned on. It was nearly noon.

"Soon we will have to stop and wait out the heat," noted

Elwin.

Colin nodded.

They would move on again when the deadly noonday sun began to progress towards the evening, and the horses were given their needed rest. Up ahead, Faraj reigned in his gray horse and waited for Elwin to catch up. He pulled his horse in next to Elwin, matching Elwin's pace.

"Are we stopping?" asked Elwin.

Faraj pointed to the east where a dark form appeared on the flat horizon. "Do you see that?"

A black cloud, thought Elwin, *perhaps it would rain tonight.* It was a welcome thought. "Will it rain?" asked Elwin in the Kambryan language. He knew the Aleash language, but he found it easier to speak Kambryan. Besides, Faraj resented his use of his language, as if it were just one more reason to dislike him.

Faraj shook his head. Then, in broken Kambryan speech, he murmured, "It is Karr al-Isma."

Elwin thought he heard a trace of fear in Faraj's voice, or perhaps it was awe. Standing up in his stirrups to get a better view, Elwin shaded his eyes. He wiped the sweat from his brow and stared out across the plains. It still looked like clouds to him, small clouds at that. It was nothing more than a black bulge against the ever-flat horizon. It would still take days to reach the sacred woods. Yet he was seeing the Woods of the Mist at last, the home of the Guardians of Light, and where Elwin hoped to find Leina. She had to be there.

What Elwin had mistaken as storm clouds were actually the dark green spruce and pine trees that covered surrounding hills and the mountain of the Karr al-Isma. As the days passed, the hills grew taller and clearer. Rising above the tree-lined hills was a towering mountain, a mountain with a single snowcapped peak, which was flattened off as if someone had cut off the top right off of the mountain. Elwin imagined that the top was a small plateau, and he wondered what the view must be from there, gazing out over the endless planes. *Thunder Mountain*, Elwin almost said it out loud.

The mountain was named after the mythical Thunderbird that the mountain's silhouette tended to suggest. According to the Aleash, the mountain was in the shape of the bird with its head tucked down between its wings. The mythical winged beast of the mountain was said to draw storms to the Karr al-Isma, but today the sky over the mountain and hills was as clear as it was over the rest of the plains. The Karr al-Isma and the great mountain reached upwards towards the blue sky. Like an island in a calm sea, the mountain and surrounding hills dominated the landscape. Elwin could see why the Aleash stayed clear of it. The people of this land lived out their lives in the flatness of the Great Plains. In all of Aleash, only the Karr al-Isma broke out above the horizon. After a month of the never changing landscape, the mountain looked dark, menacing, and uncomfortably out of place in the plains. The Karr al-Isma did not belong to this land. It was as if some dead and forgotten god had put it there by accident.

"We will camp here," stated Faraj. His tone was cold, hard, and as unmoving as the mountain.

"Why now?" asked Elwin.

"The Karr al-Isma will not vanish over the night."

Elwin tried to stay calm, but he was finding it difficult. "We could be there in two hours," he examined. "Two hours! What difference can that make?"

"Much!" snapped Faraj. "It will be dark soon. We camp here, and that is how it shall be. I command here, not the prince of soft minded outsiders. If you wish to go, then go, but we stay."

With an arrogant smugness, Faraj turned, and before Elwin could protest further, walked away.

In moments, the camp started to be set; fires were started, the evening meal was being prepared, and tents began to rise. The Aleash were going nowhere this night. Large, white tents went up as grunting plainsmen pulled on ropes attached to long brightly painted poles. The Aleash were amazingly fast. In a few short minutes, they had turned a small area of the plains into a well-organized, and defensible camp. The intense smell of smoke and roasting meat filled the air.

Elwin turned his back on the camp. Frustrated and angry, he walked a short way from camp. Reflecting in the red glow of the evening sun, a small pool of water stood at Elwin's feet. This close to the Karr al-Isma water was plentiful, and pools of water dotted the lush green landscape. It was a massive transformation in only a few short miles. Somehow the Woods of the Mist seemed to draw storms to itself. Ironically, here in the very center of the Great Plains, rain was plentiful. In all of the high plains, the few miles around the woods and mountain were the wettest of all. The grasses were now dark green and lush in water-rich soil. It would have made a good place for a settlement, plenty of water and fertile soil, but this land was not claimed by any of the clans, and no Aleash dared stay more than a few weeks.

The Aleash came here for two reasons; in years of drought to keep their horses alive and to pray to their gods that made their homes in the sacred hills. Elwin found the Aleash attitude towards the Karr al-Isma confusing. They considered this land to be holy and the most sacred of places, yet they also feared the Karr al-Isma, shunning it as a dark and evil place.

Another night. Elwin reached down and picked up a stone. It was a flat oval shaped rock that had been polished clean by years of being exposed to the wind and rain. *Another night. What can it hurt?* With a splash, Elwin threw the stone into the pool's still water, it skipped twice before sinking below the surface. Quietly, he watched the ripples circling outwards. Two sets of ripples met and joined together before they eventually vanished, leaving the pool's surface calmed once more. *It is not like the Guardians of Light will be waiting for me at the edge of the woods.* Actually, he had no idea what to expect or even how he was going to find the Guardians of Light and Leina. The Karr al-Isma was a huge area to cover. It could take weeks, maybe months to find them, but somehow, he would find them. He had to. Faynn could offer very little advice on how one would find the Guardians, only that they are said to live within the hills. As if trying to convince himself of something that he did not honestly believe, he said out loud, "I want to be rid of this sword." The words somehow felt hollow. Angrily, he slapped the blade that hung at his side in its leathery sheath. The sword felt heavy, too heavy for Elwin to carry any longer. He did not want the sword and yet at the same time he did.

"Let the Guardians have it. That has to be why they wanted me to come here, so the sword would be safe. I do not have the strength for it. What good has it done me anyway? The sword draws the nightlings like bees to honey. I have had enough of running and hiding."

Elwin placed a hand on the blades leather hilt, then just as quickly he snatched it away. He never touched it anymore or tried not to. The sword scared him. Somehow, the sword was changing him.

Every night he called upon the power of the Earth Song to protect his dreams, the sword had made that possible. Elwin could call on the song at will now. Every night, under Faynn's watching eyes, Elwin practiced, wrapping the song around him to protect his dreams. Despite his fears, Elwin knew he would keep calling on the magic to protect his dreams. Even with the growing familiarity of the magic, the power frightened him. The sword gave Elwin a power he had always been taught was evil.

Elwin tried not to touch it, yet, at the same time, he wanted it close. For a few days, he had tried not wearing the sword. Two weeks ago, Elwin had packed the sword away, but the prince had hardly taken it off before he found himself strapping the hilt back on again. That was what was truly frightening; he wanted the power, Elwin wanted to immerse and lose himself in the song.

There was also another growing fear. Once he no longer had the sword, would he still be able to access the Earth Song? The thought of losing the now familiar song of power and mystery frightened him as well as comforted him. Would Torcull again torment his dreams? Elwin also saw in himself a growing desire to embrace the magic, and was becoming more reluctant to give it up. Perhaps that scared him the most. Was he or the magic in control?

"It has to be the sword. Did it do this to you, too, Father? Did you hate it and love it? Did it sicken and enthrall you? I need to be rid of it. I want to be rid of it. I want to be free of its evil, seductive power!" *And what of Faynn? He's always watching me. Does he know? He might be able to help. The druid understands Earth Magic better than I, but would he allow me to hand the sword over to the Guardians of Light?* Elwin did not think he would. Faynn had not hidden the fact that he did not trust the Guardians of Light. However, Faynn too was hiding things. For whatever reason, Faynn wanted Elwin to keep the sword, and yet he also was willing to help Elwin reach the Guardians. Why? What was it that the druid wanted? Elwin looked into the still reflective waters of the pool. The calm, reflective surface seemed to mock him. "I have to be rid of it, I have to!"

"Rid of what?"

Elwin's head snapped up. *Faynn! How long have you been there? Always watching me. What do you want from me?*

Avoiding the muddy spots, Faynn walked around the bank of the small pool. The druid's silver and black hair shimmered in the fading light. In his hand, he held his long, crooked staff.

Is Rodan right? Are you not to be trusted? Did you know the sword would do this to me? Force me to touch Earth Magic.

"What is it you wish to be rid of?" Faynn repeated himself. Stopping a few feet in front of Elwin, the druid leaned heavily upon his staff. He stared down at the young prince. His gray eyes searching Elwin's face.

"Stop that!"

"Stop what?"

"Staring at me! You are always watching me."

The druid raised an eyebrow. "Staring? Am I? I hadn't noticed. But you still have not answered my question. What do you want to be rid of? Maybe I can help."

Elwin wrapped his dark green cloak tightly about himself. There was a chill in the air. Soon another cold night would spread across the plains. As hot as the days were, the nights were just as cold. "It was nothing," Elwin answered curtly. "I . . . was just talking to myself." *Curse you, Faynn. What do you know?* "I want to be rid of these plains and find my sister. That's all."

Faynn nodded, but he did not seem convinced. Trying not to meet Faynn's eyes, Elwin gazed off to the east. The sun touched the rim of the flat horizon. Standing out against the sun, Elwin could make out the silhouettes of tents. The tents were those of the clan's men of the Caliph. They were never too far off. Elwin had been right, the Abu Ishaq had followed them across the plains. Twice now the Caliph's clan had stopped other clans from interfering with them. The Abu Ishaq were no friends, yet they would keep protecting Elwin and the others until the Abu Ishaq could discover what these outsiders were doing out here in the very shadow of their sacred mountain.

Elwin turned back to the west. Protruding high above the tree line of the Karr al-Isma, Thunder Mountain dominated the landscape. Covered in snow, the flat summit of Thunder Mountain was still bathed in sunlight. Even in the hot summer months, snow covered the towering summit of the mountain. It was strange to think of snow in this hot, dry land. Everything about Karr al-Isma seemed out of place. It just did not belong in Aleash. While the mountain peak still danced in the light of an Aleash summer day, the plains below were growing darker.

Watching the shadows of the night gradually slide up the steep slope of the mountain, Elwin watched Faynn out of the corner of his eye. "I just need some space and time to think," the prince said. "I need some privacy. I just want to be alone for a while."

Not taking the hint, Faynn pulled out his short-stemmed pipe and began to stuff it with a dark colored tobacco. All the while he was studying Elwin. Placing his thumb and forefinger together, a flame suddenly leaped out of his closed hand. Elwin shivered. He could almost hear the sweet song of the power. Faynn held the small flame to his face and drew the magical flame into the bowl of his pipe. With deep breaths, the druid sucked the flame into the bowl until the tobacco glowed, giving off a thick smoky aroma.

"We have things to talk about before tomorrow. They cannot wait." Taking another deep breath, Faynn took the pipe from his mouth. "Tell me, Prince Elwin," he said, pausing as he blew smoke into the air, "if you had the opportunity to give the sword away, would you?"

Elwin nearly choked. "I . . . I have not thought of it. Who would want it anyway? It's a cursed thing. Why . . . Why do you ask?"

Slowly, Faynn exhaled again. A twisting cloud of smoke rose above his head. It was dark enough for the stars to start to pop out. The stars appeared so much brighter in the open spaces of the plains. A few weeks ago, Elwin told Pallas that he thought the stars were brighter than back west.

Pallas only laughed and said, "How can stars be brighter in one spot than another?" Elwin still thought they were brighter.

"The sword is a burden, is it not?" asked Faynn. "It would only be natural if you wanted another to carry it for a while."

Hesitating, Faynn took another long drag from his pipe and weighted for Elwin.

"Are you offering to take it?"

"Me? Heavens no!" exclaimed Faynn. "I think that would be a grave mistake, a very grave mistake indeed."

"Then what are you trying to say?"

"Tomorrow you will enter the domain of the Guardians of Light. It would be best to know where you stand before you meet them. If not . . ." He shrugged. "Well, they have ways of getting one to see things their way."

Elwin looked up at the druid. "By force?" He could not believe the woman, Sileas, whom he had seen in the world of dreams could be cruel. She was just the opposite. *What was the druid up to? I do not trust you.* "Are you trying to say they would steal my sword?" Just the thought made his heart beat faster as he resisted the sudden urge to touch the blade at his side.

"No, the Guardians of Light abhor all types of violence. It is at least one thing that can be admired about the Guardians. They would never force you to give the sword to them, but they have other ways to get what they want. After all, you are here, aren't you? That's already one thing they wanted."

"No one made me come."

Faynn shrugged. "Yet you are here."

"What does that mean?"

"Nothing. But remember, the Guardians of Light always do what they believe is right, yet that does not make them right. Being wrong is a human flaw, and one the Guardians are not immune to."

"And you?" asked Elwin. "Are you not human? Are you not able to make mistakes?

Faynn softly chuckled. "I have heard it said by some that I am not human. However, you are correct. I too can be wrong, and I often am. Yet there are differences, Elwin. The blind man who thinks he can see is in far more danger than the blind man who knows he cannot. I do not doubt the Guardians mean good, but I do not believe they can recognize their own limitations."

"Is there really that great of a difference between you? You both use Earth Magic." Elwin said 'Earth Magic' as if it were some type of foul disease. "And you both are interested in the sword. Certainly, they can protect it better than I. Isn't that what's really important?"

Sighing, Faynn said in a quiet voice, "They do not use Earth Magic, Elwin. Earth Magic comes from the four elements of the universe—earth, water, air, and fire. The Guardian's power comes from that which lies beyond the material world. The Guardian's power is that of the spirit and not of the earth. A Guardian can see and do things no other human can, things even a druid cannot do. The power of the spirit world is not something one can learn, but is born with."

"I thought all magic was the same."

"Not at all. But I doubt you would believe me."

"You're right, I won't."

"You have grown bold. Few would speak to me the way you are."

Elwin ignored the statement.

"What do you need?" asked Faynn. "As I have said and done, I can help you."

"What I need are some answers."

"Okay. Like what?"

"Like, will the Guardians of Light ask for me for the sword?"

"I do not know what a Guardian will or will not do. They see what I cannot see. But yes, among other things, that it is what I fear. The Guardians will try to control what they should not control. They try to bend the laws of nature to their own will. There is great danger in that. Nature is a fragile creature and can easily be broken. They will want to control the sword, and if they cannot, they will try to control you. But they are creatures of Spirit Magic and not Earth Magic. They do not have the skill or training necessary to understand the dangers of magic. Like you, they think all magic is the same, but they are wrong."

"What if the sword is safer with them? If you do not know, maybe the Guardians do. You said so yourself, they can see things you cannot. Maybe they have seen that the sword would be safe with them?"

"Perhaps." Faynn nodded. "But knowing is different from understanding. Everyone knows that birds can fly, but few understand how. They know the sword is the key to the Dark One's prison, yet I do not believe they understand it. The sword was not meant for them, but for the High King. For you."

Elwin wanted to scream, *High King? I am not a bloody High King!* Then out loud said, "Do you understand it any better?" Elwin was angry, and his brown eyes took on a hard edge. Unflinching, he met Faynn's gray eyes. "And what are you doing if you are not trying to control the sword by controlling me? From the very start, you have pushed me one way or pulled me another. One moment you say I can't go to Karr al-Isma, then you say I must. You ask me to trust you, but have you given me a reason to? You are keeping things from me. Things I should know."

For a long moment, Faynn was silent. With a bowed head, he looked at the ground. The pipe in his hand had gone out. When he finally looked up, his voice was no more than a whisper. His gray eyes appeared to be focusing on something which Elwin could not see. "Yes," he finally admitted. "You are right. I have tried to force you to take the path that I felt was the best. First, I tried to keep the sword out of Torcull's hands, by protecting you. Then I tried to protect the sword by—" he cut himself short. "I was wrong to do so, and I shall do so no more. I truly am a blind man. Though you stood before me, I could not see you. Who knows where the river shall lead? Only by following the river shall we find the sea. I will help where I can, but from this moment on, you must choose. The time has come. But I warn you to choose wisely. Your choices will be hard, and they will either save or destroy the world. If you let me, I will give you what advice I can. Yet, in the end, it will be you who choose."

"What I need is answers and the truth."

"Truth? That is an elusive word that man has chased throughout the ages. As for answers, I have few, and a little knowledge can be more dangerous than none at all. Druids are better at asking questions than answering them. It is our nature, but come sit next to me, and we will talk. Ask and I will tell you what I can."

Finding a dry rock, Faynn sat down. After a gesture from the druid, Elwin too sat down on a small border and stared at the druid. Despite his anger and distrust, a part of Elwin had grown to like the old man. He did need answers while Faynn seemed to be the only one with answers, if only a few.

"Why did you think the Woods of the Mist were too dangerous for me, then why did you change your mind?"

Laying his staff beside him, he looked up to meet Elwin's eyes. "There is a prophecy," began Faynn, "a prophecy called, 'The Songs of Tartu's Harp.'

"Tartu's harp?"

Faynn explained. "Long ago, Kambrya was known as TMor Tyre. It was the first age of man. There were few humans then, and most of the human species lived in communities along the coast of the Iar Sea. It was a time when the gods, or those who called themselves gods, still made their home upon the earth. These so-called gods were the Ancient Ones, and at the dawn of man they were still strong in numbers. Anyway, in a small fishing village, there lived a sailor by the name of Tartu. With the aid of the crystal harp, Tartu could foretell the future."

"A crystal harp?"

Faynn nodded at the sword that lay across Elwin's lap.

"Yes, and like Saran na Grian, the harp of Tartu was endowed with Earth Magic. Before Tartu, it belonged to Claidemmh."

"The goddess of music? Isn't she just a myth?"

"Perhaps," admitted Faynn. "But there is usually some truth to myths and legends. The trick, of course, is sorting out what are myths and what are not. But yes, Claidemmh, at least in the mythologies was the goddess of music, as well as a few other things. Claidemmh was a lover of life who spread happiness wherever she went. It was said that she was so filled with life that laughter was her shadow and flowers grew wherever she walked, even in the deepest winter. She was the kindest, gentlest, and most giving of all the gods. Mythologies say that she taught the birds how to sing so the world would be filled with the joy of music."

"Do you really believe that the gods are real?"

Faynn shrugged, "Most of the time I am not sure what I believe. However, I am inclined to believe there is some truth in all religions. But let me continue. The histories or myths of TMor Tyre often speak of Tartu. He acquired the harp by saving Claidemmh, from a deserted island. Why the goddess of music was on an island is not clear, nor do we understand why she could not leave on her own. The ocean should not have been a serious obstacle for the goddess. Anyway, after Tartu saved the goddess, she was overjoyed to be free once more. She promised to reward Tartu.

'Just ask' said the goddess, 'and if it is within my power, I shall give it unto you.' Tartu, being an opportunist, wanted the goddesses' crystal harp. The harp was Claidemmh's most prized possession. Its strings were made of crystal spun from the mythical glass spider. When played, the harp sang out with the voices of nature itself. The song of the harp was so pure, it could touch the darkest heart. However, the song of the magnificent instrument was as powerful as it was beautiful. The harp could also be a diviner of the future, and in the wrong hands, such knowledge can be dangerous. At first, Claidemmh refused Tartu's request, saying it was too dangerous a thing for mankind. 'Too much knowledge,' she told him, 'will destroy you. Man was not meant to know the future.' But Tartu would not listen, and he insisted upon having the harp. He pointed out that she had promised to give him anything that was within her power. So Claidemmh gave in and surrendered her harp. For the first time ever, a tear touched Claidemmh's fair face, and laughter and joy, which had always been her companions, fled."

"Why did she not say no?"

"The Ancient Ones are bound by their words in ways men are not, and so she had to give him what she had promised." Faynn let his head drop. With his gaze fixed upon his lap, he silently sat there as if he had just lost a friend. The sun had set and the darkening night was as quiet and still as the druid. It was as if the plains themselves were listening to the story of Claidemmh.

After a long moment, Elwin pressed. "What happened?"

With a distant look, Faynn nodded. "At first, Tartu used the harp for man's benefit, and he became beloved throughout TMor Tyre. Tartu advised farmers when to plant and when to harvest their crops. He warned people when a natural disaster was coming, and he helped leaders avoid wars. Kings, chieftains, and common folk alike came from all parts of TMor Tyre to ask Tartu for his advice. The gods saw what Tartu was doing with the harp.

Concerned, they approached the man. The gods tried to convince him to give back the harp. They told Tartu of the danger, but Tartu still refused to listen. The Ancient Ones offered him wealth, long life, and power, and still Tartu refused. Failing to persuade the man, the gods departed. However, before the gods left him, they advised Tartu to be careful with the harp.

'Never tell what can hurt another,' they told him, 'and never look into your own future.' Unfortunately, Tartu did not take the second part of the god's advice seriously. The temptation was too great.

Repeatedly, Tartu looked into his future, and he used what he saw in the harp's music to become a powerful and wealthy man. At first, everything was fine; he was happy, wealthy, and respected throughout the land. The Ancient One's warnings seemed foolish, and Tartu laughed at the gods. More and more, he began to use the harp on himself. Slowly he began to change. The thirst for forbidden knowledge became an overwhelming obsession, and the knowledge Tartu gained drove him into madness. It has been suggested that he saw his own death in the music of the harp, or something equaling terrifying.

Either way, Tartu went mad. He stopped caring what people needed to know, or if what he told them was harmful or not. The madder he got, the less understandable his readings of the future became. Years passed, and Tartu became so mad that he began to believe he was a god himself, so Tartu demanded that he be worshiped. He told the most hateful and hurtful things that the harp revealed to him. With the music of the harp, he destroyed the hopes and lives of the people, people who had once loved him. That love now turned to hate and fear. The kings, clan chieftains, and leaders of TMor Tyre saw that Tartu had become evil and dangerous, so they banded together and had him exiled from their lands.

"Forced to leave the settlements along the coast, Tartu vowed that one day he would have his vengeance upon them. With the harp as his sole possession, Tartu wandered inland, away from the human cities. He was never to be seen by the race of men again. For years he lived as a hermit until he came upon a race of people called the black elves."

"Black elves?" asked Elwin. "Those are children's stories."

"The legendary black elves, also known as Yorns and mountain elves, were not so legendary at that time, Elwin. The druids have a collection of their history. They are related to the wood elves. Elves have lived on this earth far longer than man has. Though now the Yorns, as some call the black elves, have vanished, they were once as real as you or me. Yet, little of their writings survived the wars and the battle of Ban-Darn. That is when they suddenly and mysteriously disappeared, though some say they journeyed from their ancient home and now live in the Northern Drygan Mountains on the very edge of the White Forest.

Anyway, the elves found Tartu living in a cave like a wild animal and took pity on the man. Befriended, Tartu lived out his last years among the black elves. For some reason, Tartu could not use the harp to see into the elves' future, so the elves did not fear him. To the elf, Tartu was a sad man who thought he was a god.

Failing to impress the black elves, Tartu turned to writing a series of prophecies called 'The Songs of Tartu's Harp.' Many of those prophecies have survived. He talked and rambled more often than not of what he had once heard in the song. He wrote of kingdoms that would rise and fall, of great mountains that were yet to be, and of a castle that would be cast out from the world of light, but mostly he talked about a time when the High Kings would rule, then vanish, and how a new High King of Kambrya would return to reclaim his throne.

The elves, of course, thought him crazy. At the time, there were no High Kings, nor the kingdoms of Kambrya. Nothing Tartu said or wrote made much sense. When the Yorns vanished from the world, they left behind the prophecies. The prophecies were discovered in the ruins of the black elves. They are now kept in the druid's homeland of An-Eilean. I have studied the surviving prophecies, though they are difficult to understand. They provide clues to what will be or might be. In 'The Songs of Tartu's Harp',

438

Tartu said this:

"The High King will return when the Sword of Light and Darkness is raised to join with the blue, and the silver crown is freed. By the hand of the High King, who crowned himself, Ban-Darn will be brought back into the world, and the Dark One will be set loose. The wise one will fail, and the Knowers will err. Darkness will meet light, and only one will remain. The power that was, will be again."

Elwin's eyes popped open. "You think I am to be that High King?"

"The thought has crossed my mind."

"If what you say is true, the High King will destroy the world!"

"That is why I wanted you away from Torcull. The prophecy also says that when the Three Eyes of Buachaille meet, the High King will once more stand within this world." Faynn pointed to three stars—one red, one white, and one blue. "Those three stars are the Eyes of Buachaille, known commonly as the Watch Men. By the end of next summer, they will meet. Torcull needs to place the sword in his pretender's hands before that time if he is to fulfill the prophecy. I thought if I could keep you and the sword hidden away until after that time, I could stop the Dark One from being freed. I was a fool. A rock cannot stop the course of a river, and I am that, a rock in the great river."

"I will not be High King!"

Faynn shrugged. "Only time will tell. The future is a hard thing to be sure of. Even the harp only foretold of possibilities."

Elwin rocked forward. "I will not!"

Faynn shrugged again. "As you say."

For a long time, Elwin was quiet. Then he said, "I still do not understand. What do the Guardians of Light want from me?"

Faynn shifted, but his mode remained calm. "As I have said, the prophecies are not easy to understand. Beli may yet be denied his victory over the light of Palling. However, you are right about the Guardians. That is why they took your sister and let you know where to find her. They are drawing you to them. I believe that they hope to make you, or perhaps someone else High King. They too have read the prophecies, and believe that the god of light will reign over the god of darkness. They have interpreted the prophecies in such a way that they see the High King as the one who will bring an end to the darkness."

"But they will make me free the Dark One! In the name of the Three Gods! This is crazy. I will never do that. Why did you let me come here? I do not want to be theirs or yours or anyone's High King. I won't! I should run from here. Hide."

Faynn tilted his head slightly to one side. "So I once thought, but can you hide? Even now, won't you enter the woods?"

Elwin knew what Faynn meant by that. He looked into the darkness. He could no longer see the Karr al-Isma, but he was aware that it was out there, and the Guardians of Light had his sister. They were using his sister to force him to come to them, so they could make him their puppet king. Faynn, of course, was trying to manipulate him too, or at least he had been, but the druid was also right. He had to go on. Leina needed him. None of this was her fault. It was not right that she should be involved. High King, Earth Magic, it was all too much. His head hurt. "I'll go, but I will not be their High King. Not for the Guardians or anyone else. I will take Leina and leave this place. I won't bring the darkness upon the world!"

Faynn gave a short single nod of his head. "As I have said, we will only know in the end. The choice is now yours. Choose wisely, Prince Elwin ap Gruffydd. You will not get a second chance. But whatever you choose, I will support you." Faynn hesitated, then went on. "There is something more you need to know. Tomorrow when you go into the woods, I cannot go with you."

Elwin's mouth dropped open, despite his anger at all the secrets, he was learning to depend on the druid's wisdom. Even if he did not like it, Faynn was usually right. He was counting on Faynn to help find his sister. "But I need you!"

Faynn smiled. "Not as much as you think. But still, I cannot enter the woods. The Guardians and the druids have never seen eye to eye. Your whole mission would be put in jeopardy if I was with you. There is too much unfortunate past between the druids and Guardians. You must go on without me, but I will be waiting here. When you return from the woods, I will be here."

Faynn looked up at the stars known as the Three Watch Men. "Now we should be returning, morning will be here all too soon, and you will need your rest for what comes tomorrow. Remember this though, you have greater strength, as well as wisdom, than you give yourself credit for. Trust yourself and you will know what to do."

CHAPTER TWENTY-FOUR

Adjusting the pillows beneath his knees, a tall bearded man stared across the spacious tent. Being careful not to meet the eyes of the man seated before him in an elegantly carved oak chair, he looked up at his lord. It was rude to look into the eyes of one so close to the Caliph. If something were to happen, this man could rule Aleash. *And if I play my cards right, he will. But first I must deal with Zafra Pasha.*

"Khalu Pasha," the kneeling man addressed the seated figure clothed in grey silk robes. "They have not met up with any of the other clans, so they must be headed for eastern Aleash or to the southern pass."

Leaning back into his chair, Khalu scratched his short black beard as he thought. "But why, Ja'var? It makes no sense. The land of the Wa-Hativa is east of the Deep Plains. The Al-Amin can't expect to find allies among them, and they would first have to pass through the lands of the Ibn Jallab. They are even more unlikely allies. And beyond the southern pass is the empire, hardly an ally for Zafra."

Kneeling, Ja'var stared at the top of the dark gray turban that Khalu always wore. The turban was a shade or two darker than his robes. "Why else would they try crossing the Deep Plains, Khalu Pasha? It is the shortest way to the east."

"Blast it!" exclaimed Khalu. "If my brother was here, he could see through Zafra's plan. They have not even tried to lose us. It is almost as if they're asking us to capture them."

"You are as capable as Banu, maybe more so."

"You are kind, Ja'var," replied Khalu, "but I think your loyalty to me has blinded you. However, that does not change my problem. What are the Al-Amin up to, and why have they brought outsiders here of all places? Zafra must have a cunning plan, or he has become desperate."

"It may be time to put an end to this chase. We could take them as prisoners. There are no more than fifty Al-Amin warriors. It would be an easy thing, and the Ibn Jallab would be pleased if you captured Jarbi and handed him over. The Ibn Jallab would make a powerful ally."

Khalu waved his hand dismissively. "Let my brother worry about the Ibn Jallab. I'm concerned with what the Al-Amin are up to. Stopping them is not enough. We must discover what they are up to, so we must wait. If I act too soon, I will never know what they are planning or why the half-bred Jarbi has returned. And it still bothers me that they have not tried to lose us. They could have tried slipping away at night. They are too content at letting us follow."

Ja'var frowned. "Do you think that it is the Karr al-Isma they have been heading for all along?"

Khalu's eyes widened, then he shook his head. "No. It cannot be that, to send an outsider to the holy mountain! Even Zafra would not allow such a thing. They are just taking the shortest way across the plains, and it's a place where they can water their horses."

"But still," Ja'var went on, "it is as if they wanted us to follow them. And they've brought outsiders to the edge of the Karr al-Isma. It would seem that they want us to be witnesses."

"I agree that they are acting peculiar, but what you are suggesting is too much. If I were to accuse Zafra of that, the other clans would think I am crazy."

"A trick!" Ja'var suddenly exclaimed.

"A trick? How so?"

"The whole thing has been a very clever ruse," Ja'var

continued, slapping his leg as the idea dawned on him. "I should have seen it sooner. Zafra wants you to act against the outsiders."

"Why?"

Ja'var smiled. "To gain strength against your brother, he must turn the other clans away from the Abu Ishaq. If you accuse him of trying to find the Dawn'lah, he will accuse you of lying, or being mad. Who would believe that Zafra would try to find the Dawn'lah, or that he would choose Jarbi or an outsider to be the Ty'Azad? Zafra is respected, and none would ever think he would make an outsider the Ty'Azad. Even the Ibn Jallab would be hard pressed to believe that."

"Ah, I see what you are saying. Zafra wants us to think that he is going to let the outsiders into the Karr al-Isma. He wants us to stop them and accuse him of plotting against the Aleash clans. That way, it will be made to look as if the Abu Ishaq made the whole thing up, hoping to destroy the Al-Amin. The clans will begin to fear that the Caliph is trying to become too powerful, and they will side with Zafra. Zafra is a clever man, but I am smarter. I'll turn his plan against him. If tomorrow they do not move on, we will then take them prisoners and bring them before my brother. I will say only that they have traveled across Aleash without the Caliph's permission. Zafra cannot deny that. If they do move on, we will follow."

"And if the outsiders enter the holy woods?"

"They won't," asserted Khalu. "But if they do, they will die at the hands of the keepers, and we will watch and make sure that the Al-Amin watch as well. They will be our witnesses to the sins of Zafra. Zafra's people will be his accusers, then we will bring down the house of Al-Amin."

The tent flap opened. A man in a dark turban ducked into the tent.

"What is it?" snapped Khalu, irritated at being interrupted.

The man bowed deeply. "Forgive me, Khalu Pasha, but there is an Al-Amin man outside who wishes to see you."

"What!?"

"He claims that Zafra has betrayed his people and all the clans of Aleash. He says he hopes to help you stop Zafra before it is too late. The Al-Amin's name is Faraj."

Khalu smiled. "So, they are sending someone to act out the part of a traitor. No doubt this Faraj will tell me that the outsiders are going to the holy mountain and that I must stop them. Do they really think I will believe an Al-Amin? Do they think I am a fool? No Al-Amin would turn against Zafra. But let us play a little with this 'Faraj'. I will let him think that I believe Zafra is trying to bring forth the Ty'Azad. Yes, send in the liar."

--

"Elwin! Wakeup!"

The voice spoke in a soft whisper, but there was an urgency to the tone. No longer a heavy sleeper, Elwin quickly came awake. It was still night and his tent was dark except for the dim light of a partly shaded lamp. "Who's there?" demanded Elwin.

The lamp shades were pulled open, casting shadows across the tent. Elwin blinked. As his eyes adjusted to the light, he saw that it was Lord Rodan. "What's happening?"

Rodan handed Elwin some clothes. "Here, you have to get dressed. We have to leave. Now!"

"Where's the druid?" asked Rodan looking around for Faynn.

Taking the clothes, Elwin sat up. "I don't know, he was here when I went to sleep." Holding the clothes in his lap, he was reminded of another time. Elwin had done this before. In the same way, his father had woken him up. That night he had escaped the

445

Ceredigion city of Llanbaedarn. In that one night, Elwin's life had changed. He had been swept away by forces he could neither control nor understand. Things seemed to have changed little in the years since then.

"What's the matter?" asked Elwin, shaking the memory from his head. "Have the Abu Ishaq attacked?"

"Nothing so simple," Rodan responded. "I will tell you as you dress, but you must hurry. Faraj has betrayed us."

Elwin started putting his clothes on, then stopped. He looked up. "What?" Faraj was a cruel man, but Elwin would never have guessed that he would go against Zafra's orders. "Are you sure?"

"Yes, now dress. I don't know how much time we have." Elwin did as he was told.

"Faraj plans to turn us over to the Abu Ishaq," explained Rodan. "He has already left for their camp. If he returns before we have escaped, we will be taken prisoner."

Elwin pulled on his shirt and began to lace up the front. "Why would he do that? Why would Faraj betray Zafra Pasha?"

Rodan shrugged. "I cannot be certain. It could be me. As you know, I am not his favorite person. In his eyes, I am Isham. However, the Karr al-Isma is most likely at the heart of it. It is a sacred place. Faraj may have decided that Zafra Pasha has asked too great a thing. To help an Isham and outsiders to enter the woods is asking a lot. It's a forbidden thing. If the Abu Ishaq knew, a thousand men would be here to stop us. However, the reason does not matter, Faraj has gone over to Abu Ishaq, so we must run. Once Faraj tells Khalu what we are planning, the waiting will come to an end. We need to escape now."

Elwin finished dressing by pulling on his brown leather boots. He strapped his sword to his side. "How do you know this?"

"Not all the Aleash are our enemies. I still have a few friends here."

Rodan frowned as he looked across the tent. "We must hurry if we are to find the druid."

Elwin shook his head. "Faynn will not be coming with us. He feels he will be a liability to us once we meet up with the Guardians. If we meet up with the Guardians."

"We can't just leave him here. The Abu Ishaq will kill him."

"Don't worry about Faynn, he knows what he is doing. I doubt they will find him until he wishes to be found." Elwin finished dressing, looking over the tent once more to make sure he had not forgotten anything, then turned back to Rodan. "I'm ready."

Turning, Rodan blew out the lantern. "Good, then lets us get moving." Carefully pulling back the tent flap, the Reidh lord looked outside. A cold breeze blew in. "We must hurry." he whispered. "Morning is not far off." Rodan appeared tense. Then again, Lord Rodan always seemed tense. Perhaps it was just the danger of being discovered, trying to slip out of camp, but Elwin suspected there was something more to the Lord's mood. It was if Rodan was feeling guilty.

"The others are getting the horses ready," continued Rodan. "They will be waiting for us just outside of camp. Come. If you see anyone, we will have to make a run for it, so stay alert."

"Okay," replied Elwin in a hushed whisper. "Let's go."

Silently, Rodan replied with a quick nod.

As he crept out of the tent, Elwin readied himself. The Aleash camp was always well-guarded. His muscles tightened as he prepared to run. Following Rodan, he stepped out of the tent and into the night. Surprised, he found that the camp was still and quiet. The only sound was the soft whisper of a cold breeze.

Strange. His gaze swept across the encampment. *The Aleash had never left their camp unguarded before.* A short way off, fires burned like bright orange stars, yet they too had been left unattended. The camp appeared to be abandoned. With a questioning look, Elwin stared at Rodan.

"They have gone to their tents," Rodan answered Elwin's inquisitive look. "What they do not see, they cannot stop nor be blamed for."

Elwin nodded. He realized that the Aleash were allowing them to escape. Rodan evidently had more friends than he was letting on.

Slipping past the last tent, Rodan and Elwin left the camp behind and headed out into the plains. Moments later they found the others hiding in a patch of tall grass. Elwin quickly climbed up into Sah-Ib's saddle. Already mounted, Pallas reined in beside him. A wry smile slid across the red headed youth's face.

"Are you always late?" he jested. "Or just when we need to escape?"

"Enough!" snapped Rodan, cutting off Elwin's smile. "We have to hurry. Faraj will be returning soon."

Aidan looked around. "Where's Faynn?"

"He is not coming," answered Rodan.

"What!?" demanded Colin. "We can't leave him back there!"

"He chose not to come," Elwin stated. "He had a good reason. I can tell you all later. We should get out of here."

With that, they headed off into the night. Elwin sat back in his saddle, wondering where Faynn was. He hoped the druid would be safe. It was going to get ugly in camp when they turned up missing.

The night was clear and the sky was filled with bright, twinkling stars. From one horizon to the other, stars beyond human comprehension stretched out across the night sky. Sitting beneath that canopy of light, Elwin felt small and insignificant. His eye caught the three eyes of Buachaille and he wondered if the prophecies could be right, and he was destined to free the Dark Lord upon the world once more. Pushing the thought from his mind, he tapped the hilt of his sword and matched the speed of the others as they rode towards the mountain.

An hour passed, and the land began to slowly rise before them. Elwin tried not to think of the Karr al-Isma or what may or may not lie ahead, but the silent night was suddenly shattered. Somewhere behind them a shout broke out, followed by the blaring of horns, then more shouting erupted.

Rodan looked over his shoulder. "It would seem that Faraj has returned and has discovered that we have slipped out of his trap."

Pallas smiled. "I wish I could have seen his face when he found out."

"A dangerous wish," uttered Kayno, "yet perhaps it would have been worth it."

"It would." Pallas laughed in agreement.

"Will they come after us?" asked Colin seriously. He saw nothing funny about this night.

"They will try," replied Rodan, "but we have a head start. If we hurry, we will make the woods long before they can catch us."

"Then what?" asked Colin, adjusting the strap that held his sword across his back. "Will they follow us into the woods?"

"No. I am the only Aleash foolish or desperate enough to enter the trees of Karr al-Isma. They will not follow. You can save your sword, Colin, until we reach the trees. It is what lies ahead that you need fear, not what we leave behind." Rodan then kicked his mount into a quick trot, pulling ahead from the others before they matched his pace.

Slowly the sounds of their pursuers grew, and with each passing moment the Aleash seemed that much closer. However, Rodan, acting as if the plainsmen posed no real threat, kept their pace at a steady trot. The whole time, Rodan kept his eyes focused on the dark form of Thunder Mountain. Like a man on his way to the gallows, Lord Rodan Macay was in no hurry.

"They're spreading out!" warned Kayno in a loud voice. "They are trying to out flank us."

"Should we not move faster?" asked Aidan. Despite his dislike of horses, Aidan hated the idea of being overtaken by the Aleash even more.

"They will not catch us," reassured Rodan.

The color of a pink rose ascended above the steep slopes of Thunder Mountain and the darkness began to give way to the coming dawn. The great mountain became a dark towering silhouette against the brightening sky. The edge of the woods was not far now. Gazing up at Thunder Mountain, Elwin felt a chill as if the mountain was calling out to him.

The shouts behind them grew louder.

"They have spotted us," warned Kayno.

"They are close enough," said Rodan. "It's time to be done with this." He kicked his horse forward.

The others did the same and the six men raced towards the mountain and the waiting trees. The Aleash tried to pursue, but they had pushed their horses hard, while Rodan had kept their horses rested. The small party of outsiders quickly put more ground between themselves and the pursuing Aleash. Breaking out over the steep southern slope of Thunder Mountain, the sun announced the day's arrival by bathing the six men in its glowing warmth. Soon the day would grow hot, but by then Elwin and his companions hoped to be in the shade of the woods and the coolness of the mountain's foothills.

As they raced eastward, the ground beneath them began to rise into rolling grassy hills and soon they were passing the first isolated trees. Like a dry savanna, the trees were scattered over a large area. These lone trees were on the outlying reaches of the Karr al-Isma. The actual Woods of the Mist still lay a short distance ahead. Leaning across his horse's thick neck, Elwin raced ahead of the others. True to its name, Elwin's horse ran like the wind. The black stallion was a proud animal and ran as if it had a full night's sleep. Cresting a small hill, the Karr al-Isma lay before him. A line of thick trees stretched out to either side. Sitting up in the saddle, he pulled in on his reins. Sah-Ib quickly responded. Turning the black mare about, Elwin waited for the others. There was no way that the Aleash could catch them now. Rodan reined in next to Elwin. His sweating horse breathed heavily beneath him. Sah-Ib danced to one side as if he were ready to start off again.

"The Aleash have given up," said Elwin, pointing down the hill to where the plainsmen sat upon their tired mounts.

The clansmen were quiet now. Their shouts had come to an end, and they were no longer racing in pursuit. Now they sat quietly upon their mounts watching the six men they had just shortly before been chasing.

A moment later, the others caught up to Elwin and Rodan. Rodan pointed. "That is Khalu there in front." Khalu's head was bare. His gray turban had been lost during the chase, but Rodan knew his face too well to ever forget it.

"Isn't that Faraj?" asked Elwin, who was pointing as well.

Rodan nodded. "Yes, I believe it is."

Faraj raced up to the Caliph's brother, he appeared angry and

451

was gesturing wildly.

Another Aleash grabbed Faraj and dragged him from his horse.

"What's happening?" asked Elwin.

Rodan gave a small smile. "Faraj seems to have gotten himself into some trouble."

Kicking and screaming, Faraj was dragged away from Khalu. "Stop them!" he yelled loud enough for Elwin and the others to hear. "They will go into the woods! You have to stop them!"

"Why are they stopping?" asked Aidan, pulling his horse around so that he could see better.

"Khalu does not believe that we will truly enter the woods," answered Rodan. "He is waiting for us to come to him. Evidently he does not believe Faraj."

"Then let him sit there and watch us enter the woods," said Elwin. He turned Sah-Ib and faced the trees.

Below, the Aleash matched their pace but made no attempt to catch them.

Swinging a leg over his saddle, Rodan dismounted with the grace of an Aleash raised on the backs of horses. Silently, he stood staring into the dense growth of towering trees. The woods were so dark that they could not see far into shadowy forest. Close to the forest's floor, a thick fog covered the earth, making the woods look like it grew out of a great cloud. Like a living thing, the misty fog twisted and flowed around the tree trunks. Staring at the fog covered ground, Elwin shivered. Even in the light of day, there was a feeling of foreboding about the woods. Before him was a place of darkness surrounded by a land baked by the sun. Here was a place that the sun never touched.

And it is here that the Guardians of Light live, thought

Elwin. *It makes no sense.* He wondered if he had misunderstood the Guardians of Light. In the world of dreams, Sileas had appeared to him and told him that he would find Leina in Woods of the Mist. Now confronted with the place that he had traveled so far and so hard to find, he wondered if it was a trap set by Torcull. Elwin remembered Faynn's warning. 'The Guardians of Light are not to be trusted.' Elwin was beginning to believe the druid might be right.

Discovering that Colin was watching him, Elwin turned his back and dismounted, only to find that Kayno, also was looking at him. "Blast it!" he mumbled under his breath. "Why won't everyone leave me alone?!"

Kayno gave a shrug. "It comes with being a prince, and someday king. You had better get used to it."

Refusing to even look at the woods, Rodan began taking the saddle from his horse's back.

"We will leave the horses here," he announced. His voice was flat and void of any emotion.

"Horses have more sense than humans. They will not enter the woods." Not too far away, the Aleash, both the Al-Amin and the Abu Ishaq, watched and waited, still not truly believing what they were seeing.

"Are they going to just stand there?" grunted Pallas.

Colin slid off his horse. "Maybe they want to see what will happen. Maybe they think that monsters and demons will jump out and drag us away."

Rodan looked over his shoulder but said nothing, yet his eyes suggested that was exactly what they were doing.

"This is a strange place," Aidan announced. The elf stared into the trees, even his dark green eyes could not pierce this darkness. "I have never seen a mist like this, or a forest so dark."

Colin nodded his head in silent agreement.

Rodan gave a short laugh. "What have I been telling you? This is not a place for the living. Nevertheless, the Abu Ishaq is still waiting for us to return. We have no choice. We go on."

And Leina is in there. "Yes," agreed Elwin. "We go on."

Aidan shifted from one foot to the other. "I'm thinking that we should wait until the sun warms the day. Maybe the fog will lift. Don't you agree?" Even he knew that would not happen, this fog never lifted. It was why this palace was called the Woods of the Mist.

Elwin hesitated only a moment before he slung his pack over his shoulder.

From across the plains Khalu laughed. "Goodbye," he called loud enough so they could hear him across the field.

Elwin turned and shouted back, "You have not seen the last of me!" He sounded braver than he felt. Taking a deep breath, he turned back and stepped into the trees. The thick mist engulfed him from the knees down. When he did not feel the fog tearing at his feet, as he half expected it would, he let out his breath with a loud sigh.

Pallas was close on Elwin's heels. Arriving quickly at his friend's side, Pallas rested a hand on Elwin's shoulder. Giving Elwin a reassuring wink, he said, "It will be a grand adventure." The redheaded youth's smile was broad, and even in the gloom, his teeth shone brightly.

"How can you be so bloody cheerful!"

"You worry too much," Pallas replied. "It's only mist. What can it do? And it is nothing like Reidh, is it? You can't have an adventure in a place like Reidh."

Elwin shook his head. "You never change."

Pallas laughed. "Why would I do a foolish thing like that?

One needs not mess with perfection."

The last to enter the shadowy woods was Rodan. The lord cast a look over his shoulder. He seemed like a man who had to choose which way he was going to die. With shoulders tense and his eyes straight forward, he made up his mind, and so he stepped forward, determined to face his end with dignity.

"I think we should head for the mountain," suggested Kayno. "It's the easiest way to keep in one direction. But of course, the decision must be yours, Elwin."

"Why me?" Elwin muttered.

"You are the prince here, and someday you will be a king. It is time you start acting the part."

"I won't be your king."

"What does that mean?" asked Kayno defensively.

"Nothing." Elwin turned to Aidan. "You lead the way. With your wood lore, you will be the best at keeping us from getting lost or falling off a cliff. With this mist-like fog, I can't even see my own feet." *And you have that feather as well. It seems to help you find paths that should not be there.*

The approaching sunny day soon became lost within the trees. A dark twilight settled over the woods. The deeper they went, the thicker the fog grew and the stranger it became. Rising from the forest floor, the fog-like mist formed into what looked like ghostly figures. Drifting upon an unfelt breeze, the ghostly images silently passed between the trees until they vanished into the gloom.

"This place looks like it's haunted, " breathed Colin.

"I have seen fog act like that on the sea," said Pallas. "It is only the dark that makes it look like ghosts."

"It doesn't look normal to me," commented Kayno in support of Colin. "And ghosts seem as likely as anything I can come up with."

"It's only fog," stated Elwin, but he was trying to convince himself as much as the others.

"I still agree with Colin," said Kayno, repeating himself. "This place is haunted. It is a place fit only for the dead."

"They are the ghosts of the dead who serve the Keepers," added Rodan. "It is said that these are the ghosts of the Aleash ancestors who have been called to aid the Keepers. It is their duty to watch and keep all others from bothering them. The holy ones do not wish us to be here in their woods."

"Who are 'keepers'?" asked Aidan.

Rodan shook his head. "Just pray you don't find out."

Pallas pulled out a lamp from his pack and changed the subject. "You were right, Rodan, we need a lamp even during the day. It is a good thing that you thought of it."

With the aid of Pallas' lamplight, Aidan picked up the pace and they quickly moved deeper into the woods.

"Do you think these woods are actually haunted?" whispered Aidan, as he slowly led the way.

Pallas shrugged, walking just behind him. "I can see why the Aleash think so, but I do not believe in ghosts." A foggy phantom passed close by and with a shiver Pallas stepped closer to Aidan. "At least I don't think I do."

Appointing themselves as sentries, Kayno and Colin marched at the rear. With intense caution, the two large men looked from side to side, keeping their hands on their weapons. Though none said it, they were all wondering if swords would be much good against ghosts, and they were all hoping they would never find out.

Around midday or what they thought was midday, it was hard to tell in the shadowy gloom of the forest, Aidan, leading the way deeper into the haunted forest, came to a quick stop.

"What is it?" asked Kayno, sounding concerned.

Aidan raised a hand. "Shhh."

Gracefully and almost completely silent, Kayno drew his sword and held it at the ready. Colin followed suit.

Holding their breaths, everyone stood still. At last, Aidan shook his head. "Sorry. It was nothing. I just thought I heard something. It's these woods. They are getting to me. Other than the trees, there is nothing alive here."

Aidan was right. The woods did seem to be without life. The eerie silence was never broken; not by the song of a bird, nor the scampering of a squirrel. They couldn't find the smallest sign that any other creature lived here. Reluctantly, Aidan started off once again.

As night approached, the gloomy twilight faded away into the blackest night imaginable. After the star filled nights on the high plains, the haunted forest seemed to close in upon them, silently watching. Even Aidan, a woodland elf, felt strangely uncomfortable in this unnatural forest of silent trees. Only with the aid of a small fire were they able to keep the blackness of the night at bay, but the silence always remained.

Not yet ready to sleep, the party huddled around the small crackling fire.

"We're being watched," Aidan suddenly announced in a whisper.

Colin and Kayno leaped to their feet with their weapons drawn and nervously searched the shadows of the forest. Even Pallas' wry smile was gone.

"Where?" asked Kayno.

"Everywhere," Aidan responded with a node of his head. "They are all around us."

"What are?" asked Elwin, not doubting for a second Aidan could be wrong.

Aidan shrugged his shoulders, "I don't know, but there is a lot of . . . whatever they are."

In the darkness, something moved among the trees. A branch snapped. Elwin found himself on his feet, holding his sword before him. Every eye tried to pierce the foggy ghost-filled night, but they could see nothing but shadows, fog, and twisted trees.

Only Rodan had not moved. He was seated, staring into the dancing flames.

"They have come," he whispered to himself. The Keepers have come." Another branch. Who or whatever was out there was coming closer.

Reflected in the firelight, a pair of yellow eyes peered between two trees. Then another, and another. All to soon dozens of shining eyes stared out of the darkness.

"What are they?" whispered Colin.

"Keepers," Rodan gowned once more. "They have come for us." There was a fear in his voice that Elwin had never heard before. Aidan slid an arrow into his bow. "What are they waiting for?"

"Gather up!" Kayno told everyone. "We need to cover our backs. And keep close to the fire."

"Should I shoot one?" asked Aidan. "Maybe it will scare the others off."

"Or make them angry," Kayno answered. "I think you should wait."

Time seemed to stop. After what seemed like an eternity, the Keepers started to move. Circling the fire, they began a rhythmical snapping noise that sounded like a thousand grasshoppers. Yet they moved no closer. Keeping away from the firelight and hidden within the shadows of the night, they began a dance. Soon a humming music joined in with the snapping sound. Not once did they come close enough to the fire light to be clearly seen. Only their glowing eyes reflected as they circled around the group fearfully huddled around their fire. Then suddenly, the fire sparked and started to die.

"In the name of the Three Gods!" exclaimed Pallas.

"The fire!" shouted Elwin. "They're using some kind of magic to put out the fire!" Yet Elwin had not sensed the use of Earth magic.

Quickly, Aidan threw more logs onto the fire and began to sing to the fire. The song he sang was in the elven dialect. Elwin immediately felt the gentle nudging of the Earth Song in his head letting him know Aidan was calling on his elven lore of Earth Magic. The fire flickered, then the logs caught. The flames slowly grew stronger.

The humming from the woods grew louder. The fire flickered, but Aidan kept singing.

Elwin felt Aidan feeding the fire with Earth Magic. The soft melody of the power flowed out of Aidan. Not caring what he was doing, Elwin reached out towards the magic. His fear of the magic had been replaced by a fear of what was in the woods. Hoping he could somehow help Aidan, he tried to grasp the power, but it slipped through his fingers like water.

Whatever Aidan was doing, it seemed to be interfering with the keeper's magic. *It has to be magic the Keepers are using, but I can't hear it like I can with Aidan's magic.* Thought Elwin as he watched the glowing eyes that danced just out of the firelight. Elwin strained to see, but whatever was out there never came closer.

"They won't come near the fire," observed Kayno.

"But what do we do when we run out of wood?" asked Colin. "We can't get more with those creatures out there." No one had an answer.

Moments passed that felt like hours. Waiting for their supply of wood to run out they watched and waited. Yet long before their firewood was used up, without warning the snapping and humming stopped. One by one the Keeper's yellow eyes faded back into the trees and back into the night, and the silence returned.

"They're leaving," breathed Elwin. "They're giving up."

Aidan stopped singing. "We'd better gather some more wood in case they come back."

Elwin stared down at Aidan. "You used Earth Magic! It was not very strong, but I heard it."

"Would you rather I let the fire go out!" Aidan snapped defensively.

"I didn't mean it that way," Elwin offered. "Thank you. You saved our lives."

Aidan nodded sullenly.

"Do you think they will be back?" asked Pallas, still staring into the darkness.

"No, I don't believe that they will be back," Aidan went on, "but it won't hurt to be ready." Aidan looked at Elwin. "What are you staring at?"

Elwin turned away and started looking for more firewood.

The next day the tired group rose as soon as the darkness was replaced by the misty gloom. After eating a cold breakfast with little conversation, they moved on ever deeper in the woods and into the mist. Throughout the day, the company remained quiet. The Keepers, if that's what they were, had put everyone into a nervous and silent watchfulness. Each set of eyes were searching for the yellow eyes of the Keepers to return. All the while, the strange misty fog swirled about them, forming into ghostly images. As the day dragged on, an uneasy mood had settled over the small party. As night once again approached, they made camp and made sure they had a large stockpile of firewood. As everyone feared, the Keepers returned. But this time, the Keepers did not try to put out the fire. Instead they just sat there. For nearly three hours, the Keeper's yellow yes watched them from the shadows of the night. Then once again they vanished, slipping back into the night.

In the morning, as he did every morning, Aidan climbed a tree to get his bearings on the mountain before heading out once more. Three more days Aidan led the party on towards Thunder Mountain, and each night the eyes reappeared.

On the fifth night Elwin asked, "How are our supplies doing?"

Frowning, Aidan threw another log onto the fire. "Not good. We have enough to last another three days . . . four at the most. We had to leave the Aleash camp in a hurry and there was little time to find more supplies." Aidan hesitated, then added. "I would never have guessed that I could not find anything to eat in the woods, but everything that grows here is inedible or poisonous."

Rodan laughed. It was the first sound that he had made in days. "What do the dead need of food? The Keepers come every night, and the ghosts haunt our days. They play with us, and they will come again and again. We should not be here. We will be punished for violating this place." For a long moment, everyone was silent. The strain was getting to them all, but it seemed worse for Rodan. With each passing day, Rodan drew further into himself. He was part Aleash, and the stories he was raised on were haunting him. In Aleash terms, they were committing a sacrilege by being here, and Rodan feared he was committing a deadly sin. It was growing harder for anyone to disagree with him.

"At least they haven't shown up tonight," noted Elwin. "Maybe we've lost them."

Pallas' face brightened. "I think we need a song. Aidan?"

Aidan consented with a nod of his head. "But I'd better keep it low. We don't need to draw more attention to us." He pulled a long wooden flute from his pack. The flute was made of a single piece of wood that Aidan had brought along and had carved while crossing the grasslands. In moments, the forest around them echoed with the soft sound of an elvish melody. Even Rodan's mood seemed to improve. Startled, Elwin looked up. Within Aidan's song was another song. It was faint but Elwin recognized it. Deep within Aidan's music was the song of Earth Magic.

He is unaware of what he is doing, Elwin was startled to realize. Aidan could not hear the song as Elwin did. Faynn said that the elves were closer to Earth Magic than other races. It's a part of them. How can one be blamed for something that is born within them?

Feeling confused, Elwin stood up and walked a short distance away. He wanted to be as far from the music as he could get without leaving the ring of firelight. Leaning against a tree, he stared back at the others. They were smiling and laughing. Pallas started to sing. Elwin knew that it was more than just the song that was making them feel better. It was the Earth Magic. Elwin wanted to tell Aidan to stop. *But then I would have to tell them why, and it does seem to be helping them.* Elwin shook his head. Caught up in his own thoughts, Elwin did not see the figure moving among the trees. Cloaked in the darkness of the Karr al-Isma, the figure drew closer, until it was right behind Elwin.

"Prince Elwin?" came a whisper from the darkness.

Elwin turned with a start. He leaped to his feet and started desperately trying to pull his sword free of its scabbard. The only thing Elwin accomplished was catching his foot on a root of a tree and falling to the ground.

Aidan stopped playing. Coming to his feet, Kayno drew his sword and rushed forward.

Colin was right on his heels.

"Who...who's there?" stammered Elwin, lying flat on his back staring into the darkness. Out of that same darkness, a man clothed in a dazzling white robe stepped into the firelight. His face was barely visible beneath his hood, but at least he did not have yellow eyes. Raising an open hand towards Kayno and his sword, he smiled, "I come in peace. You may put that away. Only the dark need to fear the light."

Kayno stopped but he did not put his sword away.

"I said put it away." The voice was gentle yet commanding.

As if he was helpless to do otherwise, Kayno slipped the sword back into his sheath.

"That is better." Turning from Kayno, the man in white faced Elwin and smiled. His robe was so bright that it contrasted against the grim background of the woods. In fact, it was so bright that it almost appeared to be glowing. Bowing low to Elwin, he said in his quiet voice, "Lord Elwin ap Gruffydd, future High Prince of Kambrya, I am Arran, a Guardian of Light, and I am a defender of truth. I have been sent by the High Counsel to welcome the next High King to our home. I have come to lead you from the dark into the light. We of the Heart are your servants." A stunned silence echoed through the party. Kayno frowned and Rodan' eyes grew wide.

"High King?" Pallas murmured softly.

After a brief moment, Elwin snapped, "I've come for my sister! Not to become your bloody High King!"

No one breathed.

"Please!" pleaded Lord Rodan. "Do not speak to a Guardian of Light with such disrespect. He has spared our lives."

"They took my sister!" Elwin gave Rodan a hard look. "I'll talk to him anyway damn way I please!"

"We did not take the sister of the High Prince. We saved the princess from a place that she did not want to be," corrected Arran, nodding his head toward Elwin. "Would you have wished us to leave her and let her be forced to wed your cousin?"

Turning hard eyes upon the Guardian, Elwin said in anger, "You took her for your own reasons! I see that now. You have imprisoned Leina to draw me here. You want to make me something that I do not wish to be. I will not be your High King!"

"Princess Leina is not a prisoner. She may come or go as she so likes. And one cannot be made into something they are not already." Arran's voice had a soft musical ring to it. The voice was soothing and called out to be trusted, but Elwin refused to give in to it. So appealing was Arran's voice that Elwin wondered if there was some type of power in his voice, but he detected no hint of Earth Magic.

"If my words have offended you," Arran went on, "I ask for your forgiveness." Once more he bowed to Elwin.

"Stop that!" snapped Elwin. "Where is my sister!?"

"She is well." Pulling back his hood, Arran revealed a clean-shaven face. He was a handsome young man with short light brown hair and matching eyes.

Elwin stood up and placed a hand on the hilt of his sword.

"She had better be."

Arran's eyes fell to the sword. For a brief moment, disbelief registered across his fair complexion. "Saran Na Grian!" he breathed in awe. "It's true!" He quickly looked back up at Elwin with unconcealed awe in his eyes. Taking a long deep breath, Arran went on. "I am here to bring brother and sister together. We are the friends of the true light." Smiling, Arran looked at the others for the first time, his eyes meeting each of theirs. "And of course, your friends are welcome too. All are welcome in the Heart."

"The Heart?" asked Aidan. "What is that?"

"My home, and the dwelling place of the Light," Arran responded.

"Are we close to this Heart?" asked Colin, hoping it would be a place that was out of this gloomy ghost-filled world. The home of light did not sound too bad. Yet it was evident to him and everyone present, that Elwin did not think this was a great turn of events.

The Guardian glanced at Colin and smiled. "Here we travel quickly. The Heart is always far, and yet it is always close. Darkness is but an illusion. With the one true power, all is light, and the Heart is that light."

Elwin grunted.

CHAPTER TWENTY-FIVE

Awakened by a warm breeze, Elwin kept his eyes shut. Something had changed. He could sense it. This was not the same place that he had gone to sleep in. Lying as still as possible, Elwin felt something that he had not felt in days—the sun. The welcome warmth of the sun beat down on the side of his face. It wasn't the scorching heat of the Aleash plains either, but rather a gentle uplifting warmth, like that of an early summer day. Accompanying the sun and its welcoming warmth was the sound of birds singing in the new day. The sound was carried on a soft whispering summer breeze was the rich earthy smells of a healthy growing forest. *This cannot be the Woods of the Mist.* Taking in a contented breath, he opened his eyes. At first, he could hardly believe what he was seeing. *I must be dreaming. Either that, or the last days in the Karr al-Isma have been a nightmare.*

Elwin was still in the woods or at least "a forest", for it no longer looked like the same woods of the day before. During the night, the dark and misty woods of the Karr al-Isma had seemingly transformed itself into a forest that was alive, healthy, and beautiful. The trees were tall and straight with a thick green canopy of leaves that softly swayed back and forth in the warm, gentle breeze. The foggy mist, which only the day before had covered the earth, had now vanished. The ghosts that had had haunted the woods were gone. The once barren forest floor was now densely covered in ferns, flowers, and green mosses that sparkled with the morning dew.

Just beyond their campsite grew thick bushes which were covered in plump, ripe berries ready to be picked and eaten. The flowers stood out the most, with their large blooms that sparkled like a spring rainbow and covered the forest floor with a blanket of colors. Other species of flowering plants wound their way up the trunks of the trees, filling the air with sweet scents. Everywhere Elwin looked, life sprang forth. It was an incredible wonderland filled with dazzling colors. Elwin had never seen woods such as the one that now surrounded him. Yet there was something wrong.

The young prince could not explain it, but he could taste the wrongness. Despite what his eyes saw, it felt as if the whole place was slowly dying. It made no sense. Sitting up, Elwin was confronted by a smiling face. The face belonged to Lord Rodan, which was glowing with happiness.

Lord Rodan smiling? Now I know that something is wrong. Elwin said out loud, "Lord Rodan? Is that you?" Lord Rodan smiling... It was almost as strange as the wood's miraculous transformation. As far as Elwin could remember, Rodan had never smiled, not even once.

"Good morning, Prince Elwin," said the man who looked and sounded like Lord Rodan but did not act like the man Elwin had known. "It is a wonderful morning. Is it not?"

Bewildered and more than a bit confused, Elwin looked up at the sun as it shone through a canopy of green leaves. Squirrels scampered and played in the branches. It was a perfect day. It was more than perfect; it was magical. But nowhere was the song of Earth Magic. Confused, he looked at Rodan. "I'm not sure. Is it wonderful, or am I dreaming? Surely this is not the Karr al-Isma?"

"But it is!" laughed Rodan excitedly.

"What has happened?"

"A miracle!"

Taking in his new surroundings, Elwin saw the white robed Guardian of Light approaching from the far side of their camp site. With a graceful stride, Arran walked across the forest floor as if he were walking on a cushion of air. With his hands tucked into the long sleeves of his flowing robe, the Guardian appeared like an angel that had just descended from above. Smiling, his fair face glowed in the morning light. Like the woods, Arran appeared perfect in every way.

Too perfect, thought Elwin.

"Good morning, High Prince." The Guardian greeted Elwin with a short, polite bow.

"Perhaps not a miracle," the Guardian added as he graced Rodan with his infectious smile, "but no doubt a welcome change." He turned back to Elwin. "I am sure you have traveled far and experienced many hardships, but now your journey is nearing its end. Today we shall be at the Heart of Light."

Elwin came to his feet. "What have you done!? Where have you taken us?"

Wide-eyed, Rodan looked up at the Guardian like a son watching his father, yet Rodan had to be at least ten years the elder of the man. To Rodan, Arran was next to a god. All the Aleash legends spoke of the Guardians of Light and their sacred mountain, and the paradise that they lived in. And this place did seem like a paradise.

With a confused sound to his voice, Arran replied, "Done? I have done nothing, High Prince."

"This is not the same place that I was last night."

"But it is." Arran spoke cheerfully, and his sing-song voice sounded as reassuring as it had the night before, and once more Elwin felt the pull of some unseen force. Whatever the force was, Elwin knew that it was not Earth Magic; the music was not there. Then he remembered what Faynn had told him, the Guardians of Light do not use Earth Magic, but draw their magic from other sources. Faynn had called it Spirit Magic.

"It is just that the falseness of darkness has been lifted and now you are seeing the light of truth."

Elwin's eyes narrowed. "An illusion? The Karr al-Isma was just an illusion?"

"All darkness is an illusion, High Prince."

"Why do the Guardians hide behind an illusion of darkness?"

Horrified at Elwin's accusing tone, Rodan gave the prince an angry look.

Arran simply smiled and replied, "High Prince, we do not hide from the world, but shut out the taint of its evil ways. Certainly, you have seen how wicked and cruel the world can be. That is not true here. Here is the world as it was meant to be. Here is a world without violence or disease. A place where truth has survived man's follies. Outside this realm, people see what they believe to be true. However, the light is truth and darkness is but a lie. When He Who is the Light returns, all shall see the truth, and the world will be remade in the image of his peace. Until that day, we guard that which was and that which will be again. From here." He spread out his arms taking in the forest. "The seed of light has been cared for and stays strong. From here, it shall spread forth throughout the world. Darkness will be stamped out, and light will reign for all the days to come. The Great Awakening is at hand."

Rodan longingly sighed and Elwin scowled.

Unlike Rodan, Elwin was not buying into the Guardian's cult. For whatever reason, Arran's strange power of persuasion was not affecting him. If anything, Elwin found it irritating. "I do not care for your dreams and illusions. All I want from you is to take me to my sister."

Arran's perfect face faltered for the briefest moment,

revealing concern and confusion. It was but a moment, but Elwin saw the confusion written there. Then Arran's reassuring smile returned. "You will see her this day, but first you should eat." Then with his graceful ways, Arran turned and walked, or floated away. Placing his hands on his hips, Rodan stood up and looked down at Elwin. His dark eyes were cold and filled with anger. "What do you think you are doing?!"

Just as angry, Elwin rose to his feet and retorted, "Doing!? I am trying to find my sister and get us all out of here without being caught up in the Guardian's traps! For reasons I do not completely understand, or care to, these Guardians have manipulated me. From the very start, they have forced me to do as they wished. They have invaded my dreams and have used Leina as a pawn. I will have nothing to do with them—Nothing!"

"Traps?! Manipulation?!" retorted Rodan. "Arran has been trying to help us!"

Elwin turned away, but Rodan followed. "You heard him last night. The Guardians saved Princess Leina, but all you can do is be rude and ungrateful! The druid has clouded your mind. If I were your father, I—"

Elwin spun around. "You are not my father! He's dead, or have you forgotten?" His voice trembled and he was barely keeping himself from shouting. Without another word, he turned his back on the lord and stomped away. This time Rodan did not follow.

In the meantime, Arran was handing out a morning meal of fruit, cheese, and rich dark bread that was spread with a generous coating of sweet honey. As he did so, he explained to Colin, Pallas, and Kayno that the Guardians do not eat meat. Kayno found that hard to accept.

Suspiciously, Kayno stared down at his breakfast. "No meat.

Why…that is uncivilized." Pallas chuckled, and Colin smiled.

Grabbing some of the cheese and a slice of bread, Elwin retreated a short distance away.

Using a fallen tree as a seat, he ate in silence as he listened to the others.

Washing down a bite with a cup of cold water, Elwin noticed that Aidan was also eating off by himself. *At least I am not the only one who finds Arran's company uncomfortable. I wonder, can Aidan also feel the wrongness of this place?* As wondrous as his surroundings appeared, Elwin knew something was not right. *I wish Faynn was here. He would know what Arran is up to.*

From across their camp sight Elwin heard Pallas ask, "What is the Heart of Light?"

"The Heart of Light is the home of the Guardians," Arran replied to Pallas' question. "It is the holiest of places, and where our hope is closely guarded until the Awakening."

"The Awakening?" Colin repeated.

"The Awakening is the day when He Who is the Light returns to the world. It is the day we Guardians of Light have worked and waited centuries for." Arran gave Elwin a quick look.

"We pray that the Awakening is at hand, but only the Light knows for sure."

Kayno choked down a piece of cheese. "Can't we eat meat? It doesn't seem fair. After all, we are not Guardians of Light.

Arran smiled. "Sorry, but it is not allowed. No person or animal has ever been murdered here. I know it seems difficult, but in time I think you will discover that your love of meat will pass."

Kayno looked doubtful.

Aidan, taking advantage of Elwin being alone, crossed over to where the prince was eating. Sitting down on the log next to him, Aidan said in a voice only Elwin could hear. "I need to talk to you."

"Yes?"

"Something is wrong here."

"I know."

Aidan gave Elwin a look of surprise. "You can feel it too?"

Elwin gave a quick nod. "It's like the entire woods are ill. I have never seen a place of such beauty and yet be so sick. I do not understand it."

"I should have known you would have felt it also. Earth Magic is a part of all living things, and you can touch the power, can't you? You can hear it as well."

Now Elwin looked surprised. A dark frown touched his youthful features. "Is it that obvious?"

"Maybe not to the others, but for me, yes. But then, I have seen you do things that the others have not. In Aonach, I saw you fend off the power of the Severed Head, and on the way to Caiplich, you shot that rabbit. Even the greatest of the elven archers could not have made that shot. You used the power. You are changing, Elwin. The power is changing you."

Elwin's frown deepened.

"Do not fear," Aidan went on. "Your secret is safe with me. Yet for how long can you hide from what is stirring within you? Ignoring it will not make it go away. You should talk with Faynn. He could help you understand what is happening and how to deal with it."

"I already have," admitted Elwin. "He has been teaching me to use the magic to guard my dreams, but that is not to say I am comfortable with the magic." Instead of meeting Aidan eyes, he looked straight ahead into the wooded forest. "It is hard to accept something that you have been taught is evil, but I'm trying." He then looked at Aidan, meeting his green eyes with his brown. "If it helps, your use of the magic no longer scares me. I see now that it is simply a part of you. How can something be evil if you are born with it? It's like saying all brown eyed people are evil. It doesn't make sense." He was silent for a moment then added, "Maybe you are right, maybe I am changing."

Aidan looked up at the trees. Shifting his gaze, he ran a long slender finger along the underside of a fern's leaf. "Strange," he murmured. "In many ways, these woods are similar to my home in the Green. As you know, we elves use a type of Earth Magic. It is somewhat different from what the druids, or what you possess. It's something, as you said, that we are born with. While it has more limits than what the druids can do, we can do things that the druids cannot. It's true that we cannot hear it, but I can feel it, and most of what we do with it comes naturally and is almost always related to nature. Yet in its own way, it is powerful.

For one elf alone, it is of little use. I can work little things like feeding a campfire to make the flames stronger, but I could not light a fire alone. Elven magic is greatest when we work together. When we are together in large numbers, we can take forest and make it a healthy and wonderful place. In such a way, we hold the Green in an eternal summer. Something similar is happening here, yet it is different. In the Green it feels right, but here it's like watching a slow death. I do not understand. Perhaps, Glas Banrion, the 'Fair Queen of the Elves', would know, or maybe Faynn. Both are knowledgeable and wise in the ways of the power."

"I wonder," thought Elwin out loud, "if the entire woods feel as wrong as this spot?"

Suddenly, Aidan fell quiet. Picking up a round stone, the elf kept his eyes cast downwards and away from Elwin. Slowly, he rolled the smooth stone in his hands. Sensing that something was bothering Aidan, Elwin waited for his friend to explain.

After some time, Aidan slowly began, "There is something I have not told you. Back in the Gobhair Mountains, before we reached Caiplich, something happened to me. It came in a dream that was not a dream."

"The feather?"

Appearing upset, Aidan nodded and replied with a simple, "Yes." As he spoke, he touched his chest where the feather was beneath his shirt. "Do you remember that night we spent in the ruins?"

"I remember. We were hiding from the nightlings."

Again, Aidan nodded. Taking a deep breath, he began to tell his story. He told Elwin of that night and of the dream that wasn't a dream, and about the mysterious child, who called herself, The One Who Never Was.

"Then," Aidan looked up at Elwin and meet his green eyes to the brown eyes of Elwin. "She said to me, 'The three must change or all will die'. I think I am the first of the three. Then this child led me to a house. It was there that I found the feather. I should have left it there or just threw it away, but I couldn't. I still can't. It has a hold on me. I did not want it to happen, yet it did. With the feather, I can see through the eyes of a hawk, the one that has been following us. Even in the Grasslands, she was never far, her name is Kestrel. Even now Kestrel is high above the treetops circling amongst the clouds. I know that sounds hard to believe, but Kestrel and I have a bond. We share each other's thoughts and can sense each other's presence. She is never far. I can hardly believe it myself, but that's how it works. It's also how I was able to find our way out of the Gobhair Mountains, and how I have been guiding us through the Karr al-Isma. Every morning I climb a tree and search out, not for the mountain, but for Kestrel. Through her eyes I can fly. I have soared above this forest and have seen the surrounding area. At first I resisted doing it and was not even sure that I could do it again. But, we were getting lost down here in the mist and had no idea where we were going or where the mountain was. From the treetops, I could not see the mountain, just an endless dark forest. It made no sense. I knew that I had to find our way or we would be lost forever. I had to do it. So, I used Kestrel's eyes to see. I have to admit, being able to fly is amazing. Once high enough, and through the hawk's eyes, I could see a different woods—a woods that was dying as if it were late fall. The leaves were falling from the branches and the land was brown. The woods we see here is as much an illusion as the one we saw last night. From above I could see the true woods. I think once I was high enough, I was away from the magic that hides the true woods. From there I could see the mountain, and that is how I have been guiding us."

"So," replied Elwin. "These woods are an illusion too?"

"Yes, and the real woods are dying. Whatever the Guardians of Light are doing here, it's killing the area around it."

"Have you been able to find the Guardian of Light's home?"

Aidan shook his head. "No, but I know where it is. It has to be on the mountain. I've tried, but I cannot get near the mountain. I can fly all around it, but I cannot get close. It's like a great dome of glass is covering it and Kestrel and I can't pass through."

After a moment of silence Aidan added, "But there is something more I need to tell you. At first I was terrified of the power the feather has given me, but now I want to use it more and more, and each time it becomes easier to do. It scares me, Elwin. What is happening to me?"

Elwin sighed. "It's me. I am sorry Aidan."

"What…you?"

"It is because of me that this thing happened to you."

"I don't know that and nor do you," said Aidan.

"I think we both do," replied Elwin. It was not an accusation but a simple statement.

"'The three will change or all will die.' Isn't that what she said?" He looked up, and glanced at Pallas and Colin. His two friends were laughing and talking over their breakfast. "Who else will I change? Change or die. It's not much of a choice." Elwin turned to Aidan. "I am sorry. You did not deserve this. Too many have been made to suffer in the name of Saran Na Grian." Elwin gently touched the sword that hung at his side. "It's a cursed thing. We both would have been better off if I had thrown it into the sea. It has made me dangerous to those I care the most about. Aidan, you should keep clear of me. Return to the Green. It might not be too late for you."

Aidan shook his head, "It's not your fault. The blame lies in the hands of Torcull and the Dark One. Until they have fallen, we are but tools in the hands of a greater power."

Elwin eyes became cold. "I will not be anyone's tool! And I will not be the High King! Not for the Guardians of Light and not for Faynn."

Aidan shrugged. "Okay, then don't. I don't care."

"Sorry," Elwin said, slowly shaking his head.

"It's okay. We are both a bit edgy lately."

"For a good reason. Do you think that the Guardians were behind you finding that hawk talisman?"

After a brief moment of reflection, Aidan responded, "No. Why would they give me something that allows me to see their woods as it truly is? I am not sure who that child was, but I do not believe that she was a Guardian of Light. A goddess, spirit or

476

maybe something else. I'm not sure, but I don't think she was a Guardian of Light. I've thought long and hard about that child, but I have not found any answers. Whoever she was, she knew me, and somehow she knew that I would be in the ruins that night."

Elwin took a deep breath. "I hate this, Aidan. There are too many mysteries and not enough answers."

"There is one more thing you should know."

"What?" Feeling the weight of the world pressing in, Elwin sighed.

"You asked if this was the only sick place in the woods. It's not. All of Karr al-Isma is ill. It is dying. And it is not just the trees; the elf in me senses it. All around the mountain the land itself is dying, and with it the Earth Magic in it. I think that is what's killing the forest. Something is killing the Earth Magic."

--

"It is time to get going. We still have a long way to go," Arran announced. "And the sooner we start, the sooner we will arrive."

Elwin could not argue with that.

Taking the lead, Arran started down a wide, well-kept path. Elwin was puzzled about that. He had not seen the trail until Arran started walking towards it. The path was so wide that it could almost be called a small road. The dirt was a rich, dark color and over the years the soil had been packed down into a hard surface. It showed no signs that a wagon had ever touched its smooth surface, and yet it was evident that the trail was one that was used frequently.

In a dark mood, Elwin followed at the rear. He did not trust Arran, yet if he wanted to find Leina, he had to follow him. Through gaps in the tree cover, Elwin caught glances of the towering, snow-covered summit of Thunder Mountain. It was there that Arran was leading them. Along the edges of the path, flowers and other lush vegetation grew. Trees, plants, and flowers were so well groomed and orderly that it was like walking through the garden of a wealthy lord's estate rather than a wild forest.

The tranquility of the woods was perfect, if it were not for the overwhelming feeling of wrongness, Elwin could have enjoyed himself. *They are killing the land. They are killing Earth Magic. Why?*

"Who's there?" Kayno suddenly called out.

Everyone stopped. Kayno suddenly had his sword in his hand.

The tranquility of the woods was suddenly shattered. A great roar burst forth, sending squawking birds into flight. Lunging out of the trees, rushed a large mountain lion. Leaping into their path, the great beast bared its long, deadly teeth. With big hungry eyes, it raised its head. A soft threatening growl rumbled out of its throat.

"Watch out!" warned Pallas.

With lightning fast speed, Aidan grabbed his bow and slipped an arrow onto its string.

"Hold!" cried Arran. "There is no need for that. We are in no danger."

Aidan took aim, but held back from letting the arrow loose. Showing its deadly teeth once more, the mountain lion snarled. The cat dropped down into a crouching position, readying itself to pounce. Then as if waking from a bad dream, the lion stood up with a jerk. The cat swung its head from side to side, looking confused. Then acting very strangely, it began purring. Arran stepped forward and patted the cat on its head and scratched it behind its ear. The lion rubbed up against his leg, as if it was a large house cat.

"Go," Arran told the cat. "I have no time to play today." Still purring, the cat turned and walked back into thick vegetation.

"Strange," responded Aidan, lowering his bow. "I thought he was going to attack." He slipped the arrow back into its quiver. "Mountain lions rarely attack men, but sometimes it happens, and he looked like he wanted to. He just changed his mind, or did you change it for him?" Aidan looked at Arran. "I have never heard of a lion changing its mind or behaving so calmly. Is he your pet?"

"Guardians own nothing, but all creatures are our friends, Aidan." The Guardian of Light smiled as he responded. "The lion did not mean us any harm. It only wanted to play. But I do not have the time today."

"So, I suppose here, even lions are vegetarian," grumbled Kayno with a touch of sarcasm.

"All who live within our forest, live in the Light of truth," replied Arran. "In the Light, neither man nor beast need to kill to live."

Silently, Elwin cringed at the wrongness of it.

It was just past noon when the party finally reached the foot of Thunder Mountain. Stopping briefly, the party had a quick meal of fruit, bread, and more cheese. Elwin, nibbling at his meal, looked about.

Here at the foot of the mountain, the landscape had changed. Surrounding the base of the great mountain was a large field of boulders. Some of the biggest ones were the size of small houses, while others were no more than a couple of feet in width. Most of the rocks had crashed down the mountainside long ago, and had been on the forest floor for so long that trees had set down roots, making their homes among the great stones, yet others looked as if they had fallen in more recent years. Looking straight up at the towering mountain, Elwin hoped no more rocks would be hurtling down the mountain face, at least not until they had passed.

After their brief break, they started off once more. The path worked its way through the field of boulders. Once past the last of the boulders, the land rapidly rose before them and the climb began. The path narrowed and turned sharply to the left as it started up the steep side of Thunder Mountain, and the going was slow. The path had been made in such a way that it gradually worked its way up the mountain side in switchback manner. Following the back and forth trail, they ascended the face of the mountain. The higher they climbed the more breaks they seemed to need. Only Arran seemed immune to the altitude. He never seemed to tire or grow short of breath. For a time, a mixture of trees lined the path, and they saw several mule deer, elk, and even a black bear. However, the higher they climbed the more the landscape started to change. First, all the trees except for the pine trees had vanished, and then slowly the pines trees became shorter and twisted. Higher up the mountain side, the trees became nothing more than shrubs that struggled to survive at the high altitude. Finally, the winded party ascended above the tree line and the last of the trees disappeared completely, leaving only the tundra grass and patches of delicate mountain flowers, all the while the air became colder and thinner. A strong wind blew down the face of the mountain. Here and there, despite it being summer, patches of snow covered the rocky soil. Still, they climbed upwards.

The view from the mountain was breathtaking. Breathing hard, Elwin stopped to catch his breath. Looking back down the way they had come, he could see the green trees of the Karr al-Isma, and a few small lakes. No longer did the trees take on their black menacing look, as they had from the Aleash plains. As

Elwin stood staring out over the vista, a flock of colorful birds rose up out of the woods. Flying just above the treetops, they formed into a dancing pattern of ever changing colors as the sun reflected off their beating wings. Elwin followed their progress until the birds disappeared beneath a low lying cloud. It was a strange sensation to be looking down on flying birds and slowly drifting clouds. Elwin wondered if this is what Aidan felt like when he flew as Kestrel. That thought still seemed strange. However, as unlikely as it seemed, Elwin had never doubted Aidan's story.

From the mountain top, the woods look healthy, yet Elwin knew they were not. Aidan had told him that the Earth Magic was dying here, and Elwin could sense it. Something was wrong. Earth Magic was indeed weaker here in the land of the Guardians, and the all life-giving power of the Earth was dying.

With a heavy heart, Elwin stood looking out over the woods. He felt helpless to stop what was happening to the land just as he was helpless to stop what was happening to himself, and now Aidan. He wished his father could be there to help him, or even Faynn.

Beyond the forest below, Elwin looked out over the Great Plains of Aleash. The flat, arid plains seemed to stretch on forever, bleak and inhospitable. Aleash looked like a hell next to a paradise. Yet Elwin knew that it was not the plains that were wrong, but the woods. He had thought of little else during the day, and things were starting to make sense. The more he concentrated on the issue, the clearer his awareness of the wrongness was becoming.

"That is the world you have left behind," Arran said, coming up from behind Elwin. "There." He pointed, out over the plains. "Beyond the trees is the land of illusion. Darkness is still strong out there. In time, you will be the High King and you shall lead the Light back into the forsaken lands."

Darkness, thought Elwin. *I live in darkness.* "I will not be your High King." It sounded halfhearted, even to himself. He was tired of telling Arran that he would not be their king. It never seemed to matter. Arran would not listen. Nobody was listening. "All I want is to find Leina."

CHAPTER TWENTY-SIX

Arran announced, bursting with pride, "The Heart of Light!"

As the weary travelers finally crested the top of the mountain, the Guardian of Light pointed down into a deep round shaped valley. What Elwin had thought was a flat-topped mountain was in reality the ridge of an extinct volcano. The bowl of the volcano lay before him. In the center of the volcano's creator sat the home of the Guardians of Light."

"Amazing," breathed Pallas.

"It's beautiful!" exclaimed Colin in a rare show of emotion.

"I have never seen anything so wonderful in my life!"

declared Rodan. His eyes glazed over as if he were having a profound religious experience.

Looking down into the valley, Elwin reacted very differently. He retreated a step. Though the valley could be called nothing short of spectacular, Elwin shuddered, he knew this place, he had seen this valley before. A dream suddenly came rushing back to him as if a curtain had been raised. In the dream, he remembered clearly standing where he now stood and seeing the view he now saw before him.

The valley was green with well-tended fields. Groups of groomed trees stood scattered across the floor of the bowl-shaped valley. On one side of the valley was a small village. In the dream, Elwin had not seen the village. In the center of the valley was a silver lake, which Elwin recognized from the dream. Even in the fading afternoon light, the lake was like a polished mirror. Reflecting off the mirror-like water was the image of a white castle. Sitting on the far side of the silver lake was the tall white castle that shimmered in the afternoon light. With its several cone-shaped towers, it looked like something out of a fairytale. At the top of each tower, there were rainbow colored flags that flapped in the wind. The flawless castle was a wonder to behold. It was almost radiant as it stood out against the green background of the valley.

Then the prince felt a strange sensation wash over him. As if he had been hit in the stomach, he staggered backwards. Before Elwin, the valley suddenly started to blur. He felt dizzy and was finding it difficult to maintain his balance. Everything was spinning. The world raced about him, getting faster and faster. In one giant blur, Elwin crumbled to the ground. Then abruptly the spinning stopped. Regaining his footing, he looked up. He was alone, the valley, the white castle, his friends, and the Guardian of

Light were gone. In their place was a dark castle on a bleak and dead plain. *Ban-Darn*, Elwin realized. In a trancelike state, Elwin stood before the fortress. A cold lifeless wind bit into his exposed skin. Above the castle, ugly grey clouds twisted and boiled. The image of Torcull appeared, rising out of the dead earth like a wrath, he was dressed all in black. The Dark Prophet looked down at Elwin, his evil eyes boring into Elwin. Torcull rolled back his head and began to laugh. Elwin screamed in horror as his nightmares attacked him now even when he was awake.

Again, the world blurred. When the world cleared once more, Elwin found himself in a dark forest. A Red Robe who seemed to be waiting for him reached to touch him. In fear Elwin backed away, then, turning like a hunted animal, fled into the forest. A shiver danced up Elwin's spine. Panicking, he tried to run faster.

A voice whispered in his head, "There is no place you can run that I cannot follow... The Dark One awaits... Surrender to your destiny."

"It's wonderful, is it not?" asked Pallas, standing at Elwin's side.

Elwin did not answer. Eyes fixed forward, he stared at nothing. Oblivious to those around him, he ran for his life. A shadow crossed Kayno's face. "Prince Elwin? Are you all right?"

Again, the prince did not answer.

"Elwin!" His call becoming louder, and he shook him by the shoulders. "Elwin!" The prince was trapped within the dark world, running for his life. He could feel nothing of the real world. Instead he felt only the rising anger and fear growing inside him.

With a sudden jerk, he came to a stop and faced the nightling. As Faynn had taught him, Elwin reached out to Earth Magic. At once the magic responded and Elwin heard its song.

Raising his hand towards the nightling, he threw the magic at the creature. Startled, the nightling staggered. Within the dream, the darkness seemed to weaken. Somewhere close by Elwin heard a familiar voice calling out to him. Elwin held onto the voice as if it were a lifeline. Clinging desperately to the voice, he wrapped the Earth Song around him, using it to search out for the voice and its source.

He blinked. "Father?"

Relieved, Kayno let out a stiff laugh and slapped Elwin on the back. "No, lad. It is not a king you see here. Just an old bar keep."

For a second, Elwin saw the face of his father. Then it was gone. "What is it, lad?" asked Kayno. "You look as if you saw a ghost." Everyone was watching him.

"Maybe I did."

Arran drew close. With a look of concern and fear he asked, "High Prince, are you well? Has something happened?" Elwin wiped the sweat from his brow. "It...it was nothing. It must be the height. I felt a little dizzy, that's all. It's gone now."

Once they reached the valley floor, the party quickly started across its wide bowl shape and headed towards the white castle, the Heart of Light and home of the Guardians. They followed a road paved in large light gray stones which cut through fields of golden grain and groves of fruit trees. The sun was descending towards the western rim of the valley, where a waterfall spilling off a cliff side lake caught the light of the fading day. The valley seemed too incredible to be real and those who had just arrived could only stare in wonder and disbelief.

This late in the day, the road was quiet and the only other person they saw was a lone farmer. Carrying a sickle over his shoulder, the farmer was heading home from a long day in the fields. Whistling a tune, the man approached from the opposite direction. He had the dark complexion and well-defined muscles of a man who spent his life working under the sun. When the man saw Arran, he stepped off to one side of the road. He gave Arran a short bow. "Good evening Lord Guardian," he called.

"And too you, good sir," Arran replied, giving the man a smile and a nod. "You are out late tonight."

"Yes," agreed the farmer. "The crop needed tending."

"Sleep well, then. And may the Light be with you."

"Thank you, Lord Guardian. And may the Light also be with you."

With unconcealed curiosity, the farmer watched them pass. Then with a shrug of his massive shoulders turned and went on his way, whistling to himself once more.

"He's an Aleash!" Rodan announced with astonishment. Rodan looked genuinely surprised to find a fellow country man here in the heart of a forbidden land.

Arran nodded. "I believe he was, once. Actually, most of the townsfolk are Aleash in origin, but there are a few from other nations as well. Some have been here for many generations. Every so often we find a brave soul wandering the forest, and we bring him or her here. We feel if a man's or woman's heart is strong enough to take on the dark illusions of the forest, they are deserving of the Light."

Skirting the edge of the lake, they headed down the last stretch of a cobblestone road that headed for the castle. Elwin should have been overjoyed, his quest was finally nearing its end, and Leina was somewhere in the Heart of Light. Yet he was not happy. In a somber mood, Elwin had said very little since entering the valley. The nightmare had left a foul taste in his mouth and left his young body shaking. No one had asked him any more questions, however, Kayno stayed close. Elwin was grateful. Still frightened, he did not wish to be alone. At last they came to the castle gate. Hanging on gold plated hinges, two bronze doors stood open. Pounded into the bronze doors were floral designs encircling a large sun painted in a translucent blue.

"There are no guards," observed Kayno. Apparently, the Guardians of Light did not worry about unwelcome visitors. Even if the doors had been closed, they were not built to keep people out. There was little chance of an attack within this valley above the clouds, and Elwin suspected that the Guardians had other means to defend themselves if the need arose. As they stepped through the splendid gate and into a large courtyard, two women appeared to greet them. Both wore the white robes of the Guardians of Light. The one on the right was a tall slender woman whom Elwin recognized. Sileas, the Guardian that Elwin had seen in his dream walk. She was a stunning woman with golden hair and fair skin...An angel in white.

The woman standing at Sileas' side was more of a girl than a woman. However, she possessed a wisdom that went far beyond her years. She had the look of a child who had seen too much and had grown up too fast. The girl was shorter than Sileas, yet no less beautiful. Like Sileas, she wore the customary white robe of their order. There was only one real difference in her dress; the smaller woman did not wear the blue rope around her waist as did the other Guardians, instead she wore a white rope about her slender waist.

Elwin was dumbfounded. He stood with eyes as wide as the lake at his back, and he felt his heart cry out with joy as his eyes meet those of the dark-haired girl.

The girl stepped forward. Cascading over her round shoulders, silky black hair shimmered in the sunlight. Taking up the hem of her robe, she gave Elwin a short curtsy and said, "Prince Elwin ap Gruffydd, High Prince of Kambrya, Welcome."

Elwin could hold back no longer. He leapt forward and pulled her into his arms. "Leina!" he breathed. "Leina."

"Brother," Leina sighed, tears running down her face to mix with those of her older brother.

"She has become a Guardian?" whispered Colin to no one in particular.

Taking a step back, Leina took hold of her brother's hands. Looking over his shoulder, she gave Colin a warm smile. "It's good to see you too, Lord Easson. And you, Lord Murray, and Aidan of the Green. I was not told that my brother's friends would be here as well. Though I should have guessed that wherever my brother goes, you three would surely follow. You are all welcome here. It is indeed a grand reunion."

Turning her head slightly, Princess Leina made the introductions. "Sileas, you have already met my brother. These are his friends: Colin Easson, Pallas Murray, and Aidan Ja-Re of the Green. However, I do not believe I have met these other two gentlemen."

Smiling down at his sister, Elwin never took his eyes from her. "This is Lord Rodan," he said with a nod of his head. "He serves under Pallas' father."

Sileas graced Rodan with a smile. "And half Aleash, if I am not mistaken."

Rodan bowed. "Greetings, fair lady."

"And this," Elwin went on, "is Kayno of Aonach."

Sileas' eyes rested on Kayno. "From Aonach, you say? Well, it is a pleasure to meet you all. Come, you are all welcome in the Heart of Light."

Starting across the courtyard, Elwin pulled Leina off to one side. "Are you well?"

Leina smiled. "Yes, brother, I am very well."

"But your clothes. You can't be one of them. I mean...you are not really a Guardian of Light. Are you?

"Yes. Well, almost. I have taken the vows of a novice. In time, when my heart is pure, I hope to become one."

A shadow crossed Elwin's face. "If you were forced to take vows, they do not count. I will get you out of here. We can go home."

Leina stopped Elwin and turned to face her brother. Tenderly, she took both of Elwin's hands into hers. "Dear brother, you sound so much like father. Like him, you tend to act before you think. I am happy here, Elwin. This is my home now. No one has forced me to do anything. For the first time since father was...taken from us, I am happy. Please, there is so much I want to tell you and show you."

Looking up, Leina's eyes met those of her brother's. "But you are not happy," she said sadly. "Are you, brother?"

CHAPTER TWENTY-SEVEN

"What will he choose?" asked Sileas. She sat on the edge of Leina's narrow bed, watching the princess comb out her long hair. "You are his sister. You must know him."

Sighing, Leina stopped combing her hair and looked solemnly over at Sileas. "I fear that he will enter the Hall of Fire. If for no other reason than to spare me. He has always tried to protect me, even when I do not need it."

"But as a Guardian of Light, you are better prepared to face the test. Surely, he must see that?"

Leina gave a thin smile. "To him, I am his little sister, and I am not yet a Guardian."

"But tonight, you will become one. Oh, that reminds me." Coming to her feet, Sileas pulled out a neatly coiled blue sash from the folds of her robe. "Here, I want you to have this. It is the one I used when I first became a Guardian of Light. When it is time, I would be honored if you would wear it."

Tentatively, Leina took the sash. Looking down at it, she shook her head and said, "Thank you. But...I do not deserve this."

Sileas looked confused. "It is normal for a Guardian to pass on their sash. I thought you would like it."

"No...I mean yes, I like it. It means a lot that you would give your sash to me, but that's not what I meant. I don't think that I am ready for the Rising. It is too soon, and I am so young. I must admit I am bit scared too."

Sileas smiled and nodded understandingly. "Yes, you are young, but in your short time here, you have learned much. The power is strong in you. The elders have seen that from the beginning. You will do just fine."

"The elders have not decided to make me a Guardian

because of what they see within me, but because of who I am, I am an ap Gruffydd, and that's what actually matters," added Leina with a slight frown.

"In part that is true. Yet still, your potential is strong, and you are ready for the next step. But you are right. The council has pushed your rising forward. It is hoped that the prince will see reason and hand the sword over to you. The rights of the rising will give you insight and the ability to touch the power within. You will need both in the Hall of Fire." Sileas shook her head. "I hope your brother will not be difficult. He should hand the sword over to you. If he doesn't, I fear he will die."

Looking sad, Leina only nodded.

"Even if he lives, he will be a hard one to control."

"He was always stubborn," added Leina in agreement.

Sileas frowned. "I hope your feelings for him will not interfere with what must be done. If he lives, he will be the High King, and he cannot be left to go wild. He must serve the Light."

Leina's eyes flared. "I am about to take the vows of a Guardian of Light and take part in the rights of the rising. I do not take that lightly! I will do what I must."

"That is good. But now we must get you ready. The ceremony will start soon, and you should get some rest afterward. If you are needed to enter the Hall of Fire, you will need all the rest you can get, and the rising is not an easy thing."

Aidan looked up from the book he was reading. "Where have you been? Kayno has been looking everywhere for you."

"I spent the morning with Leina," said Elwin, as he entered the room and then shut the door behind him. "Then I took a walk around the lake." He looked around. Aidan appeared to be the only one in the suite of rooms that he shared with Aidan, Colin, Pallas, Kayno, and Rodan. It was a rather large suite, and they each had their own private bedroom. At the moment, Aidan was seated at a large window seat with his book resting on his lap.

"How is the princess?" the elf asked.

"Fine, I guess. She is a little uneasy about something, but she would not tell me what. And she really does want to become a Guardian of Light. If I could only get her to leave, I think I could talk her out of it."

Aidan smiled.

"What are you smiling at?"

"Just the idea of you talking Leina out of something."

Elwin smiled as well. "She is stubborn. She has never been willing to accept help, even when she needs it. But this is serious, Aidan." His smile faded. "They are using her, but she refuses to see that. She cannot know what she is doing. A Guardian of Light? Why can't she see that they are using her to get to me? As long as she is unwilling to leave, the elders think that I too will stay, if only to be near Leina. They will try to make me become their High King. They're wrong. If Leina won't leave, I will have to go without her."

"You've been saying that for two weeks now," Aidan pointed out.

"I know," admitted Elwin. "I keep hoping Leina will change her mind."

"Can she use the Guardian magic yet?"

Elwin shook his head. "The Power of the Light? No. The Guardians say Leina has the potential, but she can't touch that potential until she has gone through something called a 'rising.' However, I think they are only telling her that so she won't leave. I don't think she will ever be a Guardian of Light. They're just stringing her along until they can make me their king. But I doubt they want me to truly be their king, only a puppet that they can manipulate. That is one thing Faynn got right, the Guardians of Light are not to be trusted. To think, I was going to give them the sword."

"You said something about the Power of the Light? What is that?"

"It's what the Guardians call their magic. Faynn calls it Spirit Magic. No matter what you call it, it is still magic."

"And you? Did you tell her that you have touched Earth Magic?"

"No. I'm not ready to tell her. To be honest, I am not sure what she would do with that knowledge. She might tell the Guardian's head priest, Odary. And of course, High Elder Odary will tell the rest of the Elders. Leina is too loyal to them and cannot see them for what they are."

Then Elwin changed the subject. "You said Kayno is looking for me? What does he want?"

"Arran came by earlier. He said the Council of Elders wants to see you tonight."

"Now what?"

"Arran seemed to think it was very important."

Elwin frowned. "He always does. I've told Odary and the rest of them that I don't want to be their High King. Why can't they take 'no' for an answer?" Elwin shook his head, and added with a shrug, "Oh well. Did Arran say when?"

"Not really," answered Aidan. "He just said that it had to be tonight. So, you will go? Last time you refused."

Elwin shrugged. "They don't take 'no' easily. Last time they kept asking me until they nearly drove me crazy. I guess I'll go. Besides, I really think it is time that we are leaving. I will take the opportunity to tell them so."

"And my feather? Will you ask if they will take it?"

Elwin frowned. "If you want."

"Yes. Please, Elwin, ask them. I don't care what they do with it. I just want it gone." Aidan hesitated, "You're not going to leave the sword, are you?"

"No," Elwin replied. "I cannot leave it here. Faynn was right about the Guardians. It would be too dangerous to leave it with them. I will just have to find another solution."

The door opened, and Pallas walked in. "There you are. Kayno, Colin, and I have been looking everywhere for you."

"So I hear. You can go tell Kayno and Colin that you found me," Elwin said, covering a yawn. "Tell them I am taking a nap. It's hard enough to face the elders when I am not tired. I'm going to lie down."

Crawling into his large bed, Elwin lay down for a nap. It was nice to sleep without fearing Torcull. With the skills Faynn had taught him, Elwin was improving at keeping Torcull out of his dreams, yet here in this valley. Elwin was not using Earth Magic to protect himself; he didn't need to. Elwin thought it might be because of the magic the Guardians possessed, which was another reason he had put off leaving. Here in the valley of the Guardian's, he was able to sleep in peace and not have to use Earth Magic to protect himself. Elwin also knew that he should take it as a warning that the Guardians were using magic against Torcull. Any magic that could interfere with Torcull's magic was a power to be wary of. Yet he dreaded the dreams more than the Guardian's power. He still had not completely mastered the Earth Magic and after what had happened on the mountain top, he was reluctant to try using the magic without Faynn near-by to help.

494

Elwin closed his eyes and was soon asleep.

Instead of Torcull, Elwin dreamed a new dream, and perhaps it was just a dream. Within the dream, he walked along a dark hallway. In one hand, he carried a torch and in the other, his sword.

"This way," called a voice that echoed somewhere ahead and down the hallway.

"Just stop so I can find you!" Elwin cried out.

"It is not far now."

"Where are you taking me?"

"This way."

Blast it! I thought I could sleep in peace. Well, at least it's not Torcull. Maybe this is just a normal dream. But would I know that I am dreaming then? Elwin turned down another corridor.

Before him was a door that hung on old, rusting hinges. He pushed against the door, but it did not move. "Just my luck! It's rusted shut." Grumbling, he sheathed his sword and set down the torch. Putting his shoulder to the door, he pushed with all his strength.

The door resisted opening and groaned, but as Elwin pushed, it slowly gave way. Opening just enough to slip through, Elwin wedged himself past the doorway. Blinking, he shaded his eyes. He was outside, standing in bright sunlight. That's right... It's the *middle of the day. I'm only napping.*

Elwin looked around. He did not appear to be in the valley anymore. Behind him were the ruins of a castle, but it was not the white castle of the Guardians. The ruins of this castle were covered in vines. The castle seemed to have been abandoned many years before. Turning from the ruins, Elwin stood before a grassy hill.

At the top of the hill were several tall stones that had been placed into the earth. Standing upright, the stones formed a large circle. In the center of the stone circle was a single large boulder shaped like a large oddly shaped ball. To Elwin's surprise, on top of the boulder sat a small figure. Still too far to make out the figure, Elwin started forward, following a twisting path. Climbing the hill, he approached the circle of stones and stopped just outside the circle.

It's a child! "Have you been calling me?"

The child turned her head and looked at him. *Her eyes... Such sadness,* thought Elwin.

"It is time we meet," she said, sounding too much like an adult for someone so young. "But please, come inside the circle. There are too many eyes. Within the stones, no one will be able to spy on us."

Elwin stepped inside. "Where are we?"

"In Cluain, not far from the Tyr River. I can come no closer. Your dreams are being closely guarded. It was hard just to get you to hear me."

"How did you get into my dream? I was having a rather nice one until you interrupted it."

She only smiled. It was a sad smile that made Elwin feel lonely and sad himself.

Elwin suddenly realized who this strange girl was, he took a step back, his mouth fell open, then he snapped it closed again. "You're her, aren't you? You are the girl that Aidan told me about. 'The One Who Never Was'."

"I see you are beginning to see with more than your eyes. That is good. Yes, I am One Who Never Was."

"Why did you do that to Aidan? Why did you make him take that feather? He doesn't want it."

"I merely showed Aidan Ja-Re what was already his."

Elwin frowned. "And what do you want from me?"

"I ask nothing of you. I am here only to warn you."

"Warn me? About what?"

"There is so much you do not understand, and so little I can say, but I will try." She slid off the rock, coming gracefully onto her bare feet. "You have let the one who calls himself Torcull into your dreams. That is not wise."

"I can't keep him out. Not without Faynn's help."

"You can if you want to. Guarding one's dreams is a useful thing. The Guardians of Light are doing it now, but you may not always have them near, nor should you want them near, as I would expect. You must learn how to protect yourself better. It is a skill you'll be needing." She shrugged her shoulders. "But I think you will learn it soon enough. It will be easier when you completely get past your fear of the magic. The magic is not hard, at least it would not be for you. But that is not why I brought or asked you to meet me here. I need to talk to you. You have been with the Guardians a long time already. It's been three months now, and that is not wise."

"Three months?! No. it has been only two weeks."

She frowned and shook her head.

"But..." In a wave, it came back to him. "Bloody ashes! They tricked me! Another illusion! Blast it all! It only seemed like two weeks."

"The Guardians of Light have ways of getting what they want. Listen to the earth, Elwin, and it will always show you the truth. The Earth Song has chosen you. Learn to trust it."

"What does that mean?"

Again, she shrugged her shoulders. "Hard to say really, but time will tell. More importantly, it is time for you to put the Guardians behind you. You must get away from them. They are keeping you from doing what you must do."

"Tomorrow. I will leave tomorrow. Early."

"You may try, but I think it will be longer than that. But do not fear, a few more weeks or even months will not hurt. Yet you must overcome your fear and listen to the earth, then you will see through their ways. Do so and you will not be so easily fooled again. Is the princess with you?"

"She is. But she won't leave. She wants to become a Guardian of Light."

The One Who Never Was nodded as if she was not surprised. "Be careful, Elwin. Too many people will try to control you. Not all of them mean ill towards you. However, you must learn to trust yourself, your feelings, and the power that grows within you. They will guide you. For now, I can tell you no more. Soon the Guardians of Light will discover that you are here, so you must return to your sleeping body."

"That's it? That is all you wanted to say?"

"You have learned much. You have learned you are being manipulated. If you choose to, you know now that you can see past illusions. Knowledge is half the battle. But now you most go and do what you must. Remember to listen to those you trust, but in the end, it is you who will lead the way. You are the chosen one."

"You keep saying that, but what does it mean?"

The girl responded by smiling her sad smile. The hill started fading away, and then the girl faded, too, as if she was being drawn away into a mist.

"No!" shouted Elwin. "I need answers!"

But it was too late. She was gone.

"Elwin?" It was Kayno, waking him up. "Arran is here, and

he is very persistent. Even worse than last time. He says he won't leave until you meet with the Council of Elders."

"Is he in the outer room?" asked Elwin, sitting up in his bed. "Yes."

Elwin rubbed the sleep from his eyes. "Well, let him wait. I want to talk to you first. Close the door."

Kayno softly closed the door. Pulling a chair close to the bed, he asked, "What is it?"

"We are leaving." Said Elwin seating up. "As soon as I get back from seeing the Council of Elders, we are getting out of here. Try to see if you can find a way out without the Guardians knowing it."

"Has something happened?"

"Just a little truth. Go tell Arran that I will be with him as soon as I am dressed. After I am gone, get everyone together and gather whatever supplies we will need."

"And the princess?"

Elwin frowned. *That is going to be the hardest part of all. But I cannot trust her.* It was a terrible thing to admit. "No...we will have to leave her. She might turn us in, and I doubt that she would go with us willingly. I won't force her, and she is safe here. She is probably safer here than where we'll be going."

Once he felt ready, Elwin stepped out of his room. "What is so urgent?" he demanded. "Could this not wait until some other time?"

Arran looked up from where he was sitting. Appearing worried, he shifted and came up out of the chair. "Another time? No, there is no more time. The Council of Elders is waiting for you. It must be now."

Elwin tried not to frown. He looked briefly at Kayno. The

499

big man only shrugged.

The prince looked back at Arran. He had never seen the man look so upset. "What is so important?"

"The Council of Elders will tell you. Please, High Prince. We must go. It is getting late. The sun will be going down soon."

"Very well," Elwin sighed. "Let's go, then." He looked back over his shoulder. Kayno nodded. Elwin turned and followed Arran out of the suite.

"The Master Elder honors you," said Arran, leading the way through the maze of hallways.

The halls of the castle gave off a white glow, so there was no need for torches. Trying to ignore Arran, Elwin looked down the hallways that they passed by. The castle seemed to be made of many twists and turns, and it was easy to get lost. Elwin still had not figured out the place, though he did know the way to the High Council's chambers. He always seemed to be going there.

"It is not polite to keep the elders waiting," Arran went on.

Elwin waved a dismissive hand, and sighed. "Patience is a virtue, or so I am told, and High Elder Odary is the picture of all that is virtuous. He can wait." *Three months? I can remember it so clearly now.*

"We're here," Arran announced, stopping before a large wooden door where two guards stood silently watching. They were the first guards that Elwin had ever seen in the castle. The two guards carried no weapons and wore only ceremonial armor, but they were guards nonetheless. *Something is up... They can't know that I am leaving... Unless they could hear what that child told me. But she said no one could hear us inside that stone circle.*

"His Highness, Prince Elwin ap Gruffydd of Ceredigion is here to see the High Council of Elders," Arran said, addressing the guards. "The time has come."

Time? Time for what? What is going on? Elwin was getting nervous.

The guards gave Elwin a short bow and stepped aside.

"Master Odary is expecting you, Sire," said the first guard. The other guard's eyes were wide with wonder.

Elwin had seen the look before. People were nearly falling to their knees and calling him High Prince or even High King. *I am not their blasted High Prince and I won't be their High King either!*

With his head held high, Elwin stormed into the room. Quietly, the door was closed behind him.

The chamber room of the Elders was quite large but simply decorated. There were only a few chairs lining a long table. On the far side of the table sat four elderly men and one woman. They all stared at Elwin with impenetrable eyes. Elwin hesitated. *Don't let them scare you,* he told himself. He started forward under their quiet scrutiny.

Standing before a single empty chair, Elwin stopped and looked down at the man seated directly across the table from him. "Master Odary, you wish to see me?" His voice trembled slightly.

Using the table to keep his balance, the old man came slowly to his feet.

Odary was a skinny and frail looking man. With snowy white hair and wrinkled skin, the master Elder looked ancient, but his shining blue eyes were full of life and strength. At his side, four other Guardians of Light came to their feet. They were the Council of Elders, and Elwin had already met them all. To Odary's left were Ryence and Gelon.

Ryence was a bald man who was always smiling and laughing. Elwin liked him the best. *But he also tricked me into staying here for three months and making me believe that it had only been two weeks.*

Gelon was just the opposite of Ryence. He was cold and never seemed to smile. Gelon was also the youngest of the Guardians of Light and his head of hair had not yet turned completely white. To Odary's right was Cerise and Jael.

Cerise remained a mystery behind her green eyes and half smile. She made Elwin feel uncomfortable and exposed. Then there was Jael. Jael did not talk often, but when he did, everyone around him would stop and listen. Jael was a thinker, not a doer like Odary.

"Welcome, Prince Elwin," said Master Elder Odary. "And thank you for coming."

To keep his hands from twitching, Elwin held them behind his back. He tried to look like a prince and equal to the elders, but he feared that he was not succeeding. Elwin was barely keeping himself from shaking. The Elders had an aura of power about themselves, and no matter how many times Elwin stood before them, he always felt uneasy.

"Will you be seated, Your Highness?"

Elwin took another step forward. Resting his hands on the back of a chair, he said as coolly as he could, "I prefer to stand."

Odary shrugged and took his seat. "I hope you do not mind if I sit. I am no longer a young man." Once Odary was sitting, the other elders took their seats, leaving Elwin the only one still standing. Odary looked back up at Elwin. "No doubt," he went on, "you are wondering why we have invited you here this evening."

Despite feeling nevus and vulnerable before the Elders, Elwin felt himself getting irritated. Odary always asked that, as if this time it might be something different. "To ask what you always ask," Elwin replied sharply. The anger in his voice surprised even himself. "To be your High King. As I have told you, I do not wish to be your king."

Odary raised a bushy grey eyebrow. "Perhaps, but we need a High King all the same. We did not want you to say you were not given the chance."

Elwin felt his nerves rising and was unsure of himself. *What is Odary was getting at?* Elwin felt like he was walking into a trap but could not see where the danger lay. Then he heard the soft murmur of Earth Magic. It was often there nowadays. Even here, where Earth Magic was weakening, it was always on the edge of Elwin's mind. Elwin usually pushed it away fearing it would once again overpower him. This time Elwin did not push it away. *The girl said it will guide me. I can use some guidance now. Just try not to be scared of it this time.*

Resisting the sudden urge to push it away, he cautiously let it close to him. To his surprise, Elwin felt for the first time he was in control of it, or at least able to maintain its balance so it did not overwhelm him. Then suddenly a truth revealed itself through the song of earth. He was once again being manipulated. He could see it now, feel it. The nervousness that he always felt before the council was yet another illusion. It was something they actually created to keep him off balance. Smiling inwardly, Elwin regained his confidence. Now that he could see, the illusion fell away.

He then turned his eyes onto Odary and spoke with new awareness and self-confidence. "As I have said before, I came to see Leina. If you are waiting for me to name myself High King, then you are wasting both your time and mine. I have no desire to become the High King. There is already one pretender to that title. I will not be something I am not. I will not claim to be the High King. As you know, the crown of Kambrya is lost. Until it is found, you can only have a false king like Jerran." Elwin took a deep breath. It felt good to not be tongue tied before them. "And I will never be like him."

Odary nodded, trying not to look surprised at Elwin's sudden confidence. "You have told us as much before, though now you seem surer of your position. Has something happened?"

"No," he lied. "I am just growing tired of playing games." Elwin kept his anger in check, though it was getting harder to do so. The more he saw how he was being lied to and led astray, the madder he became. *Not this time! I may not like magic, but I will use it to see the truth.*

Odary nodded. "So, you do not wish the title of King of Kambrya? In that, I cannot blame you. Being the High King is a great responsibility, and one that should not be taken lightly or without a great amount of thought. None here would want you to do something you did not wish to do. It is not our way. And so, perhaps you should not become the High King."

With the soft murmur of Earth Magic within him, Elwin could feel the truth in his words, and yet he sensed he was still being lied to. These men were leading him to where they wanted him to go. The Earth Song seemed to be warning him, but Elwin could not tell what was truly happening or what the elders were trying to accomplish. "Then why have you asked me here?"

"Time. It is something that we are running out of, but you have made yourself clear. You are free to go or to stay as you wish, and so are your friends. We will stop asking you to become the Champion of Light. In this valley, no one is forced to stay or to be something they do not freely choose."

Again, Elwin sensed the truth in what the elder was saying. *He may not be lying to me, but he has tricked me! Three months!* "So, I can leave tomorrow?"

"If you do not wish to be the High King, you can leave

504

tonight, or you may stay. Freedom, Prince Elwin. That is what the Guardians of Light are all about."

"And Leina? Is she free to leave as well?"

"She is," stated Odary. "Though I doubt she will go. She has found a home here, and she has taken the vows. She has surrendered her anger to the light. You could learn much from your sister."

"Her vows. They are not binding!"

"No, they are not," Odary agreed. "Here, we are bound only to ourselves and to our hearts. But please be seated, Your Highness. All I ask is that you hear me out. If you still choose to leave, you may go, and with our blessings."

Reluctantly and suspiciously, Elwin sat down, but now at least he had the Earth Magic to guide him, or at least show him when he was being lied to. *They're up to something. Stay angry.*

Odary smiled. "Thank you." Thinking, he scratched his head. "Now where to start?"

Folding his hands on the table before him, Elwin stared at Odary. "How about with some answers?"

Odary inclined his head.

"Why do you need a High King?" asked Elwin. "The Guardians of Light have kept to themselves for centuries. Now you are reaching out. Why?"

Odary sighed, "You are right. We have kept to ourselves. However, that time is coming to an end. A new age is upon us. To answer your question, the world's needs and our needs have become the same. We both need a High King. I believe the Awakening is at hand. The Dark Overlord stirs and will soon break free of his prison. We must be ready. When that happens, only the Champion of Light can save us from the despair of the Dark One. One last time, darkness and light will face each other.

Finally, Beli will be cast into a place where even he can never return."

"I have heard others speak of the Awakening. What is it?"

"It is the time when the god Tuatha will return and drive out the god of darkness. Tuatha awaits the coming of the High King. When that happens, the god will rise up and bless the new king with his Light, and together they will make war on the forces of darkness. Elwin, you have been out there in the world. You have seen the dark days that are falling across the land. The Dark One is awake. He wants to be free. He must be destroyed once and for all, so a new world can be created...a world of Light."

Elwin realized the Earth Magic had it limit. *It can tell me he believes what he is telling me, but it does not reveal if it is actually true or not, only that Odary truly believes what he is telling me.* "So, you think you need a High King to create your utopia. You want to make the world as you have remade the Karr al-Isma. It will not work. You know that, don't you?"

Gelon's dark eyes narrowed. "What do you know of the Karr al-Isma?"

"I know more than you might think." Elwin gave Gelon a cold stare and a colder smile. "I have been watching and learning. You have changed the nature of the woods. You have remade the land into a new type of order. In your world, all aggression has been removed and disease no longer exists. Here, nothing kills or is killed. It is a place where a lion would more likely play with a rabbit than ever think of killing or eating it."

Cerise nodded. "And is that wrong?" Her green eyes sparkled with intense interest.

For a moment, Elwin shivered under her stare. Then he shook his head, trying not to let her cloud his mind. "In itself? No. But you created an illusion around your forest, and then turned that illusion into a reality. I believe that is how your magic works. You recreate reality. But your reality is flawed. Nature is resisting the change, and something else is happening too. You are losing control over it, and it is changing into something that you did not mean it to."

Jael leaned forward. "How did you learn all this? Did the druid Faynn tell you this?"

"Does it matter how I know?" *How do I know this? Is it the Earth Magic?* "Maybe it came to me in a dream," he added with a shrug and a wry smile. "That is, when you aren't guarding and watching my dreams."

That got a few shocked stares, and a few angry mumbles. Elwin was almost enjoying his new-found knowledge.

"So, you know about that," replied Odary with a concerned frown. "It was necessary to protect you. We were not in total agreement about that, but I thought it best to give you time to adjust to our world. I only wanted to protect you."

"Like the way you protect your woods? No thank you."

"You still have not said how you know about the Woods of the Mist," stated Jael still sitting forward in his chair. "I don't think you truly learned this in a dream. As you said, we have seen your dreams. So, who told you?"

"It does not matter how I know. What is important is that it will not work."

"It matters," said Jael. "Can you see or feel the changing reality, or are you repeating what you have heard? This is most interesting." The Guardian leaned forward. Of all the council members, he seemed more curious than offended.

"Enough of this!" snapped Gelon. "He is from the shadow lands and is not one with the Light. He can't understand what we are trying to do here."

"No," interrupted Jael. "This is too important! If he can tell us what is happening, we might be able to correct it."

Gelon shook his head. "That is nearing blasphemy, Jael! Only He who is the Light can bring the land into harmony. And he," Gelon pointed an agree finger at Elwin. "Knows nothing of it! Besides, I still say there is nothing wrong with the woods."

"You are wrong," Elwin stated bluntly. He was surprised at how easily the words formed in his mouth, and how sure of himself he felt. Even Cerise's unsettling eyes no longer seemed to faze him. "There is something very wrong. You are killing the woods, the animals, trees, and everything else. In their deaths, something else is being born, and that thing is scaring you." *How do I know that? It must be the Earth Song, but how?*

Gelon's dark eyes turned even darker. "Do not tempt me, young man. I have sworn off violence, but you push me with your lies and your sacrilege. You are nothing but a sniveling..."

"Please!" Odary interrupted cutting off Gelon, with a sudden wave of his hand. "We are civilized here, let us act as such. It is time for the prince to know the truth." His blue eyes turned to Elwin in wonder and an even newfound respect. "You amaze me, Prince Elwin. We do indeed create reality out of illusion. I suspect the druid must have told you, though I do not know how he even knew. That is something that must be looked into," he mused before going on. "But for now, I will try to explain it to you. Our power, or 'gift' as we call it, comes from within us. A gift from the Light. First, we visualize a dream. From that dream, we can create an illusion. Then, with enough time, we turn the illusion into reality. I must be honest with you. You are also right about what is happening in the Karr al-Isma." Gelon tensed, but Odary ignored him. "We have overstepped our abilities, and now we are no longer sure what is happening. But you must believe me that the woods can be put right. The dream can become a reality. With the Light, all things can be done. With the death of the Dark One, the world will be remade in the image of the Light. With the Power of the High King, we will see where we made our mistake and correct it. The whole world can be remade in the true Light."

Elwin nodded. "So that's it. That is why you need a High King. To fix your mess. And to top it off, it is not really about bringing peace, but war. You want me to fight a war against the Dark One. You need me to do what you have not been able to do, or are unwilling to do. You want to bloody my hands so that you can keep yours clean."

Gelon scowled. "Odary! This is too much!"

Odary raised his hand. "Silence, Gelon!" His blue eyes were now cold and sharp. "Prince Elwin, we do want peace, but as long as the Darkness lives, there can be none. And we are not perfect. I am admitting that to you. We made a mistake somewhere. Yes, we need a High King to make the dream a reality, but it is not our dream but the Light's dream. It is the dream of Tuatha. He fills our dreams with his dream. It is a dream of how the world should and will be."

"Enough!" Gelon was almost shouting now. His face flushed with anger. "You have told him too much already! Far too much. Let us be done with this. He does not want to be the High King, and we don't want him either. Allow him to leave and he can take his friends with him."

"It is his choice, Gelon, not yours," retorted Odary. "And for him to truly and freely choose he has to know the truth. There is too much at stake to try and manipulate the outcome."

"I...we do not wish him here any longer," stated Gelon.

They don't want me, but they need their king. What am I missing?

"As I have said, you may leave any time you like, but first you must choose, Prince Elwin," Odary stated simply and to the point. "Do you wish to be our king or not?"

"This is a waste of time!" snapped Gelon. "He does not want to be the High King. Even Ryence must see that he has renounced his rights."

"He must say that. Not you, Gelon," Odary pointed out. "So, Prince Elwin, what will it be?"

They're up to something; this is too easy. "There is still something I do not understand." *Something is not right, and I have to figure it out before I renounce the claim to the crown. They are trying to trick me again, but this time they are not relying on an illusion.* "You are acting like you can make a real High King, one with all the powers of the old stories. But how is that possible? I know the legends; I've read the histories. Only when the lost crown of Kambrya is found will there be another High King."

Odary nodded, "That is true. The sword is the key, and the crown holds the mysteries which makes a High King. Only by using both can there be a King of Kambrya."

"So, what good am I? I have the sword, but not the crown. What good is a key without a lock?"

Grinning like a father to a child, Odary said, "Your Highness, we have the crown, and thanks to you, we now have the key."

Elwin's eyes widened. "The lost crown of Kambrya? Here?"

Odary gave an affirmative nod.

Elwin came to his feet. "You have had it here since the battle of Ban-Darn!? And you have told no one?"

Again, Odary nodded. "We do. Before your great ancestor, High King Coinneach went to face the Dark One, he came to us and entrusted our order with the crown. We have guarded it ever since, but none has ever seen it. The great king locked it within the Hall of Fire. The hall cannot be unlocked without your sword.

"Now, Prince Elwin, we need an answer. Do you want to be the High King? Do you want to use your sword and enter the Hall of Fire and take what is yours by right?"

"I do not want to be your High King. I will never wish to be your High King."

Odary nodded. "Then so be it. You may go."

A look of suspicion crossed Elwin's face. "Are you saying you do not want me to take up the crown? I can just leave it here?"

"Is that not what we have been saying?" asked Odary. "Isn't that what you want?"

"Yes, but..." *There is something else. What are they not telling me!?* "What is the catch?"

"Catch?" asked Odary.

"You need a High King, or at least you think so. Yet you'll let me leave. The crown will still be locked away, and still you will let me leave. Why?"

Cerise cocked her to head to one side. "Did you think that you alone could be the High ruler of Kambrya? You may leave, but another will take your place. Saran Na Grian will belong to another. The sword you wear does not belong to you, but to the High King. So you may leave, but the sword must stay to be given to another."

Elwin jumped to his feet, while his hand snapped to his side, grasping the hilt. "What!?" he roared, taking a step back away from the council. *Is this not what I wanted? I wanted to be rid of the sword and now I have the chance. Why don't I just give it to them and be done with it?* Yet Elwin felt a growing desire to keep the blade close. "It is mine. You can't take it. You have taken vows against violence. If you take it from me, you'll be stealing."

"Your Highness, someone must ascend to the High Throne," Odary said calmly as if he were only stating the obvious. "And the sword does not belong to you. In fact, it has never belonged to you or to the kings of Ceredigion, but entrusted to the prince and potential heir to the Kambryan throne. Since the last High King, the sword has been handed down through the ap Gruffydd line. As the crown was entrusted to us, the sword was entrusted to the ap Gruffydd kings. You, as all your forefathers before you, are the prince apparent to the High Throne. It is now time for the prince to become king. It is your birthright to be that king. However, you have decided to renounce your claim. That too is your right, but another must pick it up. Leave if you will, but the sword must stay with us. The sword will be passed on to the next in line.

"You're bluffing!" snapped Elwin. He was scared that they might really take the sword. Elwin felt as if a part of him would be lost. "I know the legends. It's said that only the blood of the ap Gruffydds may rule Kambrya. I am my father's only son."

"You are not the last." Gelon said with a sly smile. There was a triumphant sound to his voice that made Elwin tremble. "There is another. One who will accept the burden and has already said so. And one who is far better suited than you."

Elwin's throat felt tight. "Who?" he whispered, not wanting to know the answer, and yet he already knew it.

"Your sister, Leina," Odary replied, as calmly as he could, realizing what this would mean to Elwin. "She will be the first High Queen of Kambrya. There is no law that the high ruler of the kingdoms needs to be male."

Feeling as if he had just been hit in the chest, Elwin fell back into his chair. "You can't!" he pleaded. "You do not know what the sword will do to her."

"The choice is not mine," replied Odary. "It now belongs to the princess."

Gelon sat back in his chair and added, "Princess Leina is one of us. She knows what is needed. She will enter the Hall of Fire and be tested. She will be found pure of heart and soul."

Elwin shook his head. "No!" he suddenly shouted. "I will do it. I'll be your bloody High King." *By the Three Gods, what am I doing? I can't let Linea do this, the sword will take possession of her as it has me.*

Gelon was still smiling. "It's too late. Once you have sworn off the sword, it is done."

"I changed my mind," demanded Elwin, "I won't let you do this to Leina."

"Gelon is right," added Odary with more sympathy in his voice then had been in Gelon's. "One cannot re-take the offer once refused. It is written with in the ancient laws."

"But I do not know your laws."

"That's too bad for you," Gelon snapped triumphally. "You have renounced and..."

"No," objected Ryence, smoothly cutting Gelon off. He leaned forward, hardly giving Gelon a glance. All his attention was on Elwin. His stare was so intense that it made Elwin feel more than a bit uncomfortable. It was as if Ryence was seeing Elwin for the first time. "He has not renounced. If I am not mistaken, Prince Elwin has said that he does not wish to be the High King, but he has never said he would not be. There is a significant difference. Perhaps the Light guides your tongue, young lord."

Gelon was on his feet. "No!" he shouted, staring down his nose at Ryence. "He said it in his behavior and his desire to be done with us. He has renounced!"

"Prince Elwin?" Ryence asked in an even voice, still intensely looking at Elwin and ignoring Gelon. Not once did he turn or even indicate he had heard Gelon's protest. "Do you renounce?"

Elwin swallowed. His throat was painfully dry. *What am I doing?* The Earth Magic was singing in his head. *Trust the song*, he thought to himself. Then after a long painful pause he replied simply "I do not renounce." It was almost a whisper.

"No!" repeated Gelon. "Leina is one with the Light. I will not bow down to this unbeliever."

Odary raised his hand. "Sit, Gelon! The choice is not in your hands, but with the Light. I see that Ryence is right. The prince never said that he would not be the king. It is indeed possible that the Light has guided him to say what he did. The Light moves in ways that only the Light knows and understands. If Elwin refuses to renounce, then that is the way it must be. He will be tested."

Scowling at Elwin, Gelon sat down. His eyes turned even darker.

Odary turned now to Elwin. "But let us be clear about this. Are you saying you choose now to be High King?"

Elwin laughed ironically. "Choose? There has never been a choice. If I refuse, you will send my sister into a nightmare that she cannot imagine."

"Prince Elwin, Leina also has a choice." Odary's voice was soft and grandfatherly. "Everyone here, with the exception of Ryence, believes that you cannot survive the testing. Leina is better suited. She understands the ways of the Light. You, in all likelihood, would die. And no one has lied to your sister. She knows what is being asked of her and she has agreed. There is no shame in renouncing, Prince Elwin."

"But she doesn't know!" Elwin exclaimed. "And you don't know... The sword changes people. It has changed me. The sword will consume her. I cannot let that happen."

"Then I will ask only once," continued Odary. "Think about this carefully. If you enter the Hall of Fire, you must go through the testing. Once started there will be no turning back. If you are deemed impure or tainted by the darkness, you will die, and Leina will still take your place, but the choice is yours. Do you still wish to go forward with this?"

Elwin gave a weak nod. "I do. I will enter this Hall of Fire."

"She is one of us," pointed out Odary. "Many would prefer her over you. For centuries, the Guardians of Light have had the responsibility of guarding the crown. Many think it is only right that a Guardian should wear it. Some would like to see you pushed aside so that the princess could be queen. Perhaps they are right. You do not respect the way of the Light while your sister does. However, you are first born, and I will, must, follow the law."

"We could force him to step aside," interjected Gelon. "...for the good of the Light."

"No!" said Odary, shaking his stately head. "We won't! Even if I would allow such a violation of our vows, Leina would not go along with it. Leina's ties to the prince are still strong. She loves him, and would never take a crown that had been stolen from him."

Odary turned his head to Elwin. His voice now calm. "So, High Prince Elwin, you will be tested. May the Light preserve us all."

Elwin dropped his head. "What do I have to do?" he murmured.

"You must take the crown from the Hall of Fire. It is

written, 'The one who is to rule the lands must step forward and claim the crown. In the Chamber of Fire, the one will touch the Light and be tested. If the one is shown to be pure, the Light will bless the chosen one and show him the way.'"

"When?"

"Tonight."

"Tonight!?"

"The first two of the three stars that make up the constellation the 'eyes of the Buachaille' will meet tonight. These two stars will create a single star. This is the night the Light awakens, and will fulfill the prophecy."

Elwin lowered his head in silent resignation. *And I will bring darkness, not Light into the world. That's what Faynn told me that the prophecies say. I will free the Dark One. I will bring down the world with me.*

CHAPTER TWENTY-EIGHT

Everything happened so fast that Elwin did not know if he was coming or going. One minute he was telling the elders that he would go into the Hall of Fire to find the lost crown of Kambrya, and the next, he was being ushered down the maze of hallways that made up the Guardian's castle. As Elwin and the elders raced down the corridors, wide-eyed servants and other Guardians of Lights hurried to get out of their way. As the group sped past, Elwin heard whispers of astonishment and curiosity. Elwin mostly heard the onlookers uttering such things as 'Has the time come?' or 'The Light be praised,' but mostly he heard the same question: 'Is he going to be tested, or will Leina?' The elders never slowed down, never giving Elwin a chance to hear anyone give an answer.

"I need to tell Kayno and the others what has happened," insisted Elwin. "I want to see them before...before I go into this 'Hall of Fire."

Odary shook his head, but he did not slow his pace. "There is no need. Your friends have already been informed. While we were talking, they were taken on ahead. They will be waiting for us below."

Elwin hurried after Odary. He would not have guessed that the old, frail looking man could walk so fast. "How did you know I would do it? Enter the Hall of Fire, I mean."

"I didn't," replied Odary. "But I took the precaution. Besides, they are Leina's friends as well. She too would want to see them before entering the hall."

"Will Leina be there?"

"Yes."

"Good. I want to say..." He let his words trail off. *Blast it!*

Why don't you just say it? You want to say good-bye before you die! I will never be tested true to the Light that I don't believe in. But if I don't go, Leina will go. Death is preferable to that.

Following Master Odary and the other elders, Elwin turned another corner and headed down a set of wide stairs. Down another hall and down still more stairs. The elders were leading him into the dark recesses of the castle. As they descended, they saw fewer and fewer people, and soon the hallways were empty and they were alone. For a long time, the only sound was Gelon's grumbling. Gelon still was complaining that Elwin was unfit to see the holy hall for what seemed to Elwin like hours.

Finally, Cerise snapped at him, telling Gelon to stop his whining and acting like a spoiled child. Gelon turned bright red but held his tongue. Elwin fell in next to Ryence.

"How much further?" he asked, feeling the need to talk to someone, even if it was a Guardian.

Looking as if he had just woken from a dream, the bald headed Ryence looked down at Elwin who was now walking beside him, then he looked back as they came to yet another set of stairs.

"A little longer," he answered. "The Hall of Fire lies deep beneath the Heart of Light."

Elwin noticed that the stairs were a little narrower than the last ones. "How deep is the hall?"

"I don't really know," Ryence answered with a shrug. "Jael might know. You can ask him if you want."

"I was just wondering."

Ryence then added, "Believing is more important than knowing, anyway. Answers are for those who do not dwell in the Light. The way of the Light is the way of trust."

"Do you really think that I can pass this test? Odary said you thought I could."

Ryence shrugged as they came to the end of the stairs and started down another long passageway. "It is not up to you or me, but the Light. You will pass or fail as the Light so chooses."

"So, do you believe that the Light will test me true?"

"Truthfully, no. I do not."

"What?" Elwin was taken aback. He had thought Ryence was the one Guardian that believed in him. "But back there you... I don't understand. Why then did you point out that I had not renounced my rights?"

Ryence gave Elwin another quick glance. "Because you had not renounced." He said it as if that should have been obvious. "What I may or may not believe is unimportant. Everyone that has read the prophecies of the High King has interpreted them. Each coming up with their own ideas of what they mean or don't mean. I chose not to do that. I have read them, but I do not try to understand or try to interpret them. I only accept and watch, knowing that if my mind is open, the Light will show me the way. You see, nothing happens by chance. When you did not say that you would not be the king, I knew it was because the Light had not wished you to. Therefore, it is only logical that the Light wants to test you. So it will be done. It must be done. I did not defend you, but followed the path that the Light wished me and for you to follow. If you die, that too is what the Light needs, and Leina will take your place. If you do not die" He shrugged. "Then the Light has chosen. So you see, it does not matter what I believe. I will follow the Light whichever way it leads me." He nodded towards Gelon who was in front of them. "I am not like Gelon, Gelon tries to force the will of the Light to fit into what he believes is right. Gelon is not the only Guardian to follow such a path, yet it is not the true way of the Light."

Elwin dropped back to walk by himself, realizing that talking to any Guardian was not going to help his mood.

As they descended the next set of stairs, the strange light that illuminated from the castle walls began to fade. As the light faded to the point of needing a new source of light, Jael raised his hand out before him. A blue light flashed, then a floating ball of light appeared above his head. Guided now by Jael and the blue glowing light, the group went deeper and deeper into the earth below the main castle structure. The surface of the walls became rough as the corridors became more like caves than castle hallways. The air became damp and cold, and the walls felt moist and dewy to the touch. There were no more stairs before them. Instead, there was a gradual sloping corridor that led them deeper into the earth. After some time had passed, Elwin doubted the castle was even still above them.

"It is not far now," Odary said over his shoulder. After making a few curves that angled ever downwards, the cave floor finally leveled out. Then they came to a sudden stop. The cave-like hallway stopped in a dead end.

"Did we make a wrong turn?" asked Elwin.

No one answered. Cerise stepped out towards the end of the cave. She raised her hands so that her palms faced outward. She seemed to be glowing with a blue light. Then the cave wall started to glow as well. The wall shimmered and slowly appeared to melt away as if it were made of mist. At last, the wall completely faded away, revealing a large wooden door.

Elwin resisted the urge to take a step back. It still felt strange that he could not hear the Guardians' type of magic. Yet, the Earth Song told him that the cave wall had been an illusion.

"We placed an illusion over the door," explained Cerise, telling Elwin what Earth Magic had already told him. "This is the holiest of places."

Grabbing hold of a brass ring, Gelon pulled the wooden door open. The first thing that Elwin saw were his friends, and they all looked deathly worried.

Kayno stepped forward. "What is going on!?" he demanded, eyeing the Guardians of Light. He nodded towards the princess, who was there as well, kneeling before a small wooden altar. She did not move, nor did she even seem to have noticed that others had entered the chamber. Deeply frowning Kayno went on. "Princess Leina said that either she or Prince Elwin was going after the crown of Kambrya. Is that right?"

"One or both," corrected Ryence. "That has yet to be decided. But yes, Elwin will go forward into the Hall of Fire."

"After all these years, can the crown really here?" asked Pallas.

"Yes," Odary assured him. "It is here."

"Are you all right?" Aidan asked Elwin with a genuine look of concern.

"Yes." Elwin nodded. He turned toward Odary. "Now what?"

"First," said Odary, "we wait for Leina to finish her prayers. You may also join her at the altar and pray to the Light. That is if you wish to find his guidance."

"I'll pray in my own way." *Knowledge will help me more than a god that does not exist.*

Swinging his head, Elwin quickly took in the room. Octagonal in shape, the room was brightly lit with torches and lamps. The room appeared to be man-made with smooth white limestone walls that had been painted with blue suns. The room looked like some type of shrine. Cut into all but one of the eight walls were tall, narrow niches that held cast bronze statues. Each sculpture stood upright upon a blue marbled pedestal, and all but one of the statues had been cast to appear like Guardians of Light. The one that was not a Guardian was a knight in full armor, holding a blue sword above his head. Upon the tip of the knight's sword hung a silver crown. The one wall with no niche held a single painting of a blue sun.

"Who's that?" asked Elwin, pointing and indicating the knight.

"Shhh," reprimanded Cerise. "Keep your voice down until Leina has finished." She looked at the statue. "You do not recognize him? He is your great ancestor, the High King."

Elwin stared at the figure a long time before he turned to take in the rest of the strange room. "Is this some kind of a chapel or shrine?" he whispered to Pallas.

"Leina said it is called the Chapel to the Sun. But it seems strange that a chapel to the sun would be so deep underground. We are about as far from the sun as one can get."

In the center of the room was the wooden altar at which the princess was kneeling and praying. *It looks ancient,* Elwin thought. *It probably has some great religious significance, and not likely to be of any help.*

Kneeling, Leina was so still that Elwin started to worry, but then he saw her chest rise and fall. She was breathing. On both ends of the blackened wood altar were two large blue candles, their flames hardly flickering in the still air. Above hung an orb of shimmering blue glass suspended by a thin golden chain, making the orb appear to hover just above the holy table. Inside the orb was some kind of lamp, which was giving off a flickering blue light. Elwin turned his attention beyond the altar, to the wall with the painting. *Buon Fresco,* thought Elwin, trying to keep his mind busy. The fresco depicted a blue sun with yellow flames.

"That's it, isn't it?" he realized. "The Hall of Fire."

Jael answered with a nod of his head. "Beyond is a cave that leads to the throne of the Sun, and beyond that is the Hall of Fire, or so the histories state. None alive has ever passed beyond this room. No one even knows how long it will take to find the great hall."

Elwin stared. *They think I will die in there. By the Three Gods, am I scared. If there is a god or gods or whatever, give me strength. I can't let Leina go in there. Help me find a way to keep her out. To keep her safe.*

"Now we must pray," said Odary. "Please do not try to leave this room. It is dangerous for you to travel here without a Guardian to guide you."

Kayno pulled Elwin off to one side. Rodan, Colin, Aidan, and Pallas followed. Just behind Leina, the Guardians joined hands, forming a circle. Closing their eyes, they bowed their heads and prayed silently, slipping into a trance-like state.

"You can't go in there!" Kayno protested in a whisper. "Leina says that you will die, and I believe her."

Elwin nodded. "I know. But If I don't, Leina will. It is the only way that I can keep her safe."

"They have their eyes closed," said Pallas, looking at the praying Guardians. "We could grab Leina and make a run for it."

Elwin shook his head. "We would never make it." He glanced over at the circle of Guardians. "Besides, Leina would put up a fight. I won't take her by force."

Rodan, who had remained silent, shifted uneasily as if what was happening conflicted with everything he believed in. "I... You must think of Ceredigion. They need a king. You should go and leave the princess." His words flowed with unbelievable sadness.

"She is my sister! Forget it. I will go find this hall and find

523

the crown. I don't care about being king. Yet, I will go."

"This is where she wishes to be," stated Rodan. "I know it is not an easy choice, but you must think of your kingdom and the other kingdoms faced with war."

"I cannot leave her," Elwin repeated.

"So, you will die?" Rodan asked rather bluntly.

"If I must." Elwin was trying his best not to sound scared. "And I may not die." *Who are you kidding?*

"If you fail, the princess will go in any way," pointed out Rodan. "One of you must live to lead Ceredigion. I do not think Leina will leave this place. I do not mean to sound cruel, but..." He let his words trail off.

Elwin knew what he meant. Someone of the Ap Gruffydd line needed to survive this night. Elwin knew Rodan was probably right, but he could not make himself see that reason. Rodan was talking about turning his back on his sister, he could not do that. "Has anyone thought I just might pull this off?"

"And if you don't?' Rodan asked bluntly.

At least he doesn't seem to worship the Guardians anymore—at least not in the way he had. Too much knowledge can challenge all that we thought was true. "I don't care. I am going in. And if I can, I will find a way to keep Leina from following me. If I do not come back, Leina can go home and become the queen." He doubted that she would, but he had to hope that she could get away from the Guardians.

If only *I can find a way to keep her from following me when I don't return. If I can make it clear that it is hopeless to follow, will Leina return home?* It was Elwin's only hope. *But how am I to accomplish that? How do I make it impossible to follow me?*

"You don't plan on coming back, do you?" Aidan asked Elwin, making it sound more like a statement than a question.

Elwin tried not to shake. "I will come back if I can, but I must first find a way to keep Leina out. If I return without the crown, she will go in after it. Please do not try to stop me."

"Do you really think the crown is beyond that wall?" Kayno shook his head as if he doubted it. "It could be nothing more than a legend."

"I know," Elwin admitted. "But Leina and the Guardians believe it is in there." He nodded towards the sun door. "That is what matters, and I know that whatever is in there is far too dangerous for Leina to face alone."

"Let me go," offered Colin. "If there is really a crown behind that stone, I will find it and bring it to you."

Elwin smiled. "Thank you, but it has to be me."

"Brother," said Leina, finally ending her prayer and coming to her feet. She smiled as she joined her brother and their friends. "I did not hear you enter the Chamber of the Sun."

"Let us get this over with," snapped Gelon, coming out of his trance-like prayer.

The Guardians had stopped praying as soon as Leina stood up, making Elwin wonder if the Guardians were really praying, or only waiting for his sister to finish. Gelon did not seem like he wanted Leina and Elwin time alone to talk. *Probably fears I am going to tell her about the dark truth of their little world here. But I doubt I could change her mind. Maybe if I had more time, but I don't.*

Kayno gave Gelon a dangerous look, but Gelon did not seem to notice, or just did not care.

Pallas stepped forward, flanked by Aidan, Kayno, Rodan, and Colin who placed their bodies between Elwin and the rest of the Guardians that now joined Gelon. It gave Elwin a moment to smile and reflect upon such loyal friends. Again, the Guardians did not seem to notice. With their power, they could sweep them aside at any moment.

Leina stepped past her friends to face Elwin. Her smile almost seemed to be glowing. She also appeared to be the only one in the room who wasn't tense. "Did you decide?" Despite her happiness, she could not hide the look of worry on her face. "Please tell me you will not go forward."

Elwin did not answer. A part of him was mad at her. They had spent the whole morning together, and she had said nothing of this. At the very least, she could have warned him. Maybe then he could have found a way out. Maybe he could have saved her without sacrificing himself. Now there was no other choice.

"You can still step down," Gelon stated in his hard voice. Looking at Elwin and past the wall that his friends had created with their bodies, Gelon's eyes looked as hard as his voice sounded. Elwin could see the hate in his eyes. "It is not too late, let Leina go forward."

"No. My mind is made up. I will go."

Elwin frowned down at his sister. He had not noticed it before, but Leina was wearing a blue sash around her waist. "So, does that mean what I think it does?" Elwin asked, pointing at the sash.

Smiling, she nodded. "I am a Guardian of Light, big brother. I took part in the rising five hours ago."

"So, you are one of them now?" he asked accusingly, not able to hide the anger and disappointment from his voice.

"Yes." Her smile faded away. "Gelon is right. You do not need to do this. I know you are trying to protect me, but I do not need protecting. I am better prepared for this than you."

"So I have been told. But there are things even you Guardians do not know." The word 'you' nearly stuck in his throat.

"You are still stubborn."

"I guess." Elwin shrugged, trying to look brave.

Turning away from his sister to face Odary, Elwin frowned as his heart pounded with tension and fear. "What do I do?"

Leina stepped forward, coming closer to Elwin. She placed a slender hand upon his shoulder. "I am willing to take this burden from you, brother. Please let me."

Elwin felt all his anger towards his sister slip away. It was hard to stay mad at Leina. It always had been hard, and she was doing what she thought was right.

"No," he replied, laying his hand upon hers. Then trying to smile and sound gentle he added.

"I will do this. I think it is what father would have wanted."

Leina nodded sullenly. Her eyes glistened as if she was about to cry. "You are so much like father. He too was a stubborn fool." She took both his hands into her own and looked up into his brown eyes. "Do not leave me too, Elwin ap Gruffydd. My heart cannot take losing both you and father."

"I will return…" *If I can.* Turning his head, he gave Gelon a quick glance. "And with the crown."

"Odary?" Elwin turned once more back to face the master Elder. Still holding onto Leina's hand, he repeated, "What must I do?"

"We are not quite sure how it is done. What we do know is that you must pass through the Sun Doors." He nodded at the slab of stone. "And into the throne room of the Sun. Then you must find the Hall of Fire. There you will be tested. If you are tested pure, the Light will show the way."

"But how do I get past those?" Elwin asked, pointing at the Sun Doors. "Can you use your magic on them?"

"No. They are sealed by a greater power than ours." Odary turned to Jael. "You have been studying this. What have you discovered?"

Elwin felt his heart skip. Hope fluttered through him. *Maybe they won't be able to open the door. Maybe they don't know how.*

Jael nodded. "I believe I know the way in." Elwin felt his brief hope fading as the Guardian went on. "King Atari ap Gruffydd." Jael looked over at Elwin and Leina. "Your father was the last one to enter the Hall of Fire."

"What? My father was here?"

"Yes," replied Master Odary. "Sixteen years ago. He was a new father. Elwin, you could not have been much older than one. Your father was the new young king of Ceredigion. He came here and requested to enter the hall. We told him that the time was not right. However, he was the rightful king and had the sword. So, despite that the timing did not fit the prophecies, he opened the Sun Doors and searched for the Hall of Fire. I believe he made the attempt so that his new son would not have to. He knew the time would be coming, and he wanted to spare you the burden, but that was not to be."

As Odary went silent, Jael continued the story. "The king had Saran na Grian with him. He could not be denied his right to pass beyond the Sun Doors. However, before making his attempt, your father studied the door at great length. For hours, he would sit here alone considering the door, looking for the secret that would unlock it. Thankfully, he shared what he had discovered before returning to Ceredigion and to you. King Artair had written down what he had found and I have read his writings."

"You mean that my father passed into the Hall of Fire and returned?" Elwin was still finding it hard to believe his father had been here and said nothing.

"Not entirely," Jael went on. "He passed through the Sun Doors. He claimed to have found a great hall, but could not find a way past the great hall. There did not seem to be any way past. I have thought about that, and I believe Master Odary is correct. The correct time had not arrived. I believe that no one can pass through the hall until the time of the Light's choosing, and that is now. Your father was too early, however, he did discover the secret to the Sun Doors. In the writings, he wrote down a clue, if not the whole answer. The king wrote that there was a keyhole that he used to unlock the doors, and to hold them open until he returned. At which point he resealed and relocked the doors. However, he said nothing more about how to unlock the doors or how he was able to keep them open." Jael then pointed to a slit in the floor just in front of the Sun Doors. "I believe that is the keyhole. It is also written in the ancient prophecies that the Saran na Grian is the key to the Light, so I believe that if you slide the sword into the keyhole, the doors should open. Once the sword is removed, the doors close. If I am correct, there is no way to open the doors from the inside. So, as your father must have done, you too will have to leave the sword here in the keyhole. Otherwise you would be trapped inside."

"And the sword as well," added Gelon. "When you do not return, the door must be opened so that Leina can enter."

Kayno glared at Gelon, but Gelon ignored Kayno as if he posed no real threat or even deserved consideration.

"How long will it take to find this Hall of Fire?" asked Elwin. *Stop stalling... What does it matter? Father, why did you not tell me?*

"Again, we are not sure," said Jael. "The king never found the Hall of Fire."

"We will give you four hours," stated Odary. "Then Leina

will have to follow. We cannot afford to wait much longer than that if the prophecies are to be met."

Elwin nodded. Then he sighed. "I don't suppose you can tell me anything about this test?"

No one answered.

"I thought not." Drawing his sword, Elwin stepped past the altar. No one followed. The room fell quiet as the prince stepped forward, pulling his blade free of its scabbard.

Taking a deep breath and praying it would not work, Elwin brought the sword up before him. Holding Saran na Grian's hilt in two clenched hands, he looked down upon the keyhole. On the floor a hole was cut into the marbled surface, just large enough for a sword blade to enter. Slowly he slid the sword into the stone floor, his sweaty hands shook, there was a click, then nothing. *Broken! The door is broken!* He wanted to shout out loud in relief. *The door can't be opened.* Then shattering his short-lived hope, there was a soft groan that echoed through the room. The Sun Doors slowly began to swing open. Splitting the sun painting in half, the doors crept open until a small opening appeared to what lay beyond. Stale air blew against Elwin's face, sending a shiver up his spine. Before him was a black void. Taking a torch down from the wall, he peered into the darkness. He could see nothing but a long, narrow cave.

"Well," snapped Gelon. "Are you going in or are you just going to stand there?"

Elwin turned his back on the opened door. "If you don't mind, I would like to say goodbye to my friends."

Gelon opened his mouth, but Odary quickly cut him off. "Of course, but do not take too long. Time is running short."

"Thank you."

"Are you sure about this?" asked Colin. "It doesn't look too safe in there."

"Colin is right," added Kayno. "One of us should go with you."

Elwin glanced at the boys and men before him; they were true friends. *I will miss them.* "No. I must do this myself. They would not let you anyway." He said with a nod of his head, referring to the elders who stood watching from across the room. Elwin met each of his friends' eyes. When he looked upon Kayno's face, a memory of long-ago flashed in his head, and then it was gone. "If I do not return, take care of Leina."

"I don't need to be taken care of!" Leina snapped.

"You will return," stated Lord Rodan with more confidence than he felt. "I know you will."

"I will take care of her," added Kayno. Leina chose not to respond.

Elwin gave Kayno a long look trying to remember why he was so familiar and why his voicing his support to Leina did not surprise him.

Colin dropped his head. "A knight should protect his prince. It is wrong for me to allow this."

Elwin placed a hand on his shoulder. "My friend, you cannot stop it." Colin nodded weakly and said nothing more.

Pallas shifted from one foot to the other. He looked sadder than Elwin had ever seen him. "This is not the adventure I wanted," He said after a long moment. "I thought it would be grand and exciting. I wish we had stayed home."

Elwin responded with a warm smile. "Don't give up yet, it still may turn out okay. I will be back." *Not very likely. I will see to it that this all ends here.*

Leina looked up at her brother. Her eyes turned soft. Then acting very unlike a Guardian, Leina wrapped her thin pale arms around his neck and pulled him close. "Remember," she whispered in his ear, "you promised to return." Silvery tears raced down her check. "You promise."

Gently pulling away, Elwin stepped back from her. "I will try."

"No!" she said sternly. "You will not try! You will do it and you will come back!" There was a sternness to her voice that Elwin knew was covering her fear.

Finding no words to say, Elwin looked at Leina and tried to smile. He tried to look braver than he felt, knowing that he was shaking from the knees down. Then Elwin took a long deep breath, said his final good-byes to his friends and pulled Leina close one last time. Elwin finally stepped back, finding it hard to let go. His legs felt weak and he felt sick to his stomach. Yet he knew what he had to do. Taking another deep breath, he squared his shoulders, and turned away. He did not want them to see him crying or the fear in his eyes.

Crossing back across the room, Elwin stopped just before the door. Then in a sudden and unexpected burst of speed, he grabbed the sword. He pulled the Saran na Grian out and free of the keyhole. The door started to close.

"No!" someone behind him shouted. Elwin, knowing they were already too late, never turned his head, leaped forward, darting through the closing doors.

"Elwin!" screamed Leina. "You'll be trapped!"

"I know," he answered, turning so that he could see her one last time. "But you will be safe."

In a panic, the Guardians rushed forward. However, there was no way they would reach the door in time. Elwin clutched his sword to his chest, never once looking at the hysteric guardians. Instead, he stood there, staring into Leina's eyes. "I'm sorry," was the last thing he said as the great doors closed with a bang of finality.

Suddenly the shouting was silenced. Elwin stood alone.

CHAPTER TWENTY-NINE

The small campfire crackled as its flames devoured the dry wood. Around the dancing flames, a small island of light spread out then faded away into the deep darkness of the thickly scented forest. Beyond the comfort of the fire, the night was filled with the soft calls of owls and wolves. The mountains could be a lonely place. Despite being surrounded by his closest followers, friends, and family, the Strigiol lord felt alone. Squatting near the warmth of the small fire, trying to fend off the chill of the night air, Ruan felt the weight of responsibility much like he could feel the gray woolen blanket that was draped over his shoulders. On the far side of the fire lay a strange figure with dark hair and skin. Curled into his own blanket, the Yorn, Zann Ka Mar, was unaware that Ruan was watching him, wondering about him.

A dark elf a Yorn! Ruan thought to himself in disbelief. A creature of myths and nightmares lay sleeping no more than twenty feet away from the moody lord. *How did this come to be? How is it that I am trusting the life of my friends and family to a legend that has stepped out of the darkness of this land?* Yet Ruan had to admit the Yorn had saved his queen's life. Only hours ago, the dark elf had risked his own life by attacking a mountain troll that had nearly killed Catriono. That was something Ruan could not forget. He owed this strange creature.

Ruan wrapped his blanket closer about his tired shoulders. *Should I trust him? Tomorrow will tell. I hope I do not regret this.*

For Ruan, the morning came early. Unable to sleep, he rose and began think and brood over his situation. He was staking their lives on a dream and a legendary elf. Those two things were all that he had to lead him forward. Yet the it was now so etched into his mind it no longer felt like a dream. It was so real, Ruan was hardly surprised when the dark elf had led them to the banks of the mountain lake. Through a thin, misty morning air, Ruan looked upon the small green lake. The waterfall cascading down a stone and mossy covered cliff face left no doubt this was the place of his dreams, the place where his unborn daughter had led him. Above the lake and waterfall was a sturdy, yet ancient looking stone bridge. With the misty morning combining with the soft murmur of the flowing water, this could have been a beautiful and sublime moment. Yet for Ruan standing before the lake, it was a moment that was both surreal and disturbing. Ruan had been here before. *This is the lake my dead daughter had shown me.*

The dark elf, also rising early, stood beside Ruan. "Is this what you sought, my lord? Is this your lake?"

Ruan nodded his head. "Yes, Zann, this is the place."

Zann frowned. "This is a place of great mystery. It is said this lake is a gateway to the world beyond, to the world of the dead. The ancient kings of the Yorn are buried near here. Beyond that bridge to the east, the road leads to a boxed canyon. The Canyon is honeycombed with the tombs of our ancient kings. We once used this place to worship our ancestors, but few come nowadays. That bridge and road will lead us nowhere other than the Canyon of Tombs. It is said that this road is older than the mountains themselves. The Yorns have a belief that as the mountains grew, they created this valley and cut the ancient road in half. The road is said to be older than the mountains themselves and now only leads to our ancient tombs. It is now only a place of the dead. The road is no longer of any use to the living. It will not take us past the mountain and to my people. We should turn back."

Ruan only gave a sad and distant smile.

Once everything was made ready, he took the lead. Taking

the narrow path that rose from the lake's quiet banks and still waters, Ruan led his weary group of travelers across the bridge. He hesitated a moment to look down upon the lake one last time. Ruan smiled sadly and left the lake and waterfall behind.

From his dream, Ruan now knew where he was going. He knew that the path did not end in a boxed canyon. "Let's hurry. I fear the trolls and hobgoblins are not too far off. Let's not let them find us."

It did not take long to find the Canyon of the Dead. Like the mountains, it was a quiet and lonely place. The party walked in respectful silence. In that silence, Ruan wondered why he had not seen these tombs in his dream.

Maybe I can't entirely trust the strange dream world, or maybe it shows me only what I need to know.

All through the canyon, nothing moved. Even the mountain breeze had fallen silent. Along the cliffs of the canyon, large tomb openings seemed to stare out at them as they passed the haunted places of a lost time. Ruan had never stood in this lonely canyon, and despite missing the tombs within the dream, he knew this place. Ruan knew where to find the hidden stairs—stairs that were cut into the cliff face. The stairs would lead them to a hidden cave which cut beneath the mountain to a valley beyond. Right where he knew they would be, he found the steeply ascending staircase. The staircase was exactly as his daughter had shown him in the dream and soon they were all climbing towards the top of the cliff. It was not a difficult climb, but it was slow going up the ancient and worn stairs as one had to watch where they step.

Once he led the way to the top of the stairs and passed through the cave, Ruan found what exactly what he had already seen. Below in the lush green valley was a city ablaze with bright and colorful flags. All around the amazing city were farm fields, which added to a sense of an orderly world on the very edge of these dangerous mountains. Charming cottages dotted the landscape. If Ruan did not know better, he would have sworn he was back home. It looked like a Kambryan city, though more colorful. The surrounding countryside could have been a Kambrya landscape. However, this was the far side of the mountains. Beyond the farms, cottages, and city, was a forest that stretched out beyond the horizon. Ruan had never seen a forest so vast. It appeared to have no end. He was looking over the Great White Forest of the North. They had crossed the mountain range.

"That is my home," stated the Yorn, pointing proudly out over the valley that spread before them. "You truly are the Pathfinder. You have come to save us!"

Ruan did not have to ask from whom the dark elves needed saving from.

To the South of the city was a towering wall that stretched across the narrow section of a mountain pass. It was a defensive wall designed to keep out the creatures who lived in the high country from entering the valley. Scattered beyond and south of the wall was a vast army of trolls and hobgoblins. The city was blocked from all access to the mountain pass. The army was like a black smudge against the white limestone cliffs. Campfire smoke filled the air that seemed heavy with war.

Ruan turned to his one-eyed captain. "We'll stay here until dark, then we will enter the city. It does not appear that the troll army is aware of the mountain cave, and it is probably best they don't see us coming out of the mountains."

Zann frowned. "Even us elves did not know of this back door. If the mountain creatures had known of this path that bypasses our defensives, our homes, farms, and lives would already have been lost. We cannot flee into the White Forest. That is a place even worse than the mountains."

Ruan nodded, though he was not sure what dangers lurked in the massive forest. The city itself seemed much more concerned with the mountain pass than the woods. After all, they had built a wall across the mouth of the pass, yet there were no defenses between the city and the not too distant forest edge.

In a strange manner, the dark elf cocked his head to one side as he looked at Ruan. "We did not know of the cave above ancient tombs, or we would have left this land. I think our time here is done. You have come to save my people, to take us home. You are the Rathad."

CHAPTER THIRTY

Holding up his torch, Elwin squinted into the darkness. Slanting downwards ever deeper into the earth, the cave disappeared into a sea of blackness. The torch proved to be a poor light source and gave him little comfort, yet that was better than no light at all. Just the thought of being down here in total darkness made him shiver. The air in the cave was cold, and the silence was profound. He so very much alone and trapped in this underworld.

Elwin turned back to the Sun Door. From this side, the door looked like any other part of the cave; gray and cold. The name Sun Door seemed ironic with all the darkness that surrounded it. Elwin rested a hand on its cold surface, knowing that just on the other side were his friends and sister, yet they might as well have been thousands of miles away. Using the torch, he searched the door, floor, and walls. Nothing. *Not even a crack,* he noted with despair. There was no way to reopen the door. Turning, he leaned back against the cold stone. *Well, there is nowhere to go but forward,* he told himself, trying not to be scared. His legs felt like lead and his heart raced. The cave before him was as quiet as a tomb. *My tomb. You've locked yourself inside of a cave. At least Leina will never be able to follow me. No one will ever walk through this door again.* He gripped his sword tightly. *I have the only key, but the lock is on the far side of this door.* He pushed himself off the stone wall. *Well, I can at least see if there is another way out. If I can find this Hall of Fire, maybe I can find a back door.* Elwin took a step into the dark. It was hard to leave the door behind, but it was closed now and there was no way to open it from this side. He had to go forward.

In one hand, Elwin clutched the torch, and in the other, his sword as the cave led him deeper and deeper. The cave curved and twisted, turning left then right. There were no side passages, leaving no choice but to go down. *What will I do when the torch goes out? No. Stop thinking about that. Maybe I will find something, a lamp or something else. Maybe. There has to be more than just this cave. Well I guess I will see, and there is nothing to do now other than to keep moving.*

Around the next corner, the cave started to narrow. Twice he was forced to duck under low hanging outcrops as both the walls and ceiling started squeezing inwards. As Elwin went further, he had to squeeze past stalagmites that rose from the cave's floor and stood blocking his way. Never had Elwin felt so alone or lost.

Time slipped past, and the cave went on. Then, just as he thought the cave would never change, he came to a stop, not quite believing his eyes.

"Stairs," he breathed. A set of spiral stairs carved out of stone stretched upwards into a hole in the ceiling. Elwin looked up and saw that the stairs quickly disappeared into the darkness above. *But...they go up.*

Elwin started to climb. However, the stairs did not go up as far as he had hoped they would. Holding the torch high after a short climb, he peered into yet another dark passageway. This time, the passageway was different. It was no longer a cave but was now a man-made hallway with smooth walls painted in a now faded blue. Elwin hurried forward. The way forward neither descended nor rose, running straight and level before him. At the end of the hallway was a large white marble archway. Beyond the arch, the walls suddenly fell away. If there was a wall, it was too far to see in the dark. He strained his eyes. Still, he could only see a void before him.

Passing through the arch, Elwin went forward and into the

black void. The floor itself was covered in thick dust. Beneath the dust was a black and white tiled floor. The air smelled old and musty. Elwin found himself in a strange dark world without walls as he moved deeper into the room. He squinted into the darkness, but could see nothing. He shivered, and kept moving in what he hoped was a straight line. Cautiously creeping forward, something started to emerge out of the darkness. Just within the torch light was a shadowy white image.

"A pillar," he said out loud as he came closer and passed the white, marble pillar that stretched upward into the dark. Soon, he found another white, marble pillar and then yet another. *I'm in some type of hall. The ceiling must be pretty far up.* He looked up, holding the torch as high as he could, but he couldn't see anything that indicated a ceiling. Again, he went forward finding yet another white pillar. *This must be the large hall father found.* He stepped past the pillar. "If I could just see a little better. I wish I had more light." Something beneath his foot clicked. As if in answer to his needs, a light flashed and the darkness suddenly vanished. Stunned, Elwin blinked and quickly covered his eyes. All around him torches suddenly burst into life.

As his eyes slowly adjusted to the light, he looked up. Gasping, he saw that he was indeed in a huge hall. It was supported with the tall pillars stretched some fifty feet towards a domed ceiling. The room was immense, but that was not what had taken his breath away. At the far end of the room was a giant throne. The Dais of the Sun. "The High Throne of Kambrya," he realized. *The High King's throne. But how did it get here?* The throne was thought to have been lost in an earth quake centuries ago. Yet here it stood before him, beckoning him from the past.

Crusted in gems and valuable stones, the white marble throne stood on a round pedestal of green marble. Stairs dropped away from the throne on all four sides.

A dozen feet before the throne, Elwin saw something on the floor. Something blue was showing through the thick layer of dust. Crouching, he brushed away the centuries of dust. Beneath he found a mosaic of a blue sun with red flames. Within the sun was a small heart shaped tile with a small depression in its center. Encircling the sun were red and blue symbols and signs. To one side of the sun was an inscription carved into the floor. It was written in an ancient form of Kambryan dialect. An ancient dialect his father had forced him to learn. *You knew I would come here, that I would have to come. You made sure when the time came, I would be ready in the way you were not. Thank you, father.* He now understood why his father had forced him to learn a nearly dead and forgotten language. Elwin was one of only a handful of scholars who could still read the ancient text. Silently he read.

> *"I, King Coinneach, High King of Kambrya, leave this world with my hand upon a heavy heart. I give my life, for I am too weak to do what is needed. In the Hall of Fire, he will come. From my blood, he will be again. The Chosen One must find the Hall of Fire, and in the Hall of Fire, it will start. May the Chosen One have the courage I lacked."*

Sitting back on his heels, Elwin gave a soft whistle. "King Coinneach! A coward?" *What could he have been scared of? He was the greatest king there ever was.*

He looked up, gazing across the hall. *If this is not the Hall of Fire where is it?* He could see no doors, except for the one he had

542

come through. Unsure what he should do next, coming back to his feet, he approached the Dais of the Sun. Almost reverently, Elwin started up the marble steps to the throne of his ancestors. From this seat the High Kings had ruled, and the last of the High Kings had been Coinneach. This was the High Throne of the heroes of the past, who had defended the lands against the Severed Head and the Dark Overlord. Elwin felt small and insignificant against such a history. Sadly, he also realized that in all those years since the time of the High Kings, little had changed. The land was still fighting against the black cult of the Severed Head and the Dark One threatened to destroy the world once again. Only now there are no more heroes or High Kings, and the darkness was winning.

Tearing his eyes away from the throne, Elwin turned his back on the great chair. *There is no time for this.* He sat down on a cold marble step. *I have to find a way out of here. But how do I find the Hall of Fire? What if it doesn't exist and this all there is? I will die here!* Elwin placed his sword across his knees. *Think. There must be a way. Perhaps there is a secret door, but where?*

Standing, he began searching the walls for anything that might trigger a hidden door. He moved torches and pressed against the cold walls, but he found nothing. Working his way around the room Elwin came back at the throne. He searched behind the throne, and then started to explore the pillars. Yet they too were of no help. He was just about to give up. Frustrated, he was once more staring up at the throne. Near the top of the steps, something shimmered. Reflecting in the torch light were several golden letters.

Climbing the steps, he knelt before the chair. Brushing away age old dust, he read the old language his father had made him learn.

"When the Dark One stirs once more, the Defender of the Light must rise again. With hand on heart, the way will open for the one of the true blood. The heart will know the sign. Beyond the wall of water lies the Hall of Fire and the crystal stone."

Elwin scratched his head. It made no sense. *What wall of water, and what was the crystal stone? I thought the crown was supposed to be in the Hall of Fire, and not a stone.* He slowly retraced his steps to the mosaic and re-read the inscription by the blue sun.

"I, King Coinneach, High King of Kambrya, leave this world with my hand upon a heavy heart. I give my life. For I am too weak to do what is needed. In the Hall of Fire, he will come. From my blood, he will be again. The Chosen One must find the Hall of Fire. In the Hall of Fire, it will start. May the Chosen One have the courage I lacked."

Elwin dropped to the floor. *Could it be? Both the inscription on the throne and the one the floor mentioned a heart and a hand.* He pushed away more of the dust. "'With hand on heart the way will open'."

Placing his hand over the heart shaped tile, he pushed but

nothing happened.

Sitting on the floor, he tried again using his left hand and then his right with no better results. Elwin even attempted to pry at it with the dagger from his boot, but still nothing moved. Elwin absentmindedly tapped a finger against the bare blade of his sword. "Of course!" he exclaimed to himself looking at his sword. *This has to be it.* He jumped to his feet. It worked once, why not again? Holding his sword, he placed the tip of the blade onto the heart shaped tile and pushed downwards. Nothing.

"Blast it!" *There has to be a way. Think. King Coinneach must have set this up so that someday someone could get past to the crown.* Elwin frowned to himself as he tried to puzzle out the answer. *No, not just someone—an Ap Gruffydd.* He corrected himself. *Only an Ap Gruffydd could enter the Hall of Fire. All the legends and histories are consistent on that. Even the Guardians believe it. Only an ancestor of the Great king can enter the Hall of fire.* Standing up, he started to pace. That always seemed to help him think. *So, I must prove that I am of his blood.*

But how would Coinneach be able to keep anyone who was not an Ap Gruffydd from finding the way? And not even any Ap Gruffydd at that, but it must be the heir to the throne. How can anyone prove that they are of the blood of King Coinneach, and the rightful king? Think. What makes me so different? Nothing in my blood. All humans are pretty much the same. So, what is it that could prove that I am the right person? What do I have that would prove that I am an Ap Gruffydd? The inscription said the 'Heart will know the sign'. This must be the heart. He stopped pacing and looked back down at the red tile. "But what could be the sign?"

"My ring!" In excitement, Elwin pulled the Ring of Arros from his finger, the signet ring of Ceredigion. There was only one like it in the world, and only the king or prince would have it. *Did father know? Is that why he insisted I take it?* He shrugged, knowing such a question could not be answered. Elwin dropped back down onto the floor. "It's worth a try."

Elwin placed the ring on the heart. It seemed to fit into the small depression in the tile. He pushed. The heart-shaped tile hesitated then dropped an inch into the floor. Elwin smiled. It seemed comforting that in some way his father was still looking after him. *I always wondered why I had to wear this thing. Father had said never to take it off, keep it close at all times. Maybe he did know.* In some way, it was as if his father was guiding him, walking at his side. *He saw to it that I would have what I needed—the sword, the ring, and the knowledge. Father knew that I might have to come here and translate the old language, but how did he know about the ring? Maybe his father had told him the same thing he had told me, or he just guessed it would be needed to reach the Hall of Fire.*

Father did not know the old language himself. That is why he could go no further, and why he made me learn the dead language. Without that knowledge, I would never have been able to read the ancient text. A sad smile came to his face. *Leina could never have passed this hall. She cannot read the ancient writings and would not have had the ring. I locked myself in here for no reason. Have I thrown my life away for nothing?* Pushing the sad awareness aside, he twisted the ring. The heart tile moved. Excited, he turned harder. The heart turned completely around then snapped back up.

Hearing a soft groan, Elwin looked over his shoulder. The Dais of the Sun was slowly sliding off to one side. In the floor beneath the throne was a dark hole just large enough for a man to fit through.

Pushing his ring back onto his finger, he climbed to his feet.

Elwin laid his torch down and he gathered a few new torches from the wall. He put out their flames to save them for later. Returning to the hole in the floor, he retrieved his lit torch. Then against his better judgment, he thrust his head through the opening. Of course, beneath the floor was yet another cave. A cold, stale breeze brushed up against his face. He could hear a far-off sound, like that of running horses.

Trusting that the cave would take him where he needed to go, Elwin dropped his spare torches down through the hole and then lowered himself. It was a short drop. Looking up, he decided he could get back up if he needed to.

With the flickering torch in one hand and the sword in the other, he hurried forward. The sound of running horses that echoed through the otherwise silent world grew steadily louder. Once more the cave descended, leading Elwin gradually deeper into the earth. All sense of time was lost. The caves took Elwin deeper and deeper towards the sound below.

After what must have been hours of walking, a dim light appeared. Almost running, he rushed forward. Then the cave suddenly opened up into a large cavern. Elwin stopped and stared. Stalactites hung from the ceiling and protruded upwards from the floor. In the middle of the sprawling cavern was a small underground lake. Glowing with some type of phosphorescent material, the lake illuminated the cavern in an eerie green-white light. On the far side of the lake was a waterfall. The sound of the falling water echoed through the cavern.

"The wall of water," murmured Elwin. "Behind the wall of water is the Hall of Fire."

The lake was no more than knee-deep and Elwin had no problem wading across. The water, which had never been touched by the warmth of the sun, was icy cold. He found it was not difficult to walk across the rocky bottom of the strange lake. However, it did make him a bit apprehensive, walking among the strangely glowing water that swirled around his leg like some living thing. Elwin felt something swim past his leg. He nearly jumped out of the lake trying to get away from whatever it was. When no slimy creature wrapped around him to pull him downwards, he calmed his pounding heart. Holding his torch close to the surface, Elwin tried to see what kind of creature could live here, but he could see nothing below the glowing surface. He could not even see the bottom of the lake through the murky glowing water.

Nothing, he thought. After a moment of contemplating retreating out of the lake, Elwin went forward. *There is nothing to go back to,* he reminded himself. *If I don't find another way out, I will die down here.* Cautiously feeling his way across, he moved further into the cold waters of the lake.

At last he came to the waterfall. The underground river plummeted from a gouge in the wall about thirty feet above Elwin's head. He reached out his hand to touch the bone-chilling water. Reaching further, he stretched out his arm as far as it would go, and still he could not feel the far wall. Pulling his arm out, he studied the room one last time. Then with a shrug of his shoulders, he acknowledged that there was no choice, so he held his breath and plunged into the waterfall, letting the icy waters cascade over him. Gasping for breath, he emerged on the far side. Dimly lit by the lake, he found himself in another man-made passageway. His torch, of course, had gone out. As he had stepped through the cascading water, his sole light source had been extinguished by the waterfall. With no flint, he had no way to relight it. *Now what?* Wet, cold, and with no light, Elwin felt himself starting to panic. His only light was now the glowing lake, and he could hardly take that with him. Yet he knew his only hope was to go forward and into the dark. Staring into the darkness, he slowly started advancing down the passageway. At first the lake did dimly light the corridor, but the farther he went the darker it got. Soon he could see nothing at all. Proceeding even slower, he forced himself to swallow his fears and to go on.

Feeling his way, Elwin discovered that the passageway divided into side corridors. He tried to go straight, but he realized the place was a maze and that he was hopelessly lost. Too exhausted to go on, he curled up on the floor and drifted off to sleep.

When he woke, he was still in the dark, chilly underworld. Gathering his strength, he went on. At times, he found puddles of water, where he stopped to drink all that he could. The maze seemed to go on forever, and eventually he had to sleep again.

How many days have I been down here? Elwin could not remember. In the underworld, night and day had no meaning and Elwin found it harder to remember what it was like to see. Maybe the light was only a dream. Nearing the end of his strength, Elwin's growing hunger turned into a constant pain. His feet hurt and his legs felt as heavy as a bag filled with stones, and it was getting colder. Shivering, he leaned up against the wall. Slowly, he slid down to the floor. There he sat, too tired, cold, and hungry to go on. His muscles ached, his stomach hurt, and his head throbbed. Days had slipped by and still Elwin had not found the Hall of Fire. Depression was setting in.

I must *be going in circles. I'm going to die down here as a lost, scared, failure. I didn't have to do this, I did not have to seal the door to save Leina. She could not have read the old language, nor does she have the ring. I have trapped myself here for no reason. I cannot even find the hall.*

Lost within this dark world, Elwin was scared. Scared of failing and dying here alone. He was even scared of the dark that wrapped around him like a cold, wet blanket. Elwin then reached for the only thing he had left, he reached for his atman, the center of his being. He reached out for the Earth Song. Too weary, hungry, and scared to care or even think what he was doing, Elwin reached out for the magic. In desperation, Elwin searched for the power, but the magic would not come. Now that he wanted it, the song of power refused him and his atman fluttered away.

"Faynn where are you?" he whispered tearfully, his head cradled in his hands. "I cannot do this alone."

"Don't panic!" he whispered back to himself. "You can't fail now. If you do..." his words trailed off as Elwin realized that he could not remember what it was he was trying to do. "Okay, Elwin. Get back on your feet." *Why am I here?* Painfully, he climbed up off the floor. His toes and fingers were starting to turn numb and he was losing the feeling in them. Elwin was almost thankful for the lack of pain.

With outstretched hands, Elwin lumbered forward. He took two steps, then stumbled and fell. "I can't go on!" he cried out to the darkness. No one answered. He curled into a ball. *It never changes. It is always the same—more halls, more passageways, more darkness. I want it to end. I want to die!* He had given up. At last, his eyes closed and he once more slept. In his dreams, he could see again. His dreams always started out in a world of light and warmth, but as always, the darkness came in the end.

When Elwin finally woke, it was with a start. His heart skipped a beat. *Did I hear something?* A light flickered, or Elwin thought he saw a light. He wiped the sleep from his eyes. "Was that a dream?" He struggled to stand. Numb from the cold, he no longer felt the pain of his throbbing feet. Deep in his mind, he knew if he fell again he would not be able to get back up. Rubbing his eyes, he tried to focus. Then he saw it again. *There. It's not a dream!* A blue glowing light was ahead of him. Not caring who or what could have caused the light, Elwin stumbled forward. His numb feet would not work, and he pitched forward, crashing to the floor.

"No!" He struggled back onto his knees, but the light was gone. "No! Please no!" Then he saw a distant flash. Unable to stand or walk, he crawled forward, yet he could not get any closer to it. The faster he crawled the faster the light seemed to be moving away from him. At last, he could go no further. "Help!" he tried to shout, but it came out as a hoarse whisper. Again, the light disappeared into the darkness. Elwin let his head drop against the cold floor. It was gone, taking his hopes with it. He laid on the floor, knowing he had tried, but this was the end.

Weakly, he looked up one last time. Deep within the darkness, a blue light flashed, however, this time, Elwin was too weak to chase after it. He waited, expecting the elusive thing to fade away once more, but the glowing thing didn't vanish. Instead, it started growing brighter. It was coming towards him. Finding the strength, he crawled back to his knees. Hope filled his beating heart. He opened his mouth to cry out. but the words froze as his cry of joy caught in Elwin's throat then turned into a cry of horror. The thing that glowed with a bluish color was a ghostly figure in a flowing tattered robe. Its face was hidden within the shadows of a hood. Shimmering, the ghost with the silence of a tomb moved or floated towards him. Elwin tried to get back on his feet but his body refused to move.

The ghost came closer and closer, never touching the floor. It filled the passageway with the strange blue glow. The ghost floated ever nearer to the fearful boy. The prince could see beneath the hood of the phantom, but a full-faced helmet hid the phantom's face and eyes. Where legs should have been, only a ragged robe flowed in an unfelt breeze. Other than its strangely glowing armor and robe, the ghost seemed to have no physical form.

In a hopeless attempt to fend off the specter, Elwin raised his sword. His trembling hands tried not to drop the blade as his heart raced. The ghostly knight, at last, came to a stop. Hovering just above Elwin, it slowly swayed from side to side as if it was waiting for something to happen. "Go away!" pleaded Elwin.

The ghost swayed but did not leave. Silently, hidden beneath the hood and helmet, it stared down at the kneeling prince and waited.

"What do you want?" Elwin whispered.

Silently the ghost swayed, ever staring, ever glowing, ever waiting.

"Please... leave."

Time seemed to stop as the ghost slowly began reaching its arms towards Elwin.

"No," Elwin whimpered.

The knight moved closer towards Elwin who helplessly kneeled before the knight.

"No!" Elwin cried louder. Thrusting his sword forward, he tried to pierce the glowing ghost, however the ghost was faster— surprisingly faster. Clamping its pale hands down upon the sword's steel blade, the ghost easily stopped Elwin's thrust. Its two armored hands appeared to be formed out of the same glowing mist that had created the phantom, yet they also seemed to have a solid nature about them. Right through the ghost's hands, Elwin could see the silvery blade of his sword, yet despite

552

the lack of apparent substance, the ghost's hands held firmly. Desperately, Elwin tried to pull the blade free, but the wraith would not yield. Elwin felt the rush of power surging up all around him. It sang the song of Earth Magic, but there was something more as well, something he had never felt before. He tried to reach out to the power but he could not touch it. It was like a wall had been put up between himself and the song. Somehow, the dead thing before him was keeping Elwin from the power.

Still holding the blade, the hands of the wraith began to glow brighter. Slowly, the light grew in intensity. Brighter and brighter it glowed until it became a fiery ball of blue fire. The light was so intense that it pained Elwin to look at it, and yet he couldn't look away. Horrified, Elwin watched as the light merged with the sword. Slowly, the intensely bright light began to spread down the blade, transforming the silver blade into a glowing flame of blue fire. Terrified, Elwin watched the light creeping down towards his hands. He desperately tried to release the sword, but his hands refused to open. The light coming from the sword was like a fiery torch of searing blue fire. As the burning light reached the sword hilt, Elwin tried once again to pull free, yet he still could not. It was as if the sword was a part of him, he could not let go of it any more than he could let go of his arm. He screamed. His terrified voice echoed down the hall. The blue fire touched the flesh of his hands. He screamed again. Pain raced up his arms and surged through his body. Paralyzed, Elwin knelt with his eyes clamped closed. His head began to swim. Every muscle screamed out as power suddenly flowed through his veins like blood. Reaching every part of his body, the power of Earth Magic pulsed through him. He could hear the power, feel it, he could even taste it. But still he could not use or control the power, not even to save himself. With a final scream, everything went black.

"Lord Champion," a female voice called out from nowhere and everywhere at the same time. Elwin sat up with a start. Bathed in a soft white light, he blinked. Unlike the light before, this light was soft and gentle. Feeling as if he were floating up upon a cloud, Elwin felt strangely safe. He was floating within the gentle light.

Am I dead? Elwin wondered. Puzzled, he did not find the thought all that frightening. If anything, he felt at peace. He was no longer in pain, tired, or even hungry. Strange as it seemed, Elwin could feel the light smiling at him. As if the light could read his mind the voice responded. "No, your time has not come." The soft voice filled Elwin with wonder. "You have much to do. For that I am sorry. Too many have suffered."

"Who are you?"

"You are my champion." Not answering the question, the voice went on. "The Hall of Fire awaits you. You are to be crowned High King of Kambrya. Take the crown and return to Acair. There you will be crowned. Learn to control the power that lives within you. Gather close those who will help you. But remember, you are the one I have chosen. You are now one empowered with the earth, sky, and seas, and their song will guide you. You must learn to trust yourself and to trust the song of the earth. Neither one will betray you, yet beware of the mad ones. They will try to stop and mislead you."

"What are you talking about?"

"You will know shortly. You must learn to control the magic within you, or the madness will take hold and instead control you. You have only a short time, or the madness will win. The crown will help you in this, so hurry back to Acair. You have no time to lose. You must be crowned in the ancient halls of your ancestors. It must be on the throne of your forefathers, the Dias of the Sun."

"But the throne is here! Who are you?"

"Take the Crown, Elwin and return to Acair. I will place it upon your head, and all will know that you are my Chosen One. You are my Champion."

"Who are you?" Elwin repeated.

There was no answer.

The light dimmed, then it was gone.

Elwin found himself once again lying in the dark corridor. His face was in a puddle of cold water. Unsure of what had just happened, he opened his eyes and sat up. Thankfully, the ghost was gone. *It left me for dead. Or maybe it was only a dream. I'm becoming delirious.*

He looked down at his hands. They seemed normal, if a bit dirty. "My hands?" he exclaimed as the realization hit him. "I can see my hands!" A dim light filled the hallway, and it was not the light of the ghost, nor was it the gentle white light he had floated upon. Rather, it was a yellow light, like that of a summer day. Elwin looked up. Just a few feet away stood a pair of large arched doors. From beneath the doors, a thin line of light spilled out into the corridor. Finding his sword lying next to him, Elwin weakly pushed himself back onto his feet. He felt unsteady, but he did not fall. A new source of strength and energy was keeping him going, if only barely. He stepped forward and leaned against the doors, they swung inwards, and Elwin was bathed in a warm light.

Covering his eyes, Elwin let them slowly adjust to the first natural light he had seen in days. After a brief moment, he looked up. Elwin caught his breath. Before him was a magnificent hall. The floor was covered in golden mosaics of abstracted organic forms. Silver leaves and vines intertwined in a bed of gold. Great pillars thrust upwards from the golden floor. Painted yellow, the pillars were as wide as trees that soared upwards to a vaulted ceiling which was covered in more golden tesserae. The golden ceiling was so high above, it seemed to be floating among the clouds. Light passing through glass windows bathed the hall in a golden glow, which reflected and danced across the room. *How can there be glass windows and sunlight? I'm deep within the earth.* Yet there it was.

"It's like a glowing fire." The words froze on his lips. "Fire," he breathed at last. "The Hall of Fire!"

Grander than any cathedral he had ever seen, the Hall of Fire was staggering in its beauty.

Awed, Elwin stood in wonder. He could hardly believe what he was seeing. If he had not known better, he would have sworn that the sun was streaming through the windows above him. *But I am deep within the earth. Aren't I?*

At the far end of the cathedral, a narrow beam of white light, far brighter than the rest of the light streamed down from above. The white beam stood out like a ray of intense sunlight. In the far apse of the cathedral, the beam of white light bathed an altar. Elwin took a step forward.

The hall was warm, and he could feel sensation returning to his hands and feet. Feeling somewhat rejuvenated, Elwin took another step toward the apse. Something was on the altar.

Within the beam of light a silvery and gold colored object gleamed in the intense sunbeam. He took another step. Like some grand ceremony, taking one step at a time, Elwin proceeded down the nave of the Hall of Fire. Dwarfed by the size of the place, he walked in astonished bewilderment and respectful silence as each step echoed like the soft ringing of a crystal bell. Then he saw it,

556

resting on a red silken pillow that appeared to have not been touched by the passing of hundreds of years. Not even a layer of dust touched the brightly colored cushion. And there, resting on the pillow, was a crystal stone—a stone the size of a small boulder. Elwin studied the crystal stone and was amazed to discover that within its translucent surface was something else. Encased within the glass-like stone was a gold and silver crown.

"The Lost Crown of Kambrya," he uttered in total disbelief. Slowly, taking one step at a time, he approached the altar. Reverently, he stared down at the crown as if it were a holy relic.

"So, you have come again," said a dark voice. Elwin spun around.

In the center of the hall stood a shadowy figure. Floating, it appeared to hover just above the floor. Its voice echoed as if it came from the bottom of a deep well. The voice rippled up Elwin's spine. Upon the dark form rested a red crown inset with black glass.

"I was told you were young," the shadow went on, "but I did not expect a child." The creature's eyes were like dark pits. Its form was like shifting black smoke that swallowed any light it touched.

"Do you not recognize me?" spat the shadow.

Trembling, Elwin stepped back away from the thing, putting the altar between himself and the shadow.

"I have been waiting for you. Yes. So long have I waited, but I have not forgotten you." The shadow stopped at the foot of the stairs. "Did you think I would not remember? Did you think that I would give up?"

Elwin fell back against the far wall of the apse. He could feel a dark hand upon his heart.

"Maybe I look different? Yes, I am different. I am stronger, much stronger than the last time we met. I have shed off my physical form for one of pure power. The darkness in which you imprisoned me has made me strong. Is it not ironic? The place you thought to confine me for all time has made me more powerful, and that power will set me free. I am now stronger, stronger than you could ever dream."

Elwin realized the shadow thing was no longer talking to him. The shadow seemed to be talking to the empty space, or perhaps to the walls themselves. "You have made me what I am. You have made me one with the night." The shadow laughed, filling the cathedral with its haunting sound. "It is you who has given me the power. The power that will bring you to your knees, where you will beg to serve me."

The shadow took a step up towards Elwin who cowered at the base of the altar. "I have already won! Too young has this one come. My servants have served me well. This one will fail before he even starts, and finally, I will be free!" The shadowy thing raised its arms above its head. A smile flickered across its dark, featureless face. Then it began to change.

First, its legs joined together. Then it started to grow wider and taller. Bulging upwards, the growing shadow swallowed the red crown that rested upon a changing ill-formed head. Its arms vanished within the growing shadow. In moments, the thing had completely lost its human form, and now it appeared more like a formless black thunder cloud that was cast across the cathedral floor. Expanding, the shadow continued to grow. The black cloud spread out like the coming of a storm. The light in the hall dimmed and a shadowy night began to fall across the cathedral.

Horrified, Elwin could feel the shadow. It was killing the light, devouring the light. The hand on his heart started to squeeze, and Elwin felt his heart begin to slow.

Once the shadow had covered the cathedral floor it started creeping up the steps. Elwin's heart felt as if it was being crushed. He could not find the strength to fight any more. Sliding to the floor, he waited to die. The shadow crept closer, until it was almost touching him. Then something within him snapped. Elwin felt a great wave of Earth Magic surge upwards. The song roared within his ears.

Desperate, he reached out for his atman and the Song. It came easily. The song of Earth Magic raced through his veins like a raging river. Its wondrous beauty sang out to him. Elwin was not sure how he did it, but he was filled with the power. Then a blue light flashed near him. Elwin was certain he had not created it. The light rapidly grew brighter and began pushing back the shadow.

The dark hand upon his heart shattered into a thousand pieces, and Elwin leaped back to his feet. Unbelievable power surged through him. He felt it. Elwin was not alone. Someone was here with him.

He raised his sword to the shadow, yet before he did anything more, the ghostly blue knight formed beside him. The armor burned with a blue fire that seemed to come from within, shining out like a sun. It was the same ghost knight that Elwin had encountered earlier, yet it was different. Its ragged robe was now a cloak of shimmering light and the strange blue armor was polished and clean. Legs now formed beneath its body where nothing had been before. The once translucent nature of the phantom now looked solid and all too real.

The Earth Song raged within Elwin, yet he did not know what to do with it, how to turn it against the darkness, so he stood there in awe and fear. Unable to control the Song, a clash of powers started to unfold before him, then he could feel the knight.

He did not feel the ghost physically, but rather their two minds touched. Elwin looked into the soul of the blue knight and trembled. At that moment, Elwin knew who the knight was. The blue knight had another name.

Tuatha, the God of Light.

The god was possessed by a burning hatred. Elwin tried to fight the god, but Tuatha grabbed hold of the Earth Song, pulling it from Elwin like a toy from a child. Elwin tried to hold onto the song, but again he did not know how. In the breath of a moment, the God of Light had the power and Elwin was helpless to stop him. Now with the Earth Magic, the knight pushed Elwin back with a flip of his armored hand. The blow sent Elwin reeling backwards as the now solid and very real knight blazed with Earth Magic.

Seeing the shadow rise before him, the knight raged with a searing anger. Though Elwin could not control the Earth Song, he was still connected to it, as well as the god-like knight. Elwin could feel the great burning hatred that filled the knight. It was a hatred of everything dark, a hatred that had raged within the god since the beginning of time. A hatred that was filled with unreasonable madness. Exploding, blinding light leaped from the knight's sword, a twin sword that Elwin still held uselessly before him.

The dark voice of the shadow laughed, echoing with its own hatred. "Fool! Did you think I would come here as myself? To here, of all places? This is only my shadow. Or did you forget? I am still in Ban-Darn. But soon I will be free. The Chosen one will free me. Even you cannot stop it now."

Tuatha did not seem to hear the God of Night. Blinded by a mindless rage, the knight attacked anew, wave upon wave of thundering blue fire crashed across the cathedral. The ground shook, and walls of the white and yellow marble hall exploded as rubble flew across the room and columns came crashing down.

Thrown to his knees, Elwin dropped his sword and wrapped his arms around his head trying to fend off the collapsing ceiling. With each new blow of the knight, more of the Hall of Fire crumbled. Several of the smaller pieces bounced off Elwin, and he screamed out in pain. Cowering against a wall, Elwin was sure the whole place would soon come down, burying him alive.

"Elwin," the dark voice called above the thundering power of the blue knight. The voice seemed to echo within Elwin's head. "Now you know, the blue knight is none other than Tuatha, the so-called God of Light. Now you know he is mad. If he is not stopped, he will destroy the world. He has tried to before. Long ago, before the walls of Ban-Darn, Tuatha tried to bring down this world. However, it was I who saved it. At that time, I could only save the world by allowing both of us to be imprisoned. But now I am stronger. My servants tried to warn you, Elwin, but you would not listen. However, it is still not too late. Come to me, Elwin. Come to Ban-Darn. Come, before this mad creature before you can destroy the world. I can free the world of the mad god. Come Elwin, I am your friend. I am the world's friend, I can help you."

In the blink of an eye, the shadow was gone as if it was never there. Now that the shadow had disappeared, the blue light burst once more across the cathedral. Suddenly, the knight staggered backward as if he had been hit in the chest. He quickly regained his footing and stood frozen for a moment. The god. Seemed confused by what had just happened, then slowly he turned. Cold eyes, partially hidden under his blue helmet, stared at Elwin. In his outstretched hand, the knight pointed his sword towards Elwin.

"Do you know me?" The knight's deep voice echoed like

thunder in Elwin's head, and he trembled before the shimmering god.

"You are…the god, Tuatha." Elwin stuttered. Shaking, the young prince was terrified to be before such a being of such daunting power. But there was more. Elwin could truly see the god of light, not just his blue knightly form, but his very soul. When the god had reached out and snatched the power from Elwin, it allowed him to see into the mind of the blue knight, to touch his soul. Elwin now knew that the god was indeed mad. The God of Light was possessed by an overwhelming desire to destroy the darkness—all forms of darkness. Nothing else mattered to the god, only the destruction of the god Beli and of all things dark. The obsession was the sole reason for the god's being. He never thought of anything but destroying the darkness. The God of light was mad with hate—a burning hate, an all-consuming hate. Elwin could feel the heaviness of that hate, and he was finding it hard to breathe under the weight of the god's bottomless well of anger.

"Yes, I am the Light, and I will destroy the darkness. All darkness is evil and must be rooted out. There is darkness in you too. I can see it within you. None can hide the darkness from me; NONE! But I will not kill you. At least, not today. You have freed me from my prison." He spread out his arms gesturing to the hall, which was still bathed in the god's shimmering blue light. "For that, I shall spare your life. Now I must go and search for the hiding place of my dark brother and destroy him."

He pointed a finger at Elwin. "It was your ancestor who tried to hide him from me. I see that too. Do not think that I do not know. I know all. He, like you, had the stain of darkness about him. But I will find Beli. I will turn on this world and cleanse it of all darkness. I will remake your world into a world of my light. You have until then to purge yourself of the darkness in you.

Repent the sins of your ancestor which stains your soul. It is the one gift I will give you. It is your only chance."

Then in a flash of blue light, he too was gone. Elwin felt the Earth Song surge back under his control, but he let it go. Gasping for air, Elwin fell to the floor.

Chunks of marble, shards of glass, and dust lay across the once beautiful and shimmering room. Still, a single beam of white light streamed from the only window that was left unbroken, bathing the crown that remained resting on the altar. It was the one and only thing that had not been touched by the god's rage.

Thinking the nightmare had come to an end, Elwin let himself relax. Taking long deep breaths and only after his racing heart began to slow once more did he sit back up. He rested against the back of the altar. His eyes wandered across the shattered hall.

Looking down at himself he discovered that his clothing was torn and filthy, and he was also bleeding from several places. He reassured himself that nothing seemed broken, and he did not appear to be bleeding to death.

"Both gods are mad," he realized in despair. "And, I have set free the God of Light, but how? I did nothing." *It does not matter. By coming here, I have doomed the world to the God of Light's madness.* Despair took hold of Elwin as his fear released its grip on him. Everything had been for nothing. Tuatha could not help the world, he would destroy it. The Guardians of Light were worshiping a monster and did not even know it.

Elwin rubbed his leg where a piece of marble from the ceiling had crashed into him, cutting a deep gash along his thigh. Other than torn clothing and a few deep cuts, Elwin was surprisingly in one piece. However, he was not sure he should be thankful for being alive. He let his tired head sink forward upon his chest. *I'm still trapped down here. I will die with no way to warn anyone of what I have set free upon the world.*

In his despair, Elwin almost did not hear the doors to the hall open.

The great double doors at the end of the hall started to swing open. For a moment, he thought perhaps the mad god was returning. He feared that the crazed God of Light had changed his mind and returned to kill him after all, but it was not. Elwin stared at another figure. An old man was silhouetted in the doorway. He hunched slightly as he closed the door gently behind him. The old man wore a stained and worn white robe with a green belt around his thin waist. With slow, deliberate steps, he walked down the nave across the golden mosaics and towards Elwin.

Elwin knew he should be surprised, but he was simply too tired and sore to be surprised or even care anymore. *Will this never end,* thought Elwin. *For days, I have been alone and lived in the darkness. Now everywhere I look, someone appears in a place where there should be no one. Each time it is never good.*

But the old man who walked with the aid of a long white staff did not appear a threat, or anything nearly as dramatic as what Elwin had already seen and gone through. More importantly, he seemed human and not some mad god or ghostly aberration. *Probably some lost soul who has wandered in from above. But how did he get here?* A spark of hope passed before the prince. *Another way in! Does he know another way in? If there is another way in, then there is another way out!*

At last, the man came up to the altar. His gray-blue gray eyes seemed to twinkle as he looked at Elwin. A slight smile came to his old and wrinkled face, but he said nothing. Silently, he stood there as if he was awaiting something. *Maybe he's been trapped down here for years and thinks I am an illusion. Or maybe he is the illusion, and I have finally gone mad.*

Finally, Elwin broke the silence. "Who are you, and how did you get here?"

"I am a friend, Elwin. We need to talk." His voice was solid for such an old man. "I have waited such a long time for this moment. I am pleased you have come to me."

Elwin stared at the man in shock. "How do you know me? How do you know my name?"

"I know much, and I have been watching you for a very long time. But this is the first time I have had a chance to talk with you." With a wave of his thin arm, he gestured, taking in the long basilica hall. "This place is of the old world. It is one of the few places I can still walk as I once did. Soon I will not have the strength to come even here. I fear my days are numbered and coming to an end. Then again perhaps that is not such a bad thing."

"Your home is a mess," commented Elwin, as he looked across the ruined hall.

The man nodded. "It is indeed. Children can make such a mess, and they rarely clean up after themselves." The old man's eyes sparkled, and he gave Elwin a smile, then the aged man raised himself off the floor.

Suddenly the wooden staff came to life, giving off a softly white glow. At first, nothing else happened, then to Elwin's amazement, the hall started to change. As if time had suddenly reversed itself, the stones and glass that had laid scattered across the hall started to float into the air. Elwin's mouth gaped open as the pieces replaced themselves, restoring the hall to its former glory.

Elwin had felt the Earth Magic as the white figure repaired the hall. The prince shook his head, realizing he had been naive in thinking this was simply an old man. He doubted anything down here was as it appeared.

"Do you know the way out of here?" Elwin did not care who he was, all he wanted was a way of escaping this elaborate tomb.

The old man scratched his snowy white beard, smiling at Elwin. "There are ways, but I doubt you would be able to leave the way I will. Still, I think you will find your way. I think you will find you are not quite the same young man who entered this palace. You are capable of doing much more than you think. And you are much more than you think, young Elwin. You are much, much more."

"You're not human, are you?" *That should scare me. But this man is so kindly, like a grandfather. And I am tired of being scared.* There was something about this man that put Elwin at ease despite everything that had happened.

Again, the old man shook his head. "No, Elwin I am not."

"Are you a god, like the other two?"

Again, he shook his head. "Some have called me a god, but I am not. There was once a time I thought I was, but I have outgrown that delusion. Nor are Tuatha or Beli gods, though they certainly believe they are. That makes them very dangerous."

"They seem like gods. Mad, but gods all the same."

Again, the old man smiled "Elwin, to a dog, you seem like a god. And they were not always mad. Thinking they were gods is what brought on their madness as well as the madness in which this world now finds itself. And I too, had a role to play. They alone are not to blame."

"Tell me, Elwin, are you a good and kind person?"

"Yes, I think so."

"So, you have never done anything that could be called bad or wrong?"

"Of course I have, nobody is perfect."

"It is much the same with Beli, Tuatha, and myself. It is true that I have done things that would seem godlike, yet others may say I have done great harm, even evil. I would find it hard to disagree with them. So I ask you, can a good person do bad things and still be a good person?" He went on without waiting for a response from Elwin. "I think a good man or woman can do some bad things and still be genuinely a good person, yet I do not believe that a god can do evil things and still be a god. A god should never do evil things, even if by accident. A god should be beyond all that is evil, and thus I must not be not a god. Following such logic, I would say that none of my family could be gods either."

Elwin shook his head, confused by the man or god or whatever he was. "If you all are not gods, what are you, and why are you here?"

"What I am, or the others like me are of little importance. Elwin, it is you that is important. My days have come and gone. I am the past. You, however, are the future. I have come in hopes to undo what I have done, to help fix what I destroyed and to see that you have a chance for a future. So, Elwin, I am here to talk to you, and ask a favor."

"Me?" Elwin said with surprise. "I'm trapped here. I can't even help myself."

"You have done well so far. I am pleased with you and all that you have accomplished. It gives me some hope that the future can still be saved. Perhaps the future will not be as black as I fear. Yet I was always one to hope.

"May I sit?" the god-like man asked. "I think I have some answers you have been looking for. Though you'll probably have more questions when I leave; I must go soon. I no longer belong to this world. Still, I have to undo the evil me and my sons have done. Or to be more truthful, I have come to ask you to help me undo the evil that has been forced upon your world. I fear my kind have left you with a heavy burden to carry. For that, I am deeply sorry."

Elwin nodded. *Answers. This man has answers…Sons!* Then the shock of the man's word hit the prince. "Sons!" he said out loud. "Tuatha and Beli are your sons?!"

The man's smile turned sad. "They are. They are not the sons to make an old father proud, but they are mine nonetheless. And much of what they have become is my fault. That is why I have remained in this place." He swept his staff before him taking in the great hall. "I have stayed here, waiting here for you."

"So, you truly are not gods?"

"Once we were called gods. Still, I believe there is a god. A great god, an unseen god, a god who does not do evil, a true god of light that created us all, and a god who gave us free will. I am what the true god created, and I chose poorly how to use the gifts the unseen god gave to me. And as for my sons, they are worse than even I. Now I at last can see myself as I truly am, and all the limitations that comes with being me. My sons do not see their limitations, they do not see who they really are, and there lies the danger. They truly think they are gods and believe they have no limitations and fewer responsibilities. Believe it or not, they once wanted to do good."

"Forgive me, my mind grows frail." The old man said changing the subject. "I have failed to properly introduce myself. My name is Llyr. Once I was known as "Llyr of the Earth." There was a time I, and others like myself, called your world home. Those days are passing. There are still a few of my kind that still call this home. Their time, too, is passing, but my sons refuse to

568

see that. This was never truly our world. It is yours. My people are leaving this earth to you and the other races. It belongs to you. Where we are going, only the great unseen god knows. But I have chosen to stay because of my sons. It is long past my time to leave, yet still, I am here. After all, they are my responsibility, so I have remained behind. Though my people are leaving, we still hold this land dear and do not wish to leave it in ruins. That is why I have stayed here. I have remained connected to some places of this world in order to help stop my children from doing any more harm." He gestured to the hall with a wave of his wrinkled hand. "This is one of the few places I can still come to. Many centuries ago, this was my home. It was a time when I ruled as god and king."

Llyr gave a great sigh that seemed to come out of untold centuries. "The world is in danger, Elwin, and I can no longer control my sons as I once did. You see, your ancestor, King Coinneach, helped me trap my sons so they could be stopped from destroying this world. Most think the Battle of Ban-Darn was meant to imprison my dark son, but in truth, it was to capture both my sons. As you can see, they are both mad. Their hatred of each other has driven them insane, and today you have set Tuatha free."

Elwin looked shocked. "You mean I..."

The old man cut him off with a wave of his wrinkled hand. "In truth, you could not have stopped it. Do not blame yourself. The Earth power that you called up with the sword is what Tuatha needed to free himself. It was inevitable. In time, he would have found a way to free himself anyway, as well his brother. It is better it happens now, while there is still hope. We cannot wait for them to release themselves. When that happens they will be too strong, and no one will be able to stop them and their mad ambitions."

"But that means the blue knight will now search out his brother and destroy the world!" exclaimed Elwin.

"Maybe. Time will tell. But Elwin, Tuatha will not find his brother anytime soon. Beli is in Ban-Darn. He cannot reach him there, at least not without help. You are still the only one that can free my other son. Until then, there is little damage my misguided child of light can do. He cannot even call up as much of the earth power as you can. That is why you must learn to control it. You cannot let Tuatha or anyone else take the power from you, as my son did today. And you still have another role to play. It is with the use of your ability that you will free my other son."

"I will never do that!"

"I do not know if you can stop it. You did not mean to free my first son, but you have; no fault of your own, yet he is free nonetheless. Some things are beyond our control. It is the wise that can recognize that, and try to change what they can. Once, I too was strong in the power of Earth Magic. Strong enough to control my mad sons. But that was long ago, and my ability wanes as my time here comes to an end. You are the last who can free Beli and stop both my children. Only you have the power. And the world can only be saved through you freeing both my sons."

"That is madness! The sword should never leave this hall so that none will release that evil," stated Elwin. "I cannot free him without the sword. That is how I can save the world. Bury the cursed blade where none will ever find it."

"It is too late for that, Elwin. My first son is freed, or at least in part. But more to the point, the sword is not the problem; you are."

"What!?"

"The sword was never the source of the Earth Song, Elwin,

you are. You have always had the power within you. The sword simply released it. Though the ancient blade may still play a role, it is not the source of your strength; the earth is. It is you that the power answers to. The sword just set the potential in you free, or more accurately the sword simply showed the Earth who the chosen one is; you."

"And if I die?" Elwin asked with a coldness settling in his chest. "If I am dead, the god, or whatever, cannot be freed."

In a way, Elwin was relieved when Llyr replied, "Then earth would choose another, but by then it will be too late. You are the world's last chance. Only you. Die, and so does the world."

Llyr hesitated before going on. "Hear what I have to say, my young prince. You can judge me after that, and you can then choose if you are willing to help me or not. Know that there is great risk, and I can do little to assist you once you leave here. Rest assured, you will leave here. I can get you out of this lost world and back to yours. It is the least I can do since I am responsible for bringing you here. For that too, I apologize. However, I hope you understand my need is great, and my choices are more limited than they once were. If my sons are not stopped, their madness will destroy the world. It is a shame that no father would want. So, will you hear my story?"

Beyond amazement, Elwin stared in wonder and he could only nod. *Do I have a choice? Did I ever have a choice?*

"Thank you. Let us sit. This may take a while."

CHAPTER THIRTY-ONE

Odary, Leina, and Colin stood in the High Council chambers discussing and wondering about Elwin.

"Five days," said a frustrated Odary. "And he has not come back. You must come to accept that he won't."

"He will return," Leina said stubbornly. She shook her head with anger. Her eyes were intense and locked onto the elder Guardian. "I know he will. If he were indeed gone, I would have felt it."

Odary nodded at Colin, who was standing a short distance away. The young man was staring out a window and across the silver lake that was outside the white castle. "Even the outsider Colin knows Elwin is gone to a place where we cannot help him."

Leina gave Colin a quick glance. At the mention of his name, the youth turned away from the window. A frown was chiseled across his face. With arms crossed over his chest, he leaned against the wall. He returned Leina's stare with cold, angry eyes. Ever since Elwin had locked himself beyond the Sun Door, Colin had been at her side. He had decided that since she was the next in line to the throne of Ceredigion, she needed a guard. *As if I could not take care of myself. Blast you, Colin! You could at least talk to me. You don't have to treat me as if I wanted this to happen. He was...is my brother. You look so sad, and you are a friend. But I did nothing wrong! Elwin was trying to protect me. I didn't ask him to do that.* She turned to Odary, grateful for not having to look at Colin's judging eyes. "But he is alive, Master Odary. I know he is," Leina insisted.

Colin mumbled, and Leina could not quite make out what he had said, but she was sure he was blaming her for Elwin sealing himself behind the sun door. He had never actually said so, but she saw it in his eyes. Every time she looked at him she could feel the accusations. As she had for the last five days, Leina resisted the urge to scream at him what she was thinking. *Stop blaming me! Some guard you are. You're more like a punishment than a guard. I did nothing wrong. Did I?* Leina had to admit, if only to herself, that maybe Colin was right. Had she done all that she could have done? Was there something else she could have said to persuade him from giving up his foolish quest for the crown. *I was better prepared, why could he not see that? And to imprison himself.* Leina knew her brother's reasoning, everyone had. Elwin had seen to it that no one, especially Leina was going to follow him. *But he is alive down there somewhere. Or is that just what I want to believe? Am I unable to accept that my brother threw away his life for me? I did not need you to do that. I could have made it.*

Odary shook his head. "Even if you are right," he stated, bringing Leina out of her own deep thoughts, "he cannot be saved. That earthquake we felt two hours ago was the judgment of the Light."

"You don't know that!" snapped Leina. "We live on top of an ancient volcano. We are bound to have earthquakes from time to time."

"In truth, it doesn't matter if that earthquake was Light's test of Elwin or not. Alive or dead, he is gone and beyond our help. I know it sounds cruel, but he has not or will not survive the testing. If the prince still lives, he has sealed himself below the castle. He has no food or water, and by now no light. Even if he is never tested, he cannot survive, Leina. I am sorry. Yet the living must go on. You must go in and become our High Queen."

"How?" asked Leina. There was a harsh tone to her voice. "Elwin has locked the Sun Door from the inside, and he has the only key. I can't pass through the door unless Jael and Cerise have found another way to open the Sun Door." Her solemn face revealed a spark of hope. If only she could get past the Sun Doors, maybe she could still save her brother. If he was alive. "Have they made any headway in opening the door?"

With a sadness, the Guardian Master dashed her hopes with a shake of his head. "No, I fear neither Jael nor Cerise has had much luck. For days they have been studying the Sun Doors, yet they still have not found a way to get past the great doors. It defies all their attempts. They have tried every spell they can think of and have pored over the ancient texts, but still nothing. Last night they even tried smashing their way through. They could not even put a dent in the great stone. I don't know if they will ever find a way in. But if He Who is the Light wants you to be tested, a way will be found. In the meantime, you must stand ready."

Leina nodded, but it was Colin who spoke. "To kill her as well?" He spat with venom. It was the first thing he had said in days.

Odary looked at Colin but said nothing. He could understand the young man's anger.

Leina sadly shook her head. Colin had been her friend once. Yet, she knew he was only lashing out due to his own loss and pain. *Colin, you never did know how to handle anything you could not understand. You are only now beginning to see that your physical strength cannot always fix things. You are a soldier and have always thought like one. This is a time your muscles cannot solve anything.*

Leina tried to think of what she could say to ease his pain, but before she could speak, the floor suddenly and violently heaved upwards. An explosion ripped up from beneath them. The castle began to shake, and the walls trembled. Leina screamed. It was as if a thousand thunderbolts were striking against the castle at once. Again and again, the thunder roared. The castle trembled, tables and chairs turned over, glass shattered, and books fell off their shelving. Parts of the ceiling and walls crashed to the floor. The castle shook so violently that Colin, Leina, and Odary were thrown to the floor and could not regain their feet. This time, the earthquake was much more intense than the one they had all felt earlier in the day. Just as suddenly as it had started, the violent upheaval of the earth stopped. The castle moaned, then was still. Leina slowly climbed to her feet. With wide, fearful eyes, she slowly took in the room. Pieces of mortar and debris lay scattered across the floor, though overall, the castle still seemed intact and structurally sound.

Coming to his own feet, Colin brushed himself off. "What in the name of the Three Gods was that!?"

"The Light!" Odary exclaimed, taking deep breaths. "Elwin has been tested. That must have been the Testing, and the Light has found him to be impure. He is gone."

"No!" Leina cried out. She ran out of the room with an enormous burst of energy. Taking both Colin and Odary by surprise, the two hesitated, then chased after her. Just outside the door, Colin ran into Aidan, Rodan, and Kayno. They all looked shocked and surprised.

"Hold on," said Kayno, grabbing hold of Colin. Odary raced past. "What's going on? Where is Leina off too in such a blasted hurry?"

"It's Elwin! I have to stop Leina!" Then Colin pulled free and went after Leina. Not sure what was happening, the others followed. In moments, Colin and the others passed up the much older and slower Odary, but Leina was still far ahead.

Leina led them on a chase down into the depth of the castle and into the caves below. Colin had no doubts where she was leading them. She was going back down to the Chapel of the Sun.

Just behind Leina, Colin burst into the chapel. She had run faster than Colin would have guessed. "Leina!" he cried, breathing hard after the chase down to the chapel.

She turned her head. "Look Colin!" She pointed. Her voice trembled. The Sun Door had exploded into dust and rubble, and a dark cave lay beyond. "The Light has opened the way." Colin stopped and stared, then took a step closer. He looked at the door, or what was left of it. Colin turned his eyes down onto Leina. He narrowed his eyes with suspicion and concern. "What do you mean to do?" There was an accusing tone to his voice.

"Go after Elwin. I must!"

Colin shook his head. "You can't. I'll go."

"I have to be the one, Colin!"

"You must be kept safe! I let Elwin go, and look what happened. If I had done something, he would still be alive."

So, it wasn't just me he was mad at, Leina realized. *He blames himself too.* "You could not have stopped him." She now understood why Colin had been in such a foul mood. "It was not your fault." Finally, Aidan, Rodan, and Kayno burst in, skidding to a stop.

Leina looked over at them. Moving swiftly, Colin placed himself between Leina and the door. He squared his wide shoulders, almost daring Leina to try to get past him.

"What in the name of the Three Gods!?" exclaimed Kayno seeing the shattered door.

"I am going after Elwin," Colin announced.

"What!" exclaimed Aidan. "Are you serious?"

Pallas stepped forward. "I'll go with you."

"All of us will," added Rodan.

No one except Leina objected.

"You won't live!" Leina stated as bluntly as she could. "Not one of you would ever return. Now, let me pass." She turned slowly to face Colin. "Please, Colin. I am the only one with a chance."

Colin's eyes were hard, but Leina could see the pain behind them. Colin shook his head. "It is better for me to die in your place. It is my duty. I failed Elwin. I won't fail you too!"

"Blast your duty," snapped Leina. "He is my brother!"

Odary was the next to arrive. He was breathing hard. "The Light be praised," he managed to say between raspy gasps. "The Light has opened the way." He gulped in more air. "What are you waiting for? Go Leina, the Light awaits you!"

Leina looked over her shoulder then back to Colin. Colin shook his head. "No!"

"Please, Colin. Let me pass."

"No," he repeated. "I won't let you."

"She must," stated Odary. "Leina must go forward. The Light is calling her."

"He speaks the truth," added Cerise, who suddenly appeared, coming into the chapel. She was closely followed by the rest of the Council of Elders. "The Light has brought down the door so she could go in. Elwin thought to prevent us from entering, but the Light always opens new ways."

"No!" demanded Colin. Drawing his sword taking a menacing stance. "Elwin is still in there." He nodded his head at the shattered doorway. "If he is alive, I have to help him."

Ryence set a lantern down on the altar. "You're being a fool, young man. Elwin is no more. Your youthful heroics are wasted on the dead."

"I don't care," snapped Colin, turning his hard eyes onto Ryence. "Leina is not going in there!"

"Stand aside!" ordered Gelon. He stepped forward. Gently but forcibly, he pushed Colin aside. "The prince is dead. He has failed. Leina will be High Queen as she was meant to be."

Colin shook his head again. "I can go after him. I must. I've sworn to protect him."

Gelon's eyes had a dangerous edge to them. "The prince is dead. He came before the Light and was cast down. It was his choice. Now the Light has opened the way for Leina." He raised his right hand, his palm pointing towards Colin's chest. "I will not stand for this foolishness. Now stand aside or I will remove you. Permanently." A light swiftly enveloped him. It sparkled and danced around him. The room filled with power.

Rodan, Kayno, Aidan, and Pallas all jumped to join Colin.

Gelon scowled at them. "You cannot stand against me. I will cast you off like feathers in the wind. But if it is your wish to die..."

"Gelon?!" Odary shouted in surprise. "That will be enough! Remember your vows. Remember who…"

"My vows mean nothing!" Gelon cut Odary off. "If the Light is not set free, nothing matters."

Pallas raised his sword. "We will not yield." Aidan slipped an arrow into his bow.

The tension in the small chapel grew until Leina could take it no longer. "Stop it!" she demanded angrily. Her eyes glared as they swept across the room. "All of you." Taking a step, she put herself between Gelon and the others. "You're acting like children."

"Stand aside Leina, this is none of your business," Gelon said sternly.

Leina's turned on him. Her eyes were like daggers. "None of my businesses! Am I a child that you can send to her room?!" she rhetorically asked. "You would make me your queen, but not hear my words?"

"There is no time for this," Gelon retorted. "You must go forward."

"No," Leina returned. "I won't."

"What?" asked Gelon, taken aback. Genuine fear now registered across his face.

"You heard me! If you hurt my friends in any way, I will not go into the Hall of Fire! You will not have a queen."

Gelon tensed. Finally, he dropped his hand. "The Light must be freed, Leina." He nodded angrily at the men behind her. "They cannot be allowed to stand in the way."

"And they won't, but it will be done my way. Understand?" When Gelon gave a nod of his head, Leina then turned and looked at hers' and her brother's friends. "I know you love him." Her voice now soft. "I do too. But you cannot go. Only an Ap Gruffydd can enter the Hall of Fire. I am the only one who can go. I must go. If Elwin is in there, I might be able to help him. Please, Colin, I have to do this."

Silently, Colin returned the princess' stare, and he lowered his sword. "Let me go with you."

She shook her head. "I can't, Colin. You cannot enter the Hall of Fire."

"We can go until we reach the Hall of Fire," suggested Aidan. "Certainly, that won't hurt, and we can help you until then."

She smiled but shook her head sadly. "My brother has picked good friends. But I must do this alone. If I am to be tested, I must stand alone. So it is written."

Colin was the hardest to convince, but in the end, he nodded his head. Reluctantly, he stepped aside.

"Thank you," whispered Leina, placing a hand upon his shoulder. Staring at the floor, Colin did not answer.

"Hurry," urged Odary.

With a nodded Leina stepped forward. Then her eyes went wide. "Elwin!" she gasped.

Covered in dirt, Elwin stood in the doorway. His clothing was ripped and torn and he was bleeding in several places. Using his sword as a crutch, he limped into the torch light of the room. No one breathed. Held under his free arm was a silver crown encased within crystal stone.

Overwhelmed, everyone stood and stared at Elwin and the dazzling crown. It was Colin who finally broke the silence with a great roaring laugh.

Kayno and Rodan smiled as if their son had just turned up from being lost.

Pallas, regretting that he had missed out on Elwin's adventure, gave a long whistle. Jael dropped to his knees. The other Guardians did the same. Noticeably, Gelon was the last. Bowing their heads, the Guardians placed two fingers to their foreheads and then rested an open palm upon their hearts. Then as if on some unseen cue, they said together. "The Light has awakened. He Who Was is again."

Elwin frowned. *You may not be thanking me when you discover that your beloved god is not a god at all who will destroy the world,* the prince thought. *I have set him free, and worse is yet to come. Much worse.* But rather than say any of that, he gave his friends a weak smile and then turned a cold, hard stare onto the elders. "Rise, it is time for you to serve the High Prince and heir to the Crown of Kambrya." His voice thundered with power. "I have been tested and have spoken to the one god. I know what must be done and where I must go." For the most part what Elwin was telling them was true. He was choosing his words carefully so that later none could say that he had lied. Yet the young prince realized he was misleading them. He also realized that he did not care if he was lying to the Guardians of Light or not. After all, they had been dishonest to him. *Besides,* Elwin rationalized. *It was true that I have spoken to someone they think of as a god, and maybe he is a god. Who am I to say? And it's true that he told me what needed to be done, at least, a part of it.* However, it was Tuatha's father who had told Elwin of the danger the world was in, and not the so-called God of Light.

"Will you follow the orders of your god? Will you follow the chosen one of the Light?" The prince asked bluntly.

Reluctantly they each gave their consent. What choice did they have? They had spent their lives waiting for this moment. While it was true that they had hoped it would be Leina, who were they to question the will of their god?

"Good," Elwin replied with a cold stare. He continued choosing his words carefully, leaving out what he did not want the Guardians to know. "There is much to be done and little time. I have no time to be arguing. I have been told that the world is in great pearl. The God of Darkness will soon be set free." Elwin left out that it would be him that would set the god free. "But there is hope; the God of Light has already been set free. I have set him free." *And he will destroy us all if I do not stop him.* "Tuatha now prepares to battle the God of Darkness, Beli. But alone, the God of Light will fail. It has been shown to me. The world will be cast into eternal darkness if I do not do as I have been commanded. I must free the crown from its casing. I must become High King. To do so, I must return to Ceredigion. Only there can I become the High King and aid the Light."

His friends gasped. Elwin had insisted over and over that he would never be the High King, and now he suddenly seemed to be reaching for it, demanding it.

"How?" exclaimed Odary. His eyes were wide with wonder. "How, can you free the crown of the crystal stone?"

Elwin frowned. "When the time is right all will be revealed, but for now you will just have to trust me and the Light." The truth was Elwin did not really know himself. "I have been told of what must be done, but I cannot speak of it now. The darkness has ears." *If I told you the truth, if you knew what I am going to do, you would kill me now. Maybe you should.* "Soon, I will be leaving. I have a new journey that I must take. I am going home."

"No!" shouted Gelon "You cannot leave! We are the Guardians. Who are you to tell me— us what will be done?!"

Elwin dropped the sheath from his sword. The blade of Elwin's sword glowed with a shimmering blue light, then suddenly the light changed as it transformed into a soft green. Elwin nodded to himself as if the green light was preferable to the blue. He felt the power of Earth Magic running through him and into the sword. His whole body shivered as he realized the power no longer came from the sword but from him. *Me,* he wanted to scream, *it's coming through me! I am sending Earth Magic into the sword.* Then without so much as a blink of his cold gaze upon the Guardians, Elwin raised the magical blade and pointed it towards Gelon. "By the Light, you will heed my words."

THE END

Made in the USA
Coppell, TX
10 February 2022